MOUNTAIN ICE

by R. E. Derouin

HATS
OFF™

Also by R. E. Derouin:

Time Trial

San Juan Solution

Mountain Ice
Copyright © 2002 R. E. Derouin

Published by Hats Off Books™
610 East Delano Street, Suite 104
Tucson, Arizona 85705
ISBN: 1-58736-086-1
LCCN: 2001098339
Book design by Summer Mullins.
Printed in the United States of America.

For Marie, more than a sister—a lifelong friend.

Many thanks to Mike O'Donnell, preeminent guide, recently returned from the summit of Mount Everest. His help instructing this land lubber in the intricacies of ice climbing is much appreciated. Hats off to retired Sheriff Jerry Wakefield, for setting me straight on jurisdictional matters.

PROLOGUE

It was the sound of something falling, a chair perhaps, that startled him in his winter sleep. He was still enveloped in the grogginess of slumber and it was minutes before he found himself rising from beneath the comfort of the quilt to the edge of the rumpled bed. He was still a prisoner in the land of those inmates of his mind, the rascal story tellers who made the most absurd tales seems as natural as butter on toast. The cold floor on his bare feet shocked him to further awareness as he felt about for his slippers. Warily, feeling his way by hand, he left the bedroom and climbed the stairs to investigate. With heart racing he began to sense what he would find beyond. Her door was ajar and the chill from an open window washed over him as he cautiously approached, now somehow knowing what lay beyond. He pushed the door further but hesitated entering, as if remaining outside would somehow absolve him of responsibility for what lay beyond. The pale glow of the moon shone through the uncurtained window, casting an elongated shadow from the overturned chair.

She turned slowly, propelled by a tender breeze from the cold night air that filled the room with a chill of death. Her long blonde hair, unfastened now, cascaded about her shoulders. She had changed to the white dress, the one she'd worn to dinner that night and the hem touched the tops of her bare feet, which pointed downward. Her hands were by her sides, turned out, as if offering benediction for what she had done, as if to say, *peace at last.* The silk cord was fastened to the brass gas lamp that centered the ceiling of the room, the other end tightly knotted about her soft white neck. He could picture her, holding the hem of her gown, climbing onto the chair, perhaps even smiling, before kicking it away, and waiting the few agonizing moments until death took her hand and led her to its darkness. He was frozen to move toward her, knowing in his heart it was too late. Too late for anything. As he watched, spellbound, she revolved toward him, but he quickly closed his eyes lest he look upon her once beautiful face.

CHAPTER 1

"You have to admit it's strange," Cynthia Dean said. "The woman looked half frightened to death and the young boy with her never said a word. They were anything but typical tourists." She looked up at her husband from her position scotched down on the parlor floor and resumed sorting Christmas ornaments, packing them away as methodically as if she were returning them to the store. "Besides, she signed the register as 'Edith Jones' but her credit card said 'Edith Shipton.'"

"Did the charge go through?" David Dean asked as he sat down next to her. He had been outside, atop a ladder, removing Christmas lights when the two checked in to Bird Song, the Dean's bed and breakfast.

"Yes. It was a platinum card."

"Good. That means she's got some bucks. That's all we have to be concerned about. We collect the money, the customer gets to relax, enjoy this gorgeous mountain scenery and eat your fresh blueberry muffins. End of our responsibility."

But Cynthia wouldn't let go. "If she's so rich, why did she only book one room for herself and the boy? Don't you think that's strange? He looks to be about twelve years old. And she doesn't seem the least interested in skiing or any outdoor activity."

"She's probably coming here to meet a hot date and wants privacy. Give the woman a break."

"A liaison with her son along?" Cynthia answered.

Dean rolled his eyes in mock exasperation. "I'll talk to her and find out what's going on."

"No! She'll think we're nosy."

Dean looked up at Cynthia. "*I'm* not nosy."

She smiled. "I guess I shouldn't be snoopy either, but we've had a lot of guests in the last six months and I've never felt this uncomfortable about any of the others. It's a strange feeling something serious is troubling the woman." She hugged herself, in spite of the warmth of the cozy room.

David Dean squeezed his wife's arm and bent over to kiss her. "We're running an inn and we see a lot of different people. Some of them are bound to be a bit on the kooky side. I'm content to give

7

them fair value for their bucks and try my best to see that they enjoy themselves. The rest of their problems aren't my concern. We'll save the mysteries for Fred to solve while we try to pay the bills."

Fred O'Connor, Dean's elderly stepfather, was an avid fan of a mystery, primarily in written form, often in his imagination and occasionally in his real life world. Fred, age seventy-six, was quick to embrace any hint of mystery and attach it to the most common everyday happening. Years of devouring that fiction genre helped formulate a world where intrigue crept around every corner for the dapper gentleman. The two had shared Dean's bachelorhood for fifteen years until Dean, an ex Pennsylvania police detective married Cynthia Byrne seven months earlier. Dean met Cynthia while officially investigating her first husband's disappearance. The two had gradually fallen in love, married, scraped together funds, and together with Fred O'Connor, purchased a hundred-year-old Colorado Victorian home. After extensive alterations, Bird Song, a bed and breakfast, was born.

"Let's just be thankful we have guests," Dean continued as he wound a string of lights into a bouquet of blinking color, unplugged it, and set it aside with a dozen others. "Bird Song was an empty nest."

The inn contained nine rentable rooms, each with a private bath. The three largest of these quarters were located on the third floor. The second floor contained six, five rooms for guests, the sixth occupied by Fred O'Connor. There was an additional small guest room beneath the stairs on the main floor. This floor, bisected by a hall and stairs, contained a living room or parlor on the right, or southern side, and a dining room and kitchen on the left, with the Deans' private quarters, a sitting room-office combination and bedroom, located in the rear.

"All in all, we can't complain about business," Cynthia added. "It's one of the few times we've been without guests since we opened and we'll practically have a full house next week with the Ice Festival coming up."

In recent years, the town of Ouray had attained international acclaim for its ice climbing park, located on the southern edge of the tiny town. The Uncompahgre Gorge, a deep and narrow cut in the rock of the San Juan Mountains, hugged in its confines, a river of the same name. One hundred years ago the stream was damned by the Ouray Electric Power and Light Company. A large pipe still snaked its way downward, carrying water, via gravity, to a generator located over a mile below in town. After a century, electricity was still being generated. This pipe, called a penstock, ranged from forty-four inches down to two feet in diameter and paralleled the Uncompahgre River far above its torrent as it coursed down the deep gorge. Innovative locals, resting in the doldrums of off-season winter, noticed that when the large, ancient pipe leaked, escaping water coated the high walls of the gorge in spectacular ice. Hearty souls climbed these ice-shrouded cliffs, just for the sport of it. Later, the serendipitous drippings were augmented by additional piping, carrying excess water to spray even more surface of the rock walls. A delicate balance of local easements, public involvement and volunteer labor was slowly assembled. Thus was created a major climbing facility and, in the process, an additional invitation for winter tourists, earning the small town a reputation as a growing Mecca for this exciting and perilous sport. The seasonal highlight was a major festival held each January, attracting climbers from around the world.

"It's nice to have the place nearly to ourselves, even if it is only for a few days," Dean said, as he stifled a yawn. "Let's enjoy it."

Cynthia smiled. "If you don't fall asleep on me. Why are you so tired?"

"I had a bum night's sleep. I was dreaming."

"It must have been a corker."

"It was. There was a woman...I never saw her face. I don't think I wanted to." He looked over at his wife. "She was hanging from the old gas fixture in 2A, upstairs."

"God!" Cynthia exclaimed. "That's awful!"

"It was a very vivid dream. Not Henry Whitcomb-vivid," Dean added quickly, referring to his involvement in a strange mystery before they married. "It was a regular dream—just clearer than any I've ever experienced. I heard a noise and came up the stairs. Somehow I knew what I'd find. The room wasn't painted as it is now. There was flowered wallpaper and she was hanging there in the moonlight, twisting in the draft from an open window."

Cynthia shivered, and took a sip from her cup of coffee. "That's not a dream. It's a nightmare."

Fred O'Connor sauntered into the room, resplendent in bow tie and jacket, carrying a plate of cinnamon toast. His ears perked up at the mention of Dean's nocturnal adventure.

"It was just a dream," Dean repeated. "No big deal."

Fred was not so easily placated. "Don't be so sure," the old man said. "I hear sounds in the night, and get strange feelings sometimes. You folks don't hear 'em 'cause you sleep down here, but upstairs is different. Besides, if you remember a dream, it must be important."

"This place is a hundred years old," Dean answered. "I'd start to worry if I didn't hear strange noises. And the only reason you remember dreams is if you wake up in the middle of them."

Fred just shook his head at Dean's perceived ignorance. "There were lots of folks who passed through these doors over the last century," he said, sounding not unlike Rod Sterling. "No telling what tales their ghosts could spin and what unfinished business they left behind. Maybe some spirit is trying to contact us to set things straight." He nodded, the vision of a sage teacher. "Dreams is unfinished business. You may have seen a ghost and your conscious blocked it out while your subconscious remembered it." Fred plopped down on the sofa, set the plate in his lap and continued to eat and talk at the same time. "There's plenty of computer web sites that explain all about them dreams and visions and spirits. Very interesting stuff."

"Very uninteresting dribble," Dean grumbled. After fifteen bachelor years with Fred O'Connor he had heard it all. But periodically he forgot the utter uselessness of arguing with the opinionated old man.

Fred grumbled on. "You can make fun of that stuff, but a lot of wild things happened around this old mining town a hundred years ago." Then he added, "I should know, being as I'm in the business, so to speak."

With the proceeds of a recent stock sale, Fred O'Connor had invested in a complete computer system and was off and running. He began by selling some of his numerous mystery novels on a book finder's web site, then expanded to garage sale scouring for items of dubious value. Dean was reluctant to admit it, but the old gent had met with some success. As the esteemed Mr. Barnum said, there's one born every minute. Lately, Fred had expanded his electronic rummage sale, advertising himself as a local resource for anyone seeking ancestral information in Ouray County.

The town of Ouray, while only a century and a quarter old, was rich in history and Fred O'Connor, together with a cadre of widows with similar interests, spent many hours reading Ouray's old newspapers and written accounts. While these endeavors had produced zero income, the activities endeared him to the local ladies of the historical society who fluttered around the dapper gentleman like chicks at feed time. The sole response to Fred's electronic advertising was not a sale of services, but a questionable purchase he was conned into buying. It remained a sore point with the old man.

"Your box of junk that Chicago guy palmed off on you probably caused my nightmare. I think the gal in my dream was wearing the same white dress he sold you."

"You can make all the fun you want about that stuff, but I'm still working on selling it. I got some ideas and I have a few feelers out," Fred answered, a defensive tone in his voice. "Besides, if you don't take a chance in life, all the best opportunities will pass you by."

The box, advertised as containing Ouray, Colorado correspondence from the last century and "other items of local interest," was offered via the Internet at three hundred dollars. Fred, remembering historical items from an earlier mystery in which he and his stepson were involved, jumped at the offer. But the eagerly anticipated package was a gross disappointment. The letters, eleven in all, were not *from* Ouray, but *to* a Ouray minister's wife, from her sister, a Boston matron. The correspondence was stiff and formal and said little, certainly nothing about the town of Ouray and was totally absent any tidbits of historical nature. The "other items" proved to be a notebook with hundreds of practiced letters and numbers, a pen and dried ink bottle, a white dress with a thrift store smell that had aged to yellow, a comb, hair brush, some ancient under things and a pair of ladies shoes.

"If you keep buying 'opportunities' like Mr. Stanislaw's Salvation Army box, you'll be too broke to answer the door if a real opportunity does come knocking."

Cynthia jumped in to give Fred a hand. "It would be nice if we did have ghosts. We could advertise them in our brochure. It might pick up the Halloween season. Late October was a little slow." She bit back her smile and returned to her myriad of ornaments, carefully laying a tissue paper over a packed box of delicate pieces, merged memories of two families, joined now by a few items of their first Christmas together. "Fred might have a point," she continued. "Dreams always relate to something on your mind, don't they? What have you been thinking about? Pretty girls or just murder and mayhem?"

"Neither. It must be some movie I saw on TV or a book I read a long time ago."

She laughed. "The only thing you watch on TV is football and the last 'book' you read was a bicycle magazine."

"I'm speaking hypothetically," he grumbled. "Just because my conscious mind doesn't remember doesn't mean my subconscious didn't dredge it up with the steak and onions we had for dinner."

"Now you're going to blame my cooking," she said with burlesque severity that made him smile.

"Why are you busting my chops today?" he asked as Fred rose and wandered back to the kitchen for more food.

"I guess I'm just frisky because it's so quiet around here."

"Let's take advantage of it," Dean suggested. "Bird Song's going to be close to empty for a few more days until the ice climbers arrive. How about getting outdoors this afternoon?"

Cynthia readily agreed. They discussed their options—snowshoeing and cross country skiing—but decided to try out the ice skates that they had purchased for one another for Christmas.

When the Deans first arrived in Ouray, they weren't sure how they'd adapt to the long winters but when the first serious snow blanketed the western Colorado Mountains in early December they took up winter sports with the enthusiasm of children. Ouray County was perfect for invigorating outdoor activity, with its crystal clear air and dry, windless temperatures just below freezing. Most days were blessed by a sun that warmed you enough that a couple of heavy sweaters were more than adequate outer wear. And the Ouray County scenery, regardless of the season, always provided a spectacular backdrop to any enterprise.

Fred O'Connor strolled back to the room, his platter replenished, the garage sale section of the newspaper tucked beneath his arm. "So who's our new guest?" he asked.

Cynthia described the woman and boy. Dean was hoping his wife would refrain from expressing her concerns about the woman, but no such luck. He cringed as Cynthia described her giving two different names, allowing Fred yet another shot at constructing a mystery.

"Where's she from? I'll check her out on the web."

Cynthia shook her head. "Spying on our guests is a no-no, Fred." but then added, "Pinkville, Virginia." Dean started to protest but his wife began carrying the packed ornaments from the room and asked in her sweetest tone if he could remove the now-dried Christmas tree and finish a short list of Bird Song chores she'd drawn up earlier. Fred followed Cynthia, asking more questions about the new guest as Dean shook his head in mild frustration.

Dean had unscrewed the base and laid the tree on a drop cloth, in a shower of dry needles, when he looked up to see a thin boy standing by the archway that separated the hall from the living room. It startled him, as the lad had made no sound descending the stairs.

"Hi," Dean said, but received no response. "What's your name?" Still silence. The boy seemed attentive in spite of his muteness so Dean resumed sweeping up needles with his hand and continued to chatter. "A real tree is the only way to go but they sure are a mess, especially out here in the dry air. We try to keep water in the base but the tree drinks it as fast as a sailor on a twelve hour leave." He looked up to see the boy standing above him, holding out a small spiral notebook. On it, written in block letters, was Donnie Ryland. "That's your name?" Dean asked. The boy nodded. Dean stuck out his hand. "Pleased to meet you, Donnie Ryland. I'm David Dean."

Just as Donnie was limply shaking Dean's hand, Cynthia returned, smiled at the boy, and offered her hand as well. He accepted it with equal caution. There was a sound on the stairs and they all turned as the boy's mother paused just inside the room. Donnie turned and ran up to her, gave her a hug and then scampered from the parlor as she entered.

Dean was reminded of his prior night's dream. He hadn't seen the face of his specter, and this woman's hair was dark, not blonde, but nevertheless, there was a chilling feeling of similarity between his vision and this woman standing before him.

Edith Shipton appeared, as Cynthia had described, to be more nervous than a fifth-grader on speech day. She was not pretty, but it was obvious, even to Dean's untrained eye, that her attire, hair do, makeup and whole mien did not evolve from the poor side of the tracks. She wore white slacks, an emerald-green silk blouse and high-heeled shoes. Her long auburn hair, while looking like a magazine ad, was not enough to elevate her that step above ordinary.

Cynthia introduced her as Mrs. Edith Jones, drawing a slight smile but no offered hand.

"Please, just call me Edith." She bit her lip and began to fumble with a small purse. "I was wondering...I gave you a credit card. I'd rather pay in cash." She rummaged around and withdrew a large batch of crumpled bills, spilling several. Before stooping to retrieve them, she handed three one hundred dollar notes to Cynthia. "I don't remember how much you said it costs here. If you need more, tell me. Just give me back the credit card slip."

Cynthia took the money. "The credit card is already recorded but I'll reverse the charge if you'd rather pay in cash."

Edith Shipton looked concerned. "You've already put the charge through?"

"Yes," Cynthia answered. "Is that a problem?"

"I'm not sure," she replied, looking as if she were about to cry.

Fred O'Connor bounced into the room before the woman could comment further. He extended his hand, introducing himself and swinging into a cheery speech about the visual pleasures of wintertime in Ouray. Fred was so close to her she couldn't refuse his outstretched hand. She took it, but pulled back as if she'd touched a hot stove.

"I'm sorry," she interrupted, turned, and fled from the room, leaving Fred in mid-sentence.

"What did I say?" he asked, dumbfounded.

"It's not you," Cynthia told him. She turned to Dean, with a see-what-I-told-you look. "That woman has a definite problem." Her husband couldn't help but agree.

Dean finished dismantling the tree, cleaning up the remaining detritus of the holidays and packing away the delicate figures of a manger scene. He scraped the snow scene from the parlor window and changed the lock on the front door, an insurance company precaution mandated annually because so many keys were not returned. More of the red tape of running a lodging establishment. The phone rang twice while he worked, both times answered by Fred who sounded as if he was booking another guest. The second caller was a lady friend of Fred's by the sound of the muffled conversation. Nothing unusual about that. There was no further sign of either Edith Shipton or the boy.

Cynthia called the men into the kitchen for sandwiches. Fred was still gabbing on the phone so Dean shared with his wife the last of the turkey salad, extended mileage from the Christmas turkey of ten days earlier.

"Did you notice Mrs. Shipton's son had a different last name?" Cynthia asked as she cut her sandwich with her customary delicacy.

"Yes," Dean answered. "But we don't even know for sure Donnie is her boy."

"Yes we do. That's how she introduced him. I suppose she's divorced and 'Shipton' is her maiden name. But who is 'Jones'?" Dean shrugged and reached for a jar of peanut butter just as Fred joined the couple. He had a Lewis Carroll smile on his face.

"You look pleased," Cynthia commented as she put out a third plate.

"Which lucky lady was on the phone?" Dean asked.

"Miss Worthington. But that was no social call. Strictly business." He turned to his stepson, a smile brightening his face. "You might have to eat your words on that purchase I made of them valuable antiques!"

"So, who was the other call?" Dean asked, ignoring Fred's quip.

"I booked a room for tonight," Fred answered, a smug look on his face. "She's coming this afternoon. Just one person. It's a famous author named Miss Gladys Turnbull." Then he added, "But she don't write mysteries, just that science fiction stuff. I told her it would be nice and quiet here. She called from the Montrose airport and booked for a whole week. That will near fill us up when them ice climbing fellows get here." Fred stooped to see what goodies remained in the refrigerator and removed a plate of cold meatloaf.

"Good job!" Cynthia told Fred as she rose to pick up the dishes.

Fred sat at the table and began forking in the cold meat. "Miss Turnbull sounds fat," he mumbled as he surreptitiously dropped morsels to Mrs. Lincoln, the Dean's cat, who tried to remain anonymous behind his legs.

"How does someone *sound* fat?" Dean asked.

"It's a gift I got," he answered. "Works most times."

Cynthia turned to her husband with a look that said 'don't pursue it,' then announced, "If we're going to get in some ice skating, we'd better get cracking. Keep dilly-dallying with lunch and winter will be over!"

"No rush," he answered with a smile. "That doesn't happen until May...or maybe June." But he gulped down his milk and followed her back to their quarters.

While the Ouray winters were far less severe that one might think, they did have a way of wearing out their welcome, like company that won't go home. With the town's elevation near eight thousand feet, plenty of snow was to be expected. So were early autumn frosts and late spring freezes. And snow well into the spring. Perhaps that's why many of the citizens of the picturesque town decided they might as well enjoy mother nature's offerings rather than remain locked indoors for six or seven months. There was little hibernation in the town often called the Switzerland of America.

By the time Dean located two woolen socks that were at least the same color, Cynthia was finished dressing. She emerged from the bathroom in flashy purple ski pants, a matching wool sweater. She did a quick pirouette. "Like it?" she asked.

"Super! But you'd look super in a sack cloth and rags."

"It's the outfit my mom sent for Christmas." Cynthia's widowed mother was a librarian in a small Indiana town. They had not seen her since their wedding but Cynthia spoke to her by telephone frequently and the two were as close as the distance allowed.

"She has great taste. But it's too bad she didn't send you one of those itsy-bitsy outfits all the really cool skaters wear," he answered.

"Why would you want me to wear something so daring, darling?" she asked with a smile.

"So you could show off those incredible legs of yours and I could watch your cute little boom-boom as I followed you, gliding around the rink." He added, "When you're doing all those double Lutzes and triple Saulchows and stuff...just like on TV."

Cynthia laughed. "Dream on! Besides, I haven't skated since I was twelve. But you've got the 'following' part right. There's no doubt you'll be following me, if you're not plunked down on the ice on your own cute little boom-boom. Besides, watching someone's boom-boom isn't nice. Now that you're past forty and bordering on geezerdom, you're beginning to sound like a dirty old man."

"I've always been a dirty old man. Now I'm just an older dirty old man. But I wish you'd stop mentioning my age."

The Ouray skating rink was located on the north side of town, snuggled beneath the shade of a canyon wall to the east. The facility was funded in part by the city's recreation department, whose funds were, for the most part, generated from the highly profitable hot spring pool that operated year around at the edge of town. Private donations and an abundance of volunteer labor helped make the skating rink a success. While the facility lacked artificial ice, piped in waltz music, a snack bar and a Zamboni, there was no fee charge and it was lighted for nighttime use, making it a very popular spot. The rink was an object of pride to the citizens of the small, highly active community.

School was back in session after the holiday recess so the rink was nearly empty. The only other skaters were a mother and her four-year-old pig-tailed professional level daughter and an old man who skated like a retired gold medalist. Cynthia, whose tiny five-two body possessed far more gracefulness than her husband's, managed to look as born on blades as the other two skaters. Dean spent much time clinging to the sideboards until his wife, with a heart full of charity and an arm about his waist, supported him in slow glides around the oval. The little girl, hair streaming, offered encouragement while skating backwards, one leg lifted high and beckoning unsuccessfully for Dean to follow.

After an hour and a half of sore but thorough pleasure, they left, exhausted, with rosy cheeks, wet backsides and aching ankles for the warmth and comfort of Bird Song and mugs of steaming hot chocolate. Neither had mentioned, or even thought about Edith Shipton for the entire enjoyable afternoon.

CHAPTER 2

Fred was absent when they arrived home, but returned just as Cynthia was cutting a warmed apple pie for a late afternoon snack. Donnie Ryland followed close behind him.

"His ma said he could take a stroll up town with me," Fred explained. Cynthia offered the dessert but, surprisingly, Fred declined.

"Me and Donnie just had a banana split," Fred said, putting his arm about the boy's shoulders. Donnie smiled shyly as Fred continued. "We were celebrating."

"Celebrating what?" Dean asked as Donnie wandered out of the room and up the stairs. But before Fred could answer, Cynthia patted him on the shoulder.

"That was sweet of you to take Donnie under your wing," she said.

"Nothing to it. He's a nice kid. We get along just fine."

"I'll second the compliments, Fred," Dean added. "It strikes me the boy could use a friend. It looks as if you pushed all the right buttons with him."

"It's no big deal just because he doesn't want to talk," Fred grumbled. "If he wanted to bad enough, he probably would. It ought to be something of an annoyance to him if everybody keeps hounding him to do something he so obviously don't want to do. I talk enough for the two of us. Told him if he wanted to get my attention, just whack me on the arm."

Dean smiled and gave the old man a pat on the arm. "Keep it up." Then he added, "and tell us why you're celebrating."

The three sat at the table amid the warm smells of chocolate and apples, the Deans looking expectantly. Fred leaned back, as smug as a raffle winner. "I sold Annie Quincy's dress and letters. That's what I'm celebrating. And that's not all. I booked two more rooms for Bird Song as a result of it!" He paused, letting his pronouncement sink in and then added, "There's a couple of ladies from Boston who are shopping for airplane tickets as we sit here. They're coming to Bird Song, just because of that important merchandise you called junk! How about them bananas?"

"I think I'd like to hear the details," Dean said between bites of pie.

"I can't take all the credit," Fred added with smug modesty. "Miss Worthington was the one that actually found them ladies. She listed

Annie Quincy and Reverend Martin on one of them ancestor search bulletin boards on the computer. Sure enough, in just a couple of days she gets a message from these ladies up in Boston. When she told them the valuable stuff I had, they asked for my telephone number. I got a call from this one lady who was as excited as a bear in a beehive. Seems she and her sister have been chasing after this long lost relative for years. It was their ancestor who wrote the letters I've got! This here Annie is their great-aunt. The family knew she died out here in Colorado of the flu, but they didn't know exactly where."

"Valuable?" Dean questioned.

"What did you tell them to get them so excited they want to travel all the way to Ouray Colorado and Bird Song?" Cynthia asked.

Dean paused half way through his pie, awaiting Fred's answer. Fred picked up an extra fork. "You gonna finish that?" he asked, pointing at Dean's plate. Dean didn't answer quick enough before Fred began eating his pie. "I just told 'em the truth," he continued, his mouth half full.

Dean shook his head. "Let me get this straight. Two ladies are flying all the way from Boston to buy some old underwear, a yellow dress and a bunch of junk? And a dozen 'having-a-great-time-wish-you-were-here' letters? That's a stretch and a half, Fred."

"I didn't even have to sell all of the stuff—just the clothes and letters." Then he added magnanimously, "I'm donating the school book and ink bottle to the museum, seeing as Miss Worthington helped in locating the buyers and all."

"What did you tell these women?" Cynthia asked. "Are you sure they know exactly what your selling them?"

"I listed piece by piece what I had. I even read the letters. Told 'em what I paid for the merchandise and they didn't bat an eyebrow. You gotta understand these genealogy-type women," he added. "It's a big deal to them, to get stuff from their ancestor and find out where she lived and all. This Annie woman was their grandpa's little sister. It's like finding a long lost periodical son."

"'Prodigal' daughter, who's been dead a hundred years," Dean answered. "You could stick the junk in a box and mail it a whole lot cheaper than having them fly out here. It's not like there's a long line waiting to buy that stuff." Dean got up to get a fresh piece of pie.

"It's important for 'em to stay here—in the same place where ancestor Annie lived."

Cynthia looked at him. "You mean Ouray."

"Yeah," Fred answered, but absent much conviction.

"You didn't tell the women Annie Quincy lived here, at Bird Song, did you?" she asked.

"No. Not really. I mentioned how this here place was a boarding house in the old days and now it's a fine bed and breakfast. They said they always heard Aunt Annie lived in a fine rooming house before she met up with Reverend Martin. They seemed to think that was a first rate coincidence, especially Effie, the first sister I talked to. The other one wasn't so pleasant."

"Let me get this straight," Dean asked. "You told these ladies that this Annie Quincy woman probably lived here in Bird Song?"

"No. Not exactly. They just suspected she might have lived here, Ouray being a small town and all."

"What would lead them to suspect that? We don't know what Bird Song was at the turn of the century, just that there was a building or some sort on this site. You said so yourself when you checked the old records. The deeds tell you who owned the place, but not what use they made of the property."

"Son, Annie Quincy lived in a boarding house. This here was a boarding house, at least at one time in the past. Miss Worthington said she remembers it from when she was a girl."

"Miss Worthington was a girl in the nineteen-forties! In the eighteen-nineties Ouray had three thousand people living in town, three or four times as many as today. Even if Bird Song was a boarding house, there must have been scores of lodging places just like it."

"I never told the ladies for sure the gal lived here. They just got all excited and had me hold a couple of rooms. I wasn't about to talk them out of it. You were just belly-aching, crying poor-mouth that we were knee deep in a slow period."

"Not next week! We've practically got a full house of ice climbers starting in a couple of days," Dean answered.

"Well, now we're even closer to having a full house." Fred wiped his mouth and rose. "And I've got some research to do down at the library. I've got to bone up on the Reverend Martin and his little woman."

"I just hope these Boston ladies don't think this box of yours has some truly valuable items in it," Cynthia said. "At least let me see if I can clean up some of the things. Perhaps I can get the smell out of that old dress."

While Cynthia was off with Fred sorting his treasure box, Dean remained in the kitchen washing up the dishes. Just as he was finishing, the doorbell chimed. A red haired woman he guessed to be somewhere between thirty and sixty stood between two gigantic suitcases. Her brilliant hair topped a freckled face and mile-wide smile. Fred O'Connor's gifted powers of telephone telepathy remained in tact. Gladys Turnbull wasn't just fat, she was immense.

"Hi," she said in a high pitched voice just as a loud ringing sound came from her luggage. "Damn!" she exclaimed. "It did that in the airport, too." She sat on one suitcase, nearly bending it in two while unlatching the other until it exploded open, scattering contents about the porch. The woman rummaged through the colorful attire in a frenzy until she retrieved and turned off a large old fashioned alarm clock. Dean's offer to help was dismissed as he looked up and down the street hoping no neighbors were witnessing the growing pile of ample sized clothes. When garb and miscellany were re-packed, sort of, the two struggled indoors amid greetings and apologies just as Fred and Cynthia entered the hall.

After introductions and the necessary sign-in paper work was complete it was decided to assign Ms. Turnbull a second floor room. While the sole down stairs room would have saved considerable huffing and puffing, Dean feared the smaller quarters and especially the bed would not adequately accommodate the woman's substantial mass. A second trip to her rental car for a computer, two briefcases and a box of papers confirmed the wisdom of his choice of the larger room.

"Beautiful! Beautiful!" Ms. Turnbull called, with child-like enthusiasm as Dean heaved her luggage up the stairs behind her. His view of her sweat pants in front of him were like a sack of footballs being dragged back to the locker room after a high school scrimmage. She paused at the top to catch her breath and he did the same, before she poked around her new digs. "Me and Belfair will love it!"

Belfair, she explained, in rapid-fire falsetto, was the heroine of a series of intergalactic romances she was writing. She was an author, she explained with a puff of her ample bosom, and had just returned from Roswell, New Mexico, Mecca of the strange and alien.

"I'm so psyched!" she rambled, thrusting a suitcase on the bed. "I can hardly wait to go to sleep!"

"I'm sure you're exhausted," Cynthia said as she followed the pair into the room. "The bed's very comfortable." Fred, who had tagged along, beat a hasty retreat downstairs, making the excuse of a trip to the library.

"Oh, no! I don't mean I'm tired! Lord knows, I'm sure the bed's comfortable but sleeping is when I write! Belfair visits me in the nighttime! You see, I dream all Belfair's adventures and Roswell was such a marvelous experience! The aura there where real aliens actually roamed among us, well...it just took my breath away! I'm sure tonight we'll have scads of fun! Belfair is on the planet Draghow now and those Draghonian men are something else!" Wink, wink. The Deans followed Fred O'Connor's example. They too beat a hasty departure for the downstairs.

"What were we saying about strange guests?" Dean asked when they were alone in their quarters. "Perhaps we should charge her for a double room when Belfair shows up. Talk about out of this world!"

"Don't complain," Cynthia said. "Things have been pretty normal around here since last June." Her comments brought to mind the death of Bird Song's very first guest and the strange events that followed.

The balance of the afternoon was spent on household chores and packing away the last remnants of the holiday. Cynthia carefully hand washed the articles of clothing from Fred's box of historical goodies and hung them outside in the sun to dry. Dean reread the eleven letters he had only glanced at earlier. However, no words of century-old wisdom leapt from the pages. Each letter, written in excellent penmanship, began Dear Annie but there were no accompanying envelopes and no addresses. Each was signed, Your loving sister, Rachael Quincy. Each was nearly a copy of the others, unremarkable in its cold formality. None was longer than a page and each asked after Annie's health and well being and then added a few lines that mentioned that all was well in Boston. One note described in two sentences a Sunday trip to the Public Gardens while another mentioned three years had passed since the sisters had seen one another. Four letters mentioned Rev. Martin and the wonderful work he and Annie were doing with 'the poor mistaken souls.' The second earliest dated letter expressed sorrow that the wedding could not take place in Boston and a gift was being shipped separately. All the letters were dated between November of 1898 and January of 1900. There was nothing unusual in the final epistle to indicate why the correspondence abruptly ended. Both Deans agreed the letters were polite but of zero historical interest and strangely unloving.

Fred telephoned from the library that he would not be back for dinner, instead no doubt tasting some widow's fare. Cynthia cooked something quick and Italian for dinner, small white things that looked as they would suddenly explode into butterflies, given sufficient time. Dean doused them in enough Parmesan cheese that they looked like Mount Abrams in February. It somewhat squelched the taste, enough so they were palatable.

"David," Cynthia said, stretching out the name as she saw him masticating longer than was necessary for normal digestion.

"So I like cheese," he answered, and then added, "it's really good."

The other houseguests had left earlier and separately after asking directions to one of the few winter restaurants that remained open in Ouray. The Deans dallied over the dishes and then took a slow stroll around town, stopping at the Western Hotel a few blocks away. There they each drank a glass of Fat Tire Ale. The couple was back in Bird Song by seven o'clock.

As the Deans entered the hall Gladys Turnbull was waddling up the stairs. She looked back and with a finger wave of two chubby digits and called, "Nighty-night. Time to visit the planet Draghow!" Dean just shook his head and smiled.

"I think she likes you," Cynthia said.

"That's all I need," Dean grumbled, "an intergalactic affair."

Fred had returned and was seated in the parlor with the Quincy letters and the rest of his acquired paraphernalia spread out before him on the coffee table. He was talking to Edith Shipton who was nodding and biting her fingernails, when she wasn't wringing her hands. Dean couldn't recall the last time he'd seen someone so nervous and obviously uncomfortable. Donnie sat close to his mother doing a Denver Post crossword puzzle. A fire blazed away in the cozy room. Edith was dressed in a sweat suit, though the descriptive name appeared to be a misnomer in her case. It wasn't designed to absorb perspiration and probably cost twice the price of a David Dean suit, at least the last time he'd purchased one. Donnie was in pajamas.

"This boy is a whiz at puzzles," Fred said as the Deans joined the group. Donnie gave a nervous smile.

"Are you on school vacation?" Cynthia asked as she looked over his shoulder at his work.

The boy looked at his mother for an answer.

"No," Edith answered. "He doesn't go." Then she added, almost to herself, "I'll have to make some arrangements. Perhaps a tutor."

"Then you'll be away from home for awhile?" Dean asked. The question seemed to bewilder the woman. She bit her lip but didn't answer, causing an uncomfortable silence. She started to rise but her son tugged her down, indicating he wanted to remain.

Fred O'Connor changed the subject. "I was telling Mrs. Edith about these here letters and how the two ladies from Boston will be coming to Bird Song. They called back and will be here tomorrow afternoon. Just think, great-grand-nieces of the woman who wrote these here letters to Ouray a hundred years ago." Edith smiled, and in Dean's judgment feigned interest, but she made no further move to leave the room.

Cynthia rose. "I forgot about Annie's clothes. They're still outside drying." She hurried from the room.

"How did you make out at the library?" Dean asked Fred. "Did you locate the Reverend Martin and his wife?"

"You bet," Fred answered, pleased with himself. "They were quite a couple. He had a church here for ten years or so and his wife Anne was 'a well respected lady of social importance,' at least according to a newspaper article I found, and a paragraph in the local history. 'Course I haven't had time to do any really in depth searching, at least yet. Me and Miss Worthington are going to do a real study tomorrow. Miss Worthington's a big mucky-muck in the historical society," he said, for Edith Shipton's benefit.

Dean picked up one of the letters, glanced at it, and put it down. "Too bad we don't have the Ouray woman's side of this correspondence. Her sister in Boston wasn't very talkative."

A sharp ring from the hall telephone interrupted him. As he rose to answer it, he couldn't help noticing Edith Shipton's alarmed reaction to the ring. She looked petrified. When Dean returned after confirming a reservation from yet another ice climber, she sat huddled in the corner of the sofa.

Cynthia followed her husband into the room, holding the Annie Quincy dress in front of her, with a bundle of under garments beneath her arm. The clothes looked far brighter after their first washing in a century.

"This is the dress that came with the letters," she explained to Edith.

"That's nice," Edith answered unconvincingly as she rose to leave.

Cynthia dropped the bundle on the sofa and held the dress up in front of the woman. "It looks as if it fits you. I'm far too short myself or I'd try it on."

Edith Shipton took the garment and held it against herself. The dress was full length, rather plain, with a high collar. Cynthia had ironed it and the dress looked quite appealing in spite of its hundred-year age.

"Yes," Edith answered. "It's about my size." For the first time since she'd arrived, Edith Shipton had a peaceful look on her face. "What was she like?" she asked. "Was she a happy woman?"

"I'd say so," Fred answered. "So far as we know. She was a minister's wife and did lots of good for folks. I'd say she was happy."

Donnie tugged at his mother's hem and motioned to the dress, nodding his head.

"I think he wants you to try it on," Cynthia said. Edith smiled but shook her head. Donnie continued to tug and look up at his mother.

Edith ignored him and sat back on the sofa, the dress still spread in front of her. She picked up the letters. "She wrote these?"

"No," Fred answered. "They was written to her. She was Annie Quincy. Anne Quincy Martin, after she married the minister fellow."

Edith began to unpile the rest of the clothes, half-slips, long drawers and top coverings that Dean assumed were forerunners of bras. There were a dozen articles of clothing in all and Edith examined each carefully. Dean picked up the comb, pen and ink bottle and passed them to her as well.

She held the shoes next to her feet. They were approximately the right size but too dried and twisted to wear. Smiling, she ran the comb through her long hair.

"Look," she said examining it. "It still has some hair on it! Do you suppose they belong to that woman?"

"I'd guess so," Fred answered. "I can't think who else would have used it in the last hundred years."

"They're blonde," Edith said, sounding disappointed. "I thought they might be auburn, like mine." She extracted the few filament-like strands and held them in her fingertips.

Cynthia went to the hall desk and brought back an envelope. "If they are that old, they're certainly worth saving."

Donnie picked up a pair of long legged drawers and held them up with a smile but Edith snatched them away and shook her finger in a mock scold. She continued to examine the articles. "It makes me feel really close to her. Annie. I hope she had a pleasant life."

Donnie renewed his pantomime request for Edith to try on the dress.

"Go ahead and try it on," Cynthia said. "You'd look lovely in it."

Dean was startled to see a tear slide down the woman's cheek. She placed the dress over the back of the sofa with care and rose. "Perhaps tomorrow." She turned to Donnie and reached for his hand. "It's time for bed."

The boy pulled away with a scowl and tapped on the newspaper puzzle, indicating he wasn't finished. Edith hesitated.

"The boy can stay down here with us if it's all right with you," Dean said. Donnie popped to his feet and brushed a kiss on his mother's cheek and resumed his work. Edith seemed confused, as if she wanted her son to accompany her but was hesitant to make a scene.

"He'll be fine," Cynthia said, and then, gestured to the dress. "Take it. You can try it on in the morning."

Edith looked once more at her son and then picked up the garment and the comb. Once more, she held the dress in front of herself.

Donnie smiled at his mother and nodded his approval. Then, impishly, handed her the underwear as well.

She laughed and took them. "Perhaps," she said, as she turned a pirouette and left the room.

CHAPTER 3

Cynthia glanced at her husband, a troubled look on her face as if to express her continued concern over the departing woman. However, she said nothing in deference to Edith Shipton's son who remained engrossed with his puzzle. Cynthia took Edith's place on the sofa and began folding the ancient underwear. "I hope the Boston sisters find some use for theses awful things. The dress is pretty but I can't imagine having to wear these undies!"

"'I dreamed I married a minister in my—.'"

"Be nice," Cynthia cautioned, cutting off her husband.

Dean thought of a few more snappy comebacks but kept the rest of his thoughts to himself in front of Donnie. He just smiled at Cynthia, who could read his mind. He began helping her by handing her the clothes. "What's this thing-a-ma-jig called?" he asked, picking up one of the items.

"It's a chemise," Cynthia answered, folding yet another article. "This is a camisole. And I think you best keep your thoughts to yourself."

"It's enough to make Victoria really keep a secret."

"Gentlemen don't stare at ladies' unmentionables."

"I'm only interested in the historical implications," he said.

Fred left the room and returned with a pencil and pad. "I best make an inventory of this stuff before I turn it over to the ladies. That way, when they see how many items they're getting, they'll realize what a bargain I'm giving 'em."

"Right," said Dean, with a wink to his wife.

"Didn't the Boston ladies have any interest in the other items you're donating to the museum?" Cynthia asked, picking up the brush.

"I didn't offer 'em. But I'll show the stuff to them, seeing as it all belonged to their Auntie." Then he added, "I've got to stay on the good side of them museum folks. They're a big help in my business."

"You can say that again," Dean said, and added, "if they found a couple of live ones willing to pay for this junk!" He raised what looked like a pantaloon. "These ought to be a real crowd pleaser." Then he noticed something. "Hey, she has her name in it!" In the top seam, faded but legible, was written *Annie* in very small print. Both Fred and Cynthia looked over Dean's shoulder and agreed. They examined the rest of the garments and each, upon careful observation, was identified in a like fashion, although some of the markings were so faded they were no longer legible.

"Why would a woman write her name in her underwear?" Dean asked. "Was she afraid her hubby might wear her drawers by mistake?"

Cynthia looked perplexed. "All I can think of is perhaps she sent her clothes out to a laundry and didn't want them mixed up."

"Maybe she went to Girl Scout camp," Dean commented, winning a scowl from Cynthia.

"I used to send my laundry out, before I married a washer woman, but I never put my name on my shorts!" Dean said with a smile.

"You'd better watch what you call me or you'll be sending them out again! This was a hundred years ago. Things were done differently."

"They had these Chinese laundries in town," Fred answered. "That must be why she marked them."

"Why just the first name? Ouray wasn't that small a town." Dean answered. Neither Fred nor Cynthia had a ready answer.

"It's sort of a mystery, isn't it?" Fred said as he resumed his list.

Donnie had paid no attention to their conversation but having tired of his puzzle, picked up the notebook of letters and numbers and began to study it, turning the binder page by page. Dean sat on the floor next to the lad. "What do you make of it Donnie? Do you think Annie was practicing her letters and numbers?" The boy shook his head "no."

Cynthia bounced down to the floor to join the pair. "The letters written from Boston are answering correspondence Annie presumably wrote to her sister." She tickled her husband. "Why would she still be practicing? See how good I am at deduction now that I'm married to an ex-detective? Next suggestion, Mr. Investigator."

Dean studied the book. "There's nothing to prove the practice note-book is even in her writing. Maybe she's teaching someone else to write," he said. "Fred mentioned she was a social minded do-gooder type citizen. Maybe she gave lessons to local kids or was a tutor."

"That's possible. But it doesn't look like a child's writing to me. Granted, it's just a collection of miscellaneous letters and numbers but somehow, it doesn't look like practice work."

Dean reached up on the sofa and pulled down a few articles of the clothing. He compared the letters in the book to those on the hems of the garments.

"I'm no expert, but I'd say the writing is the same hand, wouldn't you?" he said, holding the book next to the lettering. Fred joined the trio and nodded in agreement.

"What else could the notebook be? Maybe she did write it years earlier and it really is her practice work," he offered.

It was Cynthia who answered. "It seems to me when you practice letters, you print uppercase letters first, don't you? These are all lower case. Besides, they're too random. Any practice work I've ever seen was done by rote. You write a whole series of 'A's" and 'B's" and so forth. You don't write a jejune collection of hodgepodge letters and numbers like these."

The first page of the notebook looked like this:

8m2f3km8m7ay7aa297867a88m4gkm38r366v2b7fpb452m4g5a
v2d4528m2agfam4ra38ak4692fd7j284k3n263km8848m3ab39-r3f825
b45f3fkx8m2m278 m7av22f64r2529f4r8m788m2b2fm7n262d87f9
383a4ma4j4697a367pmg99629m2f2v2f278mbp8m3fv67fs28ax
3fay3824d8m2j469385p 844y2f8m2r3f94r845398m3a544b4d
8m2ab4 s27f9rm3as2pv5278m4d8m4a2rm4n3a3829m252vg88m2
d57b23ad54z2fd7a8x 3'n28532984a622y7663fn73fx
Bpb3f9r4f'852627a2b2d54b7668m78m7am7yy2f29a3fj252nxB7583f
d35a8n3a3829b27f9jm7fk29bp63d2x

Fred O'Connor's eyes lit up. "I'll bet it's a Civil War code! Dang!"

Dean stared at the notebook. "The Civil War was over thirty-odd years before this was written." But he didn't pooh-pooh Fred's suggestion. Donnie nodded his head in agreement.

"Why would a minister's wife have a code book?" Dean asked no one in particular.

"Why does anyone have a code book?" Cynthia answered. "So someone else doesn't know what's written in it. Maybe it's a diary. If she didn't have a place she felt was safe enough, maybe she wrote her journal in code."

"Good point," Fred said, rubbing his chin like a Chinese scholar. "Now all we have to do is break it!"

Dean continued to examine the script. "Secrets from her husband the minister? I'm having a bit of trouble with that." Then he added, "If it is in code, we're the wrong crowd for trying to break it."

"Not necessarily," Cynthia answered, studying the notebook.

Dean gave her a questioning look. "Is there some activity in your background that you haven't told me about, Madam Spy?" he chided.

"No. But any code a minister's wife of the last century put together can't be all that sophisticated, can it? After all, we're not dealing with

Mata Hari. Look, there is some punctuation!" Closer study showed an occasional comma and apostrophe.

"Perhaps it's like those puzzles in the newspaper where they simply substitute a different letter for the real one," Fred offered.

Dean shook his head. "The trouble with that theory is here we have letters *and* numbers. The newspaper cryptograms are limited to replacement letters. What do the numbers mean? And the puzzles in the newspaper break the words apart. This girl's code, if it is in fact a code, is mostly one continuous line, with hardly any punctuation. That would be a dickens to solve."

"Well," Fred offered, "maybe each time you get to a number, you jump that many letters ahead in the alphabet for the replacement letter."

Cynthia shook her head. "That doesn't work. There are a lot of places where numbers follow other numbers. Besides, I think we're complicating it."

"Maybe the numbers are the punctuation," Dean suggested.

"Still too complicated," Cynthia said. "Let's see what we have. How many different numbers and letters are there?" She began counting and then reached over to the end table for a pencil and paper.

"If it is some form of code, it must have been the devil to write," Dean said but before his wife could answer, there was a noise on the stairs.

They all looked up as Edith Shipton tentatively entered the room, dressed in Annie Quincy's antique dress. She smiled. Cynthia set aside the notebook and papers and rose. Everyone followed suit, as if welcoming royalty into the warm and ancient parlor. Donnie ran up to his mother and gave her a hug.

"You look beautiful," Cynthia said as the others nodded in agreement.

The white dress scarcely touched the tops of her bare feet and fitted her perfectly. She had pulled her long auburn hair high on her head, making her appear taller and almost regal in spite of the simple lines of the garment, and the plainness of her features.

"Annie Quincy, born again," Fred said.

"I almost feel I'm she," Edith said, sounding embarrassed by her admission. "That was her name, Annie? I close my eyes and it's as if she's who I am. I'm Annie, standing in my parlor, a hundred years ago." She looked down at her son, as if just now noticing his presence. "Go up to bed now, Donnie. I put on the dress for you, just as you asked." She bent down, kissed him, and gave him a pat on his behind. He hesitated, but then followed her orders and scrambled up the stairs.

Edith stood there, neither following her son, nor making any move to enter further into the room. "I guess that's a fib. I didn't just put the dress on for Donnie. I wanted wear it."

"I'm pleased you did. It looks lovely on you," Cynthia said as she returned to the sofa.

"You'll have to model it for them ancestor ladies when they come tomorrow," Fred said. Edith just smiled.

"Come," Cynthia said, motioning to the sofa seat next to her as Dean and Fred took chairs. "Sit with us a while."

Edith hesitated, as if embarrassed but then sat next to Cynthia Dean, adjusting the dress behind her. "Look at me," she said. "I'm like some poor farm girl, barefoot as the day I was born."

"Bird Song's pretty informal," Fred said.

"It's silly. I felt such a strong urge to dress up in this, like a little girl trying to be someone she isn't—fishing in an attic trunk." She looked at Fred. "Was she happy here?" she asked again.

"I guess so," he answered, surprised at the question. "No reason to say otherwise." Then he added, "I don't know a whole lot about her. Yet."

Dean offered his two cents. "We don't know where she lived in town before she married the minister. There were lots of rooming houses but we have no idea how Bird Song was utilized at the turn of the century."

"Oh, I'm sure she was here! I can almost feel her presence. Oh, yes! She was here! I'm certain of it!" She looked at them, embarrassed at her own exuberance. "What a senseless thing to say. How could I possibly know? Wishful thinking, I guess." Then, as if to change the subject, she added, to Fred, "I'm sure you'll find she was happy, wherever she lived."

Fred answered. "I expect you're right. She was a do-gooder and a society lady, married a minister. That was a real high-up position in town. I'd guess she was real content here in Ouray."

The answer seemed to please Edith Shipton and she appeared to relax. "That would be so nice. To be happy. To have a contented life and be loved by someone." She turned again to Fred. "Did she have children?"

"I don't suspect so. Them Boston ladies would have said if they knew any cousins. And they wouldn't have had so much trouble tracing Annie down if she left heirs. No, I'd say she didn't have kids."

"Is there something troubling you?" Cynthia asked. "I don't mean to pry, but you seem on edge. If there is anything we can do to help, we'd certainly be willing."

David Dean felt a momentary twinge of the here-we-go-agains that floated by on the wings of his wife's question. Edith shook her head no, much to Dean's relief.

A rhythmic thumping echoed from the floor above. Edith looked up. "That's Donnie's way of calling me." She started to rise but Fred O'Connor rose to his feet.

"You sit still. I'll go up. It's past my bedtime anyway." Before she could protest, Fred was off with a wave good night.

Edith looked up at the ceiling once more but in a few moments there was only silence. The Fred O'Connor charm extended beyond the blue haired set to children as well. Cynthia took the opportunity to push Edith a bit further.

"Just remember we're here to help you if there's anything we can do."

Edith seemed to slump down in her seat. "No. There's nothing to be done." She looked up at Cynthia. "Donnie and I will be leaving in the morning. I've already packed."

"Oh, that's a shame!" Cynthia answered. "I understood you to say you'd be staying with us for some time. I hope nothing has happened."

The woman didn't answer for a moment of unsettling silence. She twisted her now-empty left hand ring finger and spoke, in barely a whisper. "I've left my husband." She closed her eyes, as if to block the tears.

"I'm so sorry!" Cynthia put an arm about the woman's shoulders.

"It's something I had to do. I had to get away from him."

"It must be tough on Donnie too. A little scary for both of you," Dean added. "I'm sure it was a difficult decision."

"I made such a mistake. My life is one big mistake." She began to cry, her sobs muffled as she leaned forward against her arms. "I just don't know what to do."

While Dean felt sorry for the distressed woman, he continued to hope his dearest Cynthia would let the matter rest.

Edith looked up, rubbed a sleeve across her eyes to dry them, then brushed her hands down the white dress, smoothing the fabric against her legs. She sighed. "I'll miss it here. It's so calm. Like floating back to another time."

"Why don't you stay?" Cynthia asked. "Perhaps being out here in the mountains would take your mind off all the troubles you're having. You can rest up here at Bird Song—give yourself time enough to make logical decisions. I'm sure now your mind is all awhirl. It must be distressing, trying to make logical plans about your future. Not only yours but Donnie's as well."

She shook her head. "You don't understand. I'm so afraid of what he'll do I can't think beyond the hour!" She looked from one to the other. "Now he'll know where we are. I was so stupid. I used my charge card and he'll trace us here. I know he will. That's why we have to leave in the morning."

"He didn't know you were coming here?" Dean asked.

"God no! He'd kill me in a minute! I know he would! I can't let him find me!"

"What about Donnie?" Dean asked.

She spoke, venom in her voice. "Jerome Shipton isn't Donnie's father. He may want to be and pretend he is but he isn't."

"I'm sure there's someplace you can go." Cynthia said. "Some friends or relatives."

She shook her head. "You don't know Jerome. He'll kill me before he'd let me take Donnie away. And he'll kill both of us if we go back to him."

"Has he hurt you in the past?" Cynthia asked.

Edith closed her eyes as tears seeped down her cheeks but she wouldn't answer.

"No one is going to harm you here," Cynthia said, reminiscent to Dean of another promise, another time. Dean crossed his fingers and hoped this affiance would spawn fewer complications than the last. He took a deep breath and plunged in.

"There are laws to protect women if a husband is abusive. He has no hold on you if you decide you want to live apart. Unless he claims to be Donnie's father or he's adopted the boy, I doubt he'd have any rights to see him either. You can ask the court for an order of restraint against your husband and stop him from coming anywhere near you if you're in fear of the man."

"David knows what he's talking about," Cynthia offered. "He used to be a police detective, back in Pennsylvania. He has a lot of experience in these matters."

Edith kept shaking her head 'no' as he spoke. "You don't understand. No one tells Jerome Shipton what to do. Sooner or later he always gets his way. Nothing stops him, ever." She rose. "Look, I'm sorry to bother you with my troubles. You're very kind but we'll just leave in the morning. That will be best for everyone."

Cynthia rose to join her, taking her arm. "Please. Sit down. You're safe here. I'm sure it's far more difficult to trace a credit card than it seems in the movies, even if your husband is trying that hard to find you."

Edith allowed herself to be led back to her seat. She turned to Cynthia, a pleading look in her eyes. "Just don't tell him I'm here when he calls, please!"

Cynthia gently prodded the woman until Edith Shipton began to relate her story, speaking in almost a monotone. She glanced at the door every few minutes, as if her abandoned husband might rush in and drag her back to his lair. It was a trying conversation—obvious this bundle of nerves had little experience talking to strangers. Though Dean wished to remain at hand's-length from her troubled life he quickly sensed from her disjointed description Cynthia had been correct when she assessed that the woman carried serious emotional pain. At the very least, perhaps they might be able to direct her to the help she so obviously needed.

They gleaned from her story that, as suspected, she came from a moneyed background. Dean guessed she had been pampered and protected all of her life and was now ill equipped to function independently. At sixteen, while vacationing at a New Hampshire camp for girls, she had become involved with a local boy, Donald Ryland. The result was not surprising. She managed to keep her pregnancy secret until an abortion was out of the question and Donnie was born. Ryland, twenty years old at the time, wanted to marry Edith but her irate parents forbade it. Instead, they literally forced her to wed Jerome Shipton, a widowed family friend twelve years her senior.

"Did your husband hurt you from the beginning?" Cynthia asked as Edith paused in her narration. Edith began to cry, but once again wouldn't answer. Cynthia put her arms about the woman. Rocking back and forth, head bowed, Edith began to touch herself, her cheek, her arms, her body, again and again, as if indicating where she had been struck but unable to utter the painful words.

"God," whispered Cynthia, looking up to her husband.

"You have to tell the authorities," Dean said. "This guy doesn't deserve to walk the streets. No wife beater does." He rose and crossed to the fireplace and began to bank the fire as the hall clock struck eleven times. The two women remained huddled together on the sofa.

"I just want to be away from him," Edith said in a muffled voice.

"There must be someone you can call," Dean offered.

"I'm not sure. I just don't know."

"Don't decide anything tonight. Just rest. We'll talk about it in the morning. You've had a terrible day." Cynthia spoke in a consoling tone as both women rose.

"I think we can all use a good night's sleep," Dean said. Cynthia gave their guest a hug and retreated down the hall to the Dean's quarters while Edith climbed the stairs. Dean remained in the room long enough to turn out the parlor lights and finish banking the fire. As he was closing the drapes, he glanced outside. Light snow had begun to fall—tiny crystals hardly visible in the light of the lamp across the street. The flakes drifted directly down, undisturbed in their descent by any hint of a breeze in the still night air.

As Dean was setting the hall night-light, the phone rang. As he answered the late night call, he glanced up the staircase to see Edith in the hall above, a specter in her antique dress, a look of alarm on her face. She had loosened her hair and her long tresses fell in a wave, over her shoulder and across her small breasts. Standing there, silhouetted against the upstairs light, he was once again reminded of his prior night's dream. He picked up the phone.

"Is this place called Bird Song?" asked a male voice. Dean answered affirmatively and smiled up at Edith Shipton, giving an all-is-well wave. She disappeared.

"I realize it's late out there but I'm verifying one of your guests. I don't want to disturb her...just make sure she's staying there. Edith Shipton?"

Dean heart sank. Shit! While he had dismissed in his mind, Edith's fears that she might be traced by her credit card charge as irrational, here was evidence that, in fact, her concerns were well founded.

"Sorry," he answered. He turned his back to the stairs and spoke in almost a whisper. "We don't have an Edith Shipton registered here."

"Are you sure?" asked a doubting voice.

"Yup. Bird Song is a small inn and I'd know." There followed a long pause, followed by an abrupt thank-you and a dial tone.

Dean took a deep breath and tried to consider the implications of his answer to the caller as he made his way to his bedroom. He considered not telling Cynthia about the call, but no, they didn't have secrets between them. He undressed while his wife was still in the bathroom and was in bed when she entered the room.

Six months of marriage had not diminished an iota the awe in which he held this woman he so loved. The long flannel nightgown, while perhaps frumpy in someone's eyes, was perfect for the time and season. His mind was, at least for the moment, clear of all thoughts except this beautiful petite woman. He smiled up at her and delayed telling her about the call.

"I'm a flannel kind of guy."

"As opposed to?" she answered as she switched off the light and slipped in beside him.

"Oh, there are silk guys, and cotton guys and lots of slinky guys. And there are 'teddy' guys, you know, guys who drool over those short little outfits that leave nothing to the imagination."

"And you're a flannel guy?" She snuggled closer.

"Yup."

"And if I wore one of those, 'leaves-nothing-to-the-imagination outfits' you wouldn't drool?"

Dean shook his head in mock seriousness. "You have to understand. What we're talking about here is the packaging. The most important item remains the contents. Now your 'contents' are something extra special so regardless of the packaging, you're still first class to me. It all comes down to levels of excitement."

She kissed him and smiled. "But flannel is still special?" He nodded in agreement and she continued, "Being a flannel gal is nice, too. It makes you feel all warm and cuddly, especially on a winter nights when it's snowing and especially when you're with a special flannel guy." Then she kissed him and asked, "Who was on the phone, flannel guy?" The spell was broken like a dropped mirror on a marble floor.

He told her. She pulled back and at first said nothing.

"You lied to the bastard. Thank you."

"I didn't lie," he said with feigned indignance. "Our guest registered as Edith Jones. I told him we didn't have an *Edith Shipton* registered here. I was a hundred percent truthful—same as always, almost." It was too dark to see the smile he was sure was there. "Maybe I was a bit misleading," he added.

She kissed him. "Thanks for being 'a bit misleading.'"

Dean put his arms behind his head. "It won't do any good. He'll know I was lying. He must have traced her by the charge slip so he knows she came here."

"Perhaps it will give Edith enough time to go to the authorities and force him to stay away."

"We're not going to get involved in another mess again, are we?" he asked, knowing full well the answer.

"No," Cynthia answered. "But it turns my stomach to think of a man hurting a woman like that. I feel so sorry for her. She's so vulnerable and practically incapable of doing anything on her own about her problems. And so troubled. Did you see how she adopted the Annie Quincy persona? On the one hand, she's trying desperately to escape, while she's so brow-beaten and insecure she believes it's impossible! God, what a life! It sounds like some English gothic—a naive waif married off to tyrannical older man who holds her hostage in a golden cage and beats her into submission!"

"Just remember, we can't solve all of the world's problems."

"But we can't turn our backs on them either," Cynthia answered. Dean knew both statements were correct.

CHAPTER 4

Dean's snuggled slumber drifted to wakefulness sometime in the heart of the wee hours when a metallic sound of ringing returned him to the world of the living. At first he feared it was a telephone until its uninterrupted sound told him otherwise. It woke Cynthia, too. She assumed it was morning in her grogginess until a squinted peek at their clock showed two AM. The sound stopped in a minute or so but a three AM recurrence woke them enough to hold a brief conversation on the source of the nocturnal noise, a conversation repeated at four AM, by which time the couple were fully awake.

"It's upstairs," Cynthia mumbled. "That's all I can tell. But who gets up in the middle of the night?"

Dean thought of Edith Shipton. "Edith said she was leaving in the morning. Maybe she wanted to get an early start."

"At two A M? And again at three, and four?"

"Maybe she keeps changing her mind," he answered. Then he remembered the ringing alarm clock in the luggage of their other guest. "God," he muttered. "I'll bet it's a collect call for Gladys Turnbull from the planet Draghow!" Further speculation ended as they both drifted back to sleep.

After dawn arrived at last and the couple were showered and dressed, they speculated further on the late night sounds as Cynthia filled Bird Song's breakfast table with fresh baked goodies. A quiet investigation revealed all upstairs doors closed and the sound of snoring from the Dame Turnbull's room. Edith Shipton's rental car, blanketed in six inches of fresh snow, remained out front.

Cynthia buttered her toast while Dean dribbled orange blossom honey on three leftover rolls from last night's supper. "If that was Gladys Turnbull's alarm clock, I hope she gets it fixed. Her room is right next to Fred's. If she's kept him up all night, he'll be more of a morning bear than usual."

"My guess is she sets the damn alarm multiple times every night."

"Why would she do that?"

"To interrupt her dreams."

"Why?" Then Cynthia answered her own question before biting into her toast. "So she can write about what she's dreaming?"

37

Fred The Bear joined them, later than usual, and confirmed their speculation. The old man was as nattily attired in his customary fashion, but his eyes betrayed his lack of sleep. "She was up half the night," he muttered. "The alarm clock wasn't enough. Then she shuffled around with the computer, giggled, sighed, snorted, yawned and went back to sleep. Then, as soon as it was quiet a while, she'd start the whole business over again! I don't know how I got a wink of sleep. And now she's snoring like a bum after a three day drunk." He poured a heaping bowl of Cheerios. "And I need to be top-alert today, with all the research stuff I have to do before them Boston ladies get here."

"Someone will have to speak to Ms Turnbull," Cynthia said, looking at her husband who groaned as he poured another cup of coffee.

Fred leaned close to Dean. "Seeing as I was awake anyhow, I did a bit of surfing for info about our guest." Cynthia gave Fred a raised eyebrow look but he pretended not to see her. "That town, Pinkville, Virginia? It's the base for a state-wide business of storage buildings named—get this, 'Shipton Storage!'"

"So?" Dean asked.

"Sounds like a front to me. What did Mrs. Shipton have to say after I left last night?"

Dean tried to minimize Edith's story but Fred pressed them until Cynthia related, in broad detail, all Edith had told them.

Fred nodded his head. "I'll bet he's into something illegal, using the buildings to store lord-knows-what. I read somewhere they swipe cars and ship 'em down to South America where the druggies buy 'em. Maybe that's it. Half the cars down there have USA license plates, and the models are so new they practically still have the family pet in the back seat."

Dean and his wife firmly stated, in close harmony, it was none of any of their business.

"It's going to be a busy day for all of us," Cynthia said, giving Fred no time to object. "I'd better call Janet to see if she can come by." Janet O'Brien was a local woman who remained on call to Bird Song, assisting with the domestic chores of running the bed and breakfast, at least when the number of guests required additional help.

While Cynthia was telephoning and Fred mumbling, Donnie came downstairs to the dining room. He gave no indication he and his mother were leaving and joined Fred at the table when the old man offered him a bowl of cereal. He smiled but reached for a fresh muffin instead.

"I wonder what they do with the holes," Fred mused as he spooned his breakfast and poured a glass of milk for Donnie.

"What holes?" Dean asked as he gathered up his dishes.

"The ones left over. They must stamp out these Cheerios like doughnuts. Billions and billions of 'em. Doughnuts have holes left over when they stamp them out. They sell 'em. So what do they do with the Cheerios' holes?" Fred asked the question like a learned professor, speculating on a universal problem of time, space and the creation of the universe. Donnie smiled and looked to Dean for an answer.

"That's the silliest thing I've ever heard!" he answered, as he left for the kitchen. But visions of gigantic piles of BB sized oats continued to plague his brain as he donned his coat and gloves to clear the steps and walk-ways of the over night snow.

The temperature was in the high teens but as the sun began its ascent it felt far warmer. The snow was typical; light and fluffy and a mere six inches required no more effort than a sweeping motion to blow it away. Dean never ceased to marvel at the difference of high mountain snow from the heavy, wet precipitation of the East and the endless problems it caused with man and auto. The town of Ouray was so oblivious to these frequent winter gifts from Mother Nature that snow caused not a hitch in the local activities. School was never so much as delayed. Most locals maneuvered their jeeps, Subarus or pickup trucks on the sparsely traveled roads with little notice of the winter deposits. It was business as usual. Besides, by noon the sun would have cleared all but the most shaded roadways. And, if practice makes perfect, Ouray, blessed with a beautiful but long winter season, gave its citizens ample opportunity to do just that.

By the time Dean finished shoveling, Edith Shipton was seated alone in the dining room eating her breakfast while Donnie and Fred were poring over the Annie Quincy letters and notebook in the parlor. There was no luggage standing by to indicate an imminent departure. Edith was as nervous as the prior evening, glancing across the hall at her son, as if danger lurked in every corner of Bird Song. Cynthia was busy feeding linens into the insatiable washing machine. As Dean took off his overcoat, Janet O'Brien and her young niece Martha arrived. Both had matched missing buttons on their worn winter coats.

Dean often thought if Janet O'Brien were pushing a grocery cart containing all of her belongings, she wouldn't seem out of place. Her dress was a half a step above the rag she used to polish the furniture and her hair had longer roots than Elmer Fudd's garden. She was a no nonsense woman in her thirties, time-worn to a mid-forties look, at best a five-beer take-home from an otherwise empty closing-time bar. She said almost nothing. A lengthy conversation was two grunts instead of one.

The unemployment rate in Ouray was one-point-four. Dean wondered why he kept getting stuck with the point-fours. You'd never see Janet on a TV quiz show yet the woman showed up for work, most of the time, complained infrequently, and, except for mandatory cigarette breaks, worked like a sled dog on short rations. Most importantly, because she'd burned her bridges with every other domestic job in town, Janet was available. Her presence reduced Cynthia's domestic chores and eliminated the need for Dean and Fred to pick up more than the occasional dust rag.

Martha, who was explained to be a niece, was age ten. She was a quiet girl who had taken a shine to the Deans. She wore eyeglasses, taped together on the bridge, and Dean had never seen her in more than two or three different outfits: Alice in Wonderland with a far inferior tailor. During the week before Christmas, Martha had spent an overnight at Bird Song when Janet was forced to report to court in Grand Junction, on some charges she, thankfully, did not detail to the Deans. Staying at the bed and breakfast was a dramatic change of scene for Martha from Aunt Janet's cigarette stained trailer.

"No school today?" Dean asked the young girl.

"No. I'm home schooled now. Janet got p.o.'ed at the teachers." Dean questioned Janet's scholastic ability to himself and cynically wondered if today's class was Vacuuming For Beginners or Dusting 101.

"Who's the kid?" Martha asked, gesturing toward the living room.

Dean told her Donnie was a guest at Bird Song and explained the lad, only slightly older than Martha, did not speak. She just shrugged her shoulders as if she could care less about his lack of vocalization and moseyed over to near where Fred and the boy were sitting, the notebook between them. Dean too was curious about Annie Quincy's writings but decided not to join the pair. The County Library would open soon and after Fred left, Dean would have his chance to snoop undisturbed at the hundred-year-old booklet. Besides, if any dramatic discoveries were made, with Fred O'Connor on the job, Dean would learn the results soon enough.

Instead, he sauntered into the dining room and sat next to Edith as she halved a muffin and in tiny motions spread it with butter and marmalade.

"I've decided to stay after all," she offered before Dean could ask. "You were so nice to us last night and Bird Song feels so warm." She lowered her eyes and added, "And safe." She surprised Dean by placing a hand on his arm, and letting it remain there.

"I'm pleased you're both staying," Dean said. He wasn't sure it was an entirely truthful answer. He pulled his arm back as he reached for the coffee.

"Donnie seems comfortable here," she added, as if she felt compelled to move the conversation to less personal ground.

"His absence of speech doesn't slow him down. He's a very intelligent boy. Has he always had that condition?" Dean asked."

"Only for a few years. There was an accident. His stepbrother drowned. It was very traumatic for Donnie and he hasn't spoken since." She reached out her hand again but when Dean turned away, she continued with her breakfast, a nibble at a time. Finally, after a dab at her lips, she continued. "Jerome took him to a number of doctors but nothing seemed to help. The doctors say he may grow out of it in time." She turned away, concentrating on her meal, as if signifying that was all she had to say on the subject.

"Your husband had a son from his previous marriage?" Dean asked, his curiosity overcoming his desire to distance himself from this woman who was making him increasingly uncomfortable.

"Yes," she answered, but offered no further explanation.

Dean hadn't had time for a discussion with Cynthia about whether or not to tell Edith Shipton of the inquiry about her staying at Bird Song. While he didn't want to hold back important information, neither did he wish to unduly upset the nervous woman any further. However, with a burst of uncustomary loquaciousness, she changed the subject.

"Do you believe in dreams?" she asked, but continued before he could speak. "I dreamed about Annie all last night. She was so pretty in her white dress. I think she wants me to remain here at Bird Song, at least for a while. Isn't that strange? I never had dreams back in Virginia. Sometimes nightmares, but never nice dreams." She turned to Dean. "Do you believe in ghosts? It was so real, the dream I had. It was as if she were there, speaking to me. Do you mind if we stay on? I think it would be good for Donnie. I haven't seen him this happy since...." She paused, long enough to catch her breath. "Dreams are like pretending. I used to pretend when I was young. Perhaps if I pretend Jerome doesn't exist, he really won't!" She smiled and then became serious again. "I have nowhere else to go. It was probably silly of me to believe Jerome could find me, just from one little charge card transaction. Perhaps staying here a few days will help me to get my mind in order. Do you think?"

Dean wondered if she might be on some kind of medication. Whatever the reason, he guessed she had a long way to go before her mind was together. "I think you're remaining here is a fine idea. But perhaps you should contact an attorney. You should consider taking steps to assure your husband understands that you've left him for good and want no further contact with him."

"Yes," she said, but with little decisiveness.

"That way," he continued, "if your husband should find where you're staying, you could legally stop him from coming near you."

She ate the last of her muffin, leaving Dean to wonder if she even heard him. Finally, she looked up. "I used to believe in ghosts when I was young. But they were scary. Annie seems so nice. As if she wants to help me."

He paused, waiting to see if she would respond to his suggestion but she continued eating. It was obvious the discussion, such as it had been, was over. "Well," he said, "we're pleased you're staying a while longer." He left the room, shaking his head.

Cynthia met him as he came down the hall. "What's the matter?" she asked.

He summarized his conversation with Edith Shipton, adding his opinion. "One minute she's babbling like a spring brook; the next second it's back in the shell. The woman has a serious problem." He paused before continuing. "After listening to her this morning, I'm beginning to wonder if we're getting the whole story about Jerome Shipton. She might be exaggerating. The woman has a vivid imagination."

"What makes you say that?"

"I don't know. Perhaps I'm being unfair. It's just she constantly changes. One minute she's in fear of her life, the next she's enthralled over Annie Quincy, dreaming about life a century ago."

"Don't make fun of dreams. You just had a vivid dream yourself!"

"But she's taking hers much more seriously. In her dream Annie is telling her to stick around Bird Song!"

"Perhaps we should pay Annie Quincy's ghost a commission!" Then she asked, "Did you tell her about the phone call?" Dean admitted he hadn't.

"I think I'll speak to the sheriff," he answered, "just in case. If this husband of hers is abusive and traced her charge slip to Bird Song that quickly, he means business. I don't fancy having him show up on our door step but I'm not sure there's much the law can do." Dean explained to his wife the number of times in his police career he'd seen battered women refuse to follow through when confronted by their abusive mate. "As fragile as Edith Shipton is, I just hope this jerk stays away from her." Cynthia nodded in agreement.

Fredn joined the couple. "I'm off to the library," he said as he buttoned his coat. "The kids are going with me. Donnie's Ma needed a bit of convincing but figured I wasn't going to do him no harm." Dean was pleased, for both of the children. Martha's exposure to the library was more educational than helping Aunt Janet clean toilet bowls.

"Any luck with your Wonder Woman code book?" Dean asked.

"Naw. I didn't have much time." The heavy thump of footsteps on the stairs interrupted their conversation. There followed a cheery "good morning" from the late-sleeping Gladys Turnbull. Fred O'Connor beat a hasty retreat out the back door, looking like the Pied Piper with Donnie and Martha tagging behind, the Annie Quincy notebook under his arm.

Gladys was dressed in a tiny skirt that made her look like a cheerleader for the Slim Fast "before" team. She wore those half-stockings that were supposed to be hidden by something far longer than what covered her pudgy legs, which were streaked with the stark blue of veins looking like a map of a very congested and curvy area. Her skirt rode up her ample body as if it were trying to get away.

Dean allowed Gladys to devour a platoon-size breakfast while he delayed bringing up the awkward question of the late-night alarm. All the time she was eating, Gladys prattled on about her magnificent dreams of the snow-covered landscape of far away planets and the lustful urges of their alien inhabitants. Edith Shipton sat nearby, long finished with her meal, oblivious to Gladys' tales. She rose, and to Dean's surprise, went to the hall telephone. As soon as Dean was alone with Gladys, between her second and third helping of Cynthia's pancakes, he broached the subject of the annoying alarm.

Gladys must have thought most of the world was deaf as she was quite surprised when Dean politely scolded her. Gladys was contrite, promising to "not take sleeping pills" so she would wake more quickly. She was sorry that nice Mr. O'Connor was disturbed. She would apologize to him personally and in the future at least place the alarm under a pillow so only she would hear it.

"I have to bop into town anyway. With all the writing I'm doing, I need more paper!" She added, "Perhaps I'll find one of those clocks that just flashes lights! I'll think it's Belfair's space car and wake up at once and not disturb a soul!"

Dean's morning had been filled with enough ghosts, dreams and galactic sex to last a lifetime and he excused himself. He kissed Cynthia good-bye and strolled the sun-lit streets the short distance to Sheriff Jake Weller's office behind the courthouse.

It was a beautiful day and the town seemed to be enjoying it. Dean smiled at neighbors as they brushed last night's snow from cars and walkways and went about their lives. Metal roofs, designed to slip the snow, were a common sight in Ouray. They dripped streams of water as soon as the sun began its business, the remaining moisture forming dragon-teeth icicles as soon as the cold air touched the droplets.

Storefronts facing south were opening their doors to the summer-warm sun in spite of the temperature still hovering in the twenties. Mountain winters were always a surprise to lowlanders and easterners, where the chemistry of moisture played games that produced slush and wet snow, not the sparkling crystals so soft a broom could clear a foot-deep snowfall with a few swishes. Dean chatted with a number of the merchants of the few still-open businesses he passed.

The sheriff sat with his six-foot four-inch frame wedged behind his ancient desk, about to devour a large pastry. He offered Dean coffee with a wave of his hand as he continued to eat. Dean poured himself a cup while the lawman finished his snack.

"It's been a while," Weller said.

"I suppose you consider that one of life's little blessings," Dean answered with a smile. Dean's past involvements with Sheriff Weller had always managed to cause the lawman untold grief. While the two maintained mutual respect, Jake Weller appeared unsettled in Dean's presence, a combination of insecurity over Dean's more extensive experience and memories of past encounters that had pushed the law-man into compromising situations.

"I suppose this is about Mrs. Shipton," Weller said, taking Dean by total surprise.

"How do you know about her?"

"Hubby called. Said she's a whacko. He's coming out to gather her up and haul her home. Her and his boy." The sheriff took a long sip from his coffee and added. "The guy says you lied to him on the phone. Said you told him his wife wasn't staying at Bird Song."

Dean took a deep breath. It was always the same. Every time he spoke to this guy, he found himself on the defensive. "I told a man on the phone, who didn't identify himself, that Edith Shipton wasn't *regis-*

tered at Bird Song. She registered as Mrs. Edith Jones. I just told the guy we didn't have a Mrs. Shipton listed. I didn't lie."

"And a smart big city detective like you didn't guess maybe this was the Edith he was talking about?"

Dean ignored the sarcasm. "She claims he's a wife beater. She ran away from him." He added, "I was a detective in Parkside, Pennsylvania. Parkside isn't a 'big city.'"

Weller frowned and rolled his eyes. "Here we go again. Another damn mess. Some times I think there's an epidemic of that domestic shit going around. Is she really a loony?"

"She's..." Dean searched for the right word, "unstable. Scared to death of him."

"What about the son?"

"She claims Donnie isn't Shipton's son. His last name is 'Ryland'."

"What does the boy say?"

"Nothing. He's mute."

Jake Weller let out a deep sigh. "So what's your involvement in this mess?"

"I don't have an involvement. She just checked in, used one name to register and another name on the credit charge for the room. Cynthia was concerned how nervous the woman acted. That's all."

"Then she told you her life history," he added, "and you're on a first name basis."

"She admitted she and her son had left the husband. She tried to change the credit card charge to cash later when it dawned on her the guy might be able to trace it. I thought that was TV nonsense until a few minutes later the phone rang and damned if he hadn't done just that!"

"So you lied to him."

"I explained that."

"Yeah," Weller answered as he rubbed his chin in thought. He was silent for a ten-count, as if considering his options.

Dean asked, "What was your read on the guy?"

"Honest injun? He sounded like a shit head. All business. He's drawing up papers to have her committed and flying out here to 'save' the boy. He mentioned the term kidnapping, but of course being the saint he is he wouldn't press charges against his wife who according to him was just temporarily disturbed. Like, who would even consider leaving a great guy like him? He just wants to haul her back to home and hearth, where she belongs."

"Why did he call you?"

"That's what I asked him. I'm county. Bird Song is in the city of Ouray, not my jurisdiction. I tried to get him to call Tony but he said he was just running it by me. Greasing the skids. So's I can stand out of the way while he does what he's going to do anyway, small town hick that I am."

Dean smiled. "Sounds like you maybe didn't like Mr. Jerome Shipton very much. Do you think he's a wife beater?"

The lawman thought a moment. "He's certainly domineering. A real take-charge kind of guy. I'd have to say it's a distinct possibility he's a woman thumper. What do you say? I suppose you had a raft of this abuse stuff back in Pennsylvania."

"You've got that right. If you're in the business, it goes with the territory. Ouray, too?"

Weller nodded his head. "Sometimes I feel I'm becoming an expert on domestic abuse and child molestation. We might not get the gang-bangers, car jackings and armed robberies like the big cities but we sure have our share of domestics."

"So, what are you going to do about Shipton?" Dean asked.

"I told you. It's not even my jurisdiction, even if there was something I could do. Unless the missus gets an court order on him or a good lawyer, she's back in the nest, and so's the boy. Especially if the law gives him an okay. He's not going to get her committed without a few miles of red tape but just the threat of a lockup could drag her back to old Virginia. And we both know if Shipton is a beater, chances are good she'll just keep on taking it, until he kills her or gets what he wants." Dean was silent. Weller shook his head. "You're not going to go and get us mixed up in a bucket of shit like the last time, are you?"

Dean hoped that wouldn't be the case, but he was less than sure. He skirted the question. "It seems to me, the jury is still out on this mess but if Shipton is stalking her, legally or not, she deserves reasonable protection until we know for sure. Even if she's not in your jurisdiction, couldn't you just stop by and speak to her, tell her what her husband intends to do? Suggest she get a lawyer? I didn't get to first base but you've got a spiffy uniform and a shiny badge."

"I'm not sure I don't like it better when you go off half-cocked on your own and don't involve me," he muttered, but he agreed to pay a call on Edith Shipton, suggesting she put on gloves and defend herself.

CHAPTER 5

Dean returned to Bird Song and brought Cynthia up to date on his conversation with Sheriff Weller over a quiet lunch of soup and grilled cheese. The Deans had the place to themselves. Janet finished her chores and hurried off to her afternoon soaps. Fred was back in town, treating the children to sandwiches before returning to the library for a new dose of historical research. Edith drove off in her rental car, without a word. Gladys Turnbull was walking the town, trying to glean inspiration from the towering mountains to better describe some celestial landscape.

"It's peaceful," Cynthia commented. "I just hope it isn't the calm before the storm," she added, holding up crossed fingers.

"We can handle anything they toss at us," Dean said. "After last summer's adventures, we're up to any task!"

Cynthia smiled, remembering the early-days' confusion of opening the bed and breakfast, two newlyweds and one old man, operating on piggy bank finances and not an ounce of experience among them. And then to have Bird Song's first guest turning up dead! Once the details to that "caper," as Fred O'Connor called it, were settled, life and business at Bird Song had proceeded peacefully. The Deans referred to the episode as the storm before the calm. The trio was far more comfortable now, six months later, with enough money in the bank to keep the wolves away, and expectations, if not of prosperity, of at least a reasonably comfortable coming season. But not even in the worst of times did they ever regret for a moment abandoning their life in the East for this quiet mountain hamlet they now called home and their sometimes hectic life of running a country inn.

"I'm glad in a way Edith's husband called the sheriff," Cynthia said. "It brings the authorities into the picture in case Shipton does show up and causes trouble. I know the whole business isn't our concern, but the poor woman is staying with us and God knows she looks as if she can use all the help she can get." They both agreed to let the situation take its course now that Weller was involved. There were other guests at Bird Song and enough regular problems running a country inn without creating any more.

"And," Dean added, "our life is still top priority. Let's make the most of it. It looks like we have the second afternoon in a row to ourselves."

Cynthia had received a phone call from the Boston sisters telling her their flight was delayed and they weren't now expected until late afternoon. No other guests were due to arrive for a few days and with the housework up to date, thanks to the temporary help of Janet, the Deans decided to try out the fresh snow on the cross country trails on Red Mountain. After dressing in double sweaters, wool knickers and stockings, they racked their skis atop their jeep and drove south from town into the mountains.

The village of Ouray lay snuggled at the terminus of a long valley, wrapped in a box canyon by the towering San Juans to the east, west and south. The famous million dollar highway, which climbed three mountain passes before ending seventy-odd miles later in Durango, was spectacular by anyone's definition, more so after a fresh winter snow.

The warm sun had eaten most of the snow from the roadway, leaving a contrasting black ribbon, in places still snow-patched from last night's covering. As the couple climbed to higher elevations, more caution was necessary as icy patches became more frequent. Winter mountain driving was not for the reckless or faint of heart, but the Deans were neither. They shared a respect for the high-country conditions, prudent advice at any time, but even more appropriate on these winding roads, unprotected by guardrails, and bordered by sheer drop-offs that caused sweaty palms and racing heartbeats for many a first time driver. The stone cliffs that walled the road on the opposite side wept icicles from every crevice, covering the surface in massive clusters of crystal spikes that sparkled in the dazzling sunlight. The Deans agreed it was never prettier in Ouray County than after a fresh snow. The sky was a deeper blue, the green of the spruce and pine even darker than usual against the incredible white blanket that reflected the sun so brightly one was forced to squint or wear sunglasses. As they proceeded upward, snow evaporating from the roadbed like steam rose in smoke-like puffs, wispy tendrils of ground haze that scrambled away as the jeep sailed by.

The road tunneled through a snow shed, a reminder of the frequent and hazardous avalanches that plagued the area. The highway department would periodically close the road and, using explosive devices, create slides in a controlled condition, lessening the chance for a surprising and perhaps deadly run loosed by nature on the unsuspecting below.

Eight miles from Ouray, but still four miles from the summit of Red Mountain Pass, the road leveled out. Here was nestled the town site of Ironton, a bustling community in the last-century days when silver and gold ruled the area. Now it stood empty but for a few derelict buildings. But thanks to the active involvement of a volunteer group called The Nordic Council, free cross-country ski trails were laid out and maintained. The Deans had utilized the site a half dozen times, including, in December, the council-sponsored full moon night-time outing, followed by a dip in the town's hot spring pool. While back-country skiing was also popular, the ever constant danger of killing snow slides made marked trails a safer method of enjoying this vigorous sport. The Deans, still novices, had more than enough to handle on these well-marked and relatively level trails.

The couple drove over the narrow wooden bridge that spanned Red Mountain Creek, and joined two other cars in the small parking area. After clamping on their skies and hoisting day-packs, they set out on the groomed path. There were a number of different routes, but the Deans chose the two-mile town site loop, a nearly flat path that first traversed a scented pine forest and then opened to a spectacular view of the surrounding mountains.

Cynthia leaned her head back, closed her eyes and drank in the scene. "Feel that air!" she exclaimed. "Not a grain of smog anywhere. It's beautiful!"

The January sun continued in its brilliance and the rhythmic gliding across the crystal snow, though not exhausting, warmed the couple to the point where even their limited outer cover seemed excessive. They saw others on the trail only once when an elderly couple steamed by them with a wave. While they thought themselves in better than average shape, many of the locals were dynamos when it came to high altitude athletics. Any activity ten thousand feet in the sky quickly separated the properly trained from the panting wannabes.

The trail was not difficult by cross-country standards—just enough of a challenge to stir the blood and quicken the breath. But the pristine forest and surrounding view was more than worth the tiredness that crept into the arms and legs.

They said little as they skied, content to enjoy their surroundings. At the far end of the loop, they passed the few remaining structures of the abandoned town of Ironton; empty, ghost-like buildings. Dean tried to picture the bustling town of a century past, at one time home to a dozen saloons, four restaurants, a newspaper, nearly three hundred houses and more than a thousand inhabitants. But within twenty years, it had faded as rapidly as it had grown. By 1913, the post office was closed and the town had dwindled to two dozen remaining souls, and before long, it was left to indigenous wildlife and the spirits of a boisterous past.

While there remained much of the afternoon, the shortened days of winter dipped the sun below the towering mountains as the tired couple finished the loop, returned to their jeep and left for home. Dean drove with even more caution now that the melted road sections were beginning to freeze anew, downshifting, allowing the reduced gear to slow the vehicle. As they passed the plowed pullout for the cut-off to Engineer pass, they were reminded of the past June and their mountain-camping honeymoon, up this road and into Poughkeepsie Gulch. Now the jeep road was closed, as it had been since early fall and would remain so until June, locked in its privacy by several feet of accumulated snow. Two cars were parked off the edge of the road and as they passed, Cynthia looked back with a start.

"That was Edith Shipton!" Cynthia said. "I thought the car looked familiar!" She pivoted around, as far as her seatbelt allowed, practically hanging over the seat as she looked out the back window.

"Are you sure?" Dean asked.

"Yes! And I recognized her coat, too! I wonder if the man she's talking to is her creep of a husband."

Dean had been concentrating on his business at hand, driving, and hadn't even glanced at the two cars. It was all he could do to keep his eyes on the road. By the time he looked back, they were around a curve and the cars were no longer visible.

"It seems strange she'd be out here, three or four miles from town," Cynthia continued.

"Did she act as if she knew the other person?" Dean asked.

"I don't know. But he was standing very close to her. Do you think we should go back and see if she needs help?"

"No!" he answered, loud enough to startle Cynthia who quickly turned her head to him.

"I don't mean to snoop," she pouted defensively, adjusting her seatbelt. "She did say her husband was stalking her, after all." Cynthia looked over at her husband. "We could turn around and drive by. Just to make sure. I'm positive she didn't notice us the first time."

"Cynthia, it's none of our business! Her husband called Weller from Virginia just this morning. He'd have to be Superman to fly out here this soon."

"I'm not snooping, really. I just want to make sure she's not in some sort of danger." After a brief silence she added, "If anything should happen to the woman, we'd feel terrible that we ignored her, wouldn't we?"

Dean rolled his eyes, but smiled inwardly at his wife's concern as he looked for a place to turn around the jeep. While he wanted to avoid further involvement in Edith Shipton's troubled world, he felt proud of his wife inherent sense of compassion toward anyone in trouble. Stray dogs and stray souls. It didn't seem to matter.

Just as they had reversed their direction, Edith Shipton passed them, driving down the mountain, not speeding but too fast by Dean's conservative standards. She was easily recognizable, her dark hair streaming in the breeze of her partially open window. She looked straight ahead and didn't see them. Dean caught enough of a look to see a contented smile on the face of the well dressed woman.

"She doesn't look too damn terrorized to me," Dean grumbled as he looked for another spot to yet again reverse his direction. The next opportunity proved to be the same jeep road cut off where they'd first seen Edith speaking with the man in the second car, which was now nowhere in sight.

"He must have driven south, away from Ouray," Cynthia mused. "That's even stranger."

"What's so strange? One of them probably pulled the other over to ask directions," Dean said as he backed into a K-turn. He immediately regretted fueling further speculation.

"Directions to where? There aren't any open side roads and hardly a plowed turnoff on this highway for twenty miles. There isn't even a building almost to Silverton!"

"Did you see the smile on her face?" he countered. "I'll bet I hit the nail on the head when I said she was in Ouray to meet some guy. I'll bet there's a third person involved in this mess. All the more reason for us to mind our own business."

Cynthia ignored his I-told-you-so attitude. "Are you going to report what we saw to Sheriff Weller?"

He was about to give an emphatic "no" to her question but then, in an inspirational moment of civic buck-passing, decided that talking to the law might be a pretty damn good idea. After all, every occasion in the past when he'd gotten in deep do-do with the sheriff, it was for holding back information. This time he'd bury Jake Weller in a mountain of minutiae. And maybe keep his own life less complicated in the process.

"What make car is he driving?" Dean asked the question before he remembered futility of such a query. Cynthia's ability to distinguish one motor vehicle from another was limited to trucks, vans, jeeps, limos and all others. Absent these most general distinctions, color was her only detailed observation.

"A blue one," she answered.

"And what did the mysterious stranger look like?"

"He had a beard. And he was tall." To petite Cynthia, tall meant anyone much over five-foot seven. A six-footer, like David Dean was a veritable giant from her reduced point of reference. Then she added, "He had on a red plaid flannel shirt and jeans."

"I'll give Weller a call when I get back," he said, generating a look of surprise on his wife's face.

When the Deans returned to Bird Song, the place was quiet. Gladys Turnbull was pounding away on a lap top computer in a corner of the parlor while young Martha and Donnie played a game of Old Maid on the sofa. Fred O'Connor, back from his second stint at the library and historical museum, was now poring over the newspaper and circling the Saturday garage sales in the classified ads.

"Don't know why they don't put in more information," he muttered.

"What more do you want?" Dean asked, looking over his shoulder. "This one has a whole list of junk, chairs, tables, clothes. It says it's a moving sale."

"But it don't say where they're moving."

"Who cares?"

"Look, if it said they were moving to the south, I'd know they were selling their winter stuff. Snow shovels and stuff, too. If they were going north, I could pick up some duds for next summer...."

"Are you going in the used clothing business next?"

"Not necessarily. It's just information. These are the times for information. The more you got, the better the decisions you can make. If you'd take a ride on the information highway like me, you'd know all about this stuff. Cross the digital divide."

"I get the picture."

"It's like in the case of a death. There's no reason why they couldn't put in the obituary that the deceased was a forty-two long. And maybe a conservative dresser. Makes me traipse all over the place, finding out the guy didn't have any taste."

"Who traipses? I'm the one who chauffeurs you all over Montrose!"

"If you'd let me drive, you could sit around here on your duff instead."

"You don't have a license. You can't drive."

Cynthia just ignored them, instead watching the younger, more civilized occupants of the room play their card game. Finally, Dean had the sense to change the subject.

"Where are your gullible Boston buyers? Did they change their minds?"

"Just delayed en route. They'll be here soon enough."

"Where's Donnie's mother?"

"Still not back."

"What did you find out about Annie Quincy?"

Fred sighed and put down the newspaper. Fred and his juvenile helpers had located a picture of Reverend Martin and his wife in an old museum collection of early Ouray papers and photos. While he feigned nonchalance, it was obvious he was as proud as a kid with a new toy to show them what he'd discovered.

"Miss Worthington let me take it out of the museum so's you could see it," Fred said as he presented a curled, cardboard sepia image.

The small undated photo was quite dark but showed a couple, perhaps in their thirties, standing before a church window. There was a pedestal in front of them and the man, Rev. Martin, had his hand resting on what Dean assumed was a bible. He was tall and thin and wore a mustache. His wife Annie was dour and a bit on the chunky side. Neither was smiling.

"That ought to please your Boston ladies, seeing a picture of their great-aunt and uncle," Cynthia remarked as she examined the picture.

"In spite of looking like they just saw the IRS at their front door," Dean commented.

"People were more serious back in those days," Cynthia said. "Less frivolous than someone I know."

Dean looked over her shoulder. "Looks like Annie had a few good meals since she fit into that white dress, wouldn't you say?" He turned to Fred. "What else did you find?"

Fred ignored Dean's reference to pudginess. "Poor Rev. Martin died in a flu epidemic in '04," Fred said, his voice sounding duly respectful.

"What about his wife?" Dean asked. "When did she check out?"

"No mention of her yet. But he was a widower when he died." Then he added, with a professional air, "We'll track her down."

"How are you coming on the secret code book?"

"Haven't had much time to work on it."

"If you hadn't gone and taken it to the library with you someone else might have had a shot at playing master-decoder," Dean grumbled. "How about handing it over?"

"Yes, Fred. It's time you gave someone else a chance," Cynthia said with a winning smile that offered him little room to maneuver.

Fred O'Connor reluctantly held out the century-old notebook. As Dean reached for it, Cynthia beat him to it. "Thank you, Fred." She turned, leaving the room, the notebook in hand. "Time to get out of these ski clothes and do some work."

Left with nothing else to do, Dean turned to Gladys Turnbull, more out of inn-keeper politeness than a desire to engage this strange woman in lengthy conversation. "How's your spaced-out heroine doing?" he asked.

"Marvelous, just marvelous!" she explained as her pudgy fingers raced across the computer keyboard. "The aura here is sooooo conducive! I've raced through nearly four thousand words just today!"

"That sounds like a lot," he said.

"Oh, not so much. My last book was over two-hundred thousand words!"

"Wow!" Dean said, brilliant conversationalist that he was. "So this isn't your first book?"

"Oh, heavens no! It's my seventh!" Then she added, "The last in the trilogy."

Fred jumped in before Dean could question the math. "I looked for your books in the library, Miss Turnbull, but we couldn't find them."

"Oh, I haven't had any published yet. I'm waiting until I'm finished! It's so exciting writing them, I haven't had time to send them to my publisher." Then she added, "He's anxiously waiting."

Dean decided to leave that statement alone. "Well, good luck."

Just then, the high point of excitement of the late afternoon was orchestrated by Mrs. Lincoln, Dean's cat, who had emigrated with him from Pennsylvania. The independent—if the term isn't redundant—feline trotted into the crowded parlor, a mouse in her mouth, expecting the awe and adulation of the assembled group. Instead, she was greeted by shrieks from Martha and Gladys, causing her to drop the poor creature and flee in terror, stark contrast to her anticipated moment of glory.

Cynthia rushed into the room, the notebook still in hand, and with Martha, hovered over the pending demise of the trembling rodent. Donnie viewed the encounter with mild curiosity while Gladys remained in her chair, pudgy legs elevated, looking totally petrified.

"Do something!" Cynthia said with alarm.

Dean went to the kitchen, returning with a dustpan and whisk broom, only to be rewarded with a stern lecture on his insensitivity when he made motions to pitch the little varmint out in the snow.

"No one invited him in the first place," Dean grumbled, just as Mrs. Lincoln, the successful but bewildered hunter, returned for a second round. She was promptly chased away by the mourning women and sulked off to her spot in the window. Meanwhile Donnie and Martha, with Cynthia's help, tried to revive the mortally wounded creature but the prognosis was not good. Dean's suggestion of placing the little fellow out of doors in the trash was overruled by his more compassionate wife who pointed out the resulting reduced chances of January survival. Sadly, all their attention was for naught. Monty, as he became known during his brief public life, succumbed to his injuries. A slight burst of tears followed from Martha until Dean rendered a speech on survival of the fittest, the laws of the jungle, the food chain and supply and demand. Cynthia suggested a funeral, complete with a shoebox coffin and a solemn burial, a feat Dean would have guessed impossible given the frozen earth. However, the children found the soil spring-soft next to the building foundation, thanks to the Dean's fuel-bill contributions and the poor insulation of Bird Song. Mrs. Lincoln attempted to attend the service but was chased away. The poor animal was beginning to think "Bad Cat" was her new name.

Just as the glue was drying on the small wooden cross, a noise at the front door announced the arrival of the sisters from Boston. Once again, the mysterious notebook took a back seat to the more pedestrian happenings at the Ouray inn.

CHAPTER 6

The sisters Quincy were anything but a matched pair. Little gray haired Effie wore a perpetual smile on her pretty face, a tad on the silly side but charming nonetheless, in a bewildered sort of way. Her hair was done in a pug, a style not seen by Dean since his childhood. Claire was a peanut butter blonde, gone grey, tall and well dressed, all business and definitely in charge. If she possessed a smile, she never presented it for public display. Dean managed the luggage in three trips from their rental car while Cynthia and Fred handled the paper work and showed the women their quarters. By the time Dean huffed his way downstairs from the last trip, everyone was assembled in the parlor, and introductions were taking place. Gladys had taken over as docent of the domain.

"I'm Gladys Turnbull the author, and this is Donnie who can't speak, and Martha who lives in town." Claire gave a hint of a nod, remaining under the archway to the parlor, as if entering might subject her to some vile disease from these common folk. Effie stood in the middle of the room, as if enthralled and after all the smiles and appropriate handshakes, took a deep breath and closed her eyes.

"Yes! Aunt Annie was here!" she announced like a saved soul at a revival. "I can sense it! It's so romantic! Claire, don't you feel it too?"

"Don't be ridiculous, Effie," her sister muttered, but Effie paid her no mind.

"Yes! Yes! I can feel it too!" Gladys replied. "There's such a aura here, such a celestial ambience!"

Claire rolled her eyes and changed the subject. She turned to Cynthia. "You don't have to serve us dinner," she said in sour a tone. "We ate in Montrose."

"We only serve breakfast at Bird Song," Cynthia answered, keeping her voice cheery. "But there are nice restaurants within walking distance for your other meals."

"Is this your first trip to Colorado?" Dean asked, not only trying to be polite but in hopes of dragging the conversation away from the occult, the celestial and the just plain weird.

"I've been to California. Much prettier. Effie has hardly left Boston," Claire answered while Effie and Gladys continued to become soul mates of the supernatural, blabbering away in the corner.

57

"I'm sure you'll enjoy it here. "There's lots to do. In addition to the scenery, we have a million gallon hot spring pool run by the town. It's out of doors, but even in the winter it's like taking an out door bath. Very refreshing."

"No, thank you. When I take a bath, I certainly don't want a hundred lecherous strangers staring at me."

Dean couldn't think of a polite response so for once he kept his mouth shut. He didn't even bother to search his mental library under pithy, tasteless and nasty retorts. Cynthia too was peeved. Dean could tell when she refrained from offering tea and crumpets to the new arrivals. She excused herself to prepare supper for the three residents. Claire pulled Effie by the arm and led her upstairs, after pronouncing they would return to claim their purchase after an hour's rest. The children's game broke up and Martha began to don her coat to go home but Cynthia coaxed her to stay for supper. Donnie's mother Edith still hadn't returned and the boy was beginning to look worried, glancing frequently toward the door. But he obviously idolized Martha and she seemed to be a calming influence on him. He too was invited to join them at the table.

Supper was pancakes and eggs, with conversation directed to the children, interrupted by confirming calls from ice climbers who would begin arriving on Thursday. When the meal was over, Martha excused herself to leave. Dean insisted on driving her home. While the distance to her aunt's trailer was only a half dozen blocks, once the January sun had retired after its day's work, it would be a cold walk. Before leaving, Martha whispered something to Donnie and gave him a friendly pat on the back. It was a nice gesture.

The pair drove down Seventh Street, crossed over the Uncompahgre River and followed the dirt road to the small cluster of mobile homes. When they arrived at Jane's unit, Dean noticed the trailer was dark. This didn't faze Martha in the least as she alighted from the jeep, with a wave and a thanks.

"Whoa," Dean called, "Isn't your aunt home?"

"Naw. She goes down to the bar on Tuesdays. And Wednesday and Thursdays, sometimes too. And weekends."

"When will she be back?"

"Depends."

"Look," he said. "Why don't you come back to Bird Song. You can spend the night."

Martha hesitated. "Naw, I can stay here alone. It's no big deal. I do lots of times."

"We've got empty rooms, at least until the ice climbers start coming tomorrow. You could play with Donnie some more."

"Janet told me not to 'impose'."

"It's not imposing if I ask you. It's like helping us out."

The young girl thought a moment and agreed. Dean penned a note to her aunt and Martha went inside to leave it, as Dean directed, in plain sight on the kitchen table. She skipped back to the jeep, her earlier reluctance nowhere in evidence.

To Dean, she seemed a tad pensive as she sat next to the window. She turned toward him. "You and Mrs. Dean are sort of like pals of mine, you know?" He smiled and nodded. "You're nice to me."

"You're a nice girl, Martha. We both like you very much." Then he added, "If you ever have a problem, I want you to know you can come to us." So much for all the empty words he'd been spilling to Cynthia about not getting involved, he thought. Martha just continued to nod and look straight ahead but she wore a hint of a smile.

As Dean and his young passenger neared Bird Song, Edith Shipton drove up the street, parked, and entered the inn ahead of them. A vehicle, a mud-splatted Blazer, with skis in a rack atop it, followed her and slowed as it passed the building. Dean caught sight of its bearded driver who stared in the direction of the retreating woman.

"That's Donnie's ma," Martha announced. "She's a mess."

"What makes you say that?" Dean asked, surprised at the young girl's unusual candor.

"Her old man beats her like a tin drum and he's gonna kill her if he finds where she is. She's hiding out. On the lam, sort of."

"How do you know that?"

"Donnie. He writes notes." When Dean didn't ask anything further, Martha continued. "That Donnie—he's not dumb."

"He's a very intelligent boy," Dean answered. "He just isn't able to speak. It's called being mute."

"I didn't mean he was stupid-dumb—dumb like me! I know the difference!" Dean was startled by her sharpness, chastising himself for underestimating the young girl.

"Donnie's real smart. He's good at puzzles and stuff." Then she added, "I'm not good at nothing."

"That's not true, Martha." He looked over at her, still pressed against the door. "When I was about your age, I wasn't a lick smarter than you."

"Go on, Mr. Dean! You're a real smart guy. You own a fancy place and drive a practically new jeep. You got a pretty wife. Dumb doesn't get you all that stuff."

He smiled to himself. "Smart isn't what you own, Martha. Smart comes in different packages."

"I know that."

"When I was your age, I didn't think I was very smart, but I had a father who honestly thought I was the greatest, smartest, nicest kid alive. He kept telling me that. Oh, I knew he just thought that way because I was his kid, but I figured he was a pretty smart guy himself so he couldn't be all wrong. I started thinking maybe I wasn't so dumb after all."

"I don't even know who my old man is," Martha said glumly. "And I ain't seen my ma in a long time. Besides, she knows how dumb I am. She used to tell me all the time."

"If you don't have anyone to tell you how smart you are, it's about time you start doing it yourself. Look around. You see other kids. Think about it. You're just as smart as any one of them. Maybe not always in school, but in other ways. There are thousands of ways to be smart. You just need someone to keep reminding you."

She looked over at him. "You think I'm smart, huh?"

"Yup. No doubt about it. And you said so yourself—I'm smart, so I must be right." Then he added, "But you should be in a regular school."

She changed the subject. "I think Donnie can talk." Dean looked at her questioningly as he turned off the jeep. "I made him," she said as she picked at her skirt. "I was teasing him and he yanked my pigtails. Can you imagine anyone having to wear pigtails now-a-days? Janet thinks I'm Becky Thatcher." She began to unfasten her long braids. "I like it that Donnie don't—doesn't talk. He can't make fun of me."

"Then why did you tease him?"

"Just curious, I guess."

"What did he say?"

"He said, 'Stop it'!" She paused and smiled. "At least I think he said it. I tickled him and told him I wouldn't stop until he told me to. I think he was maybe just faking."

"Then what happened?"

"He hit me. A real good one. I told him men didn't hit women but he nodded 'Yes they do.' After that I didn't try and make him talk anymore. He was more fun being quiet." Then she added, "I don't mean to spill on him or nothing. I wouldn't tell that to anyone else but you so don't tell him I told you, okay?" She hopped out of the car with a quick thanks ran into Bird Song ahead of him.

"Most men are more fun when they're quiet," Cynthia said with a smile when Dean, who was drying the supper dishes, related to his wife what Martha had said. The smell of pancakes still hung in the air of the cozy kitchen. They were alone in the room. "Do you suppose the boy really did speak?"

"There's no telling. Kids have a strong imagination. But wouldn't it be something if a bevy of psychiatrists tried everything in their books to get that boy to speak, and a little girl does it by tickling him!"

"I wonder if being away from his stepfather made it more conducive for him to speak," Cynthia mused as she drained the sink.

Dean shrugged his shoulders. "That's an area where I wouldn't even dare to speculate."

"Do you think you should tell Donnie's mother?" Cynthia asked. Dean gave her a let's-not-get-involved look one more time. Both agreed the less said, the better.

When Dean told his wife about the bearded man who seemed to be following Edith Shipton, Cynthia just shook her head.

"Edith didn't say a word to me when she came in, just whispered something to Donnie and was up the stairs. She didn't even mention being too late to take him to dinner."

"Whoever the guy in the Blazer was, he gave Edith the look-see when he drove past Bird Song."

"If the man was her husband, she didn't seem in fear of him up on the mountain when I saw them talking. If it's anyone else she's meeting, it still isn't any of our business." Dean didn't disagree.

Cynthia took a deep breath. "Well, I guess it's time we see if Fred needs any help with our guests from Boston."

"Back to the ghosts," Dean said, joining her. "Time to figure out what we're running here, a house for haunted women or just a house for 'hunted' women!"

The two ladies had joined Fred in the parlor where he was showing them the letters they had purchased from him, sight unseen. The other guests were nowhere about—the children off playing hide and seek, Edith still closed in her room and Gladys dreaming of far off galaxies.

Claire Quincy had donned reading glasses and was scrutinizing the letters as Fred O'Connor followed his notes and explained the information on Annie Quincy he had gathered at the library. "Best I can determine, she married the reverend in the spring of '99. The letter before that time talks about the wedding. I suspect the new Mrs. Martin passed on sometime a year or so later, after the last letter. I haven't found an account of her death in the papers yet but her hubby died of the flu in '04 and it didn't mention his wife in his write up."

"The poor man!" Effie said, sniffing back a sob. "He lost his beautiful wife and died so young himself." She looked from one to the other. "Anne was my grandfather's favorite sister."

"Next to Great-aunt Rachael," Claire muttered.

The Deans took seats on the far side of the room. "What do you know about Annie from your end?" Dean asked. "Did any of her letters from Ouray survive?"

"No," Claire answered. "Only Rev. Martin's note informing the family of poor Annie's death." She withdrew a single sheet of paper from her purse, unfolded it and adjusted her glasses. As she read, her sister Effie mouthed the words of the note from memory.

"'Dear Sister Rachael, it is with a sad heart that I'm compelled to inform you of the passing of the soul of my beloved wife, your sister, Annie. My beautiful bride labored to the end, administrating to the fallen and the flu stricken souls of our town until she too, fell to the scourge of this most dreaded disease. It is with tears in my eyes that I pen this note, my only solace that I will shortly be one in heaven with this woman I loved more than life itself. Respectfully yours in God, Rev. Joshua Martin.'"

She looked up. "The note was undated and if there was a return address or an envelope, it was lost over the years."

Effie Quincy sniffed as she pulled her chair next to Dean. "It always makes me cry when I hear that letter. Aunt Rachael lived with us when we were young. She used to talk of Annie all the time, tell us how brave her sister was, how she and the Reverend administered to the sick, and those women."

"What 'women?'" Dean asked.

"The sinners," Claire growled. "'The women of the night,' if you must know. Apparently this town was cluttered with them and my great-aunt and her husband had a thankless life mission to attend to the trash. I'm sure she caught that dreadful disease from one of them and it killed her. The family pleaded with her to return to the civilization of Boston, but she wouldn't listen."

"She was answering to a higher power," Effie added.

"My brother is writing a book about Annie's life and her sacrifices," Claire said.

"*Saint Among Sinners* it's called. It's nearly finished." Effie announced with obvious pride.

"Wasn't it difficult to write, knowing so little about what really happened?" Dean asked.

"No. Not at all. Edward heard the stories from father who heard them from Grandfather Quincy who took copious notes. He was Congressman Quincy. Father was a man of the cloth too, just like Edward, and Reverend Martin. Our family has a long tradition of self-sacrifice and charity."

"That's nice," said Fred O'Connor, who had zero tradition, at least as far has Dean had learned in the fifteen years he'd lived with the old man. Hell, the man changed his history like he changed his shorts.

Effie beamed. "Edward is saying the book is '*based* on the life of Annie Quincy Martin' just so he can take some liberties with the inconsequential details that have been lost in time. That's why we were so excited to come out here, to visit where it really happened!"

"That book of your brother's ought to be a big seller here in Ouray," Fred said. "This town sure likes its history. You'll be wanting to spend lots of time at the library and museum. They're real helpful folks at both places. I promised to donate this here ink well and pen that came from the box of Annie's stuff." He held the items out for her examination.

"These belonged to Aunt Annie too?" Claire asked as she took the objects.

"Yes, but I already promised to donate 'em. Before you bought the other stuff," he added.

"That was nice of you!" Effie said.

Claire's reaction was far different. "I distinctly remember buying everything in your collection," she said, a snarl of firmness in her voice. Then, as if thinking about it added, "But I'll donate these things. I'm sure the museum will be grateful and help us in our research all they can."

Dean could sense Fred was peeved. His ears were turning red. A sure sign. But to give the old man credit, he kept his cool. "The museum has already helped with this," he said, presenting the picture of Rev. Martin and his wife. "It's part of their permanent collection and I wasn't supposed to even take it out, but I'm sure if you explain about the book your brother is writing, they'll let you make a copy of it. Maybe you can use it for the cover."

Effie put her hand to her chest, as if she might faint. "Oh, my! It's truly them! God bless! What a handsome couple!"

"Yes," said Claire. She, too, was obviously moved. "I can see the resemblance. She has father's eyes." Fred reached for the picture but Claire held on to it. "I'll buy it from whoever owns it. Just tell me how much they want."

"Well, I think it's best you take that up with the museum. I borrowed it on my responsibility so I feel obligated to get it back to them first. Then you can talk to 'em but I imagine if it was a gift to the museum, they'll be obligated to hold on to the original."

Claire scowled as she looked up, about to reply. A startled look appeared on her face, causing Dean and the others to turn toward the hall.

Edith Shipton had come down the stairs and was standing under the archway. Donnie stood shyly behind her. Once more, she wore Annie Quincy's white dress. She held the comb and brush in her hand and tears streamed down her cheeks. While Claire and the Deans were unnerved, poor Effie looked on the verge of fainting.

"I...didn't mean to startle everyone," Edith said. "I just thought I'd dress up...for your guests." She turned to the sisters. "This is Annie's dress. They allowed me to model it last night. I hope you don't mind." She brushed away her tears and tried to smile. "I'm sorry. It's just that this dress makes me—feel so emotional."

"Oh," Effie exclaimed. "It's so perfect! It's as if we've gone back in time! Here we are, in this lovely parlor, just where Annie must have stood, perhaps when Rev. Martin proposed to her! It's as if she's alive again!"

Edith pirouetted, as she had the last evening. "I feel so different when I wear her clothes. Something magical happens. I'm transported back in time. Just as you said." She turned to Claire, as if acknowledging she was in charge. "What will you do with the dress?"

"I don't know. I haven't given it a thought. Why?"

"May I buy it?" she asked excitedly "And the comb and brush?"

Dean caught the look on Fred's face as Edith handed the items to Claire.

"They're part of it too?" Claire asked with a scowl directed at Fred. "What else are you holding back?"

Before he could answer, Edith replied, sheepishly. "I'm wearing her underthings, too. It didn't feel quite right, with a bra and new lingerie."

She turned and looked to Claire. "But, please, I'll pay whatever you feel is a fair price."

"Three hundred dollars," Claire snapped. "But just for what you're wearing. I'll keep the comb and brush."

"Oh, Claire!" Effie protested. "Three hundred dollars seems much too high. We only paid—" Claire cut her off and repeated the amount.

Dean hoped Edith would tell the old witch where to stuff it, but instead she looked as if she had just won an auction bid for a coronation gown.

"Oh, thank you! That's so kind! I'll get the money now!" She turned and hurried up the stairs as Donnie stood by the table, torn between curiosity and following his mother.

"About the comb and brush...." Fred said. "We never discussed anything but the letters and the clothing."

Claire ignored him as she examined the comb and brush. "Do you have a knife?" she asked Dean.

"Yes," Dean answered. "Why?" He hoped she wasn't going to play a King Solomon and cut the damn thing in half but he withdrew a Swiss Army knife from his pocket. It was a gift from a young lady whom he'd helped when Bird Song first opened. Donnie looked at the impressive impalement and Dean started to show it to him but Claire grabbed it from his hands.

"It feels as if there's something in the handle of the comb," she answered, shaking it. "There's a seam here." She inserted the blade in a crack along the edge of the brush and it separated into two pieces. A small packet wrapped in tissue fell to her lap. The others stepped near for a closer look. She unwrapped the paper to reveal seven gold coins.

"Well, my, my! Isn't this my lucky day!"

There were four five-dollar gold pieces and three two-dollar and fifty-cent coins. Each was dated in the eighteen-nineties. Everyone bent close and examined them as Claire continued to hold them in her hand. Dean figured, This bitch isn't going to let go of these newly discovered century-old coins without a hell of a fight. He was right on the money, so to speak.

"I hope you're not going to try and tell me these coins are yours," she snapped to Fred.

Fred was in his finest form, the image of polite firmness. "I don't mean to be disrespectful, ma'am, but when we spoke on the telephone, I offered you the letters and the clothing. I'd already told Miss Worthington down at the museum she could have the pen and ink bottle. We never mentioned the comb and brush." Nor the notebook, Dean thought.

"That's right," said Effie. The look Claire gave her sister would frost a barbeque.

"You wouldn't remember to put your clothes on in the morning if I didn't tell you, Effie," Claire muttered.

"Here, take them," she said, handing Fred the comb and brush, but not the coins. The others looked at her expectantly.

Just then, Edith returned to the room, holding out three crisp one hundred dollar bills, which she thrust toward Claire who reached out and snatched them, without so much as a thank-you, stuffing them in her purse.

"You could perhaps give Mr. O'Connor the little coins," Effie offered.

Claire scooped up the five dollar gold pieces and dropped them in her bag. She then pushed the three smaller denomination coins across the coffee table toward Fred.

"Here, take these, just because I'm generous. I wouldn't want to see an old man cry."

Before Fred could reply, or whack her in the mouth, which would have been Dean's first choice, the front doorbell interrupted the tense gathering. Dean opened the door to a bearded man holding a small overnight bag. "Do you have a room?" he asked. A mud-splattered Blazer was parked behind him.

CHAPTER 7

"Hi," the man said with a smile. "I'm looking for a room." Dean held the door for him and he entered.

The bearded man was younger looking than Dean had thought when he first saw him drive by Bird Song, probably no more than late twenties. He wore jeans, a ski sweater and an opened, fur collared jacket.

"Sorry to bop in so late. I just had dinner and the service was a little slow."

"No problem. It's only eight-thirty," Dean answered as they stepped into the hall.

There was a hint of recognition on the man's face as he glanced over Dean's shoulder at Edith Shipton who had just emerged from the parlor. She stopped and smiled, holding out the edges of her white dress as if to show it off. The new guest smiled in return but gave no overt sign of knowing the woman. She climbed the stairs, turning once to look back at them.

"We're a little tight for rooms," Dean interrupted. "With the ice climbing festival about to open a lot of the climbers are arriving early. We should be filled after tomorrow."

"I'll take whatever you've got."

Cynthia came out of the parlor, followed by Fred, who was still seething over Claire Quincy's appropriation of the gold coins.

"Welcome to Bird Song," Cynthia said.

"Here for a little skiing?" Dean asked. "I saw a pair on your car out there."

"Ice climbing mostly. But, yes," he answered. "I'm going over to Telluride tomorrow and give the slopes a one day try. That's about all I can afford."

"I been meaning to get over there myself," Fred replied, much to the surprise of the Deans. "I hear-tell you can ski for free once you're seventy."

"Fred," Cynthia said, beating her husband with the same question. "You can't be serious!"

The old man looked indignant. "I sure am. I've got a pair of skis out in the shed. I been meaning to tell you about 'em but it's been so busy around here it slipped my mind. I bought 'em at a garage sale right down the street. Fella had my shoe size and his wife gave me a whale of a deal." Then he added, "She made him sell 'em just 'cause he turned sixty-five."

"Smart woman," Cynthia offered.

"You're welcome to join me tomorrow," the new guest said with a smile. "I think it's great being active even after you've got a few grey hairs."

"You're seventy-six!" Dean said to his stepfather. "That's a ridiculous age to take up skiing!"

"Who says I'm just taking it up? I skied before you crawled. It's as safe as watching TV and a darned sight more fun. Besides," he added, glancing at the parlor where the Quincy sisters were still gabbing, "I feel a need to get away from here a bit."

A phone call interrupted the conversation. Cynthia answered, another guest confirming his room while Fred told his new skiing partner he'd see him in the morning. He gave his stepson an I-told-you-so look and retreated to the Dean's office and quarters in the rear.

Dean showed the guest his room, the small first floor room beneath the stairs. It had been originally designed as a maid's quarters and it was the last room they rented when Bird Song was otherwise booked. In addition to its small size, it shared a common wall to the Dean's quarters, infringing on their privacy. The room contained a single bed, small dresser and chair. Due to its location in the center of the building, there were no windows.

"Sorry about the size. I know it's a bit stuffy but it's all that's left."

"No problem," he answered in a friendly voice. "Beggars can't be choosers. I'll just leave most of my ice climbing gear in the car." He extended his hand. "I'm Donald Ryland," he said.

Cynthia was still on the phone so after Dean introduced himself he completed the paperwork, without comment or acknowledgment that he knew Ryland's relationship to Bird Song's other guest Edith Shipton and her son. Ryland listed his address as Grand Junction, Colorado and indicated he'd stay at least through the weekend when the ice climbing festivities began in earnest.

As Ryland closed his door, the Quincy sisters came out of the parlor and began climbing the stairs—Effie with a cheery 'good night Mr. and Mrs. Dean,' and Claire with tight-lipped silence.

Cynthia finished her conversation and hung up the phone. Before Dean could tell her about Ryland, she turned to her husband, "Are you going to let Fred go skiing with that man?" she asked in a whisper as they turned toward their quarters. "I know Fred means well, but you said it yourself. He is seventy-six years old! What will we do if he breaks something?"

"Shoot him," Dean answered. " I'm not his guardian, just his step-son."

"He never mentioned he could ski."

"He's never even mentioned where he was born!" Dean replied. "You know and I know Fred's past is his business. I never pressed him about it in the fifteen years we roomed together. How would I know he can ski, if in fact he really can? All I know he hasn't skied in the fifteen years I've known him."

"I think you should go with him," she answered.

Dean scowled, but then thought about it. Maybe not such a bad idea. With all the activity over the holidays, Dean hadn't had a chance to hit the beautiful slopes of nearby Telluride. Here was an opportunity to sneak away, and be a good Samaritan in the process.

"Well, I suppose I could." He tossed in a hint of reluctance, just for good measure.

"What about skis?" Cynthia asked with a knowing smile.

"I'll rent them."

"Do *you* know how to ski?"

"Better than the old geezer, I imagine," Dean answered, trying to remember the last time he himself had tried the sport. It was five years ago with a lithe red head named Ellen for a Vermont weekend. Little time was spent on the snow.

As soon as the couple joined Fred behind the closed door of their office-sitting room, Dean explained the identity of their new guest. Surprisingly, Fred O'Connor, arch fan of any hint of mystery, remained uninterested in the Donald Ryland-Edith Shipton-Jerome Shipton triangle. He didn't even mention skiing. He remained too steamed up over the Claire Quincy transactions.

"Well," Cynthia said. "Whatever is going on, it's none of our business."

Dean smiled. "If we keep saying that enough times, perhaps we'll believe it. I have to tell you, Mr. Ryland is a damned sight more pleasant than bossy Miss Quincy, the sister from hell." Fred just grunted in agreement.

The winter season precluded the front porch rocking chair conferences of last summer and since the past autumn the group's confabs had been replaced with side-of-the-bed meetings in the Deans' quarters. While the need for such meetings wasn't as dire or sinister as the first few days after Bird Song's opening, the three still gathered here, away from the guests, especially when they wished to discuss one or more of their paying customers beyond their prying ears.

"Aren't you going to give the nice lady the notebook too, Fred?" Dean asked in his sweetest tongue-in-cheek voice. If the old man was going to sulk, Dean thought, might as well get it out in the open and allow him to vent a little steam.

"They're gonna serve fresh ice cream in hell before that lady gets a sniff at this here notebook, even if it proves to be worthless scratchings. Nor is she getting any research help from me! I ain't even gonna point her in the right direction to the library, much less do her work for her." Fred snarled his response with an uncustomary growl. Most women were putty in the old man's hands, but Claire Quincy had pushed all the wrong buttons and short-circuited his good nature.

"Think of the plus side, Fred," Cynthia answered. "You recouped all the money you spent buying these things in the first place. Plus, you got a comb and brush and a notebook full of who knows what. And," she added, "three gold coins. Not a bad haul for what David called a pile of junk!"

"Plus you get to go schussing down the slopes tomorrow," Dean added.

"Schussing?" Cynthia asked.

"It's a ski term," Dean informed her. "All us mogul-jumping slalomers know these terms."

"Even the thought of skiing doesn't take away the nastiness of that woman," Fred answered, in spite of sounding somewhat placated.

"Well, at least now you can forget about Annie Quincy Martin and get on with life," Dean said.

Fred just looked at him. "Not on your tin whistle! I just said I wasn't sharing anything with that Boston shrew, I didn't say I was quitting the caper. No, sir. There's just too many questions. Not only this here coded notebook but questions like why was a minister's wife squirreling away $27.50 in gold coins in her comb?"

"Good question!" Cynthia said. "That has me wondering, too. Let's start by doing some serious work on the notebook. We've been putting it aside since last night."

Dean put on his reading glasses. He didn't really need them, but Cynthia had gone ahead and made the appointment. He just wore them to appease her. And when the light wasn't good, now that some international conspiracy was shrinking the size of the printed word.

The trio sat around the office desk, looking over one another's shoulders at the neat handwriting in the old notebook. Cynthia took up a pencil and paper again and began listing the different letters but almost as soon as they'd begun, they were interrupted by a soft knock on the door. When Dean answered it, Edith Shipton stood there, still clad in the white dress, that she now owned. Her face shone with a glowing smile like a summer sunrise.

She looked past David Dean to his wife. "Mrs. Dean? May I speak with you?"

"Certainly," Cynthia answered, coming to the door. "We were just gabbing. Come in."

Edith entered, but only a step. She smiled at the others as she spoke quietly to Cynthia. "I was wondering if you'd let Donnie sleep down here with you tonight? All he needs is the couch." She gestured toward the leather sofa against the office wall.

"We have an extra room. It's booked tomorrow but it's empty tonight," Cynthia answered. "It wouldn't be any trouble and I'm sure he would sleep much better in a regular bed."

"Oh, no! If he sleeps alone, he gets upset. The sofa in the office would be fine and you could leave the door to your bedroom open, just a pinch. It's just that he has dreams. I wouldn't ask, but I need—well, Donnie's father is here. That's who just came. I wasn't going to tell you, but you've been so kind. He hasn't seen us in years. I need some time with him." Then she added, "I'll pay for the room. And I'm sorry to put you out."

Dean and Fred pretended, without success, to not have heard what Edith was saying while she blushed.

"No problem at all," Cynthia answered. "And there's no charge. Donnie's a nice boy and we're happy to have him." There goes any chance of Mr. and Mrs. Dean doing any hugging and squirming tonight, Dean thought.

Edith Shipton gave a half smile and left. Before Dean could let loose with a torrent of pithy comments, there was another knock on the door and Donnie entered the room. He was carrying his rolled up pajamas and a toothbrush. Wrapped in his nightclothes Dean could see the edge of a Beanie Baby St. Bernard. He looked nervous and uncomfortable.

"Come over here and grab a seat," Fred said. "We need all the help we can get with this here puzzle." The boy complied, with a shy smile, and the group studied the notebook together.

"Reminds me of them crazy characters you get on your computer screen when you mess up real bad," Fred said.

"Well, they sure didn't have a computer a hundred years ago," Cynthia answered.

"It still just looks like jumble of letters and numbers," Dean said as he read the first portion. "8m2f3km8m7ay7aa297867a88m4gkm38r 366v2b7fpb452m4g5av2d4528m2agf am4ra38a..."

Donnie shook his head "no" and began listing the letters as Cynthia had suggested the night before. After some work, they found there were nineteen different letters used, with "E, I, L, O, U, Q, and W" missing. Cynthia then began listing the different numbers that had been utilized.

"I'll bet a mug of hot chocolate there are twenty-six different characters!" she said as she searched the text. She stood up and bowed when she discovered eight different digits appeared, the numbers two through nine.

"See? Twenty-six different—oh, damn!—sorry, Donnie. That's twenty-seven! And I was sure it was going to be simple! I was positive all she did was substitute a different one for each letter in the alphabet."

"I'll take my chocolate with whipped cream," Dean said but his wife made no move toward the kitchen.

Fred suggested that one of the letters might be in error so the group continued to look at the puzzle on the basis Cynthia had first suggested. It was difficult for all of them to work together so Cynthia made two extra copies of a dozen random pages of the ancient text. Donnie sat off by himself with one of the copies. While Fred, and to a lesser extent Cynthia, had solved cryptograms in the newspaper, neither were particularly adept at it. Donnie appeared to be the most talented at the undertaking but he too had little success with this ancient writing. The lack of word separation and punctuation made the task far more difficult. They realized if the text were based on substitution, the more frequently used characters were most likely replacements for more frequently used letters, such as vowels. At first they tested to see if the numbers might be the vowels but that assumption didn't seem to work out. They also looked for double characters, understanding only certain letters doubled with any frequency in English language words. However, as there was almost no break between words, they could never be sure the double characters were in the same words and not the beginning and ending of different words or sentences.

Dean questioned the rare break between characters and the near absence of punctuation. Cynthia surmised that when they did appear, they were oversights on the part of the writer who unconsciously placed them as if she were writing in a normal, un-coded fashion. It was Donnie who found the combination "8M2" and guessed it was most likely a replacement for "THE." These were the first three characters used on the first page of the notebook and the combination appeared with regularity throughout the book. Still, there were more false leads than successes before the hall clocked tolled eleven and Cynthia announced it was beyond everyone's bedtime. Even Donnie surprisingly agreed as he pantomimed skiing.

"Are you going skiing tomorrow with Mr. Ryland?" Cynthia asked the boy. Donnie nodded yes, his eyes bright with excitement. "Well, it should be quite a party!" she said with a smile as Fred left for his room.

Dean went to close up while Cynthia readied the sofa for Donnie's bed. After filling the coffee pot and setting the timer, he began turning out the lights. When he passed the parlor, he was surprised to find Donald Ryland seated in a darkened corner. When he saw Dean, he smiled and waved him over.

"Women," he said. "Who can ever understand 'em?"

Dean was uncertain how to respond. When Ryland said nothing further, Dean broke the silence. "I guess there's another skier for tomorrow's outing. It should be fun, with your son along and all."

Ryland was startled by the comment. "You know who I am?"

"Edith got a little maudlin last night," Dean answered.

The young man ran his fingers through his beard. "I haven't seen my boy in over a year and I hardly got a chance to say more than 'hi' before she scooted him downstairs. But I talked her into giving me the whole day with him at Telluride tomorrow." He turned to Dean. "How much did she tell you?"

Dean thought before answering, wondering how much to admit to Donald Ryland, regressing back to his old detective days. But, he decided, he had no reason to distrust the man. "She told us she's left her husband and you're Donnie's father. And, I guess this guy Shipton is abusive, and doesn't take rejection very well."

"It's a real mess, I gotta tell you. Shipton is a devil. He won't let me near Donnie. Edith's managed to slip out and meet me a half dozen times over the years, but that's it. The whole family thinks I'm dog-shit—always has. I know I messed up, getting her pregnant and all, but I wanted to do right by her, and especially the boy. God, we were a couple of kids when it happened. But ol' Jerome, he'd rather pretend I was the one that never happened. He treats Edith like a piece of the furniture—bangs her around too, I guess. But she's such a mouse, she stays with him, taking it on the chin, so to speak."

"But you haven't given up," Dean said.

"No. And I won't. Donnie's my son. There's no changing that fact. I don't have Shipton's dough or his connections, but I'm not going away either. Edith knows that. She manages to call me every few weeks when she can get off on her own, which isn't easy. I bought her one of those phone cards so she can call without Shipton knowing about it. I can talk to Donnie even though he can't talk back to me. Shipton would kill her if he knew I had any contact."

"What caused her to finally leave Shipton?" Dean asked.

"She didn't tell you that?" Dean shook his head no and Ryland continued. "She found out she's preg—claims he switched her birth control pills or something. Anyway, she was all set to have an abortion but he found out what she was going to do. He so adamant to have another child he'd tie her to a bed for nine months if that's what it would take to make sure. She swears she'll never have his child so she took off."

"And then called you."

"Yeah. It really made my day, I'll tell you."

"Shipton sounds like a real jerk."

"More than that. Look what the bastard's done to our son? The poor kid can't even talk anymore!"

"How did that happen?" Dean asked.

"It's kind of complicated. There was a canoeing accident, up in Canada. Macho Shipton took his son, a boy from his first marriage, and Donnie out to some remote chain of rivers and lakes, fishing and running the streams. The boy, Jerry, fell in and drowned. It was almost twenty-four hours before Shipton and Donnie got back to civilization, with the kid's body. It freaked out Donnie. Shipton claimed Jerry fell in the water while they were shooting rapids and Shipton himself nearly drowned trying to save him."

"You doubt the story?" Dean asked.

Ryland just shrugged. "Who knows? I guess I just automatically think the worst of anything that comes out of Shipton's mouth, regardless. But it was August and that river isn't exactly world-class white water. And Shipton is the only one who's doing the talking. The shrinks seemed to think young Donnie might feel he's to blame for what happened and that's why he lost his ability to speak, but Shipton disagrees. Anyway, the boy is scared to death of Jerome, according to Edith. Always has been. He treated both boys equally—like they were a couple of pansies in his mind. Now he wants to try the breeding game one more time. Like I said, the whole situation is a real mess."

Far off in the distance, Dean could again hear the ringing of Gladys Turnbull's alarm but he paid it no attention. He hoped things were more peaceful out in the galaxy that here at Bird Song.

"How did Shipton react to his own son's death?" Dean asked.

Once more, Ryland shrugged. "Stoic, I guess. He's one of these type A personality guys who's always wound up tighter than a spring—wears whatever face suits the crowd."

Dean thought a moment and then said, "Shipton is on his way out here." He felt Ryland ought to at least be warned. "He traced Edith's charge slip. He called the local sheriff in Ouray and said he plans to come out and haul his 'mentally stressed wife' back East with him. He talked about having her committed."

"That figures. Keep her hospitalized till she delivers! God!" Ryland said, putting his hand to his head. "I'll bet he could do it too, as screwed up as Edith is right now."

"Now that Edith has left her husband, where does that put you?" Dean asked.

"I wish I knew!" He began to pace the room. "I spoke with her on the phone around Christmas and mentioned I was coming to Ouray for some ice climbing. She called me a couple of days ago and told me she'd taken off and flown out to Colorado with the boy. I wanted to see Donnie. It's been over a year since I've had a peek at him. But when I met her, the boy wasn't even with her and she laid this soap opera story on me about leaving Shipton and being pregnant. Don't get me wrong, I know she's hurting, but my main concern is my boy. That's why I came over to Bird Song. But now, all she wants to do is—have sex with me, like we're still kids and she can turn the clock back to hot nights and summer camp." He finger-combed his hair. "God, what a mess!"

"It sounds to me like she needs some serious professional help." Dean said.

"But what can I do? Maybe I sound like a jerk, but it's been ten years since we were an item and I've got a life now. I don't want to be cruel or uncaring and I know she's going through hell, but I can't just jump her bones and pretend it's yesterday. Maybe some guys would just chalk it up to a nice piece of tail, but that's not me. Now she's up there bawling her eyes out, thinking I'm some kind of bastard." There was nothing helpful Dean could offer. After a few moments of mutual silence, both men rose and returned to their rooms.

The lights were out, but Cynthia was still awake, wondering what had taken him so long. He told her of his meeting with Donnie's father.

"Let's just leave it alone and let it work itself out," she said with a sigh as she snuggled against him. "Pleasant dreams," she added. "And try not to dream about hanging women."

They were quiet for a some time but could sense from each other's movements that neither was asleep. Finally, Dean spoke. "What are your dreams like?" he asked.

"I don't remember most of them," she whispered. "When I do, they're nice dreams. I dream about you. And us. Often we're in wacky places, places like the house where I grew up or schools I attended when I was a kid. Places neither of us has ever been together."

"In my dreams I'm usually in trouble. I don't mean monsters are chasing me but I have a deadline or there's some unfinished business. I'm no hero in my dreams. Sort of the opposite. Like if I'm in a ball game, I'm the one who has the ground ball roll between my legs."

"That's insecurity. Most people wouldn't buy David Dean as an insecure guy."

"What about his wife? Is she insecure, too?"

"Not any more. I'm getting to know my guy a little more each day. And loving him all the more with the increased knowledge. You're my security. My flannel guy."

Dean never even heard Gladys Turnbull's muffled alarm clock. The next thing he knew it was morning.

CHAPTER 8

Two straight days of vigorous outdoor activity coupled with a later-than-usual bedtime caused Dean to sleep through the six o'clock broadcast of Public Radio news, waking only when an extended arm felt an empty bed beside him. Even Gladys Turnbull's alarm must have been muffled enough not to disturb his slumber. The sofa was empty, too, the blanket and sheets piled neatly. Cynthia was already at the kitchen table, amid sweet smelling scents of the morning fare of fresh cranberry scones, the ubiquitous notebook and a scattering of paper spread before her.

"Where's Donnie?" Dean asked as he bent down and kissed his wife.

"Off with his father to borrow skis from a friend of Mr. Ryland. He was as excited as Christmas morning."

"And Martha?"

"Skipped home as soon as she finished breakfast."

"How's it going?" he asked, motioning to the notebook.

"Slow. But I think I'm on the right track. I skipped ahead to a page where she used more punctuation and it helped. I haven't found any new replacement letters, but I've eliminated a lot of possibilities. If I can settle on a few more characters, it should begin to fall into place." She looked up. "But even when I figure out all the substitutions, deciphering the entire notebook will be a long project. And I'm still bothered that there are twenty-seven characters used and not just twenty-six."

"Maybe one of the characters is designated as a space between words or a period," Dean offered. Cynthia looked at him and began to nod her head, considering the possibility. She methodically searched the text.

"Think how long it must have taken her to write it," Dean continued as he munched on a scone and glanced over her shoulder.

"I don't imagine it was so very difficult. Not after she'd been working at it awhile," Cynthia answered, not taking her eyes from the page as she continued to work. "As much and as often as Annie wrote, the letters and numbers must have almost become a second language to her. She wouldn't see a 'two,' she'd see an 'E.' It's difficult for us because we're just starting out."

"Why do you suppose she did it? Why would a woman hide her writings from her husband?"

"Maybe it was written before she married."

"Maybe she was having an affair with the butcher."

Cynthia just scowled. "Before we can read what she wrote, we can only guess the reason for it. But we'll know before long. I'm not going to give up until I break it!"

Dean laughed. "You sound like the Brits with the enigma code. I'm beginning to think you like a mystery as much as Fred!"

"I like a mystery without dead bodies. Besides, now that you're a retired detective, Fred and I have to carry the ball."

Dean poured himself a cup of coffee. "Edith was down here earlier," he said, a smug look on his face.

"How do you know that?"

"I set up fresh a pot of coffee on the timer last night. It's down a cup or so, and you haven't poured any for yourself yet. No cup next to your place. See? I can still detect."

"It might have been Fred. Or one of the others. Don't forget Ryland was down here."

"Nope." He smiled at her with continued smugness. "The handle's turned to the left. That's the way a left-handed person pours and Edith is the only lefty at Bird Song."

"Think you're pretty smart, don't you?"

"Once an ace detective, always an ace detective. Six months without a mystery and I'm still in top form. Otherwise, they boot me out of the fraternity."

Cynthia busied herself with the notebook once again. "It kills me to admit it, but I think you might have something," she said. "The space business doesn't seem to work but she might have used a character for a period."

Footsteps on the stairs were the Deans' signal to prepare for breakfast. Cynthia reluctantly put the notebook aside and the couple began to carry the fresh baked goods and other breakfast items to the dining room. Fred O'Conner, dressed for the slopes, gave a grumpy wave. Dean was about to ask him if his nineteen-fifties sweater came from the same garage sale as the skis but he proceeded directly to the parlor. Effie Quincy, close behind, burst forth with an animated editorial on the splendors of, Bird Song, Ouray, the sunny weather and life in general.

"I can hardly wait to start our research on Aunt Annie!" she exclaimed as she sat at the table. "I'm so excited!"

While Cynthia began serving breakfast, Edith Shipton emerged, looking as if she'd had little sleep. She said nothing, barely nodding in response to the various greetings. Fred O'Connor joined the others, looking distressed.

"What's the problem?" Dean asked. "Are you worried about the slopes?"

"It's the picture from the museum. I can't find it. It was on the parlor table last night."

Effie looked up. "Perhaps my sister borrowed it. To examine it more closely."

"I'm obliged to return the picture so I shouldn't have let it out of my hands," he muttered as he reached for a pitcher of orange juice. "I'd appreciate your asking her." Just then, Claire Quincy descended the stairs on cue. Effie immediately asked her about the missing portrait of the reverend and his wife.

"Of course I don't have it." Then she added, with a dismissive wave of her hand, "That retarded child probably stole it."

Edith Shipton looked up in shock, mouth agape. She started to say something but just bit her lip and began to cry. Dean was furious.

He stood over Claire Quincy, much too closely. "Donnie Ryland is a very intelligent young boy, with a disability. It was most unkind of you to cruelly diagnose him otherwise and accuse him of being a thief. There is no indication whatsoever he cares a flip about that picture. I think you owe his mother an apology."

"I'm sure Claire didn't mean that!" Effie said with a trembling voice.

"Well, he acts retarded," Claire grumbled disgustedly as she started to rise. But Dean stood too close to the back of her chair for her to move. "Sorry," she mumbled, not even looking at Edith. She looked up at Dean. "I just know I don't have the damned picture!" Dean stepped back and she hurriedly left the room, Effie close on her heels. Edith sniffed once, lowered her head, and continued to eat, as if ignoring what had happened might make the pain disappear.

"Way to go," Fred muttered sotto voce. Cynthia just shook her head, but never the less smiled. It was her way of saying that while he might have been somewhat more reserved in his response to Claire Quincy, she was admitting the guest isn't always right. And, by Dean's interpretation, agreeing the old bitch got what she deserved.

Fred began eating his cereal, with a serving spoon, a sure sign he wanted to accelerate the process and get on with the day's activities. Donald Ryland returned with his son. Donnie's entrance seemed to brighten Edith's morning as she clucked over him, cautioning him about the perils of his undertaking in a dozen different ways, all the while ignoring father Donald who'd fled from her bed the night before. Fred finished his breakfast in a rush and hauled out the pair of his garage-sale skis. While the equipment didn't match what was displayed on the cover of current ski magazines, they looked surprisingly good for the twenty bucks Fred said he'd paid for them, with boots and poles part of the package. With Ryland's help, the skis were attached to his vehicle. All four would ride in the same car for the fifty-mile trip to Telluride.

In the confusion of the group's departure, a carload of ice climbers arrived to register. Behind them, Sheriff Jake Weller pulled up in his official vehicle. Dean started to get out of the car but Weller waved him on and Ryland pulled away from Bird Song. Dean spent much of the trip speculating on the reason for the law man's visit.

The distance between Ouray and Telluride was less than twenty miles, on a map, or as the eagle soars, when he feels like a thrill. However, winter locked the mountain jeep roads beneath yards of snow for all but a few short summer weeks. By highway, the journey was fifty miles—ten miles north to Ridgway, then westerly to Placerville and then back toward the southeast, all necessary to circumnavigate fourteen-thousand foot Mount Sneffles and its towering neighbors.

Donald Ryland kept up a nonstop conversation with his son and front seat companion, as they whipped along the highway. Donnie responded with nods, smiles and gestures while Fred and Dean, scrunched into the back seat, politely listened. Ryland worked for the National Forest Service and regaled Donnie with tales of the outdoor splendors of the Colorado mountains. The boy was enthralled and if Dean didn't know better, he'd have thought the two saw each other daily. As the group pulled into the parking lot at Mountain Village, the upper portion of the ski area, Donnie began to look nervous for the first time. Ryland picked up on it immediately.

"Don't worry about the top of the mountain just yet, son. We won't have you skiing any place where you're not comfortable." He gave him a smile and a poke and Donnie's anxiety seemed to melt away.

The foursome rode the gondola the short distance down from the parking area to the central village complex, with Donnie looking down, wide-eyed from the swinging car. Lift tickets were purchased, at prices far higher than the last time Dean had skied. There was no charge for Fred, though the counter girl, with a wink at Dean, asked for age verification, telling Fred he didn't look a day over sixty.

Dean, the only one without skis, separated from the others and located the rental shop. He was quickly measured and fitted and rejoined the others, relieved of a few more dollars. At the top of "The Meadows," the beginner slope, he paused, took a deep breath, drinking in his surroundings.

Telluride's sixty-six trails, spread over more than a thousand acres, were an awesome change from the crowded slopes Dean had skied in the East in years gone by. Here, thanks to three-hundred and twenty-five inches of average annual snowfall, a remote location that minimized lift lines and a thirty-five hundred foot maximum vertical drop, skiing was as it should be. Conditions were perfect. The air was dry and windless. The temperature hovered around twenty-five and the sun was brilliant.

Dean skied a few tentative yards down the slope, took a couple of turns, stopped, and assessed himself. It felt good. The boots were a little tight and his legs weren't exactly locked together, but the old exhilaration of gliding over the snow returned immediately. He scanned the slope below him and located the others. Fred, Donnie and Donald Ryland were already cutting wide snowplow turns on the gradual, open slope. Dean skied down to join them.

"The number six and nine lifts service most of the double black diamond runs," Dean said to Fred with a smile as the old man glided to a wide stop. Though it would kill Dean to admit it, he was proud as punch at his stepfather's guts and ability. It was apparent that Fred had skied before at some time in his long life and, more importantly, he knew enough to do so cautiously.

"After you." Fred answered with a look that said he, too, was justifiably proud to be on the slopes at his age.

Donnie, while not demonstrating textbook form, was managing nicely to remain on his skis, and not on his butt. His father was no doubt an expert, while Dean's ability was some where in between. He was able to ski from the summit, but only on those slopes and trails designated blue or green, novice or intermediate. The black diamond expert trails were for the Donald Rylands of the world.

By the time the group stopped for lunch—two large five-cheese pizzas at Big Billie's—Donnie had progressed to the point of being able to ski alone from the top of the beginner slope. While he expe-

rienced a few sit-downs, there were no serious spills. He always made
sure one of the adults was close by, but his youth and a natural sense
of balance helped him to catch on to the sport quickly. However, when
his father asked if he was ready for a greater challenge he declined. He
was more than content to spend his first day of skiing on the bunny
slope. It was obvious Donald, and to a lesser extent Dean, would enjoy
steeper, longer and more challenging runs. Fred understood this and
volunteered to ski with Donnie while the others took a couple of runs
from the higher elevations.

The two men first boarded chair lift number ten and ten and a half
minutes later were eighteen hundred feet higher than Fred and
Donnie, at nearly eleven thousand feet elevation. Conversation on the
trip up was limited to Ryland's enthusiastic appraisal of his son's abilities and skiing in general, with no mention of Edith Shipton and her
problems. Dean was just as glad to spend the day problem free.

The view from the top was spectacular, the snow perfect and the
trail empty of other skiers. They chose an intermediate trail called
"Sundance." It was long, yet wide enough to turn easily. They skied
together and to Dean it was a long and infinitely pleasant run. At the
base they checked in with Fred and Donnie, who were doing fine
without them, so they moved to even more challenging terrain. Dean
found the deep powder beyond his limited abilities and Donald Ryland
seemed content to stay with him and ski the packed trails, sometimes
cutting off to test the moguls and deeper snow at the trail's edge.

It was mid-afternoon when the pair had just finished skiing "See
Forever" from the summit, but Ryland was anxious to return to his
son.

"It's funny," he said. "You wouldn't think skiing the bunny slope
with a kid is any fun but I got a hell of a kick out of it. I just wish it
could happen more often."

Dean nodded in agreement and the two skied back down to "The
Meadows" to join the others. They spotted Fred and the boy from the
top of the slope. Fred held a large white handkerchief to his face.

"Are you blowing your nose or waving a white flag?" Dean called as
he neared the boy and old man.

"Just wiping my eyes. They water up in the cold." Then he added,
"—when you ski as fast as I do." But Dean could see in spite of Fred's
humor, something was wrong. Both he and the boy had their skis off.
As Dean looked closer at Donnie, he could see he was crying.

"What's the trouble?" Dean asked as Ryland skied up to his son and
tried to console him. Donnie clung to him like a frightened toddler.

"I think we've had a day of it," was all Fred would answer.

Dean hurried to return his skis while the others took the gondola back to the parking lot. By the time he caught up with them, Donnie had recovered somewhat, but gone was the enthusiasm demonstrated earlier and he continued to clutch his father, as close as the seat belt would allow.

"He saw someone who scared the dickens out of him," Fred muttered as the group drove from the lot. "I was picking myself up from a minor miscue and Donnie had skied ahead of me to base. Some guy came up to him—not a skier, but whoever he was, it frightened the boy. Donnie got his skies tangled up, trying to move away. By the time I skied down, the guy was no where to be seen."

The first person Dean thought of was Donnie's stepfather, Jerome Shipton. But it was Ryland who asked his son if that was who frightened him. Donnie wouldn't respond, turning away from his father toward the window. Ryland didn't press him and the boy fell asleep before they had turned down the canyon toward the town of Placerville. The rest of the one hour trip to Ouray was driven in silence.

CHAPTER 9

It is not the chill of the night time that makes my body tremble. It's when my thoughts wander to that saintly man. I gaze from my window to the hill as I watch the warm glow from his home and pray he perhaps is thinking of me as I am thinking of him. I can scarcely wait until Thursday next when we will again be in one another's company! He walked from Oak to Main Street yesterday though he didn't see me as his head was bent against the driving snow and I, a distance away.

"See?" Cynthia said. "I told you'd I'd solve it! It is Annie's diary, written when she first met Rev. Martin! Isn't it romantic?" Dean hardly had time to detail their day's activities before Cynthia proudly showed him the transcribed text.

"That's great," Dean said, reading the century-old writing. "How much did you translate?

"Only the one paragraph. It's real pick-and-shovel work, maybe an hour a page. But you were right—'X' equals a period! That's why there are twenty-seven characters. Once I figured that out, it all began to fall into place."

"Is this the first page?" Fred asked, looking over Dean's shoulder.

"No. But I'm going to start at page one and decipher the entire notebook in order. It's like reading a novel!" Cynthia, usually much more reserved, was as excited as Dean could remember.

"It reads more like a paperback romance than a best seller," Dean said. "I've never met anyone who talked like that."

"Don't be a poop! It's very romantic, even if the language is a bit stilted."

"You gotta remember the times," Fred said. "Folks were a bit more formal back then. But this is a real find! The museum will get a big kick out of it." He scratched his head and scowled. "That reminds me. I gotta bite the bullet and go see Miss Worthington, with my hat in hand, and explain how I *misplaced* that picture she kindly lent me."

"I searched high and low Fred, but no luck," Cynthia said.

Dean frowned. "I'd still bet my last buck Claire Quincy has it in the bottom of her suitcase."

"Well, we can't very well go searching her room for it," Cynthia answered. Dean raised his eyebrows at the suggestion. "Don't you do it!" she scolded.

"I'd try to smooth over the missing picture with Miss Worthington by telling her about this here notebook, but I can't be sure she'd keep her mouth shut and not blab about it to the Quincy ladies."

"I guess the sisters spent the day at the museum," Cynthia said. "I haven't seen them since shortly after the two of you left to ski."

"The more time that Claire spends in the museum, the better, as far as I'm concerned," Dean said.

"Well," Cynthia said to Fred, "in spite of how obnoxious Claire Quincy is, you ought to let her and her sister know about the notebook. After all, it's an important part of their family history."

"I suppose you're right," Fred grumbled. "But I've got a mind to let them stew, at least for a while."

"You could wait until they return to Boston and then mail it to them," Dean suggested. "Then you won't have to listen to Claire bitching about how you cheated her when that's just what she did to you. Better yet—sell it to her, for another three hundred bucks!"

"I might make 'em a copy, but the original stays in Ouray. This here stuff is history."

"The notebook's not all the news," Cynthia said. "Jerome Shipton is in town. That's why Sheriff Weller came by this morning, to let us know."

Dean explained how they suspected it was Shipton who had frightened Donnie on the ski slope in Telluride. "He must have either seen us leave Ouray with skis or followed us over there."

"You're probably right," Cynthia said. "Weller said Shipton knows where Edith is staying."

"Does he mean to make trouble?" Dean asked.

"Weller says Shipton claims he doesn't. He was sweet as sugar—just a concerned husband looking out for his wife's welfare."

"But Weller doesn't believe him?"

"That was how it seemed to me. He kept saying Bird Song isn't in his jurisdiction and any trouble Shipton caused would be the city's problem. But that doesn't mean he isn't nosy about what's going on."

Dean was emphatic the best course of action was to play leave-it-alone. The others nodded in agreement.

"The sheriff also saw Martha wasn't in school and asked Janet why," Cynthia said. "When Janet told him she was going to home-school Martha, Weller suggested rather firmly it might be a good idea if

Martha went back to a more formal setting. He hinted Janet's teaching qualifications were a bit suspect."

"Good for him!" Dean said.

"He offered to drive Martha to school. It made Janet as mad as a hornet, but Martha's back in the classroom."

Fred smiled. "Riding in a police car is the next best thing to a fire engine. I hope he turned the lights and siren on!"

"The sheriff talked to Edith, too. He tried to get her to seek a court order against Shipton if she was in fear of him, or, at the very least talk to an attorney. Edith just withdrew and wouldn't even answer him. She spent the day in her room, in Annie's dress."

"That woman needs help and she needs it fast," Fred said as he rose to leave. "Wish me luck with Miss Worthington," he added as he left, slightly hobbled from his day on the slopes.

"You never need 'luck' when there's a woman involved," Dean called after him.

"By the way," Cynthia said, in a firm tone, "I believe I'm due an explanation from you."

"What for?" Dean asked.

Cynthia crossed to the desk and returned with a hand full of cards and envelopes. "I found these when I was searching for the picture of Reverend and Mrs. Martin. Care to explain why there are six unused Christmas cards, six Birthday cards..." she began counting, "...and seven Valentine cards, all 'To My Loving Wife,' or some variation thereof? All with unused envelopes I might add, all hidden beneath your undershorts?"

Dean shook his head. "Would you buy the answer that I ran into an incredible sale I couldn't pass up?"

"No."

"How about...."

"No." She shook her head. "Why would you ever do such a silly thing?"

"I guess I'm busted, huh?"

"Definitely."

"Well, you gave me such a hard time when I didn't get you a Christmas card, until the day after, I figured I'd stock up." He looked up at her, but wasn't exactly rewarded with a loving glance in return. "I guess that doesn't show me as a sensitive and loving husband, huh?"

"Why six cards? Why not twenty? Or fifty?"

"Styles change. See? I didn't want to get too far away from what's cool and current. I'm not some inconsiderate oaf. I'm sensitive about things like that."

"Why seven Valentine cards instead of six?"

"Valentine Day isn't until next month. I wanted them to come out even."

"And I suppose Mother's day cards weren't available this time of year?"

"I guess that one slipped my mind." Then he added, with an unsuccessful attempt at levity, "Doesn't this prove I'm looking at our marriage as a long term relationship?" She continued to glare at him, unsmiling. He pretended to hang his head. Cynthia crossed over to her husband, took his face in her hands and kissed him, hard on the lips. "Thank you, darling," she said, but the tone didn't come close to matching the words. "That's the *one* kiss you get for all nineteen cards." She turned on her heels. "Sorry you'll miss out on the other eighteen. Buy in bulk, get rewarded in bulk." She dumped the lot in the trash. "Men," she said disgustedly as she left the room, calling over her shoulder, "Go out and socialize with all those macho ice climbers."

While Dean had no desire to participate in the new and perilous sport of ice climbing, he didn't share Cynthia total perplexity at why a sane human being would even consider subjecting himself or herself to such uncomfortable danger. When her son Randy, visiting Bird Song over his Christmas college break, had expressed an interest in the sport, she had a fit. It made her dizzy just to see the magazine pictures of the climbers, she'd said.

Bird Song was now officially at full capacity and would remain so for the next few days. The three north-side second floor rooms contained Fred, Gladys Turnbull and a pretty female climber named Penny. Across the hall were Effie and Claire, with Edith and her son in the rear bedroom. The three third floor rooms contained six ice climbers while Donald Ryland remained in the small first floor quarters.

Dean introduced himself to the large gathering in the parlor, trying without success to remember names. The sole name he retained was Mick, the jolly outgoing spokesman for the group, who seemed to know all of the others.

The room was a-chatter with foreign conversation, the words having nothing to do with national roots but the fanatic avocation of the gathered guests. These mountaineering folk talked a different language. Bergschrunds, couloirs, moats and seracs peppered conversations—animated tales of past ascents of both ice and stone. These incredibly tuned climbers were as at home on rock-face cliffs as frozen water falls, the steeper and higher the better, and by the sound of it, the world was getting a whole lot smaller. They were a well traveled group for their uniformly young ages. At least Dean had heard of Quebec, the Alps, and France, but locations and climbs like Cerro Torre in Patagonia (the place, not the clothing), Frankenjura, Orizaba and Cayambe were places he never knew existed.

"God," he said at one point, "I used to think I was in pretty good shape when I was biking a lot. When I rode the *Ride the Rockies* bike tour, I was proud as punch when I finished it. You guys talk about spending overnights, hanging from a hammock sling, half way up some cliff on the other side of the world! I can't imagine trying to sleep with just a couple of little steel pegs hammered into the rock the only thing holding me from a couple of thousand foot drop!"

"Pitons," Don Ryland corrected him with a smile, as he entered the room and joined the group. "Not 'little steel pegs.'"

"At least they're embedded in rock. Ice seems a whole lot less permanent."

"That's the challenge," Penny answered. "Ice changes all the time."

"She should know," Mick answered, displaying a sporting magazine, "Penny's the one on the cover." The glossy color photo displayed a concentrated young woman, hand-climbing upside down, across a rock face that looked devoid of any hint of a hand hold.

"They just used the picture of me 'cause my butt's cuter than these guys," the young woman answered.

"Don't let Penny kid you," another climber answered. "She's a whiz on a roof. This girl can find a handhold on a sheet of glass and she's as strong as any man I know. She won't even tell you how much she can bench press. Penny always looks for the crux, the toughest place to climb."

"You gotta push," she answered with a smile. Penny, who couldn't have weighted more that a hundred and ten, picked up the magazine. "That was a pisser," she said. "We were in Alberta...." And the group was off on another round of stories.

Gladys Turnbull button-holed two of the climbers and began holding court on one side of the room while devouring a logging crew's share of Cynthia's Toll House cookies. Dean picked up Gladys's chatter in mid-conversation. It involved some sort of messages from space. The bewildered climbers looked longingly at their friends and especially Penny, but were trapped into listening to the galactic adventures of some creatures called "womps."

Effie and Claire returned, followed in by Martha and Donnie, who had been playing outside. The children raced back to the laundry room where Janet was finishing up her domestic duties. The Quincys wandered into the crowded parlor. Effie bubbled away to anyone who'd listen while Claire stood looking over the gathering with undisguised disdain. Effie explained effusively how she and her sister had spent the day resurrecting their long lost great-aunt, whom Dean wondered if they were about to dub Saint Annie. Claire took a seat offered by one of the climbers and proceeded to add to the sainthood by correcting every other sentence poor Effie tried to offer. The ice climbers smiled politely but one by one began to make excuses about leaving for dinner.

Cynthia entered the room and explained the general menus and pricing of the various restaurants in town. When the crowd began to break up in earnest, she took her husband's arm and led him to their kitchen where a chicken pot pie was still bubbling on the table. It was a sure sign he was forgiven for his irreverent try at changing the age-old ritual of greeting card purchasing. Their suppertime chatter was limited to the logistics of Bird Song and the care and breakfast feeding of its thirteen guests. Fred returned just as they were clearing the dishes, wearing a perplexed look on his face.

"What's the problem?" Dean asked as he loaded the dishwasher. "Did the Boston sisters get all the poop on Annie before you got there?"

"I don't know what they dug up but what I found is a bit of a mystery," Fred answered as he began to poke in the refrigerator. "Something doesn't add up with Miss Annie Quincy." He turned to Cynthia who was dishing out the last of the chicken for him. "Did you get to decipher any more of the notebook?"

"I haven't had a chance with Bird Song packed like a sardine can. What seems to be the problem?"

"Miss Worthington spent the day waiting on Claire and showing her and her sister the old newspapers on microfilm at the library. She claims they read everything from 1898 forward. By the way, she's a bit peeved about the picture. Asked me outright if I thought Claire might have pinched it."

"Sounds like Miss Worthington is a quick read on the old bitch if you ask me," Dean said.

"How did you answer her?" Cynthia asked.

"I told Miss Worthington I wasn't one to accuse, but I didn't argue with her none, neither. But that's not the problem." They both looked up as he continued. "I noticed the newspaper always gave a big spread for weddings, so as long as I was there I thought I'd try and find Annie and the Reverend's marriage. I started looking at earlier editions."

"So?" Dean asked, trying to hustle Fred along with his drawn out explanation.

"So all I got was the same stuff. More 'do good' business by the reverend's wife, all the way back to 1896. That's as far as I got."

"But Annie was writing her sister after that date, in 1898, and she wasn't married yet," Dean said.

Fred gave him a big gotcha smile. "See what I mean?"

Cynthia poured a cup of tea. "Perhaps there was an earlier Mrs. Martin who died?"

"Nope. The papers would have made a big deal of it."

"Maybe Annie kept her wedding secret from her family, at least for a time," Cynthia offered. "By the tone of the letters Rachael wrote to her, the family appeared somewhat estranged from one another."

"Makes reading Annie Quincy's journal a bit more interesting, doesn't it?" Dean said. "Fred, it looks like you've got yourself a real mystery this time."

"Well," said Cynthia, "I have four dozen muffins to bake and scads of other things to do like cookies and cake for tomorrow afternoon. With Bird Song being full, much as I'd like to get to know Miss Annie a little better, she'll have to wait in line."

"Tell you what," Fred said. "How's about I cook up those muffins and stuff. You can take the evening off and play decoder."

"And chase off all the guests with your cooking?" Dean said. "I'll volunteer. You can clean up after me."

Cynthia gave them both a cautious look but after explaining in detail what needed to be done, she agreed to let the surrogate cooking team give it a try. She retired to the rear quarters, leaving the two chefs to battle it out. After a few false starts, things began to move along pretty well as the evening proceeded.

The front door was in continual motion with guests coming and going, amid laughter and boisterous conversation. Edith passed by, dressed in civies, her beloved white dress temporarily put aside. She held Donnie by the hand. When they returned later, Donald Ryland was with them, chatting amicably with both of them. Just as batch number three of muffins was ready, Effie stuck her head in the kitchen, looking over her shoulder, even more nervously than usual.

"I'm not sure I should tell you this," she said. "Claire thinks I'm a silly goose about it." Dean waited, up to his elbows in flour. When he didn't say anything, Effie continued. "I got up last night. I couldn't sleep. I kept thinking I could hear an alarm clock." Dean bit his lip, assuming the little woman was about to complain about Gladys Turnbull's late night writing, but she had other concerns. "I think I saw a ghost, in the hall! She was dressed in white...."

Dean smiled. "I believe it might have been Edith," he said. "She seems to fancy that dress of your great-aunt Annie and I think she may have been up and about last night."

Effie looked somewhat perplexed, but not satisfied. "I spoke to Mrs. Shipton about it. She said she thought Bird Song held spirits, too. She didn't say anything about wandering around last night. And Miss Turnbull, the author, when I told her, said she feels things, too." She smiled. "Oh, I guess I'm just being foolish like Claire says. It probably was Edith Shipton in her white dress." Then she added, "But it looked like a real ghost. You don't suppose Annie is trying to contact us, do you?"

Mick, the ice climber, interrupted them before Dean could think up a proper reply. He announced to Dean he had answered the door and a customer was waiting. Dean brushed off a white cloud of flour and greeted a well-dressed, good-looking man in his late forties standing in the hall.

"I'd like a room," he said with a smile.

"I'm sorry," Dean replied. "We've got a full house. With the ice festival, things are pretty busy." The man looked annoyed as much as disappointed.

"Can't you move someone around—double them up? I'll pay for any inconvenience."

"Sorry. But I'm sure there are some other places in town. Do you want me to call around for you?" Dean offered, in spite of being a bit peeved at the man's abruptness.

"No. I want to stay here." Just then, Edith Shipton came down the stairs. She had reached the hall before she turned and saw the tall man standing in the doorway. "Hello, Edith," he said in a chilling voice. Edith Shipton's jaw dropped and a panicked look spread across her white face. She wilted to a heap and fell to the floor.

Dean rushed to her side, just as Donald Ryland came out of his room, in time to catch a glance at the departing man who turned and strolled down the stairs to the street.

"That bastard!" He exclaimed. "That was Shipton!"

With Fred's help, and two of the returning guests, the group revived Edith. She seemed bewildered with her surroundings and very weak. Ryland suggested they carry her to his first floor room instead of trying to maneuver her upstairs. After Cynthia came out and administered a cold face cloth, Edith seemed somewhat better, enough to decline medical attention, though she remained disoriented even after reaching Ryland's small quarters.

A batch of muffins burned in the process but things began to return to normal after Ryland indicated Edith was feeling better and had apologized for her actions. Dean called Sheriff Weller, concerned that Jerome Shipton would further disrupt Bird Song but Weller could offer little help.

"Shipton may be sleaze of the year, but until he does something illegal, there isn't anything the law can do. Tell his ditzy wife that if she won't do anything to keep the bastard away, we sure can't."

Dean considered calling the City of Ouray Police but realized they too could be of little help unless Shipton did something against the law.

It was after ten by the time the kitchen chores were finished and the place cleaned up, sort of. Fred had left a half hour earlier, to see Miss Worthington, about some business, or so he claimed. Dean retired to his quarters, bearing a warm muffin that Cynthia sampled with an approving nod. He related his conversation with the sheriff as she continued to work on the notebook. Both agreed they hadn't seen the last of Jerome Shipton.

Dean began getting ready for bed; the day's skiing had taken its toll. Cynthia, who was sitting up in bed, continued to work on the notebook.

"How is the decoding coming?" he asked, glancing over her shoulder at her writings.

"Very interesting," she replied. "Just give me a few minutes to finish this page and I'll read it to you. I messed up a couple of letters and have to go back and change them. It would have been much easier if she had separated the words."

"If you have a problem, just wait a little while and ask Annie yourself. According to Effie, she roams the halls at night. It's getting late. She should be out any time now." He told Cynthia about Effie's apparition, then added, "I'm sure it was poor Edith Shipton strolling around the place."

Cynthia laughed. "I hope it was just Edith and not some malevolent spirit that scares away all the guests."

"Don't fear," Dean answered. "I used to be a cop. If I see a ghost and it gives me a hard time, I'll pull my gun and send it packing!"

"I'm sure shooting ghosts in town must be against some local ordinance. Sheriff Weller or the police chief would jump all over you."

"It wouldn't be the first time," he answered as, Cynthia looked up.

"There," she said, putting down her pencil. "I'm not sure what Annie is saying, but I'm beginning to get an inkling."

Dean read the words Cynthia had carefully transcribed:

The night has passed at last though it will be many more hours before the sun shows its golden face to give light to this mid-winter morning. The heat has been lowered now that the men have left and it is oh so cold as I lay huddled here beneath my thin blankets. In spite of the cold, I try to open the window to rid this room of the smoke and whiskey breath of those who visited here, but the frame is frozen fast. I've tried to sleep, all in vain. My mind won't release me from all that has happened since Rev. Martin first visited me, and changed my life.

I gaze out my window as the moon is slowly slipping away and I long for the warmth of the morning. The ice is everywhere. It hangs from the rooftops like daggers nearly touching the ground. The icicles are prison bars on our windows, trapping us, prisoners to this life of sin and degradation, giving miners a few minutes of pleasure for the pittance of coins it takes them weeks to earn in the bowels of the earth, performing unspeakable labors for the wealth of others.

Dean looked up at his wife after reading the strange lines. "Damned! That doesn't sound like any minister's wife I ever knew!"

"What do you make of it?" Cynthia asked cautiously.

"It's obvious. She's a hooker. A prostitute. A lady of the night."

"We can't be sure...." Cynthia studied the words carefully. "It certainly sounds as if it might be the thoughts of one of—those girls— not Mrs. Martin. The Reverend and his wife were supposed to have administered to the working girls. Do you suppose these are just speculations about how their life might be? Perhaps they interviewed some of the girls."

"Come on! And then wrote it up in code? Listen to the words— 'smoke and whiskey breath of those who *visited* here' and look at the pronoun. '*Our*' window!"

"We can't be sure Annie Quincy wrote this," Cynthia protested.

Dean was quick to reply. "We said the writing in the notebook matched the *Annie* written in the underclothes. And the woman who wrote this, whoever she is, isn't any dunce. She is very well educated. Read the words!" He began to pace the room. "Wait until Fred gets a load of this! If he's looking for a mystery, he's sure got one now! Our little Annie is a call girl!"

"We don't know for sure," Cynthia demurred. "It doesn't add up. How could the Reverend Martin marry a prostitute without creating a world-class scandal?"

"Who knows? Maybe they managed to cover it up. Maybe she turned tricks in another city and he 'rescued her' and brought her here. I'll leave that research up to Fred. This will keep him busy for weeks! Damned! I can hardly wait to see the look on Claire Quincy's face when I tell her saintly Aunty Annie was turning tricks!"

"Don't be naughty! You'll do nothing of the kind! And remember—innocent until proven guilty," she answered as she readied for bed. "There's a whole notebook left to decipher. I'm sure it will give us some answers."

"All it's given us so far is a peck of questions," he replied.

"The Quincy family will be devastated," Cynthia said. "And what about the book the Quincy brother is writing?"

"It sounded like three-quarters fiction already," Dean answered.

"Fiction is different from an outright lie. He'll have to abandon it, if Annie Quincy really is—one of those girls."

"Let him write the truth. It would be a lot more successful. Maybe a best seller. He can just change the title from *Saint among the Sinners* to *Sinner among the Saints, The Life and Times of a Mine-Town Hooker.*" She gave him a "you're-incorrigible" look as she switched out the light.

Dean dreamed of white-dressed hookers smiling and calling to a line of seven little miners who looked suspiciously like Snow White's benefactors. Only this time, even Grumpy had a smile on his face.

CHAPTER 10

The coterie of ice climbers was beginning to gather on the front porch. A massive collection of sinister looking implements was growing—tools of their trade, all apparently necessary in order to remain aloft when maneuvering up or down perpendicular columns of frozen water. With breakfast in their bellies, the group was anxious to get going. Edith, Effie, Claire and Gladys remained in their rooms. Donnie was outside with his father. Fred had already left.

"Where's Fred off to? The museum can't open for hours," Dean asked his wife as he helped clean up the dining room.

"Miss Worthington is letting him get an early start. I think he's trying to do his research before Claire gets there." Cynthia went on to say Fred had been excited by her translation of Annie's notebook and had left in a rush.

"I keep hearing the name 'Miss Worthington' a lot lately. What goes?" But Cynthia just shrugged.

The two donned their coats and joined the climbers outside. The rising winter sun made the heavy clothing almost unnecessary. Cynthia just shook her head in amazement at the collection of gear.

"I'm not even going to ask why you do it," Cynthia said.

"Fair enough," Donald Ryland answered. "I learned a long time ago, that anyone who asks that question can't understand my answer anyway. Why don't you just come over to the ice park and watch? Edith is going with us, and so is Donnie." The young boy snuggled close to his father. "If she ever gets out of bed," Ryland added with a hint of impatience.

"I hope Edith and Donnie aren't considering taking up the sport," Cynthia replied with a shudder.

Young Donnie vigorously shook his head no. "Smart boy," Cynthia said to him, giving him a pat on the shoulder.

"I wish I'd started that young," one of the climbers said as he and two of the others began tossing their gear into the back of a pickup truck. "I was light as a feather back then." He rubbed his still-flat belly. "I'd have scrambled up the ice."

"If you lived long enough," Cynthia lectured.

"It's as safe as a stroll in the woods," Ryland answered, winking at Dean. "Just exercise a little caution, have patience, good equipment and lots of common sense." Then he added, "And hope the guy above you is playing by the same rules!" He patted Dean on the shoulder. "Give it a try, Mr. Dean. There's nothing to it. I could have you climbing before the sun sets."

"No, thanks," Dean answered.

"You'd be anchored on a line tied to a top bollard, secured in a harness. It's a cinch. Just rappel down and climb back up."

"Rappel," Dean said. "That's when you jump off a mountain with a rope tied around your waist, and hope it's long enough."

"Something like that," Ryland laughed. "You're on a belayed line that is passed under one thigh and over the opposite shoulder so that it can be paid out, nice and smooth, a little at a time...."

"Don't you even think about it!" Cynthia said.

Dean turned to his wife. "I'm afraid I'd get evicted from Bird Song, if and when I made it back!"

Penny joined the men. "Why are you guys trucking?" she chided them. "The park's practically in town!"

"We're just using it to haul the gear," Teddy, the oldest of the group, answered. "I'm just riding along so's nothing falls off!"

"Wimps!" she called, as she set off at a quick pace beneath a heap of gear that nearly buried her small frame. The rest of the climbers followed in the truck but Ryland declined to join them, turning a perturbed eye to Bird Song. There was still no sign of Edith.

Dean motioned to the odd assortment of apparatus that surrounded the young man. "Tell me why you need so much junk." He picked up a menacing looking tool.

"That's called an ice ax, or piolet," Ryland answered. "You can spend three hundred bucks on a good one. That and the crampons are the key tools" The sinister instrument was serrated on one end of its curved claw, with an adze blade on the other side of the crescent. There was a pointed pic at the base of its handle. "We use two of them, one in each hand. We embed the jagged side into the ice above us and pull ourselves up. Easy as walking upstairs, almost." He fingered a heavy strap attached to the head. "This leash, attached to your wrist, bears most of your weight."

"What's a crampon?" Dean asked.

"They're what you wear on your feet," Ryland explained. He pulled out a pair of spiked apparatuses, with lengthy teeth extending both down and forward. "These fit on the base of the boot, by a variety of means. The teeth enable the climber to scale a vertical wall by holding to the ice while pulling yourself upward. They're not much for dancing, but they are a must for climbing frozen water!"

"You trust those to hold you?" Cynthia asked.

"Ice is an incredible surface. It doesn't take much ice to give you a bomber, a firm hold, provide you set your angle right. It's always changing but it has great holding power. You get used to knowing the different types of hardness and thickness. You're always testing because surface changes, by the season, the time of day, how many climbers hack away at it, sometimes by the hour. That's what make climbing it such a challenge." He poked at the rest of the equipment. "There are all kinds of different tools, pitons, hammers to set pitons, ice screws, pound-ins, ice hooks, wired nuts and cams—different stuff for different surfaces. You're not always just on ice. You get into mixed rock and ice and there's often snow to clear away to get to a hard surface. Being able to scale a sheer wall of rock and ice while lugging this junk requires some advance planning." He held up a waist harness. The heavy leather rig appeared designed to span both waist and upper thigh. It contained a large metal ring in the center.

"That ring is called the carabiner," Ryland explained. "Its principal function is a secure attachment point for a safety line. You clip a lot of gear to your harness too. You'll also need rope, not cut from your outside clothes line, but a couple of lengths of one-hundred and fifty feet each of 9 or 10mm line. Add to this, a backpack, some food and liquid, not to mention your garments. Today it's warm, but after you've hugged ice for a few hours in the shade, you'll be glad you took time to dress sensibly. I've been on climbs in all kinds of weather, some all day, rappelling down at dusk, nearly in the dark, with wind and snow trying to blow me off the wall."

"That makes me shudder just to think about it," Cynthia said.

"It's important whatever garments you wear, that you get good protection against the elements. Your shell has to shed wind, water and snow to maintain a warm and dry climate inside. If it fails, you could be in big trouble. Add to these, specialized boots, gloves or mittens, and don't forget your helmet. While helmets provide little protection in a serious fall, they're a must to shield you from junk dropped or dislodged from above you. Believe me, that *always* happens! Sometimes you think it's raining stones and golf balls! Falling ice is rock-hard stuff!"

"You haven't told me anything to make me want to take up the sport," Dean said as Edith emerged from the building. She appeared in no hurry and was dressed in only in a light sweater.

"At least come along and watch," Ryland asked the Deans again as Edith finally joined them. He reached in his vehicle and tossed her a heavy coat, but said nothing to her.

Dean turned to his wife as Ryland and his son began packing his gear. "If we're going to host ice climbers, we ought to know something about their sport."

Cynthia still looked unconvinced at the sanity of endeavor but agreed to be a spectator. "Only if you don't get any ideas and I can close my eyes when someone starts to slip."

The group walked up to the ice park climbing area from Bird Song. Edith still hadn't spoken, but clung to Donnie's hand. The climbing area was a short distance, off the main highway, just as the roadway began to ascend into the mountains. As they strolled along, Ryland discussed the recent rise of interest in the sport. He explained that like most athletic activities such as running, climbing, swimming or skiing, ice climbing evolved from the practical necessity of getting someplace not otherwise easily accessed. As technique and equipment advanced, more and more enthusiasts took up the enterprise as a sport. In the late seventies and early eighties scaling these challenging surfaces really caught on. Ouray, he told them, was unique in the world. Here, easy accessibility, great ice in a deep, narrow gorge, facilities close by and a park run by people who understood the sport and emphasized safety, made for an ideal package.

Usually there were few cars at the site but now, with the early festival climbers in town, the parking lot at the curve of the county road was filled. A number of cars carried out of state license plates. As the group trudged up a small rise in the road, the awesome creations of the ice park came into view.

Imposing columns and pillars of ice were visible everywhere—massive icicles and mounds, built up from the spraying water tapped from the piping that paralleled the penstock. The colors were striking. A blue-green tint shone through the sunlight while frozen waterfalls, hanging from the upstream cliffs, bore a hint of the rust-orange hue from the natural deposits of Red Mountain above. As the group approached the area, climbers could be seen, bright colored flies tacked on a wall of ice.

At this spot, a bridge spanning the Uncompahgre River bisected the two main climbing sections that extended almost a mile. Once the festival was underway, this would be the prime area for gear demonstration. Now it held about two dozen people, some climbers preparing their equipment and photographers availing themselves of the excellent location where they could look straight down on the climbers below them.

"Impressive, isn't it?" Ryland said to the silent group. Donnie clung to his mother, eyes wide, pointing to a climber about to descend from the corner of the bridge. From a distance, it looked as if he leapt backwards into the abyss. Edith shut her eyes and Dean thought for a moment she might once again faint.

"I can't watch this," she said, a tremble in her voice. She turned away, looking straight ahead, back down the road.

"The ice is beautiful," Cynthia said, "but they should have a psychiatrist in residence for the participants. That's the scariest thing I've ever seen." In spite of the closeness of the park to Bird Song, this was Cynthia's first view of ice climbing. While Dean had wandered up to the area with Cynthia's son Randy on a few occasions, she had steadfastly stayed away.

Ryland just laughed as they crossed the bridge. "Let's go up river a way and you can hold my rope." While the others moved cautiously to the bridge, enthralled by the scene in both directions, Edith refused to budge any further. Ryland's pleading fell on deaf ears. It was obvious she was petrified to venture anywhere near the edge. Finally, it was acknowledged she would return to Bird Song alone.

The view down stream and directly below the bridge was awesome. The chasm appeared to Dean to be a hundred feet or more to the river below. There was ice everywhere, a panoply of shapes and forms. Climbers could be seen in pairs, groups and singles, some nearly beneath them. All seemed to be in perilously dangerous situations, clinging to the sheer walls with outstretched arms and spread legs, somehow adhered to the clear surface before them. The steady chinking of ice axes could be heard echoing up and down the deep gorge.

At Ryland's urging they crossed the bridge past the area where the main activities of the ice festival were being assembled for the weekend. Here scores of sponsoring vendors would be displaying and demonstrating their exotic wares to the multitude of visitors. The Deans were learning the sport of ice climbing is critically dependent on equipment, unique and not inexpensive. But the social aspects of the gathering were of importance to the participants as well. There would be dinners, a Saturday night dance, slide shows and hundreds of ice climbing exhibits. All access to the gorge was free, funded by the generosity of private contributors, merchants and the equipment manufactures.

"Why don't they charge money?" Cynthia asked when Ryland mentioned there was no charge.

"Colorado law exempts land owners from most liability if the land for recreational is freely offered, at no charge. That's a must nowadays, when everyone is scared of getting sued," Ryland told them. "Unfortunately, 'No Trespassing' is a more familiar sign to this sport, than this one." He gestured to a posting at the head of the trail.

Please respect the private and public ownership of this property and act in a safe and reasonable manner. Stay on the existing trails and roadways, be courteous to other users and remove all trash and equipment. All persons using the bottom of the gorge or actually climbing must use helmets and crampons. Anyone occupying the climber only area must wear crampons. Do not anchor to any man made structures including the penstock system large metal pipe. Dogs must be leashed in the climber only area and are not allowed at the bottom of the gorge. All persons under the age of eighteen must complete and mail a consent of minors use of the ice park in the box below. Enforcement of all rules will apply appropriately by the Ouray County Sheriff, the Ouray Police or by any board member of the Ouray Ice Park, Inc. Please respect the enjoyment of other climbers by not occupying more than two routes at a time. Ouray Ice Park, Inc. is a non-profit corporation and runs exclusively on the donations of sponsor members.

Donald Ryland led the troupe down the path on the west side of the river. The snow was hard-packed from heavy use but the walking was not difficult. They came up to a steel trestle that held the ancient penstock above an open gorge. It contained a plate indicating it had been built in 1928. Nearly seventy-five Colorado winters rusting away at the structure did not breed confidence. But, to Dean, neither did a 10mm line, all that bound the scampering gnats they could see peppering the icy walls of the gorge.

With exaggerated care Cynthia mounted the wooden catwalk atop the penstock, holding Dean's hand tightly. It was constructed of narrow boards and chewed by the cutting crampons of hundreds of climbers. The penstock, three feet in diameter at this point, was a long black snake, carrying its mountain water to the small generating station, while adjacent black piping and frequent taps provided the ice that coated the cliff sides in gigantic clusters below. The cliffs bulged out over much of this area so from the catwalk and path above, most of the time, they were unable to see the bottom of the gorge and only a portion of the ice, although the voices of the climbers and the sound of their axes could be heard. When the stream became visible, the flow was light, a far cry from the raging torrent Dean remembered from late spring when the melting snow increased the flow of the Uncompahgre a hundred fold. Now, mostly bound to its banks by ice, the river looked much less menacing as it wound its way downward. On the far side of the narrow canyon, the sun did its duty so there was far less snow and little natural ice. However, on this, the shaded west side, aided by the steady flow from the tapped pipe, massive icicles, bulges and clusters coated the side.

Much of the climbing activity was taking place in an area called The Schoolroom, with various routes classified and given names—Verminator, Duncan's Delight and Bloody Sunday. It was here Donald Ryland planned to tackle a mixed rock and ice climb innocuously called Rosebud. The other climbers from Bird Song were already here. All were out of sight below except for Mick and Penny who were just now scrambling up to the path.

"Where have you been?" Penny asked. "I've already made a climb."

Donnie remained with his father and his new found ice climbing friends while Dean took his wife's hand and strolled further down the snow covered path, away from the edge. Cynthia, while not as apprehensive as Edith had been, was obviously uncomfortable watching the climbers, especially from atop their precarious positions.

The giant pipe ran through a wooded area, away from the cliff edge. Here it was quieter, though the sound of the water could still be heard in the distance. While the snow was deeper here and the path less traveled, the walking was not difficult. There was a small clearing where the trail opened up to a spectacular view of winter time Mount Abrams. Someone had cleared the snow from a bench so the Deans sat, catching their breath. After a few minutes rest, they continued, first hearing, then seeing the waterfall and the reservoir from which the penstock first drew the water for its mile-long trip to town. Below the falls, a crescent rainbow gave color to the rising mist while sparkles of ice formed from the spray.

It was on the return walk to the climbing area that they saw him. Jerome Shipton was standing behind a tree and Dean caught sight of his maroon jacket just before he stepped out into the sunlight. He strolled up to them as if he was on a city street, not alone in the Colorado woods.

"Nice day for a walk in the forest," he said with a smile, looking directly at Cynthia. "You must be the innkeeper's wife. How did he get so lucky?"

"Did you find a room?" Dean asked, not in a friendly tone.

"Just for last night. But I intend to stay at Bird Song. That's where all the pretty women are. That's where you go to sleep with someone else's wife."

Dean ignored the comment. "Bird Song is full."

"So you told me," he answered, still smiling at Cynthia. He turned to Dean. "Why aren't you down there climbing up the icicles with the big boys?"

"Because he has more sense," Cynthia answered, squeezing her husband's arm and turning away.

"Oh? I thought it might be because you're scared shitless you might fall down, boom, and break something."

Dean bit his lip but had enough sense not to take the bait. "I guess your gear is back in your car."

Shipton laughed, never taking his eyes from Cynthia. "No, I don't have any of those little playthings, at least not yet. But it rather looks like fun, doesn't it? Perhaps I'll stop in town and buy a couple of those tomahawks gadgets and pointy-toe shoes and give it a try." He motioned down the pathway toward where Donald Ryland and the others were climbing. "If that pansy Ryland can ice climb, it can't be much of a challenge now can it?" He turned and walked off before waiting for an answer.

CHAPTER 11

It is Saturday night, the worst time of the week, when the miners descend from the mountains, all afrenzy with their lust for drink and acts of the flesh. I am bone-weary of the degradation, of wearing my false coquettish smile, pretending love, until they spill themselves within me. It disgusts me to know of what I've become. Night after night they come, some more kindly than others. Some near animals with their lust. The sheriff ran Happy Jake out of town, saying he was a cheat but I think he was just better at gambling than the others. He was always kindly to me and always smiled.

Frenchie was beaten badly by old Tom who Mrs. Rinaldi struck with a poker, but she was more troubled that he bled on her carpet than by sobbing Frenchie huddled in the corner and Tom, who remained near-dead when his friends dragged him out into the snowy night.

"God! It doesn't sound like a fun life, does it?" Dean said after reading Cynthia's latest translations. "There's no doubt about her occupation now, is there?"

"No. But it's so sad reading about it. What those women had to endure. Listen to this:"

Lola took the laudanum last evening. She is the third to do so since I've been in this dreadful place. It was a time before she died, though she knew she would and suffered for it. The sheriff came and laughed at something one of the men said as she lay there and it made me cry to hear him. But then Rev. Martin came too and comforted us. There will be more work for the rest of us tomorrow night with Lola gone.

Dean was silent. He thought he saw Cynthia blink back a tear. Finally, in an attempt to change the subject, he asked, "You seem to be making pretty good progress deciphering the notebook. Is it getting easier?" They were alone in the kitchen of Bird Song. After leaving the ice park, Dean had gone on to Duckett's Market for groceries. Though he was away only a half hour, Cynthia displayed three new pages of transcription.

105

"Yes. I can even remember most of the common letter substitutions." She glanced down at the pages before her and continued decoding the notebook. Dean put away the groceries and set out a tray of afternoon brownies for the returning guests. By the time he'd brewed them both a cup of Earl Grey tea and rejoined Cynthia at the kitchen table, she had finished yet another paragraph.

"Enter Rev. Martin," she said with a sigh as she handed him the page. "She's enthralled with the man. Read this."

I am the most favored wretch among mortals! God has given me a second undeserved chance at happiness! All my dreams and longings have come to fruition in a single instant when dearest Joshua held me close and my world was sunshine. I smile and the other girls look at me as if I'm daft. Mrs. Rinaldi questions me and tries to read these lines, but all for naught. Only the two of us, dear Joshua and I, know our secret and so will it remain.

"We know where this is going, don't we?" he answered.

"She only says he held her." But Cynthia's tone betrayed her disbelief in the words she was saying.

Dean gave her a raised eyebrow. "I'll bet you a night of unbridled ecstasy against a week of doing dishes that they end up in the sack."

She ignored his wager. "Do you think they marry?"

Dean shook his head. "I think he's carrying his ministry a little too far and he's already a married man. That's the only thing that makes sense."

Cynthia frowned but didn't disagree. "She writes so differently than what you'd expect, given her circumstances—where she is and what she's doing. Her rhetoric is beautiful and I've yet to find a spelling error."

"Perhaps that's one of the reasons the good reverend was attracted to her. She's certainly a cut above the usual—lady of the night."

"And how would you know that?" Cynthia asked with a sly smile.

"I was a policeman. Policemen have to know all sorts of different things."

There was a noise at the back door and Fred O'Connor entered. He was in his stocking feet, snowy boots left by the back door after his day at the library and museum. Before letting him read the translations, the Deans filled him in on their activities, including their forest meeting with Jerome Shipton. They all agreed he was bad news.

"I checked him out some more on the computer," Fred said. "He's not a poor man. In addition to the storage buildings, he owns an insurance agency, a bank and a bunch of commercial real estate. His wife is in the bucks, too. It don't look like either one needs the other's check book."

"I have to wonder why he's so obsessed with Edith," Dean mused. "He's a good looking guy, wealthy, by the sound of it, and frankly, Edith isn't the catch of the day. That, and given the fact she was in the wrong line when they were passing out brains makes me think we're missing something."

"Perhaps he's in love with her," Cynthia said, a bite to her voice. "Did you consider that possibility?"

"Than why does he beat her like a dusty rug?" Dean answered. "My guess is love has nothing to do with it. His ego just can't stand the fact that it was Edith who took the hike and not him. I think that makes him dangerous."

Cynthia didn't disagree. "I just hope he stays away from her, and Bird Song."

"The only person who can keep him away is Edith herself and it doesn't look to me as if she has the sense to do so."

Cynthia raised crossed fingers. "We can hope." She turned to Fred and handed him her latest translations of Annie Quincy's diary. The old man read them eagerly.

He looked up, with a large grin splitting his face. "This sort of confirms what we suspected, don't it?" Dean nodded in agreement but Cynthia wasn't willing to give up.

"Let's not do any condemning until I've transcribed more pages. All he did was hug her."

Dean considered pointing out that Annie's reference to their "shared secret" didn't seem to refer to a pastoral hug, but held his tongue.

Fred just grunted. "I sure wish this young lady wrote a date on her writings. It'd make my job a darn sight easier. I'm about to go blind reading them old microfilm newspapers. Some of those ads are a chuckle but it's hard work."

"I take it you didn't have any luck." Dean asked. Fred had spent his day seeking obituary information on Annie Quincy Martin.

"Naw," Fred answered, slumping down in a chair. "I guess after reading this here notebook, it was a fool's errand. Looks to me like Annie Quincy and Mrs. Martin ain't one in the same for sure." He picked up the second page. "If I had a date when this Lola lady died, I might find something, but I'm not sure what good it would do us. There was lots of stuff about the 'soiled doves' but not very many full names. Usually, if the working girls either got themselves murdered or committed suicide, all the newspaper gave 'em was a holier-than-thou write-up, pointing out the sad rewards for their sinful life. If they died a natural death, I doubt they'd even get a mention. I looked through the whole month of January but there was nothing about a girl named Annie dying."

Dean fixed his stepfather a cup of coffee. "Checking any records on the poor woman is going to be a chore. She might not have been using her own name. Maybe there were just too many deaths that winter to make news of one insignificant passing. We don't even know for certain when she died, do we? All we have is the letter from Rev. Martin, and lord knows what his intentions were."

"She received her mail as 'Annie Quincy,'" Fred noted. "And that's the name she wrote on her clothes."

"I have a better scenario," Cynthia said as she poured herself a cup of coffee and joined them. "Perhaps the reverend was the one who found her. He read the note and was so overcome with grief he covered up what she did, falsely reported her death and gave her a decent burial. Then he wrote her sister Rachael in Boston affirming her lies."

"And he visited her grave weekly, instead of her bed," Dean added, with just a hint of sarcasm.

"Don't be so insensitive, David. This was a very romantic story."

Amid a banging door and stomping feet, Gladys Turnbull entered the kitchen. Her face bore a Christmas morning smile.

"Might I speak to you, Mrs. Dean?" she said, hardly glancing at the menfolk as she tried to catch her breath. Cynthia rose, and after a whispered conversation, Gladys left and Cynthia returned, a smile on her face.

"What was that all about?" Dean asked as Fred left to change for yet another dinner engagement with Miss Worthington.

"Our guest, Miss Turnbull, has a boyfriend." Dean just looked at his wife. "She's met a gentleman, struck up a 'literary conversation,' as she tells it, and he's asked her to drinks and dinner."

"So why the whispered conversation?"

"She doesn't want us to worry if she sleeps elsewhere tonight!"

"Kind of beating the horse to the front of the pack a bit early in the race, isn't she?"

"Gladys says they *really* got along great," Cynthia said, with a smile.

Dean laughed. "I suppose if she has a chance to get lucky, she should jump on him, so to speak. I don't imagine she has a long line at her door."

"Be nice," Cynthia answered. "I think it's sweet. She says he's captivated by her writing. He's a real fan of sci-fi occult, whatever that is."

Cynthia looked down at the coded notebook, but the sounds of the returning guests caused her to reluctantly put it aside. The Deans joined the ice climbers and others in the living room for afternoon snacks and chatter just as Edith Shipton descended the stairs.

Dean was startled by her appearance, not even sure at first who it was. She was now a blonde, with her hair pinned high to the top of her head.

"I decided to change my hair color," she said. Then she added, as if dismissing the importance of so dramatic a change, "After all, if I'm starting a new life, I might as well change everything." At least she wasn't wearing the Annie Quincy white dress.

"It's very becoming," Cynthia said, although on close observation, it looked stark and artificial to Dean's untrained eye.

Edith Shipton, all abeam, took the Deans aside to tell them how thrilled she was with her son Donnie's blossoming relationship with his father.

"Donald is so good with the boy. He and his climbing friends are taking Donnie to dinner later. Donnie would never do something like that with strangers before."

"That's nice," Cynthia replied, "but you have to understand it's just a few days the two of you have been on your own. You have to look to your future. Mr. Shipton is still in town and I think it would be wise if you spoke to an attorney or someone to settle the ground rules of your separation from him."

It was as if Edith didn't hear a word that was said. "Donald thinks the boy should be in school. Perhaps Martha could take him." Then she added, "Donald is so sweet. I'm so glad we're back together. He doesn't push Donnie the way Jerome did. I felt badly that I wasn't able to watch him climb but it made me nauseated to even look over the edge. But he's so brave to do it, don't you think?" Dean started to say something, but she continued. "You know, I dreamed Jerome came here, to Bird Song, last night. He wanted a room, but you told him the inn was full and sent him away." She turned, and went up the stairs, humming a cheery tune.

"I fear for that woman," Cynthia said as Edith squeezed by the descending elephantine shape of Gladys Turnbull.

"She's playing 'let's pretend' even more seriously than Gladys and her alarm clock rendezvous. Edith doesn't have a clue about life. She knows nothing about registering Donnie in school, or anything else, by the sound of it."

"The white dress, blonde hair and her trying to emulate Annie Quincy...it frightens me," Cynthia said with a shudder.

"At least she's casting herself as a minister's wife and not a soiled dove. We don't want to give Bird Song the wrong reputation and have Sheriff Jake Weller down here busting the place."

As he spoke, the Quincy sisters entered the front door. Gladys, bedecked in an orange caftan and a fox fur jacket, smiled a knowing smile to Cynthia and was gone. Claire made a beeline for upstairs while Effie tarried to chat with the Deans.

"How is your research going?" Cynthia asked out of politeness as Effie picked up a chocolate chip cookie with dainty fingers.

"I'm leaving that mostly to Claire," she replied. "She's the brainy one. I just strolled around town, trying to imagine Annie doing the same thing, a hundred years ago."

"She'd have seen a few of the same sights you're looking at today," Dean said. "The mountains haven't changed and there are a lot of buildings still standing from the last century."

"Yes, but think of the sleigh bells and the sound of the train coming in from Ridgway, clanking and hooting, and billowing its black smoke. And, oh so many more people on the streets! I can close my eyes and see the hustle-bustle of the village, the children playing, the pack mules and miners, the ladies decked out in long dresses and fur muffs. When you read the old newspapers and see the ads, you realize how self-contained Ouray was back then. Everything you needed was right here, shops and businesses of every description. Life for Annie must have been very exciting indeed!" The Deans looked at one another and nodded.

Effie choked a tad on her cookie at the enthusiasm of her rambling and asked for a glass of milk. Cynthia directed her to the kitchen just as Edith called to them from the top of the stairs. She sounded upset as they climbed to the second floor at her summons. Fred joined them from his room across the hall, a startled look on his face as he first noted the blonde hair.

"Someone has been in my room," Edith said, sounding more perplexed than upset.

"Are some of your belongings missing?" Cynthia asked with concern.

"No. I just know someone was here."

"Janet cleaned your room and changed the linens. Perhaps she just moved some of the items around."

"No. It's more than that. My underthings were moved, and my night clothes. Jerome used to do that. It was his way of letting me know I couldn't hide anything from him." Now, a look of fear crossed her face. "You don't suppose...?"

"I think we'd better call the police department," Dean said.

"No! Perhaps—I'm mistaken." She waved her hand with a dismissive gesture. "Lately my mind's been playing tricks. I'm sorry." Edith tried to close her door but Fred deftly slipped his foot in the way.

"Let's have a little chat about this," he said, opening her door and squired her in, closing it behind the others. The Deans, left in the hall, could only retreat downstairs.

"If anyone can talk sense into her fuzzy head, it's Fred O'Connor," said Dean. "But I'm still going to call Jake Weller. I'm sure he'll give me a speech about it not being his jurisdiction but he's the one who's talked to Jerome Shipton."

"Perhaps we should talk to Janet, too. She was here alone this afternoon. If Shipton did sneak in here after we saw him, she must have seen him."

Dean agreed and telephoned Janet O'Brien from the hall but there was no answer. He spoke to the sheriff at home, but, as he suspected, Weller could do nothing without Edith's referral.

As the Deans entered the kitchen they both saw with dismay, Effie Quincy, seated at the table, milk glass in one hand, and the Annie Quincy notebook in the other. She glanced up at them, a guilty look on her face.

"It was just laying there," she said, and then added, "Annie wrote it, didn't she?"

"Yes," Cynthia answered. "We suspect so." Effie brushed back her hair and looked down at the pages.

"What does the rest of it say?"

"She wrote in a code," Dean answered. "Cynthia was just recently able to decipher it. There's only those few pages finished."

"It's a slow process replacing the letters to the text," Cynthia added.

"The notebook was with the other things?" Effie asked.

"Yes," Dean answered. He then added, "But when your sister was so snooty about the coins and other items and short changed Fred O'Connor, we decided to keep the notebook."

Cynthia gave him a quick look but Effie seemed unaffected by his sharp but true criticism. She added, "We didn't know the content of the notebook at that time. We had no idea it was anything but meaningless scribbles."

"She was a prostitute," Effie said, and a slow smile crossed her face. "It's a bit bewildering, isn't it?"

"You don't seem surprised," Dean said.

Effie just shook her head. "No, I guess I'm not."

"You had your doubts?" Cynthia asked

"I knew the picture Mr. O'Connor had wasn't Annie Quincy. Don't ask me how—I just knew. Perhaps it was the blonde hair in the comb. That's Annie. I could feel it. But the picture is too stuffy. Annie would never be like that. I knew her story couldn't be as simple as Claire made it out to be—wanted it to be." She looked up at Cynthia. "Are you going to translate the rest of the book?"

"Yes, as soon as I have the time. Do you mind?"

She thought a moment. "I suppose I should. My own flesh and blood, selling herself to half-drunk miners for a few gold coins. But, in truth, I think it's sort of exhilarating! It's sad, too, of course, but I can't help feeling an excitement that I had an ancestor who led such a different life!"

"I'm sure the news will be a disappointment to your sister," Dean said, trying to keep the eagerness out of his voice.

Effie frowned. "I'm afraid it would break Claire's heart." Then she added, "But I shan't tell her. You won't either, will you?"

Cynthia looked at her husband. It was he who answered. "We won't lie to her if she asks. But I guess there's no reason to volunteer the information to her." Then he added, "Won't it be uncomfortable for you to keep a secret from her? The two of you seem quite close."

Effie thought a moment. "No. Annie is dead. There's no mistake in that. If she lives on in my sister's mind one way, and in mine another, what's the harm in that? To me, the true Annie makes her more human, even more than before. Real people have secrets. It's as if she's sharing hers with me."

"What do you suppose caused her to leave a cultured and safe life in Boston and come west?" Cynthia asked. "She must have fallen on hard times to have been forced into the life she ended up leading. From her writing you can tell she was cultured and well educated. What would cause her to run away from all of that?"

"I suspect we'll never know," Effie answered. "Something must have happened in that Boston house to drive her away. The tone of

Rachael's letters is most unnatural. I suspect she might have known why her sister left Boston."

"You're very perceptive, Effie."

She looked away, as if remembering something she didn't care to share. "Sometimes all is not as it appears to be behind closed doors. Even the closed doors of the 'cultured and educated.' That goes for the closed doors of people's minds and thoughts as well as their elegant houses."

"Do you think it's possible to keep the truth from Claire?" Cynthia asked. "Or wise to do so?"

"It's sort of like playing let's pretend. I used to do that as a child with Claire." She thought a moment. "I still do, I guess. More often than I care to admit."

Dean decided to seize the moment. "Does Claire have the museum's picture of Rev. Martin and his wife?"

Effie gave a deep sigh. "I suppose so. I haven't seen it but I know she wanted it very badly. She tends to take that which she wants. Sometimes she does things like that."

"Steals?"

"That sounds so harsh."

"Effie, you're far too intelligent to not know Claire is constantly taking advantage of you. Why do you put up with it?"

"Why, she's my sister. I love her." Then she added, "And tell that nice Mr. O'Connor not to spend his $2.50 gold coins. The '97 and '99 are worth about four or five hundred each and the '79 should bring a thousand or more. It looked almost uncirculated. Claire's five dollar pieces are all worn—worth a couple of hundred at best." The Deans looked at her questioningly. She continued to smile. She added, almost in a whisper, "That's why I suggested Claire give the smaller denominations to Mr. O'Connor. I collected coins when I was younger." Then she added, "You will let me read the rest of the notebook when you've figured it out, won't you?" She rose from her chair, just as Fred entered the room. She patted him on the back as she left.

"What was that all about?" he asked, looking over his shoulder at her retreating form.

"Sounds like your coins are worth about three times what Claire's are," Dean said, and then asked, "how did you make out with the blonde bombshell?"

"She swears she'll see the sheriff tomorrow. She wants to talk to Donald Ryland first. He and Donnie already left for dinner. What's this business about my coins?"

"It sounds as if you're in luck again," Cynthia said as she pulled her step stool across the kitchen floor so she could reach the shelf and retrieve the breakfast dishes. She and her husband related their conversation with Effie to Fred, how she had read the notebook, her comments regarding the gold coins, and their new, more respectful evaluation of Miss Effie Quincy.

"Dang!" said Fred, his face brightening. "I been meaning to check out their value on the computer. I just been too darn busy! Looks like my Internet business is pretty lucrative, wouldn't you say?" Dean just smiled and picked up the local newspaper. He owed Fred a "gotcha" after the hard time he'd given the old man about his electronic sales adventures. Fred turned to leave.

"Give my regards to Miss Worthington," Dean said.

"That's not until later. First off, I have to go to the Post Office. It's Social Security day. God bless FDR and the Democrats."

Dean laughed. "Now that you're going to make a little money on those gold coins, added to what you took in on that Flotsam Electronics stock last June, maybe you should consider seeing the light and turning Republican."

"Not on your life! I'm a tried and true democrat. I been casting my ballot that way since Roosevelt and I'll keep doing so—even if you do cancel out my vote every dang election." The two men had carried on a fifteen-year argument on politics. Dean's marriage to Cynthia hadn't helped break the tie as she wisely refused to divulge to either of them how she voted.

Dean put down his paper. "Fred, I know you're an old geezer, but Roosevelt died during World War Two. You're seventy-six. You couldn't have been twenty-one during the war and voted for FDR. Do the math."

"I sure did vote for him," Fred answered smugly, looking from one to the other. Cynthia renewed her work on the notebook and just smiled. "I voted for Franklin Delano Roosevelt five or six times."

"That's nonsense! Even if you were a hundred, you'd only have voted four times. That's all the times he ran for president!" Fred didn't answer. "Well?" Dean asked, waiting for a reply.

Fred O'Connor sighed deeply. "You gotta understand. Where I lived, being twenty-one wasn't necessary. All you had to do was *look* twenty-one. There was a guy who'd give you the money and tell you the name of the voter you were supposed to be. Most guys were off fighting the war so there was lots of empty slots. Then you'd get on the bus or subway and go to the polling place and vote."

Cynthia laughed out loud. "Some one paid you to vote for Roosevelt?"

"Of course not! Franklin Roosevelt wasn't like that, at least when he was running for president. I got paid to vote for Patrick McGarrity for City council, but I figured as long as I was in the box, I'd give ol' FDR a boost, too."

"Democrats!" Dean grumbled, returning to his newspaper.

"Didn't they question you at the polling place?" Cynthia asked.

"Naw. Nobody bothered to challenge anyone. They all knew what was going on. Besides, I was in uniform. Home on leave."

"You were in World War Two?" she asked.

"Don't encourage him," Dean said as he read the comics. Fred left with a wave and Cynthia returned to Annie Quincy's notebook.

Later, after Dean had performed his night-closing duties and undressed, his wife handed him the results of her latest efforts.

My monthly condition excuses me from duties today so I donned my finest dress and strolled the streets of Ouray like the lady that was once Annie Quincy. Perhaps it's my past but I am more able to do so without the infliction of scorn and ridicule poured upon the other girls of my profession by the town's less sinful inhabitants. The new Beaumont hotel was all a glitter in preparation of an affair of some high social order and there was a general excitement everywhere. But this beautiful edifice was not my destination nor were its inhabitants my social equal. Instead I ambled past the house where I am to trade a damp and soiled mattress for domestic duties when arrangements are finally made by Joshua. I passed it many times I'm abashed to say. Though I so love him and trust his every word, I can't help but tremble at even the prospect I shall at last exchange this soiled and despicable life for another. It plagues my mind that my sins will continue but so in love am I that aught else matters.

"I don't suppose it means he's marrying her," Cynthia said as she emerged from the bathroom in her flannel nightdress. "But at least he's arranging for her to give up the terrible life she's been leading."

"Cynthia, you're a darling and I love you dearly," Dean said as he kissed her cheek. "But you're a full card-carrying romantic optimist. The guy is setting her up! He wants to save the few bucks the whorehouse charges and have her for his very own. He's making her his con-cubine."

"It does sort of seem that way. But she doesn't come out and say that directly."

"No, you're just not reading that. Take off the rose colored glass-es—'my sins will continue'—or better yet, wait until you decipher a few more pages and she gives it to you in black and white, chapter and verse and supplies the sinful details."

Cynthia acknowledged her reluctant agreement with a deep sigh and no further conversation as Dean extinguished the light. Later, in that languid time between lovemaking and the usual surrender to sleep, Cynthia remained awake.

"I know we'll probably never learn the answer, but I still can't fath-om what could have happened back in Boston to make Annie Quincy desert a comfortable life." She propped herself up against the back of their brass bed. Dean could see her troubled profile in the emerging moonlight. Shadows danced in tune with a slight breeze from the inch of open window and a sentinel pine tree beyond.

"It could have been anything, but I'd guess she had a serious rift at home, probably with her parents."

"But look what she had going for her! She was obviously a very intelligent young lady. Why would she become what she did? I under-stand opportunities were limited a century ago but surely she could have been a school teacher or office clerk or something above a broth-el prostitute."

"If you want me to speculate, I'd say it ran far deeper than that. My guess is she fled from some type of sexual encounter. I'm no shrink, but look at the life she later resorted to. It's as if she's bent on degrad-ing herself. She lacks any kind of positive self-image. While her writ-ing demonstrates education, most likely her background ill equipped her for the practical realities of the real world. Look at Edith Shipton. She's not stupid either, but I'll bet she'd starve if she didn't have a bank account to tap. A hundred years ago, Edith might have joined Annie, smiling her nights away at the Red Hat Saloon. And think of Annie's age. When she's writing the notebook she's been in the life some time. I'd guess she left home quite young, perhaps as a mid-teenager, with little or no dough. That would limit her options even more, making her vulnerable to coercion, finally pushing her into prostitution. That and desperation. When you're hungry and someone offers a meal, maybe you start rationalizing the price you're paying and start playing by a different set of rules."

"In spite of the reason I still can't help but feel incredibly sorry for the girl. I just wish she had been able to escape and draw a curtain on her past like Fred O'Connor and move into a secure and happy life."

"Well, I'm sure Fred wasn't a hooker but I'm content to accept him on a present day basis, regardless of why he's so protective of his past."

"I never will understand how you could know so little about Fred. Two women couldn't room together for fifteen years and, in some ways, remain virtual strangers. You must have wondered about Fred's past at times."

Dean just shook his head. "Fred married my mother years after dad passed away. I was off in the service. Then she died a few months later. I never even met Fred until a couple of days before she died. But I loved her very much and trusted her judgment. She saw the basic good in Fred and she was correct." Cynthia nodded her head in agreement. "Of course that doesn't change that half of what Fred tells me is an out and out fabrication and the rest doesn't make any sense! I love the old geezer but the few times he starts talking about the old days, I tune him out. At some point his past may crawl out of the ground and bite him on the butt, but it won't be because I did the digging."

Then there was only silence and the night sounds of the old building as Cynthia lay awake next to this man she loved. Even after Dean's rhythmic breathing told her he was sleeping she remained awake, her mind alive with thoughts of their discussion and all that had transpired. And what Cynthia Byrne might have become in a different century, under different circumstances, without a David Dean beside her.

CHAPTER 12

Cynthia must have finally slept because the noise in the hall startled her to full wakefulness, her husband as well.

"Sounds like Gladys didn't get lucky," Dean mumbled.

"Or else she brought him back here," his wife answered sleepily.

Then there were voices, Gladys with a shrill laugh, than hushed giggling, a stumble on the steps, a grunt and finally silence. Dean lay there, listening. It was his turn to hear measured breathing beside him as Cynthia drifted off to sleep. He glanced at the clock. One-twenty. Then one-thirty-four, then one-forty-six. Finally, he thought he felt a breeze and quietly rose to see if giggly Gladys and her tipsy admirer might have left the front door ajar. They hadn't, but as long as he was awake and unable to sleep, he went to the kitchen and poured himself a glass of milk. He was sitting there, in the dark, when he first heard a step on the stair. His first thought was Gladys' would-be lover having second thoughts and making a quick exit so he ducked around the corner of the dining room, so as not to embarrass the man. He peeked out and was startled by a white-clad specter on the stairs.

She moved like a somnambulist, so trance-like Dean hesitated to speak for fear of startling her. Then the awkwardness of his silent position hiding in the darkness extended beyond the point of propriety of making his presence known. He shrunk further back into the shadows of the dining room. Edith Shipton moved down the hall, causing Dean to think her destination was his and Cynthia's quarters but she stopped in front the small room occupied by Donald Ryland. She was but a few feet beyond where he stood. As Dean watched, scarcely breathing, she lifted the ancient white dress above her head in one motion and dropped it to the floor. She stood there, naked, a gaunt figure in her thinness. She was as white as the garment she now casually pushed with one foot behind a hall table. The hall night-light cast a strange and wild look on her face. Dean was close enough that he could smell the musk of her freshly washed body as she took a deep breath and let out a long and resigned sigh. She reached up to unclasp her now-blonde hair, dropping it in a cascade about her shoulders. A moment's hesitation, a quick hand on the door knob, and Edith Shipton disappeared into the bedroom of her long ago lover.

All that Dean could picture in his mind's eye was Annie Quincy, plying her despised trade in a darkened room. But Edith's Annie was a minister's wife, not a common prostitute. Then Dean remembered Donnie's copies of the telling notebook. Had the boy deciphered and shared the lines of this far different Annie?

Dean took a deep breath, half expecting Ryland to demand that Edith leave, but there was only silence. He hesitated, reluctant to return to his room, past Ryland's door from which might be expelled the naked visitor, just as he passed by. But then, in the quietness of the night, he began to hear beyond the door, the muffled but clear sounds of lovemaking. Dean crept down the hall and returned to his own bed, and, after a long time, finally slept.

CHAPTER 13

It's early morning now and the noise of the loading of the pack animals down at Ashenfelter's stables has woken me. Piano George said they lost two fine black horses that slipped on the ice of the Sneffles road and I could hear the men talking loudly about it. I had slept little as Jerome Jones' band played its brass near till dawn at The Gold Belt. I miss Frenchie and Joy-Jill and our morning coffee but they've been sent up to Red Mountain Town as the mines there are working through the winter and the men are in need of the leisure the girls are able to provide. I saw them Wednesday last when I went to Dr. Rowan's for my weekly examination and both were ill from the mountain cold and drafty quarters. I read Rachael's letter again but her words tell nothing of interest. Boston seems so long ago, and so very far away.

They say a blast at the Wanaka mine killed two. They brought the remains down in a wagon this afternoon. I saw it, with its two round sacks tied tightly and men standing nearby with their hats off. I can't say if I knew the deceased but the Wanaka and all the mines send us so many of their workers I may have. I saw Mr. Vanoli in the alley on my way to the Chinese yesterday, but I cast my eyes down and looked the other way. He was coming from The Roma. I'm trying to teach one of the Roma girls her letters as she knows nothing of reading or writing. She's Irish and they call her Flag, because of her birthmark. Fat Ella thinks this notebook is our practice! Little does she know my markings are to disguise my journaled thoughts from the prying eyes of her and others.

There is much in the newspapers about closing the saloons and dance halls and even taking away the slot machines. It seems strange to read these words of some of the men whose drawers have hung on my bedpost! I think aught will come of their rantings as the miners swear they'll flee the area for a more obliging locale if such nonsense were to happen.

121

I tremble to write these following lines. Mrs. Martin is off to a WCTU meeting in Montrose and Joshua rented a sleigh at the Union Livery that just opened. I walked by prior arrangement to the Portland Road where he met me. I fear for his reputation if we be discovered but I have never been happier than next to him, beneath the buffalo robe that covered us. I was a lady for a long and lovely Sunday afternoon while a tan mare serenaded us with her tinkling bells as the runners wooshed along on the packed snow. I hardly minded the cold and lonely walk back after evening prayers demanded my love's return.

"The guy's a bastard," Dean said as he read Cynthia's latest translations the following morning.

"Most men are," Cynthia answered, in an unusually sharp tone, and then added, "present company excepted. I just don't want to talk about it." Lack of a full night's sleep had put both Deans in less than top form as they readied breakfast. "I have enough problems with this century without resurrecting the last," she continued. "I don't like this business with Edith and Donald Ryland. It has me worried." She looked around. "Plus, Janet is either late or missing, Fred never even came home last night, I don't think I made enough breakfast rolls, and there's a stack of luggage in the hall. Some of our guests are apparently leaving early."

"Gladys and her lover?"

"No. It's ice-climbing stuff. But Gladys' *friend* is another problem. What are we supposed to say to some strange man when he comes down for his morning meal?"

"We charge Gladys for a double room and smile. It's not the first time it's happened. She's paying for the lodging. We're not the custodians of the morals of our guests, nor the taste of her lovers."

"Every time I turn around, someone is sneaking into someone else's bed!" Just as Cynthia said it, Donald Ryland appeared behind them, still in his bathrobe, much to her gross embarrassment. It was obvious he'd heard them. He smiled and rolled his eyes.

"I'm sorry!" Cynthia said. "That was uncalled for. I'm just in a grouchy mood this morning. It's none of my business what—"

"I guess I deserved that. I feel like the kid with his hand in the cookie jar."

"It's not your hand that'll get you in trouble," Dean said as he munched on a piece of whole wheat toast.

"I am sorry. It is your business. It's your inn and you've been very kind to all of us. Last night was a disaster." He joined Dean at the kitchen table although Cynthia would have preferred having her private domain to herself. "I was a shit to let her stay." Neither of the Deans disagreed. Ryland seemed as if he felt compelled to justify his actions. "I had a few drinks at dinner and I was sleeping like a log. Then I half-wake to find a naked body all over me. It was like every teen age wet dream." Cynthia gave a not-too-well disguised harrumph and left the kitchen for the dining room with a plate full of breakfast. Ryland continued, a chastised look on his face. "I told Edith we had no future together. I love Fran—this girl I'm going to marry." He looked over his shoulder. "Edith's back upstairs with Donnie."

"Look," Dean said. "I'm not your father confessor. Cynthia was right. This stuff isn't any of our business."

"Yeah, I'm sorry to unload on you. We'll be out of your hair after the weekend." Then he added, "God knows where Edith will go after it's over."

"After what's over?"

Ryland looked even more depressed. "She still wants me to help her get her abortion. I told her I'd take her to Grand Junction on Monday morning. She can't wait any longer, with Shipton poking around town. But that's all I told her I'd do—just drive her there." He rose and poured himself a cup of coffee. "Don't say it. I know I was stupid to get further involved, but damned, she's an obsessive woman. God knows what I'll tell Fran! She'll think the child is mine!" Neither said anything while Dean began to clear the dishwasher from last evening's meal. But Ryland couldn't stand the silence.

"She's upstairs now, pissed at me from not agreeing to hold her hand while they—do it. But, God, I have a life, too."

"Did she leave Donnie alone last night?"

"Yeah. I thought he was in with you, like the other night. She must have been desperate to make him sleep on his own. Damn good thing he didn't wake up." Then he added, "I'm going to miss the kid. He's really something." He rubbed his five o'clock shadow and rose. "If I'm going to get any ice climbing done, I better get moving."

Dean began to shuttle back and forth to the dining room, helping Cynthia. Janet arrived, mumbling apologies as the guests began coming downstairs to breakfast. Claire and Effie Quincy led the parade to the table. Dean pulled Janet aside and asked if she had let any strangers into Bird Song the prior afternoon. She just grunted that all the men looked alike to her and she didn't pay 'no heed.' Too busy doing her work, she added. Dean continued to wonder about the strange event. Was Edith's vivid imagination working overtime or had Jerome Shipton managed to slip by Janet O'Brien and invade his wife's room? If so, for what purpose? Like a dog pissing on a tree to mark his territory?

Two of the young ice climber descended the stairs and began gathering their suitcases and gear piled by the door.

"How come you guys are leaving?" Dean asked. "You've paid in advance. Is there something wrong?"

"No. It's great here. We're going to miss it but the guy that's bunking with the fat lady just 'bought' our room." Jeff gave Dean a smile as big as a full moon.

"Yeah, for an offer we couldn't refuse!" his friend added. "Three times what we paid you for it!"

"I know it would be tough finding a place this close to the weekend," Jeff continued, "but we've got some friends that have a cabin. We're moving down there and bunking in with them."

"I'm sorry to see you leave," Dean answered, "but I wish you'd spoken to us before making arrangements with someone else."

"Oh, he said he'd take care of everything."

Jeff began lugging his gear toward the door. "We'll be back in a week or two. With the dough we made on the room, we can afford to come over from Denver for another weekend!"

Cynthia joined her husband who explained the strange happenings. Dean began to have a sinking feeling about who had paid for the room. Just then he looked up to see Jerome Shipton sauntering down the stairs.

"Out!" Dean said before Shipton reached the bottom step or could open his mouth.

"Whoa!" Shipton answered with a smile. "Peace." He held up his arms as if giving benediction. "Look, I'm here fair and square." He held up his recently purchased room key as the two ice climbers waved good bye.

"I don't care what you *bought*," Dean said. "This is our inn and we choose who stays here. It's nothing personal. I don't even know you, but your ex-wife...."

"Wife, not 'ex-wife.' Edith is still married to me, even if she sees fit to sleep...."

"Look," Cynthia said, "We just don't want any trouble. Please leave. Our guests deserve a quiet and peaceful visit. They're paying us for tranquility, not to witness your domestic problems, which should be handled in private, in a lawyer's office. Your marital difficulties aren't our business but Bird Song is and we don't want any hint of trouble here."

Jerome Shipton's smile disappeared. "I had to ball that fat cow Gladys to get in here and then pay a hell of a premium to those guys just to get a room of my own. I have no intention of leaving and, if you'll check your law, you have no legal right to toss me out." He returned to his earlier smile. "Look, I'll be quiet as a mouse and cause no trouble. In fact, I'm off to try my hand at ice climbing for the day. You'll hardly know I'm staying here." He looked up to see a shocked Donald Ryland step out of his room. "Have a nice night's sleep, buddy?" Shipton asked. There was a noise on the stairs and they all turned to see Edith descending.

Shipton smiled up at her. "Peekaboo, I spy you."

Edith at first looked shocked, but almost at once, her face melted to a resigned look—a condemned maiden mounting the guillotine steps, Joan of Arc as the match ignited her pyre. "Hello, Jerome," she said in a tone of utter acquiescence.

"You look wonderful, darling. Nothing like a restful stay in the sticks and a good night's sleep to freshen you up, eh?" He turned to the others. "Well, I'm off to learn how to shinny up icicles. I'll see you up there, Ryland. Or, is it down there?" Then he added, continuing to coldly stare at the young man. "They say ice climbing is a dangerous sport, so remember you all, be careful out there, you hear?"

He turned and was gone. When Dean looked up to where Edith Shipton had stood, she had retreated up the stairs.

Dean picked up the telephone and called Sheriff Weller. It was an infuriating conversation, resulting in a big, fat zero. While Weller knew nothing of Dean's legal right to evict Shipton, he didn't seem to feel it was his concern and politely refused to come over and expel him.

"I don't want the bastard to sue me too. Besides, what's he done to get tossed out? He's got a point. The room's been paid for. Until he does something to warrant police action, I'd say he has every right to stay. Look, at least give it a chance. Let's not buy any more trouble than we have to. Just being a jerk isn't against the law."

Dean continued insisting but to no avail. Weller's only concession was to say he'd talk to Shipton in hopes of getting him to leave voluntarily, if he could find the time. Both men were well aware this was tantamount to a brush-off. And then, to Dean's surprise, Weller added, "Did you ever give a thought that maybe it's the wife who's the real culprit here? I mean, we're buying her book like a best seller, chapter and verse. It's her word the guy is the heavy. Maybe we should listen to him for a change. So, he's a jerk—but that doesn't mean everything he says is a lie. She's the one bed-hopping and acting like a looney."

Before Dean could comment, the conversation ended as a commotion upstairs called for his attention.

Cynthia had preceded him and stood outside Gladys Trumbull's door. The woman was sobbing inconsolably.

"He called me a fat old cow!" she wailed. "I hate the bastard. I hate him! If I had a gun I'd kill the son of a bitch!" The Deans entered her quarters, closing the door behind them. After some cooing on Cynthia's part, the crying subsided to sniffs and quiet sobs. "I'll get him," Gladys mumbled. "He just used me. He doesn't care for my stories a bit. It was all lies and deceit."

"Make him a villain in one of your stories," Dean suggested. He earned a quick look from Cynthia, but the remark hit home.

"I will," Gladys answered with a sneer that was almost scary. "The rotten, lying bastard. He ravaged me, and he used me, just to gain access...." The Deans left her to her dreams, and simmering hatred.

"We have to do something," Cynthia said, as tears began to stream down her cheeks. "It's so frustrating! I feel so controlled! That—man! He's so despicable! How could anyone go so far as to seduce that pathetic woman, just to get close enough to terrorize his wife? He's so damned manipulative! So evil!" Dean put his arm around his wife's trembling shoulders.

"Just take a deep breath. We'll get through this business, somehow." He held her for what seemed like minutes.

"It's not just Jerome Shipton. It's Edith, too. I keep trying to be sympathetic to her situation but you know how I feel about abortion. And now she's coerced Donald Ryland into helping. There are so many couples who would give anything to have that child. Just because her husband's a bastard doesn't mean her baby wouldn't be a perfect little person the right parents would cherish and love. She's just cast-

ing it away like yesterday's trash." Then, his forty-year-old wife totally surprised him. "I'd love to have a little baby."

Finally, Cynthia calmed down enough to continue serving breakfast. The two of them managed to finish attending to the chatting
guests, the late rising climbers and the Quincy sisters. Neither Gladys
nor Edith emerged from their quarters. Fred returned, a tad on the
sheepish side, and Dean filled him in on the recent happenings. He
seemed embarrassed by his overnight absence.

"Spent the night on Miss Worthington's sofa. I forgot my new keys
and didn't want to wake you folks." Dean didn't comment. He too was
troubled to distraction by Shipton's presence, enough to pass up such
an obvious chance to pull Fred's leg.

Fred read the latest transcribed pages of Annie Quincy's journal
while the Deans cleaned up the dining room. Donnie joined the old
man in the back office. Fred emerged long enough to pass on breakfast, a sure sign the widow Worthington had fed him, and he was off
to do his morning research. Donnie left with him, after supposedly
gaining his mother's approval. All of the guests, excepting Gladys and
Edith, had vacated the inn by the time the Deans finished the morning chores. Ryland and Jerome Shipton had left on their own, presumably for the ice park.

Now that the busy morning activity no longer occupied Cynthia's
mind, she again was visably upset about Bird Song's latest guest,
Jerome Shipton, and the penchant for trouble that surrounded his
presence. Dean, cognizant of this, suggested they take the afternoon
off. Cynthia protested, citing the accumulating chores and full house,
but reluctantly agreed.

"I'm not very good for anything else around here," she muttered.

"Remember our very first dinner together?" he asked. She smiled,
nodding her head in agreement. They had dined at an expensive
restaurant, at Fred's booking and in his company, when the only connection between them was Detective Dean investigating her husband's disappearance. The trio, at Fred's direction, had played an ice-
breaking game of pretending the backgrounds of the various other
dinners. "Let's pretend again," he offered.

Dean telephoned a poker-playing friend, a down-valley rancher,
whom he knew owned a horse drawn sleigh. He offered an exchange
for a later getaway weekend at Bird Song for the man and his wife. He
enthusiastically agreed to hitch up the rig. The Deans packed a quick
lunch and drove out of town to the ranch house. The building sat
amid a cluster of cottonwoods that had grown there for an old man's

lifetime, while a weather-beaten barn stood off to the side, showing its tired age. It was a scene from another time as Dean's friend and his smiling wife handed the reins to the urban couple.

"Don't worry about getting lost," the rancher said. "Daisy knows her way back."

It was noon by the time the rig was hitched, lessons given, and Deans, mittened and muffflered, were on their way. Soon they were snuggled beneath a heavy wool robe, gliding contentedly down the snow covered back roads of the Uncompahgre valley. It was colder than usual, with the sun obscured by clouds, portending the accuracy of a forecast of snow. The horse's breath made puffs of steam as she trotted along the road to the cadence of tinkling bells. They glided past snow-covered fields and occasional farmhouses, drifting smoke from their chimneys skyward and adding a hint of wood smoke to the crisp winter air. A Christmas card come to life.

There was a stillness on the tree-lined lanes that whispered peace. The tall trees were draped in a white robe that had drifted to the earth, not snarled their way downward like the wind driven Eastern storms where snow was a dirty word, not the magical hush that mother nature bestowed on the mountains of the west.

"I know why I love the winter out here," Cynthia said as she unpacked their lunch. "Back East, winters are always angry, even cruel sometimes. Here they're peaceful. Instead of everyone running around, slipping and sliding, shoveling slushy muck and shivering, here people just shift into a lower gear, listen to the quiet and enjoy the temporary peace. Winter isn't just a big inconvenience, it's really a season. A tranquil season that demands you step back a bit and accept the beauty life gives you."

Dean nodded his head in agreement, happy Cynthia's mood had mellowed. "It's nineteen-hundred, ma'am. Close your eyes and just listen."

"Are you going to make me walk back alone, sir?" Cynthia asked as she snuggled even closer, the earlier troubles of the day drifting even further away.

"No, Miss Quincy. There's no prayer meeting tonight."

"I think they really loved each other," Cynthia said.

"Even if they didn't, we'll pretend they did," Dean answered as he shook the rein. The chore of driving the sleigh took little concentration, as Daisy was far more adept at her assignment than the driver. She was as pleased as they at her freedom to trot away the afternoon.

Dean continued, "We know we love each other. There's no pretending on that point. And we're not illicit."

Cynthia looked pensive. "Imagine the overwhelming guilt Rev. Martin must have felt over this terrible sin of his relationship with a prostitute. His whole life on the brink of destruction if it were recognized what he was doing. Constant fear of being found out. But perhaps this one afternoon when they were out here together, just like we are, alone in the world, it was different. They were somehow apart from all that, the squalor and wretchedness of her life, the constant fear of being discovered. Out here, it's so peaceful. Everything else is another world. It must have been the same to them. Their love has no limits or bounds. There is only this beauty they can see from the cushions of their sleigh, these very same mountains, the valley, and especially each other." She leaned up and kissed him, with a first-kiss gentleness. "Thank you, Reverend Martin, for taking me away, even for just an afternoon. I know in my heart it can never be, but for today, it is." It was 1900, and the happy couple were the only people in the world.

Neither spoke for more than an hour, until the ranch and stable were in sight and Dean's watch reminded them of reality. Finally, it was he who broke the silence. "It was probably the happiest afternoon of her life. We know she didn't live long after that. But at least Annie Quincy had one happy day to remember. I'm not sure Edith Shipton ever has enjoyed that much."

Cynthia turned to her husband. "We'll not let Jerome Shipton spoil our days for us. No matter what we have to do. Our whole life together is too perfect to let anything as insignificant as him interfere with it."

CHAPTER 14

Miss M was much nettled when I told her I'd no longer dance to her music and I saw her talking about me to the man who owns this dreadful place. I was fearful he might try to stop me, but there are many girls willing to do as I've done, for food and shelter, so I shan't be missed. One must wonder if the young ladies realize the ordeal that lies before them. My eyes, and those of my few friends, were red with tears when I packed my trifle belongings and walked the short, but oh so long distance to my new home. Happiness should be all I feel but a strange sense of dread is overwhelming any feeling of contentment as I enter this stately home.

Here, my duties are light, even less than our Emma back in Boston. I cook, but mostly toast and tea, and soup in the late afternoon. I dust and sweep but a stern lady looks after the madam whose care is beyond my responsibilities. Heavier chores are left to others. It is a large house, devoid of boarders, though a weathered sign offers such accommodations. Most days, only the forgetful owner, this newly hired cleaning girl called Annie and a standoffish tabby are in residence. It is strange, rising early, sleeping the hours I'd worked so long in the past, and listening to the deathly quiet instead of the rowdy noises of hungry men. I count the roses on the wallpaper.

On those special nights I nervously leave the back door unlatched, and quietly steal to my bed. The house is empty except for old Mrs. Cummings, who snores away her darkness. I don't know if she is aware of our arrangement as few words ever pass between us, but her quarters are far from mine and we will be ever so quiet in our love. I tremble as I wait, more so than even when first I gave my self to a man. So many have come to my bed, but never have I been so unnerved by a nocturnal visitor than when first dear Joshua visited me in the darkest part of the night. Though countless have paid for me, never has a man risked paying so dearly for my body; his honor, his reputation, his family and even his soul.

Fred O'Connor finished reading the latest pages as Mrs. Lincoln crawled onto his lap. It was barely evening but the darkening clouds and winter season begrimed the outside as black as a slum landlord's heart. Dean started a fire for the returning guests but then joined his wife and stepfather in the kitchen.

"So far, this saga of Annie Quincy is going just like we thought. The good reverend set her up as a domestic so's he could visit her without anyone knowing about it."

"The trysting place," Cynthia said absentmindedly as she began to prepare dinner.

"Now you've got a clue to where she stayed," Dean said to his stepfather. "All you have to do is find out what property 'Mrs. Cummings' owned a hundred years ago."

"If you do find out, I'm not sure I want to know," Cynthia said. "I'm more interested in live people and guests in Bird Song, not some revenant. We have enough to be concerned with today's problems without having to clutter my mind about the happenings of a century ago."

"How's the rest of your research coming?" Dean asked Fred.

"Claire spent most of the day hogging the microfilm machine at the library but me and Donnie managed an hour or two. We did some digging in old records at the museum as well. Most of what we found was info on the dance halls and clubs. Fascinating stuff."

"Did you find out where Annie worked?"

"No, but most of the business was done down on Second street, between Seventh Avenue and Eighth. Names like The Morning Star, The Monte Carlo, The Clipper, The Cottage and The Club were on the west side. Across the street, right behind the Western Hotel, you had The Bird Cage, The Bon Ton, The Temple of Music and then Ashenfelter's stables that Annie mentions hearing the men loading the pack animals. In between were the cribs, where the girls stayed. She must have lived close to the stables but there's no telling where she worked. It could have been in any one of the clubs."

"It sounds like sin was a very big business," Cynthia offered as she stirred a pot of fish chowder.

"Supply and demand," Dean answered. "The last century Ouray sold flesh, this century it's tee shirts."

"There were some mighty interesting characters," Fred said. "Like Loco Lil, the madam at the Bird Cage, piano players and the gamblers. They came from all over. The town was teeming with 'em."

Dean turned to Fred. "Who was this Vanoli guy Annie mentions?"

Fred took on the air of a learned professor as he explained. "You can't read about prostitution in Ouray without coming across the name Vanoli. John and an older brother Dominic owned a bunch of different places. In 1888 John shot and killed a man in one of his clubs, 'The 220.' He served eight months in jail. Vanoli's Gold Belt Theater was the place that got the most attention, but he owned The Roma that Annie mentions, plus saloons up in Red Mountain and I guess other places. He owned a bunch of 'female boarding houses,' as well. In 1895 he shot another guy, but this time he was acquitted."

"No wonder Annie looked the other way when he passed by!" Cynthia said.

"Naw," Fred answered. "That wasn't John Vanoli. John died later that same year. It seems like he either shot himself or died of venereal disease. He was forty-seven."

"Then who was Annie talking about in 1900?" Dean asked.

"Probably either brother Dominick or his son Tony. The business didn't stop, although there was a lot of talk in the newspapers about closing down all the bars and clubs. The WCTU and Anti-Saloon League were active and the churches sure didn't like the kind of business going on in Ouray. The town managed to close up the dance halls in 1902, at least for a year or so, but it wasn't long before the girls were at it again, full tilt."

"Well, at least Annie managed to 'retire' from the business," Dean said.

"Yeah," Fred grumbled. "I might as well go back to my mystery novels. This caper hasn't been much of a challenge. Miss Annie's pretty much spelled it out in black and white in this here journal, even if it was in code."

"Think of the bright side," Cynthia offered. "Now you're Bird Song's resident expert on girls of the night!"

Just then, Effie Quincy poked her head into the room.

"Claire is writing up her notes about Mrs. Martin," she said in her usual shy fashion. "Do you have any more of the journal I might read?"

Cynthia handed her the latest transcribed pages of the notebook. "Young Donnie helped me do these. He's a very bright boy."

Effie sat at the table, smiling first at Fred O'Connor, then at the others, before beginning to read the pages.

"That there's some pretty spicy material for the boy," Fred cautioned.

"Oh, he just follows the code and transcribes the letters. All he sees is one continuous line."

Effie looked up, concerned. "The boy wouldn't say anything to Claire, would he?"

Dean smiled. "I don't think Claire is one of Donnie's favorite people. Besides, he's too interested in Martha to pay anything else much attention."

"Yeah," Fred said. "She's a sweet little girl. She stopped by the library after school. Those two get along right well."

Effie looked up, a broad smile crossing her face. It was not a reaction the Deans expected when Effie read the sordid confirmation her great aunt was a prostitute and carrying on an adulterous affair. "This is so exciting! Imagine being a dance hall girl back then!" They both stared at her. "Well, I guess it wasn't all pleasure, but still—it must have been electrifying! Just think—handsome gamblers, rich miners, everyone dancing with music and liquor and lively fun every night! And now my Annie has a lover who comes to her in the night!" Before they could comment, she rose, and putting a finger to her lips, whispered, "We mustn't let Claire know our little secret." She nearly collided with Donald Ryland as she practically skipped from the room.

Donald Ryland tipped his wool cap to her as he entered, still dripping snow on the kitchen floor. He plopped down on one of the wooden chairs, oblivious to Cynthia who sighed and began wiping up behind him.

"I'll be checking out in the morning," he said. "I'll ice climb during the day, then drive back up to Grand Junction."

"With Edith Shipton?" Dean asked but Ryland shook his head no.

Dean just looked at him, waiting for an explanation. Ryland raised his feet for Cynthia to clean beneath him and said, "Edith's gone back to her husband."

"You're kidding me!" Dean said.

"Nope. She's up there with him now. They're probably messing up the sheets in a fury of passion as we speak."

"Good!" Cynthia said, from her hands and knees. "Maybe now they'll all check out of Bird Song and things will return to normal."

"Only when that Claire Quincy packs up, too," Fred interjected.

Ryland continued, shrugging off his heavy jacket. "Jerome told her if she had the baby and gave it to him, he'd grant her a divorce and leave her alone."

"God!" Cynthia exclaimed. "That's no better than selling her child! Worse—she's selling it to someone she knows is scum!"

"What happens to Donnie?" Dean asked.

"He stays with his mother."

"Permanently?" Cynthia asked.

Ryland nodded. "That's the deal. She gets her freedom and Donnie."

"At least then you may get a chance to see your son more often," Dean offered.

"Yeah," he answered. "Except I'm sensing he comes as part of a package deal with Edith and quite frankly, she scares the shit out of me. She plans to move up to Grand Junction, so Donnie can be near me. That's like getting an ice cream sundae with castor oil for topping. Somehow, I can't see my fiancée Franny relating very well to Edith Shipton." He rose, oblivious to his continued dripping. "At least I'll get a head start tomorrow night, breaking the news to Fran." He added, "I'm sure it will make her day."

"When are the happily reunited Shiptons checking out?" Cynthia asked as she returned to the counter and began chopping carrots with a large butcher knife.

"After the ice festival is over," Ryland answered. "Jerome plans to climb tomorrow, so he can show everyone how much of a macho stud he is. He's as excited as a kid that's just discovered why girls are different. He can't wait to take up the sport. The bastard had the nerve to ask me to climb with him. He even laced the invitation with a ration of all-is-forgiven bullshit. I told him to stuff it."

"That's right, champ," said Jerome Shipton appearing around the corner. "What a trip! Ice climbing is more of a rush than women—almost! Sure you don't want to reconsider?" He slapped Ryland on the back before the younger man could move.

"No, thanks!" Ryland grumbled as he wasted no time leaving the room.

Jerome just laughed over his shoulder, "Don't be a poor loser!" He turned to Cynthia, ignoring Dean. "What's for supper, honey? Sex makes me ravishing."

Cynthia turned on the balls of her feet, still holding the immense knife, waist-high, pointed directly at him. The look on her face startled her husband.

"Get lost," she said. "I'm busy."

Shipton held up his hands, mimicking surrender. "Never let it be said I don't get the point!" He turned with a wave, "I'll see you later, honey bunch!"

"God, I hate that man," she said as soon as he was gone. "I can't wait until he leaves. How can Edith be so stupid to as go back to him after all he's done to her?"

"Edith is a very fragile woman. She's used to being dominated. Unlike you." He gave his wife a hug. "What would you do if I beat up on you?"

She pulled away and growled her answer. "I'd go out and buy a gun and shoot you in every part of your body that you hold dear and then finish you off right between your eyes."

He kissed her on the cheek as she continued working, chopping the carrots with a new-found vengeance. "I'd be getting just what I deserved if I hit you. Nobody has a right to hurt another person, especially a defenseless woman." She turned, still holding the knife. "I withdraw the 'defenseless' part," he added, stepping back. She returned to her chopping.

"I thought you didn't believe in capital punishment," he said, trying to lighten the situation.

"I don't. And I don't believe in abortion either. Or killing in general."

"But you believe in blowing out the brains of a woman beater. Isn't that a wee bit inconsistent?"

She thought a moment. "No. I didn't say I *believed* in it—I don't. I just said that's what I'd *do*. It's not the same thing."

"You mean you'd start blasting away on the spur of the moment—in the heat of passion."

"Not necessarily. I might even plan it."

He just looked at her, waiting for her to explain, but she said nothing. "Plan it, but not believe in what you were doing?"

"Believing in it and doing it are two different things."

"You're confusing me. What's the difference?"

She put down the knife and thought a moment. "I'd know I was doing wrong. I'd even feel terrible about myself after I'd done it and most likely be devastated. And I'd accept whatever the consequences were and never be the same for the rest of my life, but I'm not sure knowing all that would still stop me from going ahead and doing it." She looked up at her husband. "Sometimes you just do things, because you feel they have to be done. That doesn't mean you believe in them, believe they're right. Maybe just the opposite. You know you're doing wrong, but you sort of admit to your own imperfections."

"But you do them anyway?"

"Yup." She paused, trying to find the right words. "We're not perfect, us humans. God knows, we're not even close. Yes, I think I could kill someone, given the right circumstances. But I hope I'd have the gumption not to rationalize my actions by pretending I believed what I did was right. I'd know damn well it was wrong. And be totally sorry later."

"What could happen so terrible to cause you to do something you felt so strongly against?"

She smiled, breaking the tension. "Probably nothing. I guess I'm just blowing off steam."

Dean was wondering about her answer, as the telephone rang. The call was for Cynthia. As she answered it, he pondered what she had said. He wondered if this beautiful, loving, compassionate wife of his whom he loved so dearly, was really capable of killing another human being. But when she returned and he saw her concerned look, his mind went to real-time matters.

"Who was that?" Dean asked.

"My mother," she answered.

"I hope she's coming to visit. I miss her cooking." Cynthia's mother, a widowed librarian, telephoned from Indiana frequently. While the independent woman had only been to Ouray once in the six months the Deans had been married, she and her son-in-law got along spectacularly. The lively woman was fun to be around.

"No, she's not coming down. She says they have plenty of snow up there." Then she added, "But she didn't sound her usual self. I'm worried."

"Is she ill?"

"I'm not sure. I pushed her and she did admit to having some tests but then dismissed them, saying the doctor was just running up his bill." Cynthia looked up at her husband. "Any admission by her usually means a lot more than what she says."

"Do you want to take a quick trip up there and visit?"

"Lord no! How could I get away with an inn full of guests? Besides, I'm sure I'm overreacting. It's just that lately everything keeps piling up. I'm a bundle of nerves with all that's going on around here. I've been a bundle of nerves since Edith Shipton first showed up on our doorstep. We go months with normal, pleasant guests, then all of a sudden we pick up a conflated collection of crazies! Alarm clocks ringing in the middle of the night, ghosts walking around, everyone hopping into someone else's bed, half the people wanting to kill the other half! And it's been getting worse daily."

Dean felt compassion. Cynthia was definitely not herself. "I'm insulted," he said with mock severity. "How could you think for a minute I couldn't handle this place? Go in the parlor and pour yourself a glass of sherry and put your feet up. I'll cook dinner." He opened the refrigerator and took out the fish that had been thawing. "Go on! Scat!" Cynthia rewarded him with a hundred dollar smile as he looked at the label on the package.

"It's orange roughy," she offered. "Perhaps Fred could help you."

"Come on! Fred thinks orange roughy is a hoodlum from Northern Ireland! I'll cook for all of us. Go in there and keep Gladys company. I just saw her come out of hibernation."

"There's some rice..." she offered, "and the carrots..." but he continued to shoo her out of the room.

Fred wandered into the kitchen as Dean was reading the label of a Campbell's soup can in hopes of creating an exotic sauce for his broiling fish. "Are you off to Miss Worthington's again?" he asked.

"No. She begged off. She's been a mite tired lately. Are you cooking supper?" He opened the door of the stove to peek.

"You got a problem with that?" Dean asked.

"Nope. It'll seem like old times. Besides, I still have some of my old supply of Tums." He smiled when he said it, and added, "Just don't go trying to get fancy. Where's Cynthia?"

"Feeling out of sorts." Dean explained the phone call from Indiana and Cynthia's general displeasure, particularly with Jerome Shipton.

Fred looked over his shoulder before speaking. "I been trying to find out some poop about that guy on the Internet but it's a whole lot easier checking out hundred year old folks than living ones."

"Any luck?"

"There was a biography on him from some local storage shed association that made him some kind of muck a muck a few years back. It didn't say much more than what we already knew." He withdrew a piece of paper from his pocket. "This here's the phone number of the current muck a muck. His name is Able Whitehouse. I know Cynthia don't fancy you snooping after our guests but I thought you might...."

Dean grabbed the paper, gave a glance to the parlor and picked up the portable phone.

"I hope it's not too late on the east coast," he said as he dialed.

A grumpy man answered and Dean tested his sweetest voice. He ad libbed a ridiculous story of wanting do a magazine piece on Shipton and began to flatter the listener, saying he was recommended as a prime source of accurate information. After a lengthy pause, the man asked. "You a cop or something?"

"Oh, no!" Dean answered, "I just want...."

The man cut him off. "Listen. Don't tell the bastard I talked to you, but here's the short version. Shipton is a son of a bitch in anyone's book. He was raised on a South Carolina farm by a red neck father who didn't have two cotton balls to rub together. He used to beat the shit out of his shack full of kids just to keep in shape. Jerry took off at about age thirteen. The rest of 'em are all still down there, eating grits and keeping away from the law."

"Jerome doesn't have a southern accent."

"He works at it. Like everything else."

"So how did Mr. Shipton get to be a gazillionaire?"

"Stomping on everyone in his way, I guess. Plus the old right place, right time." Then Whitehouse added begrudgingly, "And I guess he's smart. But 'gazillion' is a bit heavy. He and his wife, who's as nutty as Planters, aren't on anyone's top one hundred list of the rich and famous. Both of them are at that level of not worrying about missing any meals but they're not big spenders—maybe five to ten mil bracket, give or take—no real debts. Nice cars, nice enough house, but the tour bus doesn't bother to point out their digs."

"Anything else?"

"Ol' Jerome would bonk anything that wears panties. I don't know why, but a lot of the dames let him. He probably got an early start on his own sisters down on God's little acre."

"What does his wife say about that?"

"If she opens her mouth, he either doesn't listen or whacks it shut. He's king of the double standard."

Dean, crossing his fingers at being on a roll, decided to ask about the death of Shipton's son. "I hear he had a boy who drowned."

Able Whitehouse paused a moment before answering. "Yeah, I'd forgotten about that. Seems to me the kid was someplace swimming, fooling around when he shouldn't have been."

"I heard he died on a canoeing trip with his father."

"I don't think so, but wherever it was, it shook her up."

"Edith?"

"She tried to commit suicide. But I guess that wasn't the first time. She's always doing something melodramatic—a real nut case. I don't know what he sees in her." He added, "Look, I've got to get going. Whoever you are, if you're thinking of selling this 'magazine bit' to all of Jerry's friends, you'll starve to death!" He cut off the conversation with a hearty laugh.

Dean turned to Fred. "I don't think Mr. Whitehouse likes Jerome Shipton." He then highlighted the conversation, adding, "He cut it off just when it was getting interesting. It seems there's some confusion on how son number one died."

Dean returned to his gourmet preparations. After dinner, and obligatory rave reviews by the other two-thirds of Bird Song's management team, Dean joined Cynthia in the parlor. He'd coerced Fred into doing the dishes. Dean didn't tell Cynthia about his phone conversation with Whitehouse. No point in even introducing a mention of Jerome Shipton. Instead, he steered the conversation toward Gladys Turnbull, who was the only other occupant of the cozy room. The others were all up town for dinner. She was prattling on about the planet Zzz where some arch villain who closely resembled Jerome Shipton, was to meet his due while climbing an icy cliff, in hot pursuit of a fair maiden whom Dean took to be a greatly slimmed down version of the author. She eagerly informed the pair how she planned to attend tomorrow's ice festival activities, in search of first hand research for what was sure to be a winning chapter. Dean tuned her out when she described the miscreant becoming impaled on a giant icicle while fair what's-her-name laughed in his face as he slowly bled to death before her.

Dean had to give Cynthia credit. She pretended so well to be interested in the recitation of the saga that he almost believed she was becoming a fan. However, when the phone rang—one a reservation, the other a lengthy call for Fred from his current beloved—Cynthia jumped like a startled rabbit. In an attempt to calm his wife's progressive nervousness, and because he too felt like a snort, Dean broke out a jug of left over Christmas cheer. It didn't last long as it was within Gladys' frequent reach.

The others returned in a group, the climbers boisterously chatting, but any sign of camaraderie among the others was absent. Ryland made a beeline for his room, and the Quincy sisters tromped up the stairs, Effie giving a three-finger wave and Claire looking as if she'd punch out the lights of anyone who got in her way. The reunited Shipton family stood like a Saturday Evening Post cover. Jerome held Donnie's hand while his other arm was about Edith's shoulder, in a grasp that looked to Dean a tad too tight for simple affection. Cynthia cast her eyes downward while Gladys glared at Jerome with unfettered hatred, looking as if she wished she had a giant icicle to do her research here and now. Edith stared straight ahead, looking as zonked as Gladys was well on her way to becoming.

"Donnie's going to sleep with Ryland tonight," Shipton said with a smile, as if he was sending the boy off to a slumber party. The look on Donnie's face indicated this was news to him. The look on Edith's face said she was off visiting the planet Zzz.

"There's only one bed there and the room's small," Dean said. "Donnie can bunk in our office." The boy smiled at the suggestion, but Shipton shook his head no.

"He can sleep on the floor. Just make a pallet with some blankets." He let go of Donnie's hand and turned to his wife, with more of a leer than a look of love. "Edith and I need privacy." He turned, and was off up the stairs, propelling his bewildered wife before him. Donnie ran off to Ryland's room. Cynthia began to quietly cry out of sheer frustration while Gladys Turnbull started to loudly snore.

CHAPTER 15

I have a diamond ring adorning my finger, just as a bride might wear! My Joshua gave it to me last night, when he came a-visiting! It belonged to one of the girls who took her life and died in his arms. She gave it to my darling out of gratitude for his compassion at her passing and he wanted me to have it as a token of his feelings for me. I wear it always when we're together as it gives comfort to him about our situation which I know troubles him greatly. I wear it too, when I'm alone, and pretend that we are one forever.

Sometimes I fear my mind may be going as I often pretend my circumstances are far different than they truly are. I perform the duties of the house as if it is our home and I am awaiting the tread of my darling's foot upon the stair as he returns from his ministrations to the arms of his dutiful wife. There is a spring in my step and a note on my lips, until I realize the awful truth of my situation and am forced to hold back my tears.

Cynthia sat up in bed as she read the brief passage, an uncommon glass of amber liquid in her hand "Donnie deciphered it. Don't you think it's sad?"

Dean had brief thoughts of the errant preacher robbing a dead hooker but kept them to himself. Instead, he gave a more neutral response. "She certainly is taken with the guy. But I wonder what he's thinking. He can't expect to keep sneaking up to visit her indefinitely and hope to get away with it." He stripped of his clothes, donned his pajama bottoms, and sat on the edge of the bed. Cynthia lifted her glass and drained it. Liquor was something Cynthia used infrequently and not very well.

"You have to stop plying me with booze or I'll think you have evil intentions. My head is starting to whirl."

"At least that stuff seems to have improved your blue mood."

"Thanks to you. That was sweet to cook supper. I do feel better but I'll still be glad when things get back to normal and I'm comfortable my mother is her old self again."

"Would it make you feel better to give her another call?" he asked.

"No. It's two hours later in Indiana. I'd just wake her. I'm fine. I just need a good night's sleep. And thanks," she said sweetly as she bent over and kissed him. "I'd make you come over here and cuddle me but I'm afraid I'd get dizzy and be sick." She fluffed up her pillow and turned away as he turned out the light.

Dean's mind was still turning. He wasn't quite ready for sleep so he wandered back to the parlor, sat in the back corner and picked up a biking magazine. In spite of good intentions, he must have dozed as he woke to the sound of someone on the stairs. Effie Quincy stepped into the room, startled when she saw Dean, sitting there in his bathrobe. She wore silk pajamas and a woolen sweater.

"I didn't mean to startle you," he said.

She joined him, sitting on the sofa and pulling one of Cynthia's quilts across her lap. "I can't sleep either."

"Insomnia or excitement at learning all about your great-aunt?" he asked.

Effie paused, tugging her quilt higher. "Neither. I'm worried about Claire. I think that awful man Mr. Shipton told her the truth about Annie."

"How would he know?"

"Little Donnie has been helping your wife transcribe the notebook so his stepfather may have seen some pages. And I've confided to poor Edith a little about Annie. She seems so taken with her, dressing like her and coloring her hair and all."

"Why would Jerome tell your sister? He's never even spoken to Claire that I know of."

"Just spiteful, I guess. The five of us sat together at the restaurant this evening and after Edith and I went to the ladies room, we came back to find Claire livid and Mr. Shipton laughing. Poor Donnie looked very uncomfortable. I think the boy is frightened of the man."

"Did you ask your sister what happened?"

"Oh, yes. I tried to. But she wouldn't even talk to me. She just muttered. She'd like to kill the...she used a term very uncommon to her usual vocabulary." Effie snuggled deeper into the cushions. Join the line, Dean thought. Good old Jerome has a knack for making enemies.

Neither said a word as the hall clock began striking midnight. As it tolled its final gong, Edith Shipton appeared, in her late night attire—

the Annie Quincy white dress—her hair loosened about her shoulders. She didn't seem surprised to find others in the living room and took a seat next to Effie, looking less a nighttime specter than an exhausted victim. Dean noticed a darkening bruise on her left cheek.

"Jerome likes me to wear this," she said by way of apology, spreading her hands to feel the fabric of the old dress.

"You're hurt," Dean said.

She touched her cheek. "Yes. It's quite tender. Do you think it will leave a mark?"

Dean ignored her question as Effie moved to look closer at the injury. "Did he do that to you?" Dean asked, a no-nonsense tone to his voice.

Edith hesitated, as if pondering her answer. "No. I bumped into the door." She then added, with a hint of silly smile, "Foolish me." She bit her lip. "Foolish, foolish me."

Effie looked to Dean, as if for guidance, but said nothing. Dean wanted to question Edith further but she rose, with Effie following, her arm on Edith's elbow and the pair returned upstairs. Dean sat a while longer, amid night sounds, the ticking clock, and the muffled ringing of Gladys Turnbull's alarm.

Foolish Edith, Dean thought as he returned to his room.

CHAPTER 16

It's begun to snow. Usually I enjoy seeing the gentle flakes and they cause me little aggravation with their accumulation as I seldom travel more than a block or two when I secure provisions. But today is different. Something ominous hangs in the winter air, a darkness and trepidation that well matches my mood. The snow seems to trap me, as it does with the small squirrel I am watching from my window. The frightened creature is as ill prepared for the season as I and scurries about frantically in the deepening snow in search of sustenance. I've tossed him a scrap of bread but I fear it will be inadequate to meet his long-term needs. My time of the month has passed without its usual affliction and I am dire fearful of the consequences of why this might be so. What am I to do if my darling has made a new life within me? My circumstances are without solution and his life would be ruined if the world were to know the truth of our love. And what of the dear creature unborn and unknowing who may dwell within my womb? Surely if it be blessed with even a fraction of the goodness and kindness of its father, the child deserves all the blessings of life; far more than might be offered by this wretch of a woman God may deem to mother it into the world.

The snow began falling before dawn, drifting down with an urgency that heralded a serious accumulation. The darkening sky matched the mood of Bird Song's guests and inhabitants as they woke to a busy Saturday morning, the main day of the ice festival.

Cynthia was troubled with a headache and tried to catch an extra half-hour of sleep as Dean served breakfast to the early risers, Penny, Mick and two of the other climbers. Donnie had scampered down at first light and dropped off his un-separated but translated letters of Annie's notebook, which Dean penned to completion over breakfast. Donnie had pretty well taken over the project as the chores of Bird Song limited Cynthia's time. Fred joined Dean in the dining room, taking up the duty of chatting with the guests, a task Dean was not yet ready to perform after a less-than-complete night's sleep.

Ryland's gear was piled by the door by the time the others were pouring their second cup of coffee. Jerome appeared, overly chipper, talking up the other climbers as if he was a life-long participant in the sport, not a second day novice. The Quincy sisters sauntered down. Effie bubbled over with verbal celebration at the beautiful snow, so much prettier than Boston's slop, while peeking out of every window, and collaring each passing guest to share her unabashed enthusiasm at each limited vista. Sister Claire bitched at the weatherman and anyone else she could blame for 'this horrible stuff' while shooting daggers at Jerome Shipton and pretending Fred O'Connor hadn't been born. She did attempt to engage an uninterested climber in a conversation about her Great-aunt Annie being one of the founders of the Ouray Woman's Club, back in 1897 and how she helped form the Ouray Library, with her friend, the famous millionaire, of Hope Diamond fame, Tom Walsh. Dean took this to suggest Annie's true past remained a secret to the sharp-tongued woman.

Edith Shipton remained unaccounted for, and unmentioned. Young Donnie munched on his fourth or fifth muffin, ignored by and ignoring his stepfather. Late-sleeping Gladys Turnbull was still dreaming of the vengeance of the inhabitants of Zzz. Janet was late again and Cynthia's bedside attempt to call her mother in Indiana resulted in unanswered rings, causing her further concern.

Cynthia ambled out as Dean was clearing away the dishes. She apologized for her tardiness to the balance of the accumulated climbers who were tarrying over coffee and herb tea. She responded to Dean's hug, saying she felt better, but was still concerned about her mother.

The climbers grumbled about the negative affect of the snow on their anticipated activities, all except Penny, who considered the weather a new and exciting challenge. Mick asked about the weather forecast and Fred responded that in Ouray, any prognostication was speculative and definitely regional—for real accuracy, one looked out the window or guessed. In the next town over, the sun might be shining. He went on to add judiciously that elevation changed Mother Nature's rules about the weather every few hundred feet. There were markedly different conditions just a few miles away. A typical year saw four hundred inches of snow fall atop Red Mountain, a hundred and seventy-five inches in Ouray, and perhaps a foot in Montrose, all within fifty miles.

Edith emerged, dressed for the great out doors, ready to accompany her man on his macho adventures. Gladys waddled down, her jaw set like a drill Sergeant, looking as if she'd like to spit in Jerome's cof-

fee. Last to arrive was Donald Ryland. After milling about until nearly nine o'clock, the entire group began to trek up to the ice park and,
as Claire Quincy put it, view this craziness. Even Fred O'Connor was
taking the day off from his historical research to watch the festivities.

It looked as if the Deans might have more time to themselves, even
if Janet's absence meant they'd spend their leisure changing sheets
and cleaning toilets. But their wayward helper finally arrived, stomping off snow and apologizing profusely as the others began gathering
their mountain of gear and leaving.

Dean answered a phone call—a six-month-early summer reservation—while waving to the departing guests. Ryland shook his hand
goodbye as Dean cradled the phone to his shoulder. Ryland was the
last to leave, or so Dean thought. As he was finishing his conversation, a loud sound came from the kitchen, followed by a sharp cry in
a man's voice, and then laughter. Jerome Shipton passed Dean in the
hall, holding the side of his head, and left the building as Dean hung
up the phone.

When Dean rushed to the kitchen, he found Cynthia, her hands to
her face, in tears, grease covering the floor. He comforted her, as best
he could, trying to learn what happened. She swiped an arm across
her face in an attempt to brush away the tears.

"The bastard! She growled. "I hope I killed him!"

"What in God's name happened?"

Cynthia just shook her head, not answering, until Dean held her at
arm's length and insisted on a response.

"He grabbed me," she finally blurted out. "He thought he was
being funny. He grabbed my breast. I...I whacked him in the head
with the frying pan." She began to cry anew as Dean rushed from the
room and out the front door.

He caught up with Shipton on the sidewalk where the man was
holding a handkerchief to the side of his head while loading gear to
his vehicle and chuckling to himself. Dean turned him around as he
was swinging, knocking Shipton flying into a snow bank with a right
hand that started at ground level. The other guests, standing nearby,
gaped in utter shock. Dean leaped on Shipton, clawing away at the
soft snow, pummeling him like an eight grade schoolyard brawler
while Shipton, still clutching his ice ax in one hand, swung at Dean,
catching him on the cheek and face with the side of the solid handle.
Two of the climbers clawed them apart, pulling Dean from him, just
as Cynthia reached the front door, screaming for him to stop.

The next fifteen minutes were an embarrassed blur as Dean tried
to stem his bleeding face at the kitchen table. The others beat a hasty

retreat as soon as they learned there were no fatalities, finally leaving Dean and his wife alone, with only Janet obliviously scrubbing away somewhere above.

"Good God!" Cynthia whimpered. "How could you? He could have killed you! That's not the way a grown man would respond! He could sue us! We'd lose Bird Song! Everything! Everything I love! The bastard is just not worth it. Just leave it alone. It's my problem. It's my breast he grabbed. If I want to smash the bastard's head, that's my decision! I just want him gone."

Dean tried to hold his wife but she pulled away. "Just clean yourself up. You're bleeding on your Christmas sweater. And don't mop up the floor! It's my grease!"

Back in his bedroom, Dean wondered through a dizzy fog if his nose and cheek were broken. The nose felt like it. There was a loud bang as the front door slammed with Cynthia's violent departure. He felt helpless and ineffective in dealing with this scoundrel who dared grope his wife in Dean's own house! He couldn't even get the son of a bitch out of his and his wife's life. Now all he'd accomplished was to piss off the woman he loved and make a public fool of himself! God, he thought, as he laid back his aching head, get me through the next few hours and maybe they'll all be gone! Then maybe, thank God, we'll have a bit of peace.

In spite of Cynthia's admonition he returned to the kitchen and cleaned the bacon grease from the floor, using half a roll of paper towels in completing the task. He did the dishes as well, hoping for an early reprieve from her justified anger. When he finished the chores, he swallowed three aspirins and went outside to shovel the accumulating snow, hoping further activity might dissipate the anger he felt, not only at Shipton, but at himself for losing it in so public and childish manner. By the time he finished, it was after eleven and Cynthia still hadn't returned. Bird Song was as quiet as a tomb, with Janet either the most silent domestic on record or snoozing away in an unoccupied room. Dean took a deep breath and decided he'd better trudge up to the ice park, wool hat in hand, and attempt to make his amends.

The crowd had grown since Dean's Thursday trip, both in numbers of climbers and spectators. The largest group was assembled below the bridge where some activity was taking place. The crowd seemed clustered at one particular spot. It was difficult to see as the intensity of the falling snow was increasing by the hour. Dean wandered up the penstock trail, the path he and Cynthia followed earlier, where Donald Ryland had climbed. Small clusters of people were gathered at every vantage point. Piles of gear were stacked about while partners called out to those below, fed line and encouragement, while others watched, a number with anxious looks on their reddened faces as they looked downward. Dean searched for his wife but didn't spot Cynthia's colorful ski jacket among the pockets of viewers. He continued to trudge forward, leaving the river and crowds behind.

It was peaceful on the path, in spite of the snow and increased inconvenience of trudging in its depth. Once beyond access to the river below, the seldom-used path presented an unbroken cover of fresh white, now blanketed in more than a foot of fresh powder, as it followed the large pipe toward the reservoir. Nevertheless, Dean waded forward, enjoying the peace of being alone in the woods.

When he reached the waterfall at the base of the storage pond, the mist rose up from the cascade, creating a myriad of icy fingers of crystal in the cold air. He paused, leaning against a concrete abutment, mesmerized by the never-ending torrent as it flowed over the edge of the dam. Finally, with a sigh of resignation, he began the fifteen-minute walk back to the awaiting problems of civilization.

After the trail bent toward the cliff, Dean could see down the gorge, all the way to the roadway bridge where ghost-like spectators continued to mill about in the whirl of falling snow. He was surprised to spot young Donnie Ryland, recognizable by his small stature and familiar jacket, running down the end of the trail. The boy was too far away for Dean to hail but Dean hurried his pace in hopes of stopping him and asking if he'd seen Cynthia. A short distance further, he was surprised for the second time when he caught sight of Janet O'Brien. She was standing at the rail, peering down river, dressed in only a sweater, clutching her arms to her body against the snow and chilling cold.

Dean called to her and she turned, startled. "What are you doing up here?" he asked. "You look half frozen to death."

"I came for Cynthia. Her mother's sick. She had a heart attack. Someone called." She turned, peering again down the river, as if the message she'd delivered was as perfunctory as a call to supper.

"Did you find her?" Dean asked.

"Yeah. She's run down to Bird Song." Dean turned to leave, but Janet called after him. "You haven't heard?"

"Heard what?" he asked, anxious to get going.

"Mister Shipton's dead. He fell in the river." She waved her hand down the trail where she was looking at a large gathering.

Dean took off at a run, past more gawkers staring over the edge. As he came out of the trees and crossed the bridge, he passed the sheriff's car and emergency vehicles, their bubble gum lights still turning red or blue in the thickening snow. He glanced back, far below, down at the water where a group was huddled, presumably around the victim. But Dean's first priority was his wife Cynthia and he continued to jog, forced to concentrate on his footing if he were to remain upright in the gathering snow. Any thoughts of Shipton could wait until later.

When Dean rushed into Bird Song, Cynthia was standing in the hall, the phone at her ear. While she wasn't crying, she was biting her lip against doing so, and kept blinking her reddened eyes. He put his arm around her as she continued to talk. Dean could tell from the conversation she was speaking to her son Randy. As soon as she hung up, she held Dean close.

"Janet told you?" He nodded. "It happened last night," she murmured. "A neighbor friend tried to call me but they didn't know my married name. Finally someone from back in Parkside told them."

"How is she?" Dean asked.

"I don't know. Not good. No one seems to know, not really. She's in the hospital, still unconscious." She began to cry. "Where were you? When I came back, I...wanted you here."

"I was up at the park, looking for you," he answered, holding her closer.

"Shipton, he's—?" she said.

Dean cut her off. "I heard. But that can wait. We have to get you up to Indiana." He reached for the phone book. "You go pack some things. I'll make a plane reservation."

"Can we afford—?"

"Cynthia, it's your mother. She needs someone and you're the only person she has. We're not paupers, at least not completely."

Effie Quincy rushed in the door while Dean was drumming his fingers, listening to waltz music on hold. She was all a-babble over Shipton's fall and dismayed that she couldn't find her sister. Dean told her about Cynthia's mother. She offered her sympathies but seemed more concerned with finding sister Claire and hurried outside to see if any of the other now returning guests had seen her. The Deans then retired to their quarters to make airline arrangements in private. A half hour later, with Dean never having removed the phone from his ear, they were ready to leave for the airport. By that time, most of the ice climbers were back at Bird Song. Not only did the intensifying snow make climbing even more dangerous than usual, but Shipton's accident had cloaked a pall over everyone's activities.

Dean had been successful, for a four-figure charge, in securing a one way ticket with an open ended return, from Montrose, via Denver and

Chicago, to Indianapolis. Cynthia would go alone—that was a given with Bird Song requiring Dean's attention. From Indianapolis, Cynthia would rent a car for a two-hour drive to her mother's small town. It would be a very long day and night. She paced as Dean finalized the arrangements with scarcely enough time left to reach the airport before the first leg of the trip was scheduled to board.

Fred returned, was informed of the situation, and gave Cynthia a warm and silent hug. He then reached into his pocket for his snap-top purse and extracted five worn twenty-dollar bills. He forced them into her hand, closing her fingers.

"You might need a stiff drink or two. And don't you worry none about Bird Song. Me and David here will have the place running as smooth as a Shanghai subway." Before Dean could remember what Shanghai offered for public transportation, Fred set about taking care of the needs and concerns of the returning guests.

"How's she going to fly in this stuff?" Fred asked at one point, on his way to deliver cookies and hot chocolate to the parlor. Dean continued to make sandwiches the pair would eat on the road.

"They say the flight isn't canceled yet so let's hope Montrose stays clear enough, at least for another hour or two."

The trip to the Montrose airport was slow. The roads were nearly empty but low visibility made driving treacherous. Cynthia sat huddled in the corner of her seat, away from Dean, her tiny size looking child-like as she trembled, in spite of the fact the Jeep's heater was set on high.

"I'm sorry about this morning," he said as they crawled up the road from Ridgway. She looked away, outside, at the blur of snow as he continued. "It was stupid of me to lose it and act like a school kid. Whacking the bastard wasn't the way to respond. God," he said, as it began to sink in, "and now he's dead!"

She just shook her head. "I don't know what's right and wrong anymore. It's been a terrible few days." She took a deep breath, "I'm glad he's dead. He was an evil man. I know I shouldn't say it, but it's the truth. I just hope God doesn't punish me by...taking my mother."

"It doesn't work that way." He added, "I wish I were going with you."

"I'm scared."

He reached over and pulled her toward him and she snuggled against him and he could feel her shake. "He's dead now. It's all past us."

"No, it isn't," she answered, her voice muffled against his shoulder.

"What do you mean?" But she wouldn't answer. He let her snuggle there in her silence, the only sound the swish of the windshield wipers blowing away the snow. Neither spoke until the lights of Montrose glowed through the snow.

"Shipton was an ass. Don't let him continue to bother you now that he's gone."

"I don't want to talk about it," she answered. "I don't want to answer any questions. Please, don't even ask me any questions." She looked up at him. "I just want you to love me."

When they reached the airport it was snowing heavily, but the accumulation here was far less than in Ouray. Much to their dismay, the incoming plane for Cynthia's scheduled flight had been diverted to Grand Junction, sixty miles further away. They had no alternative but to drive the additional distance. After a call to Fred at Bird Song and the necessary schedule changes, they once again boarded the Jeep for the one-hour ride. Dean suggested Cynthia try to catch some sleep as it was nearly dark as they passed through Delta, Colorado and the open stretches of desert-like country beyond. Surprisingly, she did so, as he could tell from her measured breathing. Cynthia was still sleeping when a speeding Ford Explorer passed them and Dean caught sight of Donald Ryland, with his son Donnie sitting beside him. There was no sign of Edith.

After a kiss and a hug, but no further conversation of consequence, Cynthia boarded the plane for the first leg to Denver. Dean pitied his wife, knowing the grueling trip that lay before her over the next several hours, not knowing what awaited her landing.

The long ride back to Ouray reminded Dean of another trip after dropping Cynthia at the airport. She had visited him in Ouray, nearly a year and a half before, while he was recuperating from a gunshot wound. It was the first time they had made love, and were newly committed to one another. That too was an upsetting time, but for a far different reason—fear of commitment and an unknown future they wanted together.

As Dean blinked at on-coming headlights, he considered what a glorious future they were having. The past half-year was the best six months of his life. They both loved Ouray, the Colorado mountains and hosting the guests of Bird Song, at least most of them. He remembered the day, just before they first opened the bed and breakfast, when he'd picked up this Jeep, the first new vehicle he'd ever owned. Now, six months later, in spite of the windshield pockmarked from the gravel roads of Ouray County, it felt like an old friend. A friend, but empty without Cynthia beside him. And worse yet, he felt a strange shiver of discomfit at Cynthia's odd reaction to Jerome Shipton's death.

CHAPTER 17

Illness plagues me each morning, causing me difficulty in accomplishing my chores, as simple as they may be, though failing Mrs. Cummings hardly seems to notice. I am sure now that I carry my beloved Joshua's child in my womb. At times my heart soars like an angel at the gates of paradise at the mere thought that a part of him is now a part of me. At other moments, I am as distressed as the sinner that I am, being dragged to hell's fire beyond. There is a woman who would scrape this life from my body if I don't tarry much longer. She has done this deed for so many others, but I can't bear to heap more sin on my blackened soul and kill unborn this result of my Joshua's love.

I long to share my secret with the one I so love, but then fear and doubt overtake me before the words will leave my lips. I plan well what I will say when we are together, but dread of so burdening this dear and gentle man with the troubled future before us causes me to only hold him close and retain my silence.

He has spoken to me in whispers, in the dark of the night, how waves of guilt over our relationship are with him every waking moment, and yet he loves me so as to risk all for my embrace. He prays for an answer and I cry for his pain. But all too soon my condition will be displayed for all to see, and then, only dear God can help me!

The snow continued to fall as Dean pulled in front of Bird Song, angled his Jeep as best he could in the drifts, and climbed to the porch. In spite of the lateness of the hour, he turned and stretched the stiffness from his limbs. There was a lingering smell of wood smoke in the night air and all earlier efforts at shoveling the walkway and stairs were lost in the smooth swirls of new fallen whiteness. It had now been snowing steadily since after dinner yesterday—no, the day before, now that it was long after midnight. From the very beginning there had been an intensity, a seriousness to the falling flakes that spoke of accumulations far in excess of anything the Deans had seen to date. A true introduction to Colorado mountain winters, the ones you read about in the books and think are the exaggeration of some faulty memory. The flakes were not large, but unlike most gentle Ouray snow storms, they didn't drift to the ground like tiny dust motes. Instead they swirled, at first slowly, then with a vengeance, churned by an uncommon wind that drove down from the mountains with an increasing fury. By now, more than two feet was packed against the door, though the exact depth was difficult to determine in the wind-driven drifts. Dean stomped his feet and entered his home, for the first time absent his wife.

Fred O'Connor sat in the parlor, a Sue Grafton novel in his lap, snoring softly. It was one-thirty. The return trip from Grand Junction had taken Dean twice the usual two hours, a slalom of ditched autos, snow plows, ice and stopped traffic. It snowed for the entire trip, but all but a few other drivers had the sense to remain home for the last fifty miles. Fred awoke, rubbing his eyes.

"Just nodded off a second ago," he grumbled.

"You didn't have to wait up," Dean said, as he slumped into a corner chair.

"I figured you needed bringing up to date," he muttered. "Cynthia called from Denver. She made it that far at least. Sheriff Weller spent half the night here. He wants to talk to you."

"That's no surprise. Jake probably thinks I kicked Shipton over the side. How did the accident happen?"

"There's a bunch of different stories, but I'm not sure anyone knows. I was down stream, on the other side of the bridge, watching Penny and by the time I noticed the crowd and got there, they were getting ready to haul Shipton out. He was climbing alone, something I guess you're not suppose to do, especially if you're a beginner like Shipton was. Mountain Rescue had him on a litter, all wrapped up like an Egyptian mummy. They took Edith along, too."

"Where's everyone else? Ryland and Donnie passed me on the way to Grand Junction."

"The others are upstairs. The climbers are checking out of Bird Song tomorrow. Gladys is happy as hell about Shipton's swan dive. She darned near did a jig and couldn't wait to write about it—didn't even take time to dream it. I'm not sure Claire Quincy isn't just as pleased as Gladys. Effie is plain bewildered."

The front door Dean had neglected to lock opened and Sheriff Weller strolled in without knocking.

Dean scowled. "You know, Jake, at least you could give it a rap. That doesn't seem out of order, wouldn't you say?"

"I saw your car. I knew you were back."

"Is your watch broken? It's pushing two o'clock in the morning. I just drove two hundred very nasty miles and I'm going to bed. Why don't you come back in the morning? Say, about eleven?"

Weller ignored Dean and his sarcasm as he flopped down on the sofa. "Evening, Mr. O'Connor. Staying out of trouble?"

"Always," Fred answered.

Weller turned to Dean, "I thought you might be interested in the welfare of your guests."

"From what I hear, one ex-guest doesn't have any more welfare and the welfare of the rest of the group can wait until morning."

"Your face is a mess. It looks like Shipton got in a few good whacks. I'm surprised he could do that to you."

"The bastard had an ice ax in his hand when I slugged him," Dean answered. He felt the puffiness about his cheek and cringed at the touch.

"That doesn't sound very smart on your part, taking on a guy with a tool like that in his hand."

"I wasn't thinking at my highest level of logic. I just wanted to beat the shit out of him."

"Did you?"

"I'm not sure. If I didn't, it wasn't for not trying."

"I suppose you've got a good reason why you tried to beat the brains out of a guy holding an ice ax, in the middle of the street with a bunch of people watching."

"The bastard had just grabbed my wife's breast, for God's sake! I was furious!"

"You wanted to kill him, I suppose."

"Damn right! Wouldn't you?"

"But I didn't."

"Neither did I. The jerk managed to do that himself. Just don't ask me to be a pallbearer."

"Nope." He turned to Dean, ready to read his expression. "'Nope' to both points."

Dean stared at the lawman, who said nothing. "Are you telling me someone killed the son of a bitch?"

Again, Weller ignored Dean's question. "Just where were you when Shipton took a dive?"

"Come on, Jake! You sound like cops and bad guys 101. What the hell's going on?" When Weller didn't answer, Dean finally said, "I was looking for Cynthia. I hiked up the path, all the way to the reservoir."

"Alone."

"Sure. Everybody else was watching the climbers, at least what they could see through the snow."

"And since it's snowed a foot or two since then, I'd guess there aren't any footprints to prove you were strolling alone in the woods."

"That would be my guess. Come on, now! What's this all about?"

"A few folks saw you running from the scene."

Dean sighed. "Janet O'Brien had just told me my wife's mother had a heart attack, for God's sake! What the hell else would I do? Saunter home as if I'd all the time in the world? Of course I ran."

"I'm sorry about Cynthia's problems," Weller said. "I guess it's been a shitty day all around."

Fred asked the sheriff. "Did someone really kill Jerome Shipton?"

Weller rocked back and at first Dean didn't think he'd answer. He looked Dean in the eye. "Let's just say his climbing rope was cut, near-ly all the way through. It was cut up at the top, within reach of where it was tied off. It's a long way down to the river. Now, given that, wouldn't you say whoever did the cutting might suspect it would cause Mr. Shipton a bit of bodily harm?"

Dean stared back at him. "And you think I did it?"

Weller squirmed his large frame around, reaching into his pocket, retrieving first a handkerchief, then a set of keys and eventually a red Swiss Army knife. "This look familiar?" he asked holding it out for Dean's inspection.

Dean took it from him. "Yeah," he answered. "It's mine. At least it looks like mine. They're not exactly unique." He examined it closer. "It's mine. It has a chip in the handle."

"Got any booze around here?" Weller asked. "I think I'm gonna need it."

"A couple of bottles of cheap wine, and half a jug of Tequila some guest left," Dean answered as he fingered the knife. Fred rose to get the liquor.

"Bring me the south-of-the-border stuff. No ice—just the bottle." Then he muttered, "I've seen enough ice already today."

"Does your boozing it up make this little meeting unofficial?"

Weller just snorted. "I don't suppose you happen to know how this knife got up in the ice park, next to the cut end of a rope?"

It was Dean's turn to ignore a question. "Any fingerprints?" he asked.

The sheriff just shook his head. "You been outside lately? It was five above at my place this morning. Folks around here tend to wear gloves in the winter when it gets that nippy." Once again, Weller had found a way to make Dean feel stupid.

"You can't seriously think I'm a suspect."

Weller smiled and began counting off on his fingers. "Let's see. It was your knife. You tried to beat the shit out of Shipton only hours before and instead he damned near beat the shit out of you. You were practically the last person to see him before he fell. He was trying to toot Cynthia. You were seen running from the scene. You used to be a big city detective. What do you think?"

"'Toot' Cynthia? Don't be silly! Cynthia didn't give the bastard the time of day!"

"No offence sport, but when is the last time you looked in the mirror? If you were in a beauty contest with Shipton, it wouldn't be you taking home the medals. That guy was a mighty handsome stud. The ladies were crawling all over the ice park for a peek at him."

"He was an egotistical wife beater. Cynthia couldn't stand the guy. She could hardly keep from sticking a butcher knife in his belly the other night in the kitchen!" If Dean had given any thought to how that statement sounded before he opened his big fat mouth, he would have practiced a little restraint and kept it shut.

"Oh? And just where was Mrs. Dean when Jerome found himself on the short end of a cut rope?"

"Why don't you arrest both of us?" Dean said. "Toss in Fred, too," he said as the old man returned with a bottle and three glasses. "He probably sharpened the knife."

Fred poured a full glass of Tequila for Weller but left the other two glasses empty.

"Look," Weller said as he reached for his glass. "I'm the law and I've got to ask the questions. What do you think some prosecuting attorney would say with this evidence? Or the state boys? They'd have you sitting down under a hot light, spending a few hours while a gang of suits practiced twenty questions on you."

"If I was going to kill the bastard, I'd do it face to face!"

"You didn't make out too well the first time you tried a face to face." Weller said with a smile that said he couldn't resist slipping one in at Dean's expense. Dean just scowled and looked away. Weller continued. "Someone cut the son of a bitch's line and I'm the one who's stuck trying to find out who did it."

"Where was Mrs. Shipton at the time?" Fred asked. "If you want my opinion, I'd have to say, look to the wife. Nine times out of ten, in these here capers, it's the she who's doing the deed. It nearly always comes back to the spouse."

"Edith claims she never got further than the road next to the bridge. Couldn't stand the height. A bunch of people confirm it. That's where she was when they hauled her husband out."

"Where's Edith now?" Dean asked.

"They took her to the Montrose hospital, too. I guess they'll keep her overnight."

"Why? I can't see her as the grieving widow."

Weller just shrugged. "It wasn't my call. I haven't spoken to her. Not that she's made any sense the other times we've had a conversation."

"What about the others? My read is Shipton didn't exactly make friends at Bird Song."

"Yeah" said Fred. "I thought I was gonna need funny hats and party favors for the celebrating going on around here."

Weller put his feet up on the coffee table and took a long swallow. "The way I see it, someone from Bird Song cut his rope. That sort of narrows it down, doesn't it?"

Fred reached for an ever-ready pad and pencil and began making a list. "There's the boy's father, Ryland, Gladys Turnbull, Claire Quincy...."

"Look," Dean said. "I'm exhausted. I didn't sleep worth a damn last night, I got rapped in the head pretty good this morning, and I just drove a couple of hundred miles in a blizzard. I'm worried sick about my wife stranded who knows where. Can't we do this shit tomorrow?"

Weller tipped his glass high. "Jerome Shipton was still alive when I got down there," he said, arresting the attention of the others.

"I thought he was dead," Dean said.

"Nope. I'm surprised he wasn't, as far as he fell and I guess he is by now. The medics were talking about looking in his pockets for an organ donor card. But he wasn't dead when I saw him."

"Did you talk to him?" Fred asked.

"In a manner of speaking."

"What's that mean?" Dean asked sharply, tired of Weller's game playing.

"He just whispered one word."

"And that was...?"

"Dean," Weller answered, as he rose to leave.

CHAPTER 18

My heartless mind will not allow my aching body the sleep it so desperately craves and I wander this near-empty house throughout the night. The winter wind has come a-calling and moans through cracks and crevices like so many ghosts visiting from hell, wailing and beckoning for me to join them. I surely may accept their morbid invitation and although seared by the flames of eternal damnation, I'll at least be free from the anguish and heartache of this abominable life.

My baby stirred within me today and were I not so bundled in winter garb the few times when I venture out, surely all the wagging tongues in town would know of my maternal state. Mrs. Cummings, I think, suspects, though low health now keeps her to her bed and back, except for bodily duties, and to sit up for soup and toast a time or two a day. She talks forward of the spring; seeing the flowers and the young people riding on these new wheels called bicycles, but I think to myself she'll not last the winter. I've grown to think kindly of her these last weeks as I've spent much time in her company, though mostly she sleeps and our talk is only of trifles. Perhaps I too will join her, before the lilacs and forsythia give color to this white and lonely landscape.

Joshua visited me last evening though he stayed just long enough. If it wasn't for the naivete of his sex, he too would surely sense my secret, the secret I've still dared not divulge to this man I love. He continues to anguish with guilt and I fear in my heart the burden of his sins will soon cause him to flee in exile from these quarters he has arranged for us to share together. And then all threads of hope will finally vanish from the fabric of my life.

Dean slept fitfully, once he managed to count sufficient sheep to do so, with dreams and mind games interchanging so rapidly as to blur the borders more than a map of Africa. He heard Gladys' muffled alarm at least twice, and someone rummaging around the kitchen, all well before the light gave a hint of welcoming Sunday. In between, his sleep-movies starred Annie, huddled and pregnant as she walked the penstock trail in tears, and Shipton plunging down to the rocks and river below, amid scores of viewers clapping and cheering his bloody demise. The wind blew the entire night, creaking and groaning about the old building in a mournful dirge. Cynthia telephoned at two-thirty, fulfilling her promise to let Dean know when she'd safely arrived. Her voice told him she was as bone-weary as he from her exhausting trip. Mom was "resting comfortably," the only news a night volunteer at the hospital would convey. Cynthia was staying at her mother's apartment with plans to visit the hospital first thing in the morning where she could speak with the doctor and learn more of her mother's condition. He called her again as soon as he rose, but she had apparently left earlier as there was no answer.

Fred had taken care of the early morning chores as Dean poured himself his first cup of coffee, dreading the inquisition he knew would be forthcoming from the old man. Fred couldn't resist a mystery and here was a riddle on-site. The ever-present list and pencil were poised on the kitchen counter, as if ready for action. But Fred was being unusually patient. He held his conversation to mundane chit-chat.

He informed Dean the climbers, who were due to check out later, had left for the ice park, grumbling at the heavy accumulation of snow which was abating to a last-ditch flurry after depositing thirty inches of fluffy white. Gladys Turnbull was sleeping late, as usual. She was the sole guest remaining in the building as the sisters were off for a Sunday tour of the town. Claire had informed Fred she and Effie would be leaving Tuesday. It was the first words spoken to him by the sharp-tongued woman since the prior Tuesday evening when she'd first purchased the letters.

"If she knows the true story about Annie, she's sure keeping it to herself," Fred muttered as he stacked the breakfast dishes. Dean knew the old man was itching to raise the more important topic of Jerome Shipton's death. He could read Fred like a book—start the conversation with a few benign topics, then ease in. "Looks like it's going to be a mite empty around here in the next few days," Fred continued as he began washing the plates.

"I can use all the peace the good Lord can offer," Dean answered, as toast popped up in a puff of smoke. "Did you set this toaster to 'black' again?"

Fred ignored the question and sat at the table, his patience expired. "The way I see it, we best get ourselves involved in setting this Shipton business straight. If you don't come up with some answers, you're going to find the police at our door, asking you some pretty pointed questions. And when I say police, I don't just mean Jake Weller."

Much as Dean hoped otherwise, he couldn't disagree with Fred. During the night, he'd turned the matter over in his mind, and kept coming back to the fact that someone from Bird Song had killed Shipton and any objective viewer would be taking a long and hard look at David Dean as that person. "This is still Weller's case," he replied. His statement did nothing to slow Fred down.

"There's no doubt in my mind it's the wife who did him in," the old man continued. "It's the only solution that makes sense. I made this here list of everyone I figured who could have done it, and Edith Shipton is right on top."

"Look," Dean said. "We've got about three feet of snow out there that needs shoveling. Why don't you come on out and ask your questions while I'm getting something done? Just give me two minutes to digest this piece of charcoal," he said, biting into the blackened toast. Fred didn't have a chance to bellyache at the compromise before the phone interrupted.

It was Jake Weller, sounding annoyed at the world. "You're sticking around town, right?"

"Why?"

"You're not thinking of going up to Indiana are you?"

"If my wife needs me, I am," Dean answered, getting a bit annoyed himself. "What's this all about?"

"'Cause the CBI boys want to talk to you. That's the Colorado Bureau of Investigation, the State cops. They're sort of moving in on this," he answered.

"Fine," said Dean. "If I'm here, I'll talk to them. If I'm not here, screw 'em. My wife comes first. Let 'em arrest me if they think they have a case but I'm not making any schedule to accommodate some jerk's whim to play TV cop." He hung up the phone and stormed out to the hall and donned his winter coat. Not only was he miffed at Weller's attitude, but at the short length of his own fuse. Fred followed but there was little time for conversation. Dean had hardly begun clearing the walk of the deep snow before Jake Weller drove up.

"Am I under arrest?" Dean asked, as he leaned on his shovel.

"Stop being a dickhead. I'm on your side." Dean returned to the job of moving the mounds of white. Weller continued, "That's why I'm in deep shit." Dean stopped and looked up. "The state boys are real interested in this. I got a nice strong feeling they're blocking me out of the picture."

"Why? It's not supposed to work that way, is it? How did they get involved?"

"It's all jurisdictional bullshit. I was on the scene of Shipton's swan dive with Mountain Rescue but it happened inside the city line so it's the City of Ouray's territory. They called in CBI when they heard about the cut rope and smelled a major problem."

"What 'problem'?"

"I got the word from this friend, an old maid clerk who likes me 'cause I didn't treat her like shit like everyone else does. She tells me I'm out of the loop. The state boys figure I'm too close to you to be what somebody calls 'objective'."

"Is Shipton still alive?" Fred asked.

"No one is even saying that much. That's another funny thing."

"So, it's my turn in the barrel?" Dean asked. "I thought you said they were getting ready to spread Shipton's body parts around to the sick and needy and then plant what was left. What happened?"

"Damned if I know. The whole business is hush-hush. My guess is Shipton either said something to someone before he croaked or he's still alive and talking. I thought he was a goner before we even got him out of the gorge. Everyone was pretty damn busy wrapping him up to haul him out of there, just trying to keep him alive. His head was bloody, he looked like shit, and at least one of the medics thought he was already dead. It doesn't make a whole lot of sense. That's a hell of a distance to fall and live to chit-chat about it." The lawman climbed into his Cherokee. "Don't tell the big boys I gave you a heads-up on this." He started the vehicle and left.

Dean managed to whistle down a young boy who agreed to use his snow blower on Dean's unfinished sidewalk, for an amount Dean considered ridiculous, but he knew he needed to get up to snuff on Shipton's fall before he was totally on the defensive. Thankfully, Janet arrived to take up the inside tasks of Bird Song. Dean let Fred follow along, list in hand, as he poked into Edith's room, which Jerome had recently shared.

The room remained basically unchanged. Most of the climbing gear was absent, presumably picked up by Weller at the ice park. There was an empty sack which had contained the climbing rope but it was empty and Dean put it aside. There remained a second rope, various books on the sport of ice climbing and a few pitons. All of the luggage was still strewn about the room. Only Donnie's clothes were neatly stacked. Neither Shipton appeared to consider tidiness a high priority. A half-burned candle sat in a dish on the bureau, perhaps signs of Edith's fascination with the last century. Dean found nothing useful until he looked in the trash.

Crumpled in the waste paper basket was a small piece of white paper with a telephone number. It began with the digits 3-2-5, indicative of a Ouray number. Dean recognized the rest of the number as belonging to Janet O'Brien.

"What in hell would Jerome Shipton be doing with Janet's telephone number?" Dean asked, as much to himself as Fred O'Connor.

"Maybe she dropped it herself, when she was cleaning," Fred answered.

"Janet's not Jeopardy material but she ought to be able to remember her own phone number."

Fred peered at the paper. "It's not her writing. She writes itsy-bitsy numbers. I've seen her grocery list. I wonder where Shipton got it."

"Probably from the men's room wall at a local bar," Dean grumbled. " More importantly, I wonder why he has it."

"Let's ask her," Said Fred. But before they could do so, they were interrupted.

Gladys Turnbull, wrapped in a scarlet robe, stuck her head in the room. "Oh, she said, rubbing the sleep from her eyes, "I thought Mrs. Shipton was back." Before they could answer, she turned on her heels and stumbled back to her quarters, diagonally across the hall.

Dean frowned, perturbed at being discovered scrounging through Shipton's belongings, but he continued. However, his endeavors were unsuccessful. The pair returned to the first floor where they located Janet O'Brien dusting the parlor. While she denied any knowledge of her phone number being in Shipton's room, Dean questioned if she was telling the truth. He and Fred retired to Dean's quarters, having made no progress.

"I figure the killer planted the knife, just to throw the cops off the trail," Fred said as he slumped on the edge of the bed. "She cut the rope, then high-tailed it back to the bridge."

"Without being seen by anyone?" Dean asked, more to humor Fred than anything else.

"Maybe she wore a disguise," Fred offered as the phone rang. It was Cynthia.

"She looks terrible," she said when he asked about her mother. "She has all these tubes and wires coming out of her. It was really upseting. But then she woke up and smiled at me. That was worth the trip. The doctor says the next few hours and days will tell the difference. They are yet to assess the amount of damage to the heart."

"I wish I could be there with you," he answered. He didn't tell her of his escalating concerns over the Shipton case, nor, surprisingly did she ask about it. They spoke for a few moments and she promised to call again in the evening when, perhaps, she'd have more information.

Dean decided to take matters into his own hands. He left Bird Song, telling Janet where he was going and together with Fred, hiked up to the ice park to where Shipton had fallen. The crowds were lighter than yesterday, due to the heavy snowfall making not only climbing difficult, but viewing a wet and laborious task. A yellow police tape blocked off the area where Shipton had belayed for his ill-fated drop. The pair tramped further to the next closest point where they could see his line of descent to the river far below. A large outcropping of rock made it impossible for a climber more than just a few feet below the edge, to see anyone above him. The location was somewhat isolated from the rest of the path and climbing area.

"Long way down there," Fred commented, as he cautiously peered over the side. The observation mirrored Dean's thoughts precisely.

"He couldn't have fallen all that way and survived," he answered.

"Maybe he bounced on some of that snow and it broke his fall."

"There wasn't near as much snow early yesterday and it's too loosely packed to provide much of a cushion. Besides, the last fifty feet is still straight down."

"Maybe the rope didn't bust loose until he was part way. She could have partially cut it."

"Either that, or someone up here waited until he was out of sight before they took out the knife. That would be less risky and make more sense."

"Kind of lets you off the hook, don't it?" the old man said with a smile. "If Shipton was far enough over the edge, close enough to the bottom and the river to survive the fall, how could he see you hacking away at his rope? If he wasn't that far, how come he's still around to point fingers?"

"Good observation," Dean answered, nodding in agreement. He walked back from the edge and looked around. Even though the position was more isolated than a number of the other starting points, it still was in relatively plain view of the walkway, both up and down stream.

"Someone would have to be damn gutsy to sit here and hack away at a rope and hope no one saw them," Fred said. Dean smiled at a pair of climbers rounding a bend in the trail and waited for them to pass before responding.

"I suppose no one would pay much attention," he answered. "Most of the climbers have partners up here with their gear, ready to help. There aren't many fools climbing alone. The big problem would be hoping no one remembered seeing you."

"It was snowing pretty heavily about that time. Makes recognizing anyone a tad more difficult."

"Yes,' Dean said. "And damn near impossible to see anything from down below, even if the overhang didn't block the view." He added, "It conveniently covers up any footprints or evidence up here too. I'm surprised anyone found the knife in the snow." He took one last look and started back down the path.

As Dean and his stepfather neared the bridge, they looked up to see a uniformed City of Ouray police man pointing at him. Next to the officer was a stern looking man in a suit and tie, arms crossed, staring straight ahead.

"Cheezit, the cops!" Fred said.

"Ten bucks says I know who he's looking for," Dean answered.

"No takers here." Just then, the man waved the cop away and began moving toward the pair, but not before giving a nod to second man Dean hadn't noticed. The partner, the younger of the two, began to circle to his left. Dean supposed this was his idea of being subtle while trying to cut off the open path.

"Looks like they've got us desperadoes. Ready for the big shoot out?"

"Naw," Fred answered. "Let's turn ourselves in and get a high priced lawyer."

"Mr. Dean?" The first man asked.

"Officer Livingston, I presume," Dean replied.

"No. It's Fitzgerald, Detective Fitzgerald," he said, without a hint of a smile. "Would you please come with us?"

"Only if you're going where I'm going, and for me, that's home."

The detective, who looked to be about fifty, started to take Dean's arm. Dean glared at him. "If you touch me, I'm liable to get really pissed." The man seemed to consider, aware of the small crowd whose attention was drawn to the group.

"Listen, Buster...." Fred said, moving closer to the tall lawman.

"Take a hike, pop." Fitzgerald answered but Dean intervened, grabbing the old man's arm. "Come on, Fred. It'll be just like reading a cheap thriller." He began walking down the road before Fitzgerald could protest further.

"Your home is fine," Fitzgerald answered, sounding irritated as he moved to follow them. Cop two remained a dozen steps behind them as if to let the pair know they'd better do as they were told.

Dean knew from his prior life the pair were just doing their job but that didn't mean he had to like being watched like a street felon. He and Fred walked down the road, unfortunately meeting a half-dozen friends from town en route. Fred grumbled, but Dean just slapped his back and began to whistle, as if he didn't have a care in the world, while his mind turned like a racecar piston on the final lap.

Two unmarked State cars were parked in front of Bird Song, along with, to Dean's surprise, Edith's rental car and Donald Ryland's Explorer. As they came in sight of the building, two men were lugging Shipton's belongings to a waiting car.

"Hail, hail, the gang's all here," Dean said as he climbed the front stairs.

Janet met him at the door, looking ready to cry. Dean wasn't sure if it was her natural aversion to anything involving law enforcement or concern for her boss's future. He tossed her an it's-all-right and, ignoring three more strangers in suits and the crowded parlor, went directly to the phone. Fitzgerald made a move to stop him, but John Wayne's twin with a bigger belly in a grey suit shook his head. Dean telephoned Cynthia's mother's number and his wife answered on the first ring.

He stared the others away while he spoke with her. He had been fortunate to catch her on lunch break from her bedside vigil at her mother's apartment. Mother slept constantly, Cynthia said, but according to the doctor, her progress was "as expected." No, she still wasn't out of the woods, but everyone seemed pleased at her responses to date.

"How is...everything there?" Cynthia asked. Dean didn't want to lie, but he had no intention of causing more concern than Cynthia was already carrying.

"The cops are here to do their bit. Most of the guests are ready to check out. The place will pretty much empty out by morning. Everything's under control." He crossed his fingers on the last statement.

As he finished the conversation, Donald Ryland emerged from his room, looking as if his dog had died.

"Welcome back to Bird Song," Dean said.

"Yeah, thanks. Do you always provide a police escort?" He moved closer to Dean, out of earshot of the waiting investigators. "What did you do, waste the bastard? All these guys want to talk about is David Dean. When I heard someone killed Shipton, I was sure it was Edith, but the cops aren't even looking at her. All she does is bawl. What an effing zoo!"

Penny and the balance of the climbers stomped in the door, led by yet another suit. They too were not pleased and, to Dean's chagrin, tracked the front hall with the remnants of the piss-poor shoveling job on the front walk.

"Why don't you tell Heinrich here we don't know shit about Shipton so we can get back to enjoying ourselves?" Penny said, glaring at the officer as she tapped the handle of a sinister looking ice ax. "The Gestapo is making noises about keeping us here overnight, if you can believe it! Like some people don't have to go to work tomorrow."

"I'll see what I can do," Dean answered. He turned, and entered the parlor.

Edith Shipton was standing by the fireplace, sobbing, Ryland was ready to swing on Fitzgerald, Claire Quincy was protesting something in the corner while Effie just looked bewildered. Gladys Turnbull, all smiles, was frantically taking notes. Fred was snuggled up on the sofa, next to the only woman member of the law-folk group.

The John Wayne look-alike with the big belly was in charge and held up his hand for attention. He cleared his throat, as if ready to address a Rotary luncheon. He introduced himself as Emile Corday, with the Colorado Bureau of Investigation.

"Please, everyone, return to your rooms except Mr. Dean. Just wait there. We'll call you when we need you."

"Look," Mick said. "Most of us have to get on the road. How long is this going to take?"

"We'll work as quickly as possible but this is an important and serious investigation." He stared at Dean. "It depends how cooperative everyone is."

"Anyone got a good recipe for cake-with-file?" Dean asked with a smile as the others began to follow the orders to leave the room.

"This isn't a laughing matter, Mr. Dean," Corday said sternly, although most of the departing guests thought otherwise.

"No, I don't suppose it is. But I've got to tell you, it looks pretty funny to see this many suits and uniforms in Ouray on the same day. I bet that hasn't happened since they buried the last mayor."

Mick, trailing behind with Penny, called over his shoulder, "Why don't you just round up all of Shipton's enemies, rent a stadium and interview them?"

Penny laughed, then covered her mouth. Corday glowered at her. "Well," she said, "he hit on me the first time I set eyes on him. I laughed in the jerk's face. He was a total asshole."

Fred sat down on the sofa, staking out his territory, letting the world know he had every intention of sticking around. Gladys paused by the door.

"How do you spell your last name, officer?" she asked the leader of the pack.

"Emile Corday, ma'am. C-o-r-d-a-y."

Gladys smiled some more. "This is so exciting," she giggled as she backed out of the room.

Fred squirmed to a more comfortable position. "Aren't you supposed to ask him if he wants a lawyer?"

"Do you?" Corday asked, directing his question to Dean.

"Only if you're paying for it."

"You don't look indigent."

"I'm not. I'm just cheap. Why should I pay a hundred bucks an hour for some guy to tell me not to answer questions I don't mind answering in the first place?"

"You're willing to voluntarily speak to us?"

Dean realized from his past experience that being forthcoming and subjecting himself to interrogation without an attorney was naive but the entire idea of his trying to kill Shipton was so ludicrous in his mind, he tended to minimize the seriousness of the situation. He sat next to Fred on the sofa. "Sure, let's talk. But shouldn't Sheriff Weller be here?"

"Your very good friend Sheriff Weller is busy chasing speeders and bike-nappers. This is our investigation. We're here at the invitation of the Ouray Police Department," Fitzgerald said, not even attempting to hide the chill in his voice.

Dean stared at him, but was lost for a snippy response. "Why don't you cut down on the troops here? We don't need the entire brigade. If about eighty percent of your help left town maybe my nice country inn wouldn't look like Dillinger's hideout and we could get down to business and wrap this up. But please, let's not play silly games like good-cop, bad-cop and all that bullshit."

Corday nodded to the others who slowly left the room until he and Fitzgerald were the only two officers remaining. Corday looked at Fred, seemed to consider asking him to leave and then decided he'd best leave well enough alone. Fred had his pencil and pad at the ready.

Dean got right to it. "Maybe we can all save some time if we skip the part where you ask the questions and I just go ahead and answer them. No, I didn't kill Shipton, or try to kill him by cutting his rope. Yes, I was up at the ice park when he fell, but no, there's no one to alibi me—I was off alone on the upper trail. Yes, I did try to punch his lights out in front of half the town. Yes, it's my knife Weller found up there and no, I don't have any idea how it got there. Yes, I despised the son of a bitch, especially after he grabbed my wife's breast ten feet away from me. No, I don't have any information on who killed him, but yes, there's a pretty damn long list." He stopped to catch his breath.

Fitzgerald slumped, with an annoying roll of his eyes and an "I've-seen-it-all-before" look on his chubby face. He pulled out a fingernail clipper and began clipping his nails, sending little white crescents flying about the room. Dean glared at him, with no result. He was in no mood to exercise patience.

"Get the hell out of my inn," he said with a snarl, finally getting the detective's attention. He looked up. Dean repeated his demand.

"Look, asshole," Fitzgerald grunted. "If you haven't noticed, I'm a cop and I'm here investigating a crime. And I'll stay put as long as it takes."

"You may be a cop, but you're also an obnoxious slob who's soiling a clean carpet with your discarded body parts. Corday is the only one doing any investigating and he's the only one I'm inviting to stay. You were not invited and I'm telling you to get out. Now."

Fitzgerald started to say something but Corday grimaced, let out a long sigh and nodded for the younger detective to leave. Fitzgerald looked mad enough to take a swing.

"There's nothing I hate more than a cop who thinks he can make his own rules, Dean. Your ass is grass and I'm a lawn mower. Remember that." He ambled out of the room, but Dean didn't hear the front door close and assumed he was an earshot away in the hall.

"Do you guys bother with a trial around here or do you just draw lots and send us blood thirsty killers directly over to Cañon City?"

"Don't mind Fitzgerald. He gets a bit vexatious at times."

"Let's get on with this," Dean said.

"Were you sleeping with Mrs. Shipton?" Corday asked the question as casually as if he was inquiring about the weather.

Fred, who had been taking it all in, gave a snort of laughter. Dean himself smiled and shook his head. "Of course not. That's preposterous!" He added, "And offensive."

"Why did Mrs. Shipton choose Bird Song to visit?"

"Ask her. She chose Ouray, at least according to Ryland, because he was her son's father and he was coming here to ice climb." He added, "I have no idea how she picked my inn."

"Why did you tell Jerome Shipton his wife wasn't registered here?"

Dean sighed. "Look, Edith Shipton had just poured her heart out to my wife and me that she had run away from an abusive husband and was hiding. She was petrified he'd follow her, by tracing her credit card receipts, so much so she'd registered under an assumed name. I thought she was just being paranoid, like some bad TV nonsense. Then five minutes later, some guy calls asking for her, by name! I didn't lie to him when I told him no one named *Shipton* was registered at Bird Song but I saw no reason to go out of my way and help him either."

"You know," Corday said. "Us guys in law enforcement see so much shit, sometimes it gets to us. I can't really blame the ones that step over the line once in awhile. We know, we're the damn law, aren't we? That ought to count for something, give us a little leeway. Sometimes we just have to act on what we see, don't we? Screw the rules. Some asshole like Shipton, he doesn't deserve to be around. Just waste him. Nobody much gives a damn anyway. Right? I bet you've seen stuff like that back East, seeing as you were a big city cop and all. We know you and your good buddy Jake Weller played it fast and loose last summer when that guy Glick got killed. Who's gonna blame you here? You say this shithead was feeling up your wife right under your nose. Hell, I'd have been pissed too if someone was trying to pork my woman. I'd probably have wasted him myself."

A myriad of emotions flooded over Dean as Corday spoke. First and foremost was an overwhelming urge to punch his lights out but past similar responses hadn't produced positive results. He could feel himself getting redder as the man spoke, but for once, he held his temper. "I won't even give that speech the benefit of a response," Dean answered, trying to sound calm.

Corday just shrugged and began asking questions about Dean's background. Dean assumed Corday already knew most of the answers. The conversation droned on for twenty minutes but Dean was never read his rights nor, surprisingly, was the interview recorded. Corday never volunteered any information and when Dean asked him outright if Shipton was still alive, the officer ignored the question and changed the subject. Few queries were related to the other guests and

Dean withdrew from volunteering as much information as he had in his opening monologue.

Finally, his patience wore thin. "Is Shipton accusing me? Because if he is, he's either grossly mistaken, a damned liar or setting me up! Someone cut that rope, but it wasn't me." Corday gave Dean an I-don't-believe-you look.

"Have you been in Shipton's room?" Corday asked.

Dean remembered Shipton's luggage and the container that held the rope. His prints would be on them and they were now in the possession of the police. "Sure," he answered. "This is an inn and someone has to keep it cleaned." More raised eyebrows.

Corday rose, and asked, not quite casually enough. "When is your wife returning?"

Of all the questions Corday had asked, for some reason, this one made Dean's heart do an extra skip.

CHAPTER 19

The police spoke to Fred next, while Dean strolled back toward his quarters, with Corday's question concerning his wife's return echoing in his mind. That, coupled with Cynthia's strange behavior at the news of Shipton's fall bothered him far more than he'd allowed himself to believe. Yes, Shipton whispered the name *Dean* to Jake Weller, but perhaps he didn't mean David Dean! He kept remembering Cynthia's earlier revelation that, in certain circumstances, killing someone wasn't a totally preposterous idea. But then he pictured his beautiful wife, her unfailingly sweet and kind nature, and refused his mind's picture of her kneeling there in the snow, calmly sawing Shipton's rope until it parted, plunging him to his bloody death.

Most of Bird Song's other guests remained, as requested, in their own rooms but Ryland hung around the kitchen, sharing a snack of take-out pizza with Donnie while Edith sat nearby, wringing her hands and looking petrified. Dean stuck his head in the room as he passed. He hadn't spoken to Edith Shipton since her husband's accident and felt, as the host of Bird Song, he owed the woman some sort of condolence. However, in view of the Shipton couple's unconventional estrangement, he wasn't sure what words might be appropriate.

"Sorry for your troubles." That sounded general enough, but her strange response set him back a beat.

"Do you think he's dead?" she asked, looking as if the words 'Boy, I hope so!' were on the tip of her tongue. She looked terrible—red-eyed, no make up and dark roots beginning to show through her Annie Quincy blonde. She wore a tee shirt with no bra, perhaps in some vague attempt to emulate Penny, but with only a fraction of the appropriate equipment.

Dean caught his breath before answering her inelegant question. "I don't know if your husband is still alive. The police aren't being very candid with me. They're too busy trying to lock me up and toss the key."

"Oh, they can't be serious! You didn't do it!" Then, with a total change of subject she rambled forward, "I've been reading about Annie. My Donnie's been showing me her writings. Your wife let him make a copy. It's so sad. The poor woman is just like me. We both have a child in our bodies and don't know what to do about it." She turned to Ryland, who looked like he wanted to volunteer for disappearance in the witness protection program. Dean itched to ask her how she was so sure it wasn't Mr. David Dean who dropped her hubby into space but she began to sob anew, making any further conversation impossible.

Dean returned to his quarters where in less than five minutes Fred joined him, annoyed at the brevity of his inquisition. Effie Quincy was next in the hot seat, according to Fred. It appeared, excepting Dean, the line was forming in descending order of potential culpability. That ought to make Edith Shipton dead last by Dean's calculation.

Dean knew Fred was chomping at the bit to dig into this caper, as he called it, but just to flip his switch a bit, Dean started the conversation with the old man's love life. "Are you giving Miss Worthington another night off?" he asked as Fred sat across from him at the office desk.

"She's off to Hawaii to visit her daughter, but you and me have got more important things to do. Look, son," Fred continued. "This here business is serious. These boys have tunnel vision, you're at the end of the dark and the train's on time."

"I'm beginning to believe you," Dean grumbled. "They don't have a strong case, but if I'm the only one they're looking at, someone's going to get away with murder. I wish I knew Shipton's condition and what, if anything he saw or told them he saw. The police haven't even informed his wife if her husband is dead or alive!"

Fred wet his pencil and frowned like a college professor. "It's not like they're dealing with a couple of novices here. You and me have beaten this bush a few times before, partner. Now, let's put our heads together and do this right. Proper detective work calls for an orderly investigation." Dean smiled, in spite of himself as Fred continued. "Now, when's the last time you saw that jackknife Claudia gave you last summer?"

Dean had pondered that very question during his sheep-counting hours the prior night. "In the parlor," he answered. "The same evening your picture from the museum turned up missing. The night you got screwed out of the gold coins by Claire Quincy. Last Tuesday. Remember? She used the knife to open the comb."

"I'll bet she swiped it, too," Fred said. "I'm sure she took the picture of the Rev. Martin and his missus."

"Don't jump to conclusions. We're supposed to be tackling this business in an orderly fashion, remember?"

Fred made appropriate notes, then asked, "Who was in the room when the knife disappeared?" He answered his own question. "The three of us, you, me and Cynthia, plus the two Quincy gals, Edith and her son, young Donnie. Jerome Shipton didn't show up for a day or two and Ryland hadn't arrived yet either."

"Ryland came later that same evening," Dean added. "He could have picked up the knife from the table. Don't forget Gladys Turnbull was registered, too, even though I think she stayed in her room. And Tuesday night Martha slept over."

"Criminy," Fred said, "I'm running out of paper!"

"Think positive. The ice climbers hadn't shown up yet. But let's be reasonable. We can't suppose the knife was originally taken with any murderous intent. Shipton wasn't even in Ouray yet so no one could have been planning to use it to kill him. If that's the case, then why would someone take the knife in the first place? Who would want it? The logical answer is a child—Donnie or Martha, picking it up out of curiosity."

"You're not saying they...?"

"Tried to kill Shipton? Hell, no. But if one of them was just playing with it, then he or she might have left it anywhere. The killer could have found it days later. Better get more paper. Your list is getting longer." Fred grumbled a bit, but Dean just laughed. "Back to reality. Just thinking a guy's a jerk doesn't usually result in your killing him. Let's look for the person who would either benefit from Shipton's death or hated him strongly enough to cut his rope. That should make for a shorter list."

"I got my pencil ready. Give me your short list."

Dean thought a moment. "While I'm not disagreeing with you that Edith looks like the best candidate, in my mind she's still the flavor of the month at the fruitcake sale. My guess is someone did a bit of planning for Jerome Shipton's big fall, and Edith hasn't demonstrated any real talent for long-range thinking. The killer brought the knife up there and made sure they weren't seen. Unless I'm off base, the knife wasn't left by accident. It was left to implicate me. In my mind, that speaks of organizing, not the kind of behavior Edith Shipton has demonstrated."

Fred rubbed his chin in contemplation. "Maybe being so dizzy is an act with her. I read a story once where this here woman pretended to be crazy, eating bugs and stuff like that...."

Dean tuned Fred to the off position until his stepfather floated back to reality and continued. "Here's my short list Fred, for what it's worth. Edith, up top, in spite of what I said. Donald Ryland, although I haven't quite figured why. Gladys, because I saw the venom in her eyes after Shipton took advantage of her."

"Never underestimate a scorned woman," Fred said.

"True, but playing the devil's advocate, I have some problems with Gladys. Whoever cut that rope managed to do so without being seen. Can you picture Gladys sneaking anywhere? It would be like trying to hide a yellow school bus in a Volkswagen showroom. She is one huge and colorful woman."

"Maybe she cut the rope ahead of time."

"We went down that road earlier. The rope was cut at the top, within reach of where it was fastened. Either Jerome Shipton would have seen the cut and not used the rope, or he would have fallen so far he'd be whispering to Lucifer, not Jake Weller. No, whoever sliced Jerome Shipton's line did so after he'd partially descended. That's the only scenario that makes sense."

Fred nodded in agreement. "Let's get back to the list. Claire Quincy is another one who should be there. She's on all my lists—short, long and in between."

Dean smiled. "Claire Quincy is no saint in anyone's book, but her motive is a mite on the thin side, isn't it?"

"These here genealogy folks take that stuff mighty seriously. Remember, she said her brother was writing a book about the family. If Shipton let her know he knew all the dirt on Annie's past, that might throw a kibosh on the whole business. Maybe she decided to snuff him out, to keep him quiet."

Dean laughed. "If Shipton did, in fact, bust her chops over the fact Annie Quincy was a hooker, who knows, she might hate him enough to do something nasty. But kill him? She'd have to realize if Shipton knew about Annie, so did a bunch of us. I don't see her plotting to knock us all off. I suppose if she were mad enough at him, she might kill him but I could visualize her whacking him over the head with a library book more than sneaking up to the ice park and cutting his rope—and then going to the trouble to blame it on me."

"Maybe, but trying to put the blame on you would be right up her alley. What about her sister?"

"Sweet Effie? Come on, Fred. Now, that's a full-length stretch. Why? To protect her sister?"

"I'll put her on my middle list, not the short one," he grumbled. "Who else?"

"I suppose we have to list young Donnie. He's a troubled kid and we know he has no love for his stepfather. The boy is smart enough to see what Shipton was doing to his mother and he's the most logical one to have taken the knife in the first place. I'd hate to think a child his age would try to kill someone, whatever the reason, but I have to admit it's a possibility. Given his size, he would have been less conspicuous up on the trail."

"I saw the boy with his father earlier. He and Ryland were taking pictures. Donald bought him a camera at the Variety store." He scratched his head. "Until we talk to these people, we won't know who was off on his own enough to have an opportunity and who has an alibi."

"That's what the police are supposed to be doing," Dean said, his voice heavy with sarcasm.

"By my read, all the police are doing is making a case against David Dean. That means it's up to you and me to solve this caper." He looked up, his face somber. "That's all of your list?"

"Yup. I can't see any of the ice climbers taking Shipton seriously enough to bother to dump him. He didn't have any significant contact with them that I could see."

Fred rose and began pacing the room. "What about the three of us? We'd sure all be near the top on anyone else's list—anyone who was looking at this business objectively. You're sure number one with them State guys. Maybe Fred O'Connor ought to make the list too." He turned to Dean, and added, "And Cynthia. She sure had a top-notch motive."

Sometimes Dean wished Fred O'Connor wasn't so damned perceptive. This was one road he didn't want to travel. "You're serious, aren't you?" he asked.

"I don't want to be. I love her like she was my daughter, but you said it, a woman's scorn and all that stuff. She sure hated Shipton. With good reason. I didn't want to say it, but I saw her, real close to where Shipton fell. She was hurrying away and looked frightened to death." There was no conversation for a long minute. Then Fred asked, "What did she have to say about Shipton's fall when the two of you drove to the airport?"

Dean just shook his head. "Nothing. She wouldn't talk about it." Then he added, "She was upset about her mother's condition. I didn't press her." Dean leaned back his head. "God, I can't be sitting here considering for even a minute, my wife might be a killer! This is ludicrous!"

Fred put his hand on Dean's shoulder. "Look, if she did go and do something rash, we both know the jerk deserved it. I'm not saying she did try to kill him, but I'm just letting you know I'm with the both of you, all the way, no matter how it comes out. I'll help any way I can."

"Cynthia didn't do it," Dean answered, trying to make his statement sound forceful, but unsure of whom he was trying to convince. "The knife was left up there to implicate me. That certainly wasn't my wife's doing."

"I thought about that too," Fred answered. "That Edgar Poe guy wrote a story about the obvious being overlooked. Why couldn't whoever cut the rope have just dropped the knife by mistake? Especially, if they was in a hurry? Maybe it was left up there to implicate you, but there's a good chance it was just plain dropped by accident."

Before Dean could answer, there was an almost inaudible knock at the door. It was Effie Quincy. She came into the room, glancing over her shoulder like a spy on over time.

"I...I found this," she said, holding out the missing picture of the Reverend and Mrs. Martin. "It must have been picked up by mistake."

Dean couldn't help raising his eyebrows at the obvious lie but when he looked at her tear-stained face, he felt compassion. "What's the problem, Effie?" he asked.

She let herself be led to a corner chair. "It's nothing, really. That policeman upset me, I guess. And Claire is in there now. I don't know what she's going to say."

"Is there something about the accident she knows?" Fred asked, but Effie just shook her head.

She bit her lip. "Claire won't talk to me about it. But she's so pleased Mr. Shipton is dead, it frightens me. It's so unlike her."

"Seems to be some question about that," Fred said. "'bout him being dead, I mean."

"He may still be alive?" she asked. Fred nodded. "Oh, my! Claire will be livid!" She rose and started toward the door.

"Has your sister given any indication Shipton might have told her the truth about Annie Quincy?" Dean asked. Effie just shook her head, turned without a word and hurried from the room.

Fred examined the picture as Dean slumped back in his chair. "She never did say where she *found* it, did she?" Dean said. "Probably in Claire's suitcase. I guess she was afraid the police might search their stuff."

"I'm beginning to wonder which of them ladies is the strangest!"

For the second time in a few minutes, there was a knock on the door. It was Janet O'Brien, telling Dean he had a visitor at the back door. When Dean kicked the door loose from the accumulated snow blown against it, he found Jake Weller dressed in civilian clothes, huddled against the frame of the unshoveled rear entrance.

"Come on in," Dean said. "Why didn't you use the front door? You look like the poor little match boy." Weller had tromped through several feet of snow and was white to his thighs.

"Naw," he growled. "Get a coat. Let's walk and talk."

Dean donned coat and boots and joined the lawman. Both high-stepped their way through the deep snow to the plowed alley in the rear of Bird Song.

"So why the cloak and dagger stuff?" Dean asked as he paused beneath a streetlight. Weller prodded him further to the shadows beyond before he answered.

"They cut me out of the investigation. Corday would write me up for just talking to you."

"Why? You haven't done anything wrong. Besides, you don't report to Corday or those guys—he's State, you're County."

"It's all political bullshit. I have to sit back and look like I'm the grateful little kid getting help from the benevolent teacher. What's happening is they don't trust me. Shipton's told them I'm in bed with you against him and if they haven't bought what he said in total, they've sure banked the down payment."

"So Shipton is alive?"

"Yeah. Mums the word on his condition, but he definitely hasn't croaked."

Dean stamped the snow from his boots. "And he's pointing his finger at me."

"And maybe the missus, his wife. He's gone ahead and drawn court papers for the first steps to have her declared a looney and I guess he's hinting at the possibility the two of you are banging each other."

"Corday asked me that directly," Dean said. "I couldn't believe it! The idea is as crazy as the rest of this business!"

"Not if you look at it through Corday's eyes. Corday doesn't know any of the players. Given what he's hearing and seeing now, it makes a heap of sense. Especially if he buys the garbage Shipton is selling. Lord knows what Edith Shipton might say."

"Why the lack of candor on Shipton's condition? They didn't even tell his wife if he's alive or dead. That's pretty unbelievable."

"My source tells me they've snuggled Shipton someplace cozy because he's afraid you'll try to kill him again. You and his wife, maybe. Besides, if they buy the fact Edith Shipton is nuts, maybe they don't feel they owe her the normal concern they'd give a sane spouse. Plus, she *did* leave him."

Dean mopped his brow with his arm, in spite of the cold of the evening. "Thanks for sticking your neck out. Talking to me like this can't be doing your career any good."

Weller just grunted. "What career? Besides, I'm not just doing this to be a real neat buddy, you know. Someone out there is a killer and if Corday has his head up his ass over your guilt, somebody needs to be taking a hard look at what really happened. This is still my county and if I'm the law, nobody is going to get away with murder on my watch."

"Thanks anyway, whatever the reason," Dean answered.

"It pisses me off being shut out. My source with the CBI isn't that privy to what's happening and it's damn tough acting on what I'm not supposed to know."

"Unless they arrest me, I'm still in Bird Song, and that's where all the action is right at the moment. I'll keep you posted on what I hear." Dean slapped his friend on the back. "Besides, you're not alone. Fred O'Connor is busy making a list and checking it twice as we stand here. It's only a matter of time until justice is served."

Weller just rolled his eyes and smiled, but then turned serious. "You watch your ass," he told Dean, pointing his finger for emphasis. "And keep an eye out for Cynthia, too. Your wife's the only other suspect in the eyes of the State boys."

Dean nodded his head, shuffled his feet, but said nothing. A dog barked down the alley and Dean turned to see a man walking a collie as his wife looked on from a doorway. Just a quiet family scene—no murder, no accusations. He looked up to see the stars beginning to twinkle as the clouds moved out. He took a deep breath of the clear evening air. But Dean had no time to enjoy this tranquility. There was work to be done before the return of this sense of small town peace could to be fully embraced. "Thanks, Jake," he said. "We'll make it through this mess somehow."

"Keep poking and listening," Weller said as he turned toward the street. "You never can tell what might crop up."

Dean returned to his quarters without being seen and found Fred still at work on his notes. He filled in his stepfather on his conversation with Weller as the two shared a macaroni dinner Fred had heated up. When they finished eating, Dean sat back to think.

Fred lowered his voice. "I been peeking out the door when I hear someone coming down stairs. They've talked with Ryland, Gladys, Edith and even Janet. They're starting on the ice climbers but they're only taking about five minutes with each of 'em. I think Penny is in there now."

"She'll give them their money's worth," Dean commented.

There was a knock on the door and before Dean could respond, Corday entered.

"When's your wife due back?" he asked, absent any preamble.

Dean answered him with a cold stare. "Her mother had a heart attack. She'll come back when she's satisfied her mother's condition warrants it."

"We want to talk to her."

Dean gave him a that's-your-problem shrug, then added, "If she had any information she would have told me." I think, Dean thought to himself.

Corday wasn't a happy camper. "Look," he said. "I went along with your silly nonsense and kicked Fitzgerald out. Frankly, I agree he was being a pain in the ass, but you quit being a detective when you left the East—we're the guys still on the job. Why don't you just let us do our work and stick to answering our questions? Give me her phone number in Indiana." Dean hesitated. "Don't give me any shit that you don't have it," Corday added. Dean had no ready alternative. He considered switching a digit and feigning a mistake but he knew these guys would figure he was hiding something and be all the more aggressive when they questioned Cynthia. He tore a sheet of paper from Fred's pad and scribbled the number. Corday left without so much as a thank-you.

There was ample evidence of Cynthia's reluctance to discuss some element of Shipton's accident and Dean was just as reluctant to subject her to police interrogation. He tried to convince himself the reason was the burden she carried with her mother's illness, but deep down, he knew that was only partially true. He hastily dialed Cynthia's mother's number, as Fred stood guard at the slightly opened door. He crossed his fingers that he was ahead of the police, and his wife would be there to answer. Miracle of miracles, Cynthia picked up the phone on the first ring. Dean told her the police wanted to question her. "I had to give them your number," he said, trying to keep his voice low.

"I don't want to talk to them," she answered, the nervousness apparent in her voice. "At least not now. Not yet." Then she added, "I know I'm not being fair, but please, let me do this my way. I haven't had time to even think about it."

He thought a moment. "Don't answer the phone when it rings. When I call, I'll only ring twice. Then I'll do it again, twice. The third time, answer it—it'll be me."

She let out a deep sigh. "Did you give them mother's address?"

"No. But when they can't contact you by phone, they'll come back to me. I'll try to make myself scarce." Dean wondered if his phone might be tapped. While this seemed a bit absurd, the more he thought about being the prime candidate in an attempted murder, with his wife a close second, the more he considered the phone tap a real possibility. Perhaps not yet, but soon.

"I'll use our phone card and call from uptown," he told his wife. After mutual love-you's, he hung up.

Fred suggested the pair speak with Edith, Ryland and the others, but Dean pointed out the difficulty in doing so while Corday continued his interviews in the parlor. Fitzgerald, too, was lurking somewhere about the premises. Besides, the long day had blurred both their minds to the point of uselessness and Fred punctuated every sentence with a yawn. As the mistress of Tara had said, tomorrow is another day.

Dean felt the beginnings of a headache creep along the base of his neck as he tried to concentrate on who, among the cast of characters cloistered snugly in Bird Song, might have been responsible for Jerome Shipton's fall. He admitted none of the mental scenarios circling his tired brain made a lick of sense. He closed his eyes and leaned back his head. Fred, seeing that further discussion was fruitless, excused himself. He was obviously as worn out as Dean, feeling all of his seventy-six years. Dean put out the office light and undressed for bed. As he reached for the bedside lamp, he noticed Annie Quincy's notebook where Cynthia had been working on it. Between Cynthia's and Donnie's efforts, only a few pages of the journal remained undeciphered. As tired as Dean was, he still felt a pang of curiosity about the life of this long-ago prostitute. He picked up the pencil and word key and, stifling a yawn, began to decode the notebook.

CHAPTER 20

Mrs. Cummings was taken away to the Sister's hospital this forenoon and I fear she shan't ever return. Her son has been called from Denver and is to arrive tomorrow on the afternoon train. My heart is empty as I have no doubt he'll dismiss me if his mother does, in fact, pass on to her final reward. This I am sure will occur if he is to guess my condition, which grows more noticeable as my time draws closer.

My dearest Joshua has been absent for near a week now, bound to the duties of his calling, and those of his wife who is much involved in the charities of our city. I am alone in this house, with only a cat for company though he gives me little solace. My world shrinks with each passing day. On Monday I dared venture to Main Street to replenish our near-empty larder. I passed Skinny Nelly who looked the other way as I neared her. It made me cry that I, who so short a time past was one of their ranks, is now shunned by a member of even this, the lowest profession.

I've nowhere to turn. These last days I've begun to understand this and come to the dreaded decision of what is to become of me. Of us, our child and me, as now we are one.

I read a passage in a novel last evening as I sat by the fire, trying to wile away these idle hours. A woman, dreaming of her pending marriage, scratched in tiny letters with her diamond, 'So in love, says everyone,' on the pane of her bedroom window. The words fell from my lips as softly as the tears from my eyes, I so wished the world could know of the love I hold for you.

With loving hands, dear Joshua, I did the same. I took the ring you gave me and I too scratched that identical message on my bedroom window, the very same room where you and I have stolen our few hours together. My letters are so small none will ever see my mis-

sive, but there it will remain and give me strength for what I am now resigned I must do.

I have unfastened the silken cord from the drapes and knotted it to the gas fixture above. It hangs there, waiting for me to step upon this velvet chair where I sit, tie its far descending end to my neck, and step from this world, freeing it from the guilt and troubles Annie Quincy has caused.

I only ask this of you, my dearest Joshua; that you not tell my family how I lived, and that you mourn not my passing. I would choose not to alter a single element of my life if in so doing it would eliminate even an instant of the time we're spent together. But you have your life and your duties to others and I must stop wounding your conscience and let you go your destined way. I thank my God that I too had you, if only for a little while. Believe in your heart forever how very much I loved you.

Dean awoke Monday morning with Annie Quincy's words still ringing in his ears, and the phone ringing on his nightstand. He answered it, muttered a few words, and hung up. Still half asleep, he glanced at the clock and was shocked to see he'd failed to set his alarm. It was after eight, long past his usual wake-up time. With a disgruntled look on his face he hurriedly dressed and shuffled out to the kitchen where Fred O'Connor was munching on a doughnut and holding a glass of Ovaltine.

"Good afternoon," Fred said with a smile.

"Thanks for covering for me," Dean muttered as he poured himself a cup of coffee.

"Who was on the phone?"

"Get ready to grab your dust mop, Harriet. Us upstairs maids are on duty today."

"Janet?"

"Yup. That was Martha on the phone. It seems her aunt is a bit under the weather, again."

"Too much time bellying up to the bar?" Fred drained his glass and stacked it in the dishwasher.

"Give the poor woman a break. She only goes tavern-traipsing on days that end in Y." He sat at the table and picked up a piece of pastry. "Where is everybody?"

"Let's see," said Fred, counting on his fingers. "The ice climbers decided to get in a quick climb and blame their delay returning home on the cops. Donald is out ice climbing, too. He flew out of here like a rock off a kid's sling shot. His son went with him. My guess is any place Edith ain't is where you'll find Ryland for a while. Edith is, as them English novels say, 'in seclusion'—probably plotting how to wrap up Donald and take him home. Miracle of miracles, Gladys is awake and it ain't even noon yet. She's pecking away on her story—has been, most of the night. She came down long enough to eat a dozen biscuits before she beat it back upstairs. The Quincys are out, taking pictures around town and then off to the library. So says Effie. Claire still's not talking to me."

"No sign of Corday and his army of storm troopers?"

"Nope. At least not yet." He looked over to his stepson. "You in the mood for a suggestion?"

"Sure. My mind isn't donating any words of wisdom that make a lick of sense."

"Take off for the day. It's beautiful out there, as warm as Patty at a picnic. I've got this place under control. If you ain't here, Corday and the police can't ask you questions you might not want to answer, like what's Cynthia's Indiana address. Stuff like that."

Dean smiled at the generous offer. "There's a lot to do around here with Janet AWOL and a bunch of newly empty rooms."

"First off, all the ice climbers are leaving so there's no hurry cleaning up what's going to be empty rooms, probably until the weekend. Ryland and the Quincys won't be back until dark."

Plus, Dean thought, it would give the old man a good excuse and ample time for some world-class snooping. He'd even have a shot at Gladys' and Edith's rooms. They would have to be absent for lunch.

"I'll take you up on that offer," Dean answered. "I owe you one."

Fred dipped his voice to a whisper. "It'll give you a chance to telephone to Cynthia, too." Then he added, "Why not give her a long-ring call from here? She won't answer, but just in case the law's got a tap on the line it'll keep 'em off base. They might get a mite suspicious if you didn't try to give her a call." Dean chuckled at the intrigue, but the suggestion made sense. When he finished eating, he called the Indiana number, letting the phone ring a dozen times.

It was after nine when Dean stepped out on the porch. A breath of almost spring-like weather assailed him. It was a signature day in Ouray, better than the best of the area's finest painted or photographed images with the sky so blue, the pines so green and the snow so white, you couldn't paint truer colors with an art store's inventory.

Thursday's storm had roared into town with uncommon severity, bringing with it not only more than two feet of fresh snow, but a wind that set the white stuff a-dancing and swirling about the town, like a wild rhumba or some native fertility rite. But Monday, the dance master played a different tune—a beautiful Viennese waltz of warm air and sunshine that teased of spring, still months in the future. The town's promenaders were clothed in sweaters at most, with only tee shirts adequate in the brilliant sun. One hearty soul was clothed in shorts, as if trying to wow his neighbors with an out of season, near full body tan.

Dean took a look at the thawing street in front of Bird Song and went out back and unhooked his bicycle. Why let a hint of spring pass by unutilized? He donned biking clothes, packed a jacket and sweater in his pannier and set off in pursuit of a few peaceful moments in one of his favorite worlds. Hoisting the lightweight bike to his shoulders, he walked to the paved Main Street before mounting. It was a long, slow glide, mostly downhill toward Ridgway ten miles distant and Dean leaned his head back, as if to clear his over-burdened brain of the confusion of the past few days. While the air remained chilly, especially in the shaded patches, it was so clear and unseasonably warm Dean hardly noticed. He didn't even mind the rooster tail spray of water from his back tire, the product of the run off from melting snow. If anything, winter biking was more pleasant without playing dodge ball with rushing tourists and campers along the summer-busy, shoulder-less highway. The local vehicles that passed him invariable gave him a wave and a wide berth.

A breeze pushed the last of the storm up the valley, moving it south, toward the mountains behind him. Clouds from the retreating storm looked like a triumphant army, hauling away its ordinance for another engagement—with only white-gray stragglers tagging behind. As he peddled downhill toward Ridgway, he could see the east side of the valley, exposed to the southern sun, had melted nearly clear of snow while across the valley, draped in shadow most of the day, the western slope retained almost all its recent covering.

Dean sped downhill, the temperature dropping in the breeze he created as the steep sides of the narrow valley blocked out all the mid-morning sun. Three or four miles from town, the roadway opened and he slowed, allowing the warmth of the day to soak into his stiff body. He hit a comfortable pace and stayed there as he peddled past the cemetery and the open meadows where a herd of elk grazed near the river to his left, standing at attention near the edge of the tall cottonwoods that lined the bank. Here the road was dry and only a few cars passed him before he drifted past a private hot spring, along the wide curve and by the County fair grounds before entering Ridgway.

Just as he neared the intersection, Dean recognized Corday and Fitzgerald driving toward Ouray. He instinctively ducked his head but the two were paying no heed to a passing biker as they sped south. He was pleased he'd accepted Fred's offer to stay away from Bird Song. He was in no mood to talk to the pair.

Dean paused at the County's sole traffic light, a recent addition and, in some minds, a reluctant bow to progress. Just west of the intersection, he pulled up to Cimarron Books, a small combination bookstore and coffee shop. He asked Priscilla, the owner, for a cup and filled it from one of the coffee dispensers. He then asked if he might use her telephone with his phone card. She obliged with a smile and was polite enough not to question his eccentric dialing pattern and cutting the connection twice before letting it ring. He muttered some lame excuse, feigning making an error. Cynthia finally answered.

There seemed to be improvement in her mother's condition but Cynthia's mood remained subdued. She questioned how the investigation was proceeding and her pointed questions forced him to admit he was the prime suspect.

"That's ridiculous," she exclaimed. "You were a police officer yourself."

Dean pointed out the obvious reasons he was suspected of cutting the rope. He let her know he and Fred were sniffing about in an attempt to determine the real killer. This, however, gave Cynthia little solace.

"I wish the whole business would just go away," she muttered.

"That's not going to happen."

"No," she answered with a sigh. "I don't suppose it is."

Dean wanted to ask when she might return but was hesitant about appearing to hurry her from her mother's bedside. "I miss you," was all he said.

Dean turned at the sound of the shop door opening to see Sheriff Jake Weller standing, hands on hips, staring down at him. "Gotta go," he said to his wife and hung up.

"How's the little lady?" Weller asked

"What do I have, some sort of tracking device stuck in my shorts?" Dean asked.

"Naw. I just recognized your bike. Is your phone at home busted?" he asked as he sat down and asked Priscilla for a coffee. He then added, "Or do you figure it's tapped?"

"Is it?"

Weller smiled. "I'm a law man. I wouldn't be giving out that kind of information now, would I?"

Priscilla handed the Weller a coffee cup without being asked, a sure sign the sheriff was a regular. Then, sensing the need for their privacy, she moved to the far room and began shuffling books.

"Which one of these damn contraptions is the real thing?" Weller asked, eying the dispenser suspiciously. "If there's anything I can't stand it's tutti-fruitti coffee."

Dean motioned to one of the units. "If you're looking for an update on what's happening at Bird Song, you're out of luck."

The sheriff filled his cup. "Today I'm delivering information, not collecting. I got the poop on Shipton's condition. He banged himself up fairly badly—broke a couple of ribs, did something to his knee and leg, whacked his head pretty good and cut up his face. Lots of bruises. The word is he fell a pretty fair distance and bounced a couple of times."

"But he's not in critical condition?"

"Naw. He's bitching a lot about headaches, double vision and memory loss, and wants to see his own doctor but he ain't gonna die." The big man pulled up a chair next to Dean.

"Thanks for telling me. I know you're sticking your neck out just talking to me."

"I been giving that matter a little thought too. I've come to the conclusion I don't really give a shit if I have this job or not." Dean looked up at him, surprised.

"Come on, Jake. You can't be serious. Don't let these state guys get you down. It's just politics. That can't be anything new to you. You must have been fighting bullshit like this since the day you first pinned a badge on your shirt. Give it a couple of days and we'll laugh about it over a beer."

"Naw, it's more than that. Given enough time, I could eat Corday and Fitzgerald for lunch. I've still got some friends and these two will get tired of messing around out here in the boonies. It's just me. I don't feel the same as I used to come Monday mornings. Maybe it's time I hang 'em up. I'll be sixty in the fall. It'd be kinda nice to just think about fishing and TV and not having to wonder what suit is all over my ass because of some dumb new rule. I could collar a dozen perps and someone'd bitch because I didn't line 'em up in alphabetical order."

"You're just mouthing off."

"Maybe. But I never have been worth a damn over the details. I run a good office, but I do it my way, but my way isn't good enough now-a-days." When Dean didn't respond, Weller continued. "I'm not sure I'm up to this job anymore. It's not only the politics." Dean was startled by Weller's seriousness. "Something happened last fall. It kinda stuck in my craw. I was busting up a Friday night drink-out. A bunch of under-agers were boozing it up on beer. They were out in the woods in this spot we all know about. It was going down as usual. I was reading them the riot act and they weren't believing it any more than they ever do, except for maybe the first-timers. Then this one snot-nose gives me the finger. I made a move toward him, and he high-tailed it out of there. I chased him down this bluff but then I started getting pains in my chest and short of breath until I just had to stop."

"Hey, Jake. None of us is as young as he used to be."

"It's wasn't that—I know I'm lugging around thirty extra pounds. But I glance up and this little shit, who looked to be about twelve, is standing on a rock about fifty feet away, laughing his ass off. He knew damn well I couldn't chase him down even if I killed myself trying."

"Did you know who he was?" Dean asked.

"It didn't matter. I was so mad, I unholstered my piece and pointed it right at the little son of a bitch. I know I was doing wrong, but I was so mad, I didn't give a shit. I think I even considered blowing away the little bastard."

Dean sighed. "I imagine you got his attention."

"He wet his pants. But that's not the point. That's the one time I've ever pointed my piece when I had no business doing it. I don't deserve to carry it anymore. What if someone pissed me off enough that I did blow them away?"

"Come on. You were hot. Chalk it up to poor judgment."

"Would you just brush it off?" Dean scratched his head, but didn't answer. Weller continued. "The election comes up in August. It's just the primary but that's the whole ball of wax 'cause this is pretty much a one party county. I don't think I'm going to file."

Dean could see Jake Weller was dead serious. He didn't know how to respond. Weller continued, the trace of a smile on his face. "If they don't stick your ass in jail, you should consider filing. You were a pretty damn good detective back East. I know, 'cause I checked you out when we had that business last year."

"You've got to be kidding! I retired from that stuff, remember? Besides, I've got a bed and breakfast to run."

"Cynthia and the old man do more running Bird Song than you and I'll bet you could use the dough." He named his salary, a figure that surprised Dean. "Vote for David Dean, ace detective," Weller said with a grin as he pulled himself from the chair. "Think about it."

Dean thought about it for all of ten seconds after Weller left, but once more on his bicycle, all thoughts of his future were restricted to immediate concerns of removing himself and his wife from the list of prime suspects in Jerome Shipton's attempted murder. He biked away from the highway, up the gravel road to the west. In years long gone it was the rail bed for the line that ran to terminus in Ouray and now a favorite path for bikers. It climbed gently along the escarpment above the river and was devoid of traffic. However, unlike the highway, the snow here had not yet melted and Dean was forced to return to the main road at the first opportunity to cross back over the river.

As he peddled the road to Ouray, he tried to formulate a scenario of Shipton's ice park fall that made sense. It didn't work. He concluded there was a major element he was missing.

The logical suspect was the person who possessed the most reason to see Jerome Shipton dead. That had to be Edith Shipton. Putting aside her obvious mental problems, Dean guessed she still possessed the ability to try and kill her husband. But, by all accounts, she was not near the spot where he fell, a fact confirmed by enough people to make it believable. And, if she had cut the line earlier, it would have either been noticed by Shipton or he would have fallen the entire distance of more than a hundred feet from the edge to his certain death.

Might have Shipton faked the accident in some sick attempt to place the blame on David Dean whom he obviously despised? By all accounts his injuries were far too severe to have been logically self inflicted.

Somehow, considering Gladys, Effie or Claire seemed to stretch common sense more than an overweight bungee jumper. Dean couldn't bring himself to think of any of them seriously, given their lack of reasonable motive. Unless one of these people had a reason to kill Shipton beyond the apparent. Janet? Even more of a stretch, in Dean's mind. He considered Donald Ryland. Perhaps in cahoots with Edith? Not if outward appearances meant anything. Ryland gave no indication of having any interest in furthering his relationship with the mother of his out-of-wedlock son.

The remaining possible suspects were young Donnie and Cynthia. Dean was reluctant to even consider either option. He wanted desperately to dismiss Cynthia from consideration. Regardless of what she had said, he couldn't conceive of her killing someone with the possible exception of self-defense or protection of another. Shipton's fall did not fit either category. While she despised the man, her feelings still lacked a motive to sever his rope in cold blood and watch him plummet down to the rocks and churning river below. And yet, Cynthia was disturbed about something moments after the incident.

Suddenly, he had a thought. Might have his wife witnessed the attempted murder? That made some degree of sense. But why not immediately tell someone? Logic began to drift back into Dean's thought process. The obvious answer was to protect that person. But whom? Her husband? No. Dean hadn't been in the vicinity of Shipton's fall. There was no reason for her to even think he might be involved. Fred? Again, no. Fred's life was a mystery in some respects but he was honest and his report of Cynthia after Shipton's fall was certainly not a fabrication. There was no reason for Cynthia to protect any of the other adults. That left Donnie Ryland. The young boy would be the only person Dean could think of who Cynthia would care enough to at least consider protecting.

While he hated even speculating about a child murderer, it was the first time Shipton's attempted killing began to make any sense. There was one way to settle the matter. As Dean drew close to Bird Song, he resolved to ask his wife point blank if she witnessed Donnie Ryland cutting his stepfather's climbing rope in an attempt to send him to his death.

A small red sports car skidded to a stop in front of Bird Song as Dean dismounted his bike. A tiny red haired woman, under five feet, Dean guessed, emerged from the vehicle that bore Colorado license plates. She stamped out her cigarette in the snow before pulling a large suitcase from the small rear seat, nearly yanking off the handle and serenading the action with a chorus of curses. Dean moved to assist her after setting his bike against the porch.

The woman, a few steps from girlhood, was attractive in a cute, but no-nonsense way. She was dressed for spring in only a light sweater and glared at Dean as if he were a street mugger before surrendering her torn and ancient luggage.

"Welcome to Bird Song," he said as they climbed the steps.

"You don't look like an ice climber," she called over her shoulder as Fred O'Connor met them at the door.

"I own the place," Dean said, extending his hand. She smiled, for the first time. Dean introduced himself and his stepfather.

"I'm Franny Mulligan," she said, looking around, and then added sharply, "where is that bastard Donald Ryland?"

So this was Ryland's "Fran", his Grand Junction fiancée. No wonder the young man feared her! In spite of her pussycat size, she looked as if she could scratch your eyes out as quick as a tiger. Dean sighed. More trouble in the making, certainly for Mr. Ryland. He wondered how much Miss Mulligan knew about the aggressive Mrs. Shipton.

"Out ice climbing," he answered. Then he added, "Is he expecting you?"

"Hell no! He would have scrammed in a minute, the coward. Is the bitch with him?"

So much for her not knowing. "No. Mrs. Shipton is in her room. Donnie is with his...with Donald."

"I know he's the boy's father. You don't have to pussy-foot. Donald brought Donnie up to meet me, before the cops dragged him back down here." Then she added, "What kind of a mother lets her son do something stupid like climbing icicles at the age of twelve? The poor kid!"

"Donnie just watches the climbers," Fred answered.

"The jerk. He'd better be damn careful with Donnie! He can kill himself if he's fool enough to want to but the boy has no business up there."

"Ryland seems to be very cautious," Dean offered.

Franny ignored his comment. "Do you know, she had the nerve to call me! The conniving bitch!" Then added, in a mocking voice, "'We were intimate, and all our old love came flowing back!' The bitch! She said the wedding is off and Donald is staying with her! Fat damned chance! And the whore hung up before I could tell her what I thought of her and her ancestors back to Mrs. Adam!"

"Edith telephoned you?" Fred asked, stepping back from the petite woman's fury.

"Hell, yes! Can you believe it? I suppose she thought I'd roll over and cry in my pillow. Wrong guess! I'd kill the pair of them, if I hadn't already bought my wedding gown."

"Look," Dean said. "I'm sorry about all this but we don't need any more trouble at Bird Song. The police are already investigating Jerome Shipton's accident and—"

"Accident? That's a peck of bullshit! The bitch cut his rope so she could grab Donald. She's not fooling me." Then she thought about it a minute, and calmed down. "Don't sweat it, Pop. I won't get any blood on your carpet or bother any of the other guests. It's just between Donald and me. I should have known better that a jerk like Donald could pass up a free bounce in the bunk—the bastard." She glared at Dean, and Fred. "Men. You're all alike. But I'll be real generous and let the nutty bitch self-destruct. Okay?" Her smile lit up the room. Dean couldn't help but return it.

"Edith Shipton doesn't have a chance against you," he replied. "But—"

"No 'buts.' I'll be a good little girl and keep it quiet. You'll never even hear him scream when I cut his balls off." She grinned. "I'll gag him and mop up the blood, too. Deal?" Dean looked unconvinced. She continued. "Look, my parents even rented the hall. If I gave the bastard the boot now, like he deserves, my old man would have my hide. I'm here to protect my family's financial investment."

"I can put you up on the second floor, in the corner," Fred offered before Dean could make a decision.

"Don't bother. Just don't tell the Iceman I cometh when he shows up. I want to surprise him. And don't let him escape! No separate room needed, I'll bunk with deceiving Mr. Donald Ryland and make sure that hissy butch doesn't jump his bones or she'll land on me." Then she added, "Don't worry about two singles sharing a room and having illicit sex before marriage and all that shit. It'll be a long damn time before that bastard lays a finger on this gal without getting even more of his body parts severed!"

Dean shook his head in resignation. "Have you ever tried working for a collection agency? I bet you'd be great at it."

"Ryland's room is this way," Fred offered, leading the petite guest down the hall.

Dean sighed. "I suppose letting someone into a guest's room is against a bunch of innkeeper laws but considering the circumstances, I'll stick my neck out." He picked up her bags and followed the pair to the small room.

"Nice and cozy," she commented, bouncing the bed, and then added, "I suppose Bird Song is a tree-hugger-type joint and you don't let a person smoke here."

"Sorry," Dean said. "Outside only."

She gave a groan, but then smiled again. "By the way, you can bill the bastard for a double now. I suppose you should have been billing

him that way all along, if this is where he's been corking the widow."
She turned and began pushing them out of the room and closing the
door. "Thanks, guys. Remember now, mums the word. I want to play
jack-in-the-box and pop out of the closet."

"Why do I think letting her stay here was a really stupid thing to
do?" Dean said as he entered his quarters, with Fred close on his tail.

"I always like a wears-it-on-her-sleeve type gal a whole lot better
than the sneaky-Pete kind," Fred answered. "No trouble guessing
where you stand with Miss Mulligan." He reached in his pocket and
unfolded a sheet of paper and held it out to Dean. "Miss Franny
would never resort to writing something like this."

CHAPTER 21

Belfair crept away from the castle of the lovely Queen Sinthee and her lazy mate Dorvad, past the kindly Fird of Kornor, mingling on the street with the commoners. She disguised her beauty as an old man, a ragged peasant, and no one paid heed as she carefully moved up the narrow pathway until she finally reached the edge of the cliff and sighted the spot where Jership the Terrible had secured his line. The rope was taut with his evil weight and she could hear his movements as he carefully climbed down the sheer wall to his ice-bound lair below. Cautiously she moved forward, allowing herself a peek at this amalgam of evil, this seducer of virgins, who had so ravaged her body. She recalled with bitterness how he'd plied her with potion, falsely igniting her deep seeded passions until there was no turning back from his rampant lust. Now, she knew, he'd never let her alone. Now that he'd tasted the fires that burned in her voluptuous body, no other woman could ever so satisfy him. He'd be obsessed with her, stalk her to the ends of the galaxy as long as he lived. As long as he lived. Slowly she extracted the knife she'd found and with her long and lovely fingers began to methodically cut away at the line. Again, she stole a look below and this time, he glanced up at her, a questioning look on his handsome yet ugly face. He tried to crawl upward toward her, but she just smiled down and doffed her beggar's hood so he'd recognize her. Panic slowly crossed his craven countenance. There was a moment of realization as he understood her brave actions, and then a snap as the line let loose and he tumbled backwards like some mortally wounded game bird shot from the sky, arms outstretched, scream muffled in his mask. Belfair watched, a sneering smile painted on her beautiful face, revenge was hers, as Jership the Terrible crashed in a bloody heap on the rocks below. Her laugh echoed down the rocky canyons of Zzz as the essence of abomination breathed his bloody last below her.

The two men were seated in the parlor as Dean finished reading the photocopied paper.

"Where did you get this? Did you just swipe it from Gladys?"

"It's just a copy I made. I didn't take the original. It was sort of lying around when I was dusting her room. She'd left to clean out some restaurant for lunch. Besides, it's evidence," Fred added. Dean didn't bother to mention certain rules of evidence that looked askance at pilfered items. Fred continued. "Gives a whole new dimension to poetic license, don't it? Didn't much like the guy, did she?"

"Dorvad the lazy mate? Where does she get off, talking about me like that? I work my butt off around here," Dean muttered.

"Right," answered Fird of Kornor. "But what about the rest of it? She sure gives a lot of detail, the borrowed knife, him looking up, her wearing a disguise. My bet is she disguised herself as you—that's why Shipton said your name to Jake Weller!"

Dean had to smile at the picture. "The only disguise she could pull off would be an over inflated sister of the Michelin Man!" He tapped the page. "This stuff is pure fantasy."

"Maybe. But she sure has a way with words. And she makes herself a tad more attractive than real life."

"Yeah, and she has a pretty hot thirst for retaliation."

"Hey, it was your suggestion to her to make Shipton the villain in her book," Fred said. "I still think this stuff is important evidence."

"It's the rambling of a disturbed woman but you'd better bury it somewhere before you have to start explaining your upstairs cleaning habits. By the way, where are the cops? I passed Corday and his sidekick headed this way."

"Come and gone. They were mostly looking for you, and kinda ticked when you weren't here. Corday talked to Edith for about ten minutes, then skedaddled. The ice climbers are gone, too. They were sorry to miss you but most of 'em will be back later in the month. Gladys and Edith are both upstairs, the Quincys are at the library and young Donnie and his dad are still out someplace." Then he asked, "Did you get to telephone 'the lovely Queen Sinthee?'"

Dean brought Fred up to date on not only the telephone call to his wife, but his meeting with Weller and his speculation that Cynthia might have seen Donnie Ryland near the accident scene. The two fixed lunch—a tuna salad sandwich for Dean and a bowl of soup for Fred.

"Seems like talking to Donnie might be a tad productive," Fred said, rubbing his chin like Charlie Chan. "Suppose we could get Martha to feel him out? Those two kids get along like salt and pepper—different as black and white, but always on the same table. She came by a while ago, looking for him. I sent her up to the ice park."

"Why isn't she in school?" Dean asked.

"I asked her that. Seems she took off to take care of Janet, but I guess Janet made a miraculous recovery. I asked Martha back for supper. Maybe that'll give us a chance to talk to her."

"I'd like to hear Donnie's side of the story about the drowning of Shipton's son, too. What that guy Able Whitehouse said on the phone still bothers me. His version of the accident was entirely different from the story Ryland said Edith told him. I'd like to know which version is true." Dean rose to pour himself a glass of milk.

"Donnie knows but he ain't talking. Maybe I can fish around on the Internet and dig up some poop. There must be a newspaper account of the drowning someplace."

"Good idea." Dean reached for a piece of pie. "You didn't find out anything else, 'cleaning' the rooms?"

"I read Claire Quincy's notes on her great aunt Annie. If she knows the truth about Annie's past, she isn't admitting it. She's buying Mrs. Martin as her kin. All her information is on that woman, all the good deeds she did, with nothing about the real Annie. But Donnie's been transcribing Annie's notebook. I saw the copy Cynthia made for him in his and Edith's room." He put down his spoon. "It was real sad how Annie ended up. I wish I had the date so I could look again to see if I maybe missed it in the paper the first time I checked."

Before Dean could answer, there was a knock on the front door and he rose to answer it. It was Franny. She stood on the front porch, cigarette in hand, huddled in the corner so as not to be seen by Ryland when he returned Dean guessed.

"Sorry. I left my key on my bureau," she said, extinguishing her smoke in the provided ashtray.

"No problem. Lots of people forget them." Dean noticed a marked change in Frannie's demeanor—she looked as if she might have been crying. "We only lock up at night," he said, to make conversation. "We didn't even do that at first but some of the guests were nervous. It gets to be a pain at times."

"I suppose half the people run off with the key," she said, her back toward him but making no move to return inside. The afternoon sun bathed them like summer, and Dean, in spite of being coatless, was embraced by the warmth.

"We lose lots of keys. We were about to run out so I got smart and just changed the front door lock after Christmas. This time our keys say 'Bird Song' on the key fob." When she turned and he looked down at her, he could clearly see her reddened eyes. "What's the problem?" he asked.

She managed a sweet smile. "It shows, huh?" He nodded. "Damned! I don't want that bastard to know." She wiped her eyes vigorously. "I'm just a little up tight."

"You have every right to be," Dean answered. "But my guess is you don't have any reason to doubt Ryland loves you. Edith is a very manipulative woman. She crawled in bed with him while he was asleep. He didn't instigate anything—just the opposite."

She looked away. "It's not just that. It's Donnie, too. Donald talked about some sort of joint custody when he brought him up to meet me. I'm not sure I can be a mother so soon, even if it's only part time. I'm an only brat-child. I haven't even had any sibling practice. Donnie's got a bundle of problems and I know I'll love him, but it scares me to think of the responsibility." She sighed. "But worse, I know if we don't get involved with the boy, that bitch will screw him up for good." She turned and looked at Dean. "Having a child nowadays is tough enough but jumping in in the middle of the game is bewildering. How would you like to become an instant father? Scary prospect, isn't it?"

Dean nodded. "He's a nice little boy, a bit immature, but very intelligent." Dean glanced up the street to see Donnie and Martha coming toward them, hand in hand.

Franny smiled and left the porch and to meet them. Dean couldn't hear what she said, but the boy gave her a hug and gestured to Martha who had hurried ahead to where Dean remained standing on the porch.

"Who's your girl friend?" Franny asked Donnie as the two joined Dean and Martha.

Donnie blushed and Martha pretended she didn't hear so it was up to Dean to introduce her. "This is Martha Boyd. She's our friend." Dean gave the girl a hug as she shyly took Franny's outstretched hand. Martha, although half her age, was taller by two inches than the elfin Franny.

"Pleased to meet any friend of Donnie's and Bird Song." She turned to Donnie. "Where's your old man?" she asked. He motioned with a turn of his head back toward the ice park. "Come on. Let's wait in his room. Surprise him." She winked at Dean.

"Let's you and me get an ice cream," Dean said to Martha as the others entered Bird Song. The young girl hesitated but he took her hand and didn't give her time to decline.

Dean continued to hold Martha's hand as they walked uptown and found a place open on Seventh Avenue, a couple of blocks from Bird Song. On the way, Dean chatted about inconsequential things but pointedly asked about school.

"It's okay, I guess. There're some jerks."

"You'll never run out of dopes and ninnies," Dean answered.

"I do pretty good at most stuff and the teacher is nice enough but Janet doesn't like her."

"Janet doesn't have to go to school. You do. Besides, you don't have to like a teacher. Then he added, "But it does help if she likes you."

"I like most people well enough. I didn't like Donnie's stepfather." Her reference seemed to be an invitation for Dean to discuss Shipton.

"Why?"

"He seemed sneaky. Besides, Donnie didn't like him."

"Has Janet ever mentioned Mr. Shipton?"

"A couple of times. He called her, at least once. And maybe met her at a bar. He wanted her to do something but then he went out and got killed, I guess."

Dean didn't mention that Shipton was still among the living. "You don't know what Mr. Shipton wanted Janet to do, do you?"

"No. But I don't think Janet did it, whatever it was. It had something to do with Bird Song and I think she was afraid you'd fire her."

Dean guessed Shipton wanted Janet to somehow intercede in getting him into Bird Song, before he was able to obtain a room on his own. Or, perhaps he wanted access to Edith's room. It didn't appear Shipton had a relationship of any kind with Janet nor did she seem to have any logical reason to try and kill him. Over a hot fudge sundae Dean changed the subject to Donnie Ryland.

"Has Donnie 'spoken' any more?"

"Naw. But it don't matter. He's cool anyway."

"How did he act when his stepfather had his accident up in the ice park?"

"I don't know. Kind of strange, I guess." The young girl looked up at Dean. "Do you think Donnie cut the rope?"

"Do you think he did?"

She took her time before answering, as if rolling the question around in her mind. He reached over and brushed some chocolate from the side of her mouth. Finally, she answered. "Naw, I don't think so. But he did have the knife. I saw it last week—the day we buried the mouse. He showed it to me but he wrote on his pad it was yours and he just borrowed it 'cause you left it around. He was gonna give it back."

"I'm sure he was. Do you think he'd tell you he cut the rope if you asked him?"

"I don't know. Maybe. He likes me. He didn't tell the police he had the knife 'cause he thought he'd get in trouble over it." She thought some more. "If he was still scared of his stepfather, he might have done it. I know he wasn't real sad when Mr. Shipton fell but now that his real father is around, he isn't as scared as he was. That's why maybe he didn't cut the rope."

"Who do you think did?"

"Donnie's ma," she answered without hesitation. "She hated him. She wants to get back with Donnie's pa but he doesn't like her no more." Then she added, "Besides, Mr. Ryland's got Fran now."

They took their time over the ice cream, making soup of the last few spoons full, but Dean learned nothing further. He excused himself and asked the owner if he could make a phone card call and did so, but was unsuccessful in reaching Cynthia. When the two returned to Bird Song, Donnie met Martha at the stairs and tugged her up to his and Edith's second floor room. Bird Song was as quiet as an empty church with none of the remaining guests in evidence, nor was there any sign the police had returned. Count your blessings, Dean thought. He wandered back to his office, listening to only silence as he passed Ryland's door.

Dean spent the balance of the afternoon doing bookkeeping for the lodging establishment. Just before five o'clock he went to the kitchen to begin preparing spaghetti for Fred and himself, and Martha, whom they had invited to again stay for supper. He could hear the strains of some lost cowboy lover coming from Fred's room, a sure sign the door to the old man's room was open. Fred O'Connor strolled into the kitchen a few moments later, all smiles, carrying his ever-present notebook.

"You forgot to turn off your radio. The guests will think we're having a hoe-down."

"The kids are listening to it. I'm converting them from that rip-rap stuff."

"You look like you just won 'Wheel of Fortune'," Dean said as he emptied a package of pasta into a boiling pot.

Fred began setting the small kitchen table. "I been busy surfing the web." He had a look that begged to be asked about his success. Instead, Dean changed the subject.

"Is Ryland back?"

"Yeah. He trotted in while you and Martha were out. I ain't heard a peep out of his room since." Then he added with a smile, "Don't suppose little Franny slit his throat, do you?"

"Could be," Dean answered. "Dead bodies don't make much noise." He began to hum a Dave Brubeck piece as he reached for a bottle of virgin olive oil.

"Ain't you going to ask what I found on the net?"

"I figured you'd get around to it. I'm all ears." He put a tray of garlic bread into the oven and the pungent smell of warming cheese filled the room.

"Well," he said, little-kid excited, "I got the real poop on the death of Shipton's son! Believe you me, it weren't easy. First I tried calling that Able Whitehouse guy, but I couldn't get him. Then I looked up the Pinkville newspaper but it was merged into a countywide paper four years ago. I spoke with a nice lady at the new paper but she said all the old records were in some basement. Then I—"

"Can't you just hop to the facts?" Dean said as he strained the spaghetti into a colander.

"Well, I figured the drowning of a child ought to make a big city paper and sure enough, after I checked a few of my sources and a couple of papers, I hit pay dirt!" He checked his notes, wetting his fingers as he turned each page.

"Pay dirt being...?" Dean prompted. Lord, he thought, listening to Fred was like watching a sloth race.

"Pay dirt being, that Whitehouse guy was right. The drowning happened right there in Pinkville, Virginia, not on some far off canoeing trip, like Edith said! It happened in a swimming pool, not some river. And Shipton was out of town. Both boys were swimming and Edith was watching them, or was supposed to be. The paper didn't give a whole lot of details but the boys got in trouble and Edith saved the youngest one, Donnie. There was no one else around. The paper says she was extremely distraught and sedated, and under a suicide watch."

"Interesting," Dean said as he drizzled the olive oil over the pasta and sprinkled it with pepper and Italian spices.

"Edith's version is as far-out fiction as some of Gladys Turnbull's stuff," Fred said like the learned professor.

Dean thought a moment. "So the whole business about Shipton lugging a dead body back to civilization was a total fabrication. The questions is, whose fabrication? Edith's or Ryland's? He's the one who told me—not Edith, even though he claims that was what she told him." Then he added, "Good job, detective O'Connor."

Fred nodded at the compliment. "That raises the question about Donnie not being able to talk. And why would he fear his stepfather."

"The drowning in a pool could have been just as traumatic as Edith's version, especially if Donnie felt some responsibility for his stepbrother's death. Maybe Jerome Shipton has never forgiven both of them or, at the very least, that's how Donnie reads it. I could see how Shipton might hate his wife. Maybe he blames her for both not watching the boys and then for saving her child and not his."

The pair was interrupted from further speculation by the sound of Martha's laughter and footsteps bounding down the stairs. The two children bounced into the room. Martha held a twenty-dollar bill.

"His ma wants to know if Donnie can eat with us." She held out the money. "She's just sitting in the room, in her white dress. She says she ain't hungry. But Donnie is. And she wants Donnie to sleep over with me and Janet for the night! She's paying Janet, too!"

"We've got plenty of food," Dean said. He turned to Fred as he began dishing it up. "Set another plate." He pocketed the twenty dollars.

The four ate with gusto and animated conversation, led by Fred O'Connor, who won the contest of sucking up the longest spaghetti strand without dribbling oil on his chin. He even managed to coerce the children into doing the dishes. After the chores were finished, the group emigrated to the parlor for a game of Scrabble.

Gladys waddled downstairs, strung in more beads than the draped back room doorway of a Turkish dope den. She 'ta-ta'ed a greeting, and was off to dinner. The Quincy sisters strolled by moments later, arm in arm. Effie smiled and Claire snarled. Dean wondered how Effie would accept the final chapter of Annie's diary, once he had a chance to share it with her as Cynthia had promised. He wondered, too, about the sister's relationship, so close in some respects and so distant in others. Effie the realist, Claire, her head in self-made dreams of a pretend ancestor, as make-believe as Gladys Turnbull's creatures from Draghow and Zzz.

Donnie won the first game with "cant" which Dean questioned, unsuccessfully, assuming the boy meant the more common version, "can't," which was unacceptable. It was never clear if that was the case and the kid lucked out, but Dean used the excuse of mock consternation to excuse himself and walk uptown to telephone Cynthia.

As he strolled away from Bird Song, Corday pulled up in front. He didn't notice Dean, who continued walking. The night had cooled but it remained winter-pleasant as Dean sauntered into a Main Street bar. While he knew he'd have to speak to Corday sooner or later, he hoped to first learn the reason for his wife's reticence about discussing the ice park fall. Was she perhaps, as he had speculated, covering for young Donnie Ryland?

Once again, the phone rang unanswered at the Indiana location. Dean spent the next hour nursing two beers and telephoned again, still without success. As he was about to leave, Corday entered the dimly lit establishment. He spotted Dean at once and joined him on the next stool.

"Down here to call the little woman?" Corday asked.

"Down here to have a couple of beers," he answered. "And get away from the pressure of the hotel business."

"I'll bet. I want her address. Now." He waved for a beer.

"Drinking on duty, Officer?" Dean asked, a decibel louder than necessary, causing a head-turn or two.

"Now."

Dean looked directly at him. "Do you know the exact street address of your mother-in-law?"

Corday thought a minute. "I've got a car right outside. I'll drive you back to Bird Song so you can look it up."

Dean showed his irritation. "Look. It's two hours later in Indiana. I don't want a gang of storm troopers invading my mother-in-law's house at midnight to ask my wife a few simple questions. I gave you the phone number when you asked for it, didn't I? Now you can wait until morning for the address. Come by after nine and I'll give it to you." He continued to sip his beer, then added, "Besides, you shouldn't be drinking and driving." Corday tossed two dollars on the bar and rose without a word. He left his beer untouched. Dean drank it.

After trying Cynthia one more time, he gave up and returned to Bird Song. Donald Ryland and Franny were on the front porch. She was finishing a cigarette.

"You should give those things up," Dean said. "I hear they stunt your growth."

Franny laughed. "Maybe I will. Now that I'm going to be a weekend ma, I shouldn't be puffing around kids."

Dean followed them back inside. Ryland sported a black eye but, in spite of it, was smiling.

"I wasn't going to hit him," Franny said, "but I couldn't help it. At least I did it quietly." She gave his arm a squeeze. Ryland looked relieved that the shiner was the extent of his injuries.

"Peace prevails?" Dean asked.

"Yup. We even had it out with Miss Bed-hopper. You should have seen the look on her face when she came a calling in her antique duds and found me there! I thought she'd shit! She looked as if she could kill Donald!"

Everyone else was apparently asleep as Bird Song was as quiet as a tomb. Only Mrs. Lincoln roamed the halls, purring for a pat, as Franny and Ryland walked hand in hand to his room. Dean was sure the young woman's promise of a platonic night was already forgotten.

Dean read before going to bed, earlier than usual. He worried about not hearing from Cynthia, but there was little he could do. He turned out the light. Dorvad the lazy mate hopelessly missed his Queen Sinthee.

CHAPTER 22

I have unfastened the silken cord from the drapes and knotted it to the gas fixture above. It hangs there, waiting for me to step upon this velvet chair where I sit, tie its far descending end to my neck, and step from this world, freeing it from the guilt and troubles Annie Quincy has caused.

I only ask this of you, my dearest Joshua; that you not tell my family how I lived, and that you mourn not my passing. I would choose not to alter a single element of my life if in so doing it would eliminate even an instant of the time we've spent together. But you have your life and your duties to others and I must stop wounding your conscience and let you go your destined way. I thank my God that I too had you, if only for a little while. Believe in your heart forever how very much I loved you.

The Annie of Dean's dreams had long blonde hair but kept her head turned from him as she wrote in her journal. He kept wanting to see her face but was unable to do so. She closed the journal and began her preparation. Stopping her seemed not to enter Dean's mind as she placed a chair in the middle of the room, looking up to make sure it was directly beneath the hanging brass fixture. Then, with her back still turned toward him, she unfastened the drape cord and began tying the knot. When she completed her task, she stepped up on the velvet chair, after modestly lifting her skirt ever so slightly.

Dean woke with a start in the darkened room, as wide-awake as mid-day of a grade school vacation. His body was damp with perspiration and his breath labored. Rubbing his eyes, he peered at the blurred figures of his clock, (more evidence of the necessity for his glasses). The time was just after two. Fully alert, he listened, but heard only night noises, the ticking of the hall clock, a slight breeze, the ever-present furnace rumbling heat to the old building. The dream was drifting away from conscious memory, into that pit of forgotten remembrances that somewhere dwells in our deepest subconscious. While he'd failed to save Annie from her moribund actions, he now labored to retain the phantom vision of her final memory.

He lay back and closed his eyes, trying to picture the sad death, the end of the sad life of a woman, now resurrected to importance after a hundred years of total obscurity. Perhaps, he thought, we are all owed contemplation of our actions, as a parting gift to those who succeed us so they might somehow learn from our deeds and mistakes. But what a price to pay! What price love? he thought, to take one's own life for the simple expedient of protecting the other participant, a co-sinner, no less responsible for their sins together. And yet, if Cynthia should be in need of an ultimate expression of his love, how would he respond? He knew full well the answer.

It was if Annie bade him turn his thoughts beyond her long forgotten cares to the no less pressing concerns of today. Dean's mind churned the details of the recent happenings, trying to make sense of Shipton's orchestrated plunge to the river, and the strange reactions of those still sleeping beneath Bird Song's roof, and elsewhere. His thoughts were a carousel that like repeating ponies progressed in circles no closer to conclusion than the start of the ride. No golden ring of an answer. The last time he glanced at the clock it was three-thirty and he'd still not closed his eyes. Nor had he made any sense of his deliberations but finally his mind quit the task and allowed his exhausted body to sink into a deep sleep. This time, it was Cynthia who visited him in his dreams.

A warm touch began to arouse Dean. It was only a slight brush, not enough to fully wake him from the depth of his stupor. He failed to register the familiar, yet not familiar glance of fingers on the bareness of his body. He must have reached an arm across the warmth next to him and her nearly soundless mewl began his slow but steady rise to the surface of consciousness. Like a sunken object freed from the ocean floor, Dean began to ascend to the surface of wakefulness. It was then he began the slow realization that it was not his beloved wife who spooned against his back in nakedness, sharing his bed!

He woke with a start, to find Edith Shipton, with only her long blonde hair covering the body that was snuggling against him! He tried to turn and raise himself to a sitting position while pushing her away, but she held back his arm in a strong grip and locked a crooked arm about his neck.

"Shhh," she hissed in his ear. "You'll wake the others." Her arm tightened about his neck as, vice-like, she pulled her body against him while swinging a bare leg over his. "Be quiet! No one knows I'm here."

"Edith! This isn't right! I don't...." He turned but she pressed her open mouth against his lips, muffling his words, fiercely kissing him.

He pulled back, having to exert considerable force against her surprising strength. "Edith, you have to leave! Please!" She continued to hold him about the neck until he slowly pried her arm away and pushed himself to a half-sitting position, her leg still tightly locked over him."

"Edith, look," he said, his voice containing a hint of the panic he felt. "I'm married. Happily. I've been married less than a year. I don't want this. Please go back upstairs!"

At first she said nothing but when he tried to rise, she grabbed his wrist and held it, her long nails cutting into his flesh. Then she whispered, "It's all right. I know what men want."

While he possessed sufficient strength to pull away, he was fearful of hurting her, and even more so, of her crying out. "Please, Edith. I know you're upset, but this doesn't answer anything. It's wrong, for both of us."

"Make love to me," she said with a huskiness that made Dean feel if he could clearly see her there would be a coldness in her eyes, like a winter mountain wind. "And don't make a sound," she added, in a higher voice that hinted of her ability to bring the other guests a-running.

He tried another tack. "You're being unfair to me, Edith. I love Cynthia and I don't want to cheat on her. If anyone sees us together like this, I'm done. You don't have any reason to hurt me like that, do you?"

"The police know about us," she whispered.

"Edith, there isn't an *us*. Please."

"He's going to stay with *her*. They're getting married." She began to cry.

"Look," he said, his frustration growing. "I know you don't know where to turn but there are places that help with problems like yours. You have the whole rest of your life to live."

"I'm pregnant." She said it with a sad finality, like someone admitting to having a terminal disease.

"Yes, but your husband...."

"I wanted to kill him. He knows I hate him. They let him fly back to Virginia. He's gone. I can't even go back to him."

She rolled away from him and released his arm. He sat up and started to rise. "No!" she said, in a voice Dean thought loud enough to wake the house. He tried to put his hand over her mouth but she pulled away. "Don't leave me. Lie back down." The tone was not as

loud as before, but near a snarl. He hesitated but remained half sitting
on the edge of the bed. "I don't want to be alone," she continued. "If
you make me leave, I'll scream. I swear to God I will!" He laid back
down, leaving a space between them. She turned her back to him. The
headlights of a slow moving car washed her white body, shadowing
the curve of her buttocks, the roundness of her shoulder, painting her
golden hair in its light. "I'm Annie," she spoke, her whore-voice quieter now. "You can do anything you want to—things you wouldn't do
at home." She turned and in one motion straddled him, pinning his
arms above her head, the heat of her body pressed against him. "I'm
worthless. It will mean nothing to me. I'm just here to please you—
Joshua. We can be together, always. We can leave Ouray, leave your
wife behind. She has her life—we can have ours. I'll be good, so good
for you." She paused. "You don't have to pay me the two dollars." She
moved down to press her face to his.

Dean had no alternative but to force her hands away and flip her
from him, onto her back, reversing their positions in a single thrust
that caused her to loudly gasp as she landed soundly on her back,
Dean now above her.

"Listen," he snarled. "I'm not Joshua Martin! I'm not having sex
with you! I have no intention of having sex with you! Your coming
down here was cruel and unfair and I think you know it! You're not
Annie Quincy—you're Edith Shipton. You may be hurt and feeling
helpless and desperate and God knows what and I'm sorry as hell but
I have a life too, and I'll not have you ruin it!" The alley light shone
through the partially open door, interrupting the darkness just enough
to illuminate the frightened look on her face. "Now, please go back
upstairs."

"I just want to be with someone." Her voice a child-like whimper.
"I need to talk to someone, please."

Dean paused. "If you go back to your room and dress, we'll talk.
But in the parlor. With the lights on. And clothes on."

"I have my dress here," she answered meekly. "My white dress."

Before Dean could respond, he heard the sound—the front door
opening! Who? Then he remembered Franny and her too frequent cig-
arettes. He remained motionless, wondering if she could possibly have
left hers and Ryland's room nearly next to his without hearing them. A
slow smile crept over Edith's face.

"You'll have to let me stay now," she said in a sharp whisper. "I'll be
quiet." Before he could answer, the bedside telephone shrilled, its
shocking ring penetrating the late night stillness. It rang a second time

before Dean released Edith's pinned arms and answered it. It was Cynthia. Dean's heart sank.

"Did I wake you?" she asked. "I can never remember which way the time goes, earlier or later." Then she answered her own question. "Lord, then it's only, what? Four-thirty! I'm sorry."

"It's all right," he answered, his nerves tingling. He then added, "I've been trying to call you all day."

"I guessed you were, but ma doesn't have an answering machine. I've been at the hospital all day. Randy hitch-hiked out from college."

"Has something happened?" Dean assumed if Cynthia's son had traveled to see his grandmother, she had taken a turn for the worse. His heart continued to race as he glanced over at Edith. She smiled and began to hum, ever so quietly.

"No. Mother's better. Much better. She was awake off and on, most of the day. The doctor says long term, it looks good. She's weak and needs time and rest, but she has her old zest. Apparently the attack didn't do too much damage to the heart."

"That's great!" Dean said, trying to force a tone of normalcy into his strained voice. "When do you think you might be able to come home?" Any thoughts of questioning Cynthia about the happenings in the ice park never entered his mind. He just wanted his wife back in Bird Song. Edith leaned closer to him and began to run playful fingers down his bare chest, and lower. He grasped her wrist with his one free hand but she used the other.

"I don't know," Cynthia answered. "Maybe after a few more days." She paused, and he could picture her biting her lip. "Are the police still there?"

"Yes. I promised to give them your Indiana address tomorrow morning—this morning." Edith moved her fingers lower and he tried to turn away. When Cynthia didn't answer, he added, "I miss you."

Edith let out a sound of disgust, loud enough that clearly said she didn't care if Cynthia heard it or not.

"Is there someone with you?" Cynthia asked sharply.

Dean thought later how pivotal that moment was in his marriage. He answered by instinct, yet, in spite of not thinking of his answer, had he been given more time to consider, it would have remained the same. "Yes," he answered honestly.

"Who is it?" Cynthia's voice was steady, but concerned.

"Edith Shipton. She's—upset."

"Are you in the bedroom?" Before he could respond, Edith laughed. There followed silence, then a dial tone.

Dean closed his eyes in despair. "Get out!" he snarled. Now Edith was afraid. She knew he meant business. To Dean, the worst had already happened. Now that Cynthia knew, he didn't care who else found Edith Shipton in his room. All he wanted was to be alone so he could call his wife back and beg for her understanding. Edith scrambled from the bed as Dean turned on the light. She turned her naked body away from the glare and his eyes, as if expecting to be hit. When she saw he wasn't about to strike her, she whirled back toward him, a sneer on her face as she exposed herself to him. "Two dollars, mister. It's no matter if you can't perform. It's two dollars anyway. Just for the looking." She spotted his wallet on the bureau, extracted two one dollar bills and waved them in his face.

Dean made a move toward her, but she scurried out the door with a loud laugh, still naked, dragging her white dress behind her. Dean angrily followed her as she scurried upstairs. There, at the top, in tightly bundled robe and, yes, a Mother Goose stocking cap, stood Claire Quincy! Edith had her back to Dean so he couldn't see the look she gave Claire but she passed her haughtily and was gone. Claire stood there, mouth agape. Dean turned away and like a beaten boxer long after the bell had sounded, slowly returned to his room.

The telephone in far away Indiana rang, first in their agreed sequence, then twenty times before Dean gave up and turned out the light. The time would be near sunrise later in the year, but now the night and his world was as dark as midnight.

In spite of all that had transpired, Dean couldn't think. He slept, fitfully, though this time he remembered no dreams. Suddenly, a loud sound from above awakened him with a start. He lay there, trying to comprehend if the noise were in his mind's fantasies or in the real world of Bird Song. And then he recalled an earlier dream!

Dean leaped from his bed and charged up the stairs to Edith Shipton's room!

His heart raced as he began to sense what he would find. Her door was ajar and the chill from an open window washed over him as he approached, somehow knowing what lay beyond. He pushed the door further but hesitated entering, as if remaining outside would absolve him of responsibility from what lay beyond. The pale glow of the moon shone through the uncurtained window, casting an elongated shadow from the overturned chair.

She turned slowly, propelled by a tender breeze from the cold night air that filled the room. Her long blonde hair, unfastened, cascaded about her shoulders. She had once again donned the white dress, and the hem touched the tops of her bare feet. Her hands were by her side, turned out, tranquilly, as if to say, *peace at last*. She had tied the silk cord to the brass gas lamp at the ceiling in the center of the room, before knotting the other end about her soft white neck. He could picture her climbing onto the velvet chair, perhaps even smiling, before kicking it away, and waiting the few agonizing moments until death set her free. For seconds he was frozen to move toward her, knowing in his heart it was too late. You couldn't be a cop for four-teen years and not look death in the face and recognize its gruesome glare. Too late for anything. As he watched, spellbound, she slowly revolved toward him, but he closed his eyes lest he see her face. But he was too late for even that.

Two crumpled dollar bills lay on the bed.

CHAPTER 23

They were all gathered, either in Edith's room or nearby in the hall—Corday, Fitzgerald and a number of uniforms who seemed to come and go. Even Sheriff Jake Weller was there, and the city police chief and, in various costumes of night-wear, Fred, the Quincy sisters and Gladys Turnbull who'd let out a banshee scream that woke everyone but poor Edith Shipton, who'd never wake again. Her body had been cut free and moved to the downstairs to await a hearse from Montrose. Sheet-covered, her remains lay in Dean's office, only feet from where she had lain naked against him so short a time before.

Only Ryland and Franny were missing from the scene. Together they had hurried to Janet O'Brien's trailer in hopes of catching Donnie before he wandered unexpectedly into the macabre turmoil his mother had caused in her violent exit from life. Franny had been first on the scene behind Dean, dressed only in panties, her arms covering her tiny breasts, shivering as much at the sight as the chill of the early winter morning. The others followed quickly. Dean had a memory of Fred draping a flannel shirt over Franny's bare shoulders, though no recollection of the order of arrival or any real details of what followed.

Dean was a wreck. He still wore only pajama bottoms and couldn't even remember who'd dialed 911 to summon the troops. All he knew now was his bare feet were cold, standing on the hard wood floor at the perimeter of the carpet in the death room. He moved closer to the center, where Edith had died. The suspended cord brushed his shoulder and he could close his eyes and still see the protruding tongue, the open, frightened eyes, a body stiff and lost of life. Others had tried to administer to her but he knew it was pointless and turned away. He could no longer look at the two crumpled bills on the bed, the stark reminder of her fury when he'd sent her away.

Corday stared at Dean as if he were something on his shoe, utter disgust written on his unshaven face. For a long time he didn't say a word. Then he turned to the assembled spectators. "Scat," he ordered, and the Bird Song occupants all slowly complied—all but Fred O'Connor who defiantly sat on the bed, taking notes.

It was Fitzgerald who spoke. "Maybe we should check the body for semen," he said, smirking at Dean.

Dean spoke for the first time since the investigators arrived. "Go ahead," he muttered.

Corday turned away, steaming. "You know what I think, Dean? I think your wife caught you two together and took off. That's why you don't want us contacting her. Then you ditched your new honey and she's stupid enough to think that's a big loss and goes and hangs herself."

"So you now have a suicide to handle," Dean said.

"We don't handle suicides, asshole," Fitzgerald snarled. "We leave them for the locals. Even when some scumbag drives the victim to it. We figure it's her choice if she wants to take the big trip. Even if it's over some total jerk like you."

Corday gave Dean a chilling stare. "Unless it wasn't her choice. Maybe you snuck up here and helped hustle along your sweetie on her trip to never-never land."

"And wrote her note for her?" Jake Weller asked, with raised eyebrow. He held a paper in his hand. It had been on the nightstand, partially hidden by the base of a lamp.

They all looked over his shoulder at the penned missive. It was on plain white notepaper, lined and firmly creased, written somewhat shakily with an ink pen, in the dainty script of a woman. Weller read it aloud.

I'm going to hell for what I did. It's where I belong. Please, don't tell Donnie the truth about how I died. Donnie, Donnie, I love you so. I'm not fit to be a mother. Daddy will take care of you now. Mommy.

Corday looked at Dean. "Too bad. She didn't even say good bye to her lover."

Fitzgerald gave a scowl. "Who says she wrote it?" He gestured to Dean. "Maybe he did."

It was Jake Weller who spoke up. "Don't be a shit head, Fitzgerald. Check her purse for something she wrote and compare it. Check the register downstairs. It's a suicide note she wrote 'cause she killed herself. Stop playing prime time TV. It's a damn shame she's dead but so are a lot of things in life."

Dean began to move away. Corday started to grab his arm, then thought better of it. "Not so fast. I'm not through with you. When did you and Mrs. Shipton last talk?"

Dean turned, and glared at Corday. "My feet are cold. I'm going down and get dressed. I've got an inn to run. This is a suicide and you guys don't handle suicides, remember? Unless you're going to charge me with something, get the hell out of Bird Song and leave me alone." He turned and went down the stairs. No one made a move to stop him.

Dean had a fleeting sense of relief that Corday hadn't pressed him for Cynthia's address. The last thing he wanted now was for the police to interview his wife so soon after she'd hung up on him as he lay in bed with the now-dead Edith Shipton. God, how he wanted to put things right with the woman he loved.

Dean tried to ignore Edith Shipton's body as he passed the temporary catafalque erected in his office. But he couldn't avert his eyes from the white-sheeted form, the last remnants of the warmth of life slipping away. He paused and said a silent prayer for the spirit of this person who had brought so much grief to Bird Song and his previously contented life. Once in his bedroom, he closed the door and again tried to telephone Cynthia. The only response was the echo of an unanswered ring. He dressed but instead of returning to his duties, lay back on his bed, depressed and exhausted.

Later, Dean heard the movement of the mortuary men coming for Edith—the hushed conversation and the bumping and thumping as the lifeless shell of this troubled woman was bagged and forever removed from Bird Song. Only silence remained as he lay there, wanting to escape from all that was happening, surrender in the peace of sleep, but even sleep eluded him. At length he heard the sound of a soft knock on his door. He assumed it was Fred, with a tray of food and a peck of good intentions, but just now, even his stepfather was not a welcome visitor. "Go away," Dean said, unmoving.

In spite of his admonition the door opened, not to Fred O'Connor, but to Claire Quincy who closed the door behind her and stood with nervous defiance at the foot of his bed.

"I saw her, naked, after you two...had your pleasure together." She waved her hand at the bed, as if to indicate the location of his foul deed. Dean looked at her but made no effort to rise. He knew better than to deny anything to this tunnel-visioned woman. "The police are still here, but I haven't told them." Then, she added with a snarl, "Yet."

"Why not?" Dean asked, out of no more than a mild curiosity. Claire could shout it to the world, for all he cared. Tell them that naked Edith Shipton came out of his room and moments later hanged herself. After all, Corday had already painted him an adulterer. The investigator might as well have his "proof." To Dean, his reputation mattered only in the eyes of one person, his wife. He didn't give a flip what Corday thought.

"You're just like her and she was a whore."

"I guess you've been learning a lot about women of street this week," Dean muttered, sick of the pretentious woman.

Claire stiffened and turned away. With her back still toward him, she asked what must have been the most difficult questioned she ever voiced. "Are you going to tell everyone...those awful stories about my great-aunt?"

He laughed, half-aloud. "Listen," Dean said. "Right now I don't give a damn about what happened a century ago and I'm in no position to make judgments of a situation I know so little about. I care even less if your brother writes *Saint Among the Sinners* or *Sinner Among the Saints*."

Claire Quincy turned and stared at him, as if waiting for the quid pro quo of an if-you-don't-tell, I-won't-tell agreement of some sort. That was a game Dean had no intention of playing and the silence draped the room like a spring fog.

Claire tried to muster a schoolmarm firmness that didn't work. "I want assurances from you and that horrid old Mr. O'Connor that the integrity of my family name will not be stained with unproven lies! Mrs. Martin did much good and she deserves to be honored for it. My brother's book will give her the credit she so richly deserves." It sounded, as Dean didn't doubt it was, like a well-rehearsed speech.

"Get out of here," was all Dean answered. He was in no mood to argue against Claire Quincy's selfish interests in preserving the strained moral reputation of the long-dead ancestor. He turned toward the wall and, after what seemed like minutes, heard the bedroom door close.

It was hunger that later returned Dean to reality. A little after noon he emerged from his room. Corday and Fitzgerald were gone. The only representative of officialdom remaining on premises, in even a semi-official capacity, was Sheriff Jake Weller. He was holding court with Fred O'Connor in the parlor, a plate of potato chips and a tuna salad sandwich on his ample lap. Gladys Turnbull was the only visible guest. She was wedged into a corner chair with one hand in a bag of cookies while the other took notes. Dean wondered if her throat was sore after her pre-dawn glass-breaking scream upon first seeing Edith Shipton's body slowly turning from the end of the sash. Dean had tried to telephone Cynthia once more with no luck. He fixed himself a cheese sandwich and joined the parlor confab.

Fred looked up from his notes and answered Dean's unasked question. "The Quincys are off somewhere and Franny and Donald took Donnie to a motel. They're going back to Grand Junction tonight."

"Thanks for doing all the chores," Dean mumbled. Fred acknowledged with a nod.

Gladys just smiled and munched, and munched. Weller took another bite of his sandwich, waved Dean to a seat as if he were the host, and continued with his discourse.

"The way I figure it, Edith took the knife the night when she first tried on the dress. We can't say if she planned on killing him with it or was just protecting herself but later she used it to cut his line. Like the note says." He sat back with a hint of smugness.

Fred nodded his head, scribbled on his pad, and asked, "You figure the note's a confession, of sorts?"

"Sure. It says, '*I'm going to hell for what I did*,' doesn't it? If she didn't try to kill Jerome, why would she kill herself? There's no doubt the note is in Mrs. Shipton's handwriting—even Corday agrees with that. As far as I'm concerned, that wraps it up." Weller sat back and took another chaw from his tuna salad sandwich, brushing a few crumbs from his chin.

"Is the handwriting definitely Edith Shipton's?" Fred asked.

"No doubt about it," Weller answered. "She even used the same fountain pen she used when she registered here at Bird Song, when she signed 'Edith Jones.' And there were papers in her purse in her writing that matched, too." He leaned across the coffee table and reached for Bird Song's guest register, handing it to Dean.

"I thought I was the only one who uses an old-fashioned fountain pen," he said. Cynthia had given him such an instrument at the time the couple signed papers acquiring Bird Song. "Where's the suicide note?"

"Corday has it. He's sending it and the samples of Mrs. Shipton's writing over to CBI in Denver, just to make sure. But it's just a formality. Even he knows she wrote it. He's closing the case, and the open case on her husband's fall as well."

"In spite of Shipton saying 'Dean?'" Dean asked as he fingered the stubble-beard he'd never gotten around to shaving.

"Corday filled me in, at least a bit. According to Corday, Shipton doesn't remember anything about the fall and doesn't even remember saying anything to me at the scene. He's claiming head injury and all that shit...stuff—sorry Miss Turnbull."

"That doesn't answer why Shipton said my name to you."

"My read is he just wanted to cause you some grief after you tried to beat his brains out. Or maybe he honestly thought it was you who cut him loose."

Dean didn't respond but in his mind agreed the answer made a certain amount of sense, giving the situation.

"Come on!" Weller said. "You're off the hook. You came out smelling like a prom queen on her first date. Why are you mopping around like your dog didn't make it across the Interstate?"

"A woman just died on my watch, Jake. And it makes me feel guilty as hell."

"Hey," Weller said, his tone conveyed a surprising note of sympathy. "Stop beating yourself. You weren't her answer. She needed a lot more than you could give her."

"That still doesn't absolve me from feeling like a bastard," Dean muttered.

"I suppose not. But we do what we do, at the time. We don't get much chance to turn the old clock back. You've got a inn to run."

"It's pretty tough trying to rent a room with a piece of yellow tape strung across it." Dean knew in time, he'd get over the sudden death of Edith Shipton but he also knew the fact he failed to stop her from killing herself would remain with him forever. Regardless of Weller's kind words, he realized deep down if he had been more understanding of the troubled woman, she *might* still be alive. Though he harbored no regrets in declining her invitation to sex, he knew he could and should have handled so obviously unstable a person in such a mental state far better than he did.

"Where is Jerome Shipton, Sheriff?" Fred asked.

"He flew back East to Virginia yesterday. They gave me the job of running him down to tell him the missus killed herself."

"Why did Shipton go back to old Virginia?" Fred asked. "I thought he was at death's door."

"He was limping and hurting, but not in bad enough shape to keep him hospitalized. He said he wanted his own doctor to take care of him. I guess he wasn't the ideal patient so the doctors weren't inclined to put up much of a fuss. He agreed to come back and testify if CBI needed him, when they pinned his accident on you. Corday wanted Shipton to hang around but couldn't stop him from leaving. After all, he was the victim, not the perp."

"So there's no unanswered questions?" Fred asked.

"I don't know why she hanged herself when she had a bottle of sleeping pills right next to her bed but wacky people do wacky things."

Gladys Turnbull, almost forgotten in the corner, spoke up for the first time. "Edith thought she was Annie," she said. Dean and his stepfather looked at her, surprised she was privy to the Annie Quincy saga. She explained. "Effie told me about the prostitute whose diary you're reading. The one Mr. and Mrs. Martin were trying to save."

"Oh, that one," Fred said, realizing Effie was perpetuating the misinformation about Annie Quincy's past, creating Annie the prostitute as a salvageable soul of Reverend and Mrs. Martin, a separate person from the true Boston ancestor.

"Who?" Weller asked. Fred O'Connor gave a brief—unusual for him—explanation of Annie, careful not to identify her as a Quincy and the sisters' ancestor.

"Well," Weller said smugly, "That locks it up even tighter. Mrs. Shipton was packaged a little loosely to start with, so the white dress and her being pregnant and all just pushed her all the further." He looked at Dean. "Too bad she decided to do it here at Bird Song."

What bothered Dean most was his misread of Edith Shipton. If he'd thought for a minute she was suicidal, he'd have taken some steps to protect her from herself.

"I was a cop for a lot of years. I should be able to react professionally to something like that. I was trained to defuse desperate situations, not sit around and be blind to their development."

Gladys shrugged. "It was all his fault. He drove her to it. He was a terrible man. I'm glad he's gone from here. If she'd killed him, I'd be glad of that too." She brushed away a tear, leaving a streak of smeared rouge and mascara. "He was nasty to everyone. Even Miss Quincy."

"You heard him arguing with Claire Quincy?" Fred asked.

"No, no. Not Claire—her sister Effie." She leaned forward. "I heard them talking at night." The large woman had Dean's attention. "She whispered something to him and he just laughed in her face and said, 'Try and stop me'. He was that way with everyone he encountered, brutish. He was a cruel and nasty man."

Dean turned to Weller. "So tell me how Edith Shipton tried to kill her husband," he asked. "And why."

Weller looked as if the answer should have been obvious. "She cut his rope, figuring on hooking back up with that Ryland fellow but then his girl friend showed up and in no uncertain terms pointed out why that was a dead end. First, she gets brooding about it, knows she's pregnant, knows Shipton is still alive and won't let her go. And now he'll be all the more pissed off at her, seeing as he knows she tried to kill him. Donnie's father cares for his son. He's someone who will take care of the boy, maybe better than she can. So she—"

Gladys read from her notes, "...stepped up on the velvet chair, tightens the silken cord about her neck, and closed her eyes...."

Dean rose and began to leave the room, disgusted that Gladys Turnbull would trivialize Edith Shipton's death in fiction, even before the shattered woman was cold in the ground. "That was a human being they hauled out of here, Gladys. You might not have liked Edith Shipton, but her death is still a tragedy." He immediately felt bad for snapping at the woman who in some ways didn't demonstrate the good sense to blow on hot soup.

"What's a matter?" Weller asked, changing the subject. "Isn't that the way you read it?"

Dean stopped. "I'm not sure I'm *reading* it at all. A woman killed herself in my inn. If I was a bit more sensitive, I might have stopped her." The others looked at him, surprised at the depth of his reaction. He continued, "She came down to my room last night."

"That was rather forward," Gladys said, "with your wife out of town and all." She continued to take notes, as if Dean's scolding had fallen on deaf ears.

"Forward, yes, but desperate, too. Cynthia telephoned while Edith was there and I tossed her out."

Weller's cheek twitched noticeably and Fred looked up. "So, you were the last person to see her alive?" the old man asked.

Dean thought about Claire Quincy standing on the top of the stairs, as Edith ascended, naked as the day she was born. He didn't answer.

"Well," the sheriff said, rising and stretching. "It's over. We can all talk about a bunch of 'ifs' but the past is past. Maybe now you can get back to the future, and running Bird Song."

"Amen," said Fred O'Connor.

"On that note, I'm out of here," Weller smiled. "Time to go back to keeping the county safe, 'from speeders and bike nappers'." He gave Dean a knowing pat on the shoulder as he left.

"How come you're still taking notes?" Dean asked Fred, after Gladys left the room and they were alone.

"There's still a couple of things that bother me a mite. It's kind of spooky. Edith Shipton commits suicide just like Annie Quincy did."

"Why does that bother you?" Dean sighed. "She mimicked Annie from the beginning—wearing the white dress—dying her hair—candles in the room. Why not how she killed herself?"

"Plus, you had your dream," Fred said.

"My dream was just that—a dream. It doesn't mean crap."

Fred shook his head, still not satisfied. "I might could buy the Annie Quincy look-alike scenario but to me, it's a hard sell to do something horrible like strangling yourself when you have a bottle of perfectly good sleeping pills a hand's reach away."

"I can't answer that. There are a lot of questions about Edith Shipton I can't answer, but they don't make any difference. She killed herself. It's over and done with."

"Like what questions do you have?" Fred asked, pen poised.

Dean sighed, realizing Fred would want all the answers pat. "Like why did she bother to put her dress back on after she left me?"

"She came down to your room naked?" Fred asked, with eyes upturned.

"Yes," Dean answered, with some reluctance. He filled Fred in on the details of Edith's visit and Cynthia's late night phone call and the abrupt end to the conversation.

"She'll come around. Cynthia can't think you'd cheat on her. Mark my words."

"She's not answering my calls," Dean said but Fred just waved off his response.

"There's more questions," Fred added, glancing at his notes. "I didn't say anything to Weller 'cause he's so positive everything is all wrapped up and tied with a bow, but I knew you and me would want to make double-dipped sure."

"I'm sure. Edith killed herself. I don't care if she cut her husband's rope or not."

Fred shrugged him off. "You're just not up to your usual detective-sharpness so I'm taking on the bulk of this here investigation. But see? Deep down, you still don't think Edith was the one who cut the line!"

"I don't much give a flying you-know-what who cut her husband's rope as long as no one is blaming me, or any of us."

Fred checked his notes again. "Then there's the matter of the pen."

"Edith's fountain pen? What about it?"

"There ain't no pen." Fred smiled proudly. "Least there wasn't a pen in her room. You tell me how you write a suicide note when you don't have a pen."

"Maybe the police took it. Or one of the others. All of Bird Song was in the room."

"Nope. I was there right off the bat, right behind screaming Gladys. I'd have seen if someone swiped it."

Dean thought a minute. "The white dress. I'll bet she put it in her pocket. It probably went out with the body." Fred looked crestfallen.

He quickly recovered. "But that just goes to prove what I been saying. We got to look at all these loose ends and satisfy ourselves about 'em." He wet his pencil. "Like what time was it when the victim left your room?"

"Damned, Fred! I was trying to get a naked woman the hell out of my bed, just after my wife caught her there! I sure wasn't checking the time and writing it down!"

Fred seemed less than satisfied with Dean's answer but didn't push it. Like any good mystery novel detective, he'd bide his time. He carefully put a star next to the unanswered question. Dean, in turn, began trying to remember the time sequence in his own mind. But Fred was right about one thing. Dean wasn't thinking at near his usual high level. Cynthia Dean kept pushing away all other thoughts from his tattered mind.

CHAPTER 24

Dean spent the afternoon busying himself with the chores of Bird Song, partially out of guilt for having dumped the morning duties on Fred and in part to take his mind off the ever-present feeling he'd caused long term or, heaven forbid, permanent damage to his seven-month marriage. He cleaned the kitchen, dusted the entire downstairs and, as the weather remained mild, even washed the first floor windows, hoping when and if Cynthia saw them it would not be in the sun. In between, he telephoned Indiana a dozen more times. Dean even called the hospital—"No, Mrs. Dean was not there, thank you. I'll convey your message. Yes, her mother is much better and sleeping." In spite of all his cleaning, Bird Song didn't seem to have the same shine as it did when Cynthia was in residence. He considered flying to Indiana, but decided against it, at least for a day or two.

Gladys flitted back and forth, like a moth in a lamp shop, alternating with Dean for the hall phone, apparently conversing with an editor who was expressing interest in the lurid tales of Belfair of Draghow and her sexual mischief about the stars. There were whispered conversations about money—hers, Dean presumed—followed by excited talk of the man driving up from some obscure New Mexico town to meet her at Bird Song. The inn needed the business. Donald Ryland and Franny Mulligan were checking out this evening, as soon as he returned with Donnie, followed by the Quincy sisters scheduled departure in the morning. With only Gladys on board, that left eight rentable rooms, one wrapped in yellow tape, and a winter heating bill on the office desk.

Dean dumped some sort of casserole, frozen and packaged, into the oven without bothering to read what would emerge as their supper. While he fancied himself at least an experimental, if not good cook, in his present state of mind he found himself reverting to bachelor days of quick-is-best.

"Sort of like old times, ain't it?" Fred commented as he poked about the kitchen.

Dean thought back to the fifteen years the two of them had shared similar meals and chores, with each sure he was doing more work than the other. It had seemed a contented life at the time, but not so much so in retrospect. Dean didn't answer his stepfather.

"Don't mean old times are better than new times." Fred said as he turned to Dean. "I miss her, too." He waited for Dean to respond but when he didn't, he continued eating. "But I can't say I miss that Shipton lady none."

Dean wanted to shout, "I killed her, Fred. As sure as if I tied that cord around her neck and kicked out the chair." But he said nothing. Mrs. Lincoln mellowed into his lap, as out of character as a clown at a wake. She even commenced to purr, as if to say, "Get on with it, you jerk. So you screwed up. Like it's the first time? Deal 'em again. We're still in the game." He knew she was right, but even her feline comfort didn't seem to help.

After the bland meal was over and the tin foil discarded, Dean donned his coat and walked up town. Darkness had fallen and the streets were silent. He passed the recently restored Beaumont Hotel, a beautiful structure that after several decades of disuse and deterioration had finally been returned to its past glory. The building was a superb example of craftsmanship from an era when quality was meant to survive those skilled men who proudly worked it. The building stood there, gazing down on the quiet town like some magnificent matron, watching over her citizens as she had for a hundred years.

Dean wondered if Annie Quincy had ever entered through its portals. Probably not. Rev. Martin and his socially conscious wife must have dined there many a time, perhaps as poor Annie, like some wayward match girl, hovered outside. It seemed to Dean she'd spent her life on the outside, in some respects by choice, somehow driven from one social plane down to another, much lower, until there was nothing left but death. In her mind, at least. It bothered Dean, the choice Annie had taken. He was, by nature, a fighter, not someone to toss in the towel in despair, regardless how trying life had become. He always tried to govern his thinking by logic. While he knew he couldn't duplicate the feelings and situations of another, in a far different time and circumstances, he was nevertheless disappointed at the actions of this young woman whom he'd come to admire. Her writing showed she was intelligent and perceptive, though she demonstrated incredibly poor judgment at times. What would he have suggested she do? That she give birth to the baby and march up to the parsonage steps? He had no ready solution, but continued to believe the ultimate solution she chose to these insurmountable obstacles was a cop-out. Love. That was the overpowering emotion that had come to rule poor Annie's life. It drove her to final despair. Blind, illogical love. Would Dean ever make such irrational and illogical decisions if faced with a test of his love? He wondered, and hoped he would not. He considered stopping for a beer or two but realized bellying up to the bar was no solution to life's problems. Instead, he returned to Bird Song to once more try to contact his wife.

Fred O'Connor sat alone in the parlor, notes spread around him on the couch and coffee table. A Country and Western singer was mourning a lost love on Fred's mini boom box. Mrs. Lincoln formed a pillow behind the old man's head. Dean nodded on his way back to his quarters but didn't stop.

Dean had no more than hung up from yet another unsuccessful telephone try when the phone rang.

"Hi," said a subdued voice he nearly didn't recognize. It was Cynthia. "Come get me?"

"Where?" he answered anxiously.

"Montrose."

"I'll be right there!"

"Hurry," Cynthia answered and hung up.

Dean had all he could do to maintain reasonable proximity to the speed limit after letting Fred know where he was going. The usual forty-five minute trip took little more than a half hour. Cynthia stood at the airport curb, her suitcase by her side. They stood there together, holding each other, with her head against his chest, saying nothing, for what seemed like minutes. When she looked up at him, she was crying.

"Welcome back," was all he could say, grossly inappropriate for how strongly he'd felt her absence.

"I missed you too much not to come home."

Cynthia's mother was recovering nicely. The long-term prognosis looked good and arrangements made for a friend to stay with her during her convalescence. Cynthia's son Randy was on his way back to college. Neither mentioned the late night phone call during Edith's nocturnal visit nor Cynthia's sudden, unannounced return. They began the drive back to Ouray with Cynthia snuggled against him.

It was Dean's turn to talk. "A lot has happened in the last twenty-four hours," he began. "Edith Shipton is dead." He could feel her tense against him as he explained in detail the late night suicide and the termination of the police investigation. She was shocked and disturbed by his announcement but said little, allowing him to describe the happenings without interruption. He delayed mentioning Edith's visit to his room as if that encounter deserved its own time and chapter in this bizarre scenario.

"It was Edith who tried to kill her husband?" She sounded surprised.

"That's what the police believe," Dean answered, surprising himself with so qualified an answer. Cynthia didn't press him on the point but continued to act very nervous. "They didn't say anything about still wanting to talk to you." He could feel her sense of relief.

Dean explained how Annie Quincy too had ended her life, in a carbon copy fashion, with Edith mimicking the century-old life to its final extreme. He quoted from memory, verbatim, Annie's final passage. Cynthia grimaced but seemed to understand. He glimpsed the sparkle of a tear in the flash of on-coming headlights.

When they arrived in Ouray there was a mutual understanding all that lay between them had not been discussed. Nor had Cynthia eaten dinner so they stopped at The Buen Tiempo. The Main Street Mexican restaurant was uncrowded on this winter evening.

"I suppose you're wondering why I hung up," she asked after they were seated in a quiet booth, beneath a ceiling of dollar bills stapled above them.

"No," he lied as he chip-dipped salsa.

"I didn't take time to think," she continued. "Once I did, I came home."

"I'm just happy you're here. Nothing else matters," he said as he leaned across the table and kissed her.

"I didn't want to lose you."

"I called dozens of times." She just nodded. He could picture her sitting there, listening to the ringing telephone, but not wanting to answer it.

She looked away. "I should have talked to you, asked you why she was there, but I didn't want to. Not on the phone, at least. So I just came home."

"She came down to our room when I was asleep," he said. "I turned her out. She was hurting. Hurting terribly. She had no one. But what the hell could I have done?"

"You could have slept with her," Cynthia answered, brushing back a hair and looking down. "Some men would have. Maybe most. Ryland did."

"Yeah."

"But you didn't. I don't think you would have, even if you weren't married." It was his turn to look up at her. "Once I stopped to think," she continued. "You're smart enough to know that having sex wouldn't have solved any problems for Edith Shipton, and probably not stopped her from taking her own life."

"I feel like a shit about the whole business."

"Why?"

"Because she's dead. Because I should have seen it coming. Because I should have dragged her to a shrink or someone who could have talked some sense into her, or at least watched her more closely-protected her from herself."

Cynthia seemed to understand his hurt. "Edith Shipton was a very troubled woman, from the first time she stepped into Bird Song. Long before she came to Ouray, I guess. I don't know what would have helped her. Like Annie Quincy. I guess that's why she identified so much with Annie." Then she added, "Did Edith wear her white dress when she came to...your bed?"

"Yes. No. Sort of."

Cynthia smiled for the first time. "That rather covers all the bases, doesn't it? But I'm not sure it answers the question."

"She had the white dress *with her*," he answered, embarrassed. "I suppose she wore it down stairs. When I saw her, she...didn't have it on."

"She was naked?"

"In a manner of speaking."

Cynthia didn't say anything. Dean couldn't stand the suspense. "Aren't you going to ask me all those stock questions like 'Weren't you tempted? Were you aroused? Didn't you at least *consider* doing it?' I mean, it was the quintessential traveling salesman's dream, a naked and willing woman hopping into his bed, wife in another town, a freebie, so to speak."

"No." He looked at her as she spoke. "No, I don't have to ask. I know you too well."

Dean sighed, feeling more contented than he'd felt in days. But then he remembered the doubts. He'd even considered his wife might have killed Shipton. She had doubted, too—she had hung up the phone. Perhaps they both were human after all.

Over a desert of flan he asked her about Jerome Shipton's ice park fall. "Why were you avoiding the police?"

She took her time before responding. "Donnie was right there. I saw him clearly. I could tell something happened because everyone was running up to the area but Donnie was just skipping down the trail. I've never seen a child so happy. When I found out Shipton had fallen, it frightened me to death."

"You thought he killed him?" She nodded.

"He must have seen his stepfather fall. It doesn't mean he cut the rope."

"I didn't know what to do. He's just a boy. I was sure he was there. My mind was all awhirl and then Janet came up and told me mother was ill—I didn't know what to do. I was frightened to death to talk to the police. I didn't want to tell on Donnie yet I couldn't lie about it." She looked at him, big brown eyes incredibly sad. "I'm sorry. I should have confided in you. I wasn't being fair."

"You were just upset. Your mind was on overload." He took her hand.

"It was more than that. I hated the man. I truly did, for the way he grabbed me, like I was some street whore. Annie, maybe. I guess in a way I bonded with Donnie, thinking he did what I wanted to do. How awful his life must have been living with that shit Shipton. I truly want-ed to do it myself! God, I was so confused!"

They were silent for a few moments before he asked, "If you were that close to where Shipton fell, you must have seen Edith."

Cynthia looked up and shook her head. "When I came back down the trail, Edith was still standing at the bridge. She couldn't have been back there." Dean rubbed his chin but said nothing. Suddenly, Cynthia looked startled. "Do you think I was right? Does that mean that Donnie did cut the rope?"

"No. All it means is Edith didn't."

Cynthia fumbled with her napkin. "If she didn't try to kill Jerome, then why did she kill herself?"

"Everything piled up, I guess. She had no one. She obsessed with the Annie Quincy story, and...."

They both knew the other obvious answer. Edith Shipton was pro-tecting the one person she truly loved, her son Donnie. She was admit-ting to a crime she didn't commit, knowing it was her son who did it. Knowing her suicide would put the matter to rest.

"What are we going to do?"

"Let's not jump to conclusions," Dean said. "Did you see anyone else up there? Near where Shipton fell?"

She shook her head no. "It must have been Donnie. God, he's just a kid! He can't even realize the seriousness of what he did!"

Dean didn't answer but remembered Edith insisting it wasn't Dean who'd cut her husband's line. She must have known at that time who really did it. Her son.

"What can we do?"

"Officially, there isn't even an outstanding unsolved crime. There's a good chance Donnie is finally about to get some psychiatric help—help a long time coming. Regardless of what we suspect, it's still just conjecture. Hopefully, what happened will come out and Donnie will be able to have some sort of normal life, away from both of the Shiptons. It's not as if there's some crazed killer running around loose. Jerome Shipton is no longer in the hospital and was never hurt critically. He's back in Virginia, playing with his storage garages and probably chasing every skirt he hasn't already lifted."

"Do you suppose Shipton suspects what Donnie did?"

"According to Weller, the answer is no."

"He is such a hateful man. Lord knows what he did to Donnie over the years to cause the boy to despise him so." She sighed. "So, it's all over." It wasn't a question, just a statement.

"As far as we're concerned. Everyone thinks its finished, except Fred who is still taking notes."

She smiled again. "It'll give him something to do now that the Annie Quincy business is over and the sisters are returning to Boston." Then she asked, "You're not going to tattle on Claire about the real Annie, are you?"

He laughed. "She isn't worth the effort. Let her play 'let's pretend' with her ancestors. Good riddance to her."

"I think if you were going to squeal, I'd be forced to protest." She quickly added, "Not for Claire's sake certainly, but for Annie Quincy. Rev. Joshua Martin perpetuated her fabrication as she requested. The lie held up for a century. Who are we to make it public now? Besides, we have to accommodate the wishes of the guests of Bird Song, don't we? Annie *is* a guest, at least in spirit!" She smiled. "But you're right. I'm glad all of it is behind us."

"Do you think Annie ever told Rev. Martin she was carrying his child?"

"I'd guess he learned from the notebook, after she was dead. Her belongings that Fred bought probably came from his estate. At least her words influenced the Reverend enough to carry on her lie and write her family in Boston," adding, with a hint of sarcasm, "without him using his return address."

"She wouldn't have minded his retaining his anonymity. Annie acknowledged his need to do so by her suicide. But I'm sure she was pleased he abided by her wishes and didn't betray her life to her family."

"Well, at least her secret is still intact, even if it's now being preserved by Claire for all the wrong reasons."

"Do you think the reverend loved her? As strongly as she loved him?"

"Who knows? I'd guess he cared for her, in his own way. But beyond that, I don't have much sympathy for him or what he did."

"I'd like to believe he truly loved her. It makes the story much nicer."

"Cynthia, you are a confirmed romantic. You're letting this saintly man of the cloth off a bit easy, aren't you? He *was* a married minister, preaching the good book on Sunday and boffing a hooker a couple of nights a week! He probably had a charge card up and down Second Street!"

"Nonsense! It's not as if he visited the cribs and houses, looking for prostitutes!" she said sternly. "He simply fell in love after he met her, while doing God's work."

"Okay, let me get this straight," Dean said. "You're saying it's sinful if you go to a whore house, but take-out service is acceptable?"

"I'm not condoning what he did, but I'm not completely condemning it either! Only God judges."

"Rev. Martin was one of God's employees. He, if anyone, should have known better. Annie's death was a direct result of him and his actions."

"I don't care. It's a beautiful story. She really loved him. He gave her a diamond, didn't he?"

Dean wanted to add the cheapskate didn't even buy it—he swiped it from a dead hooker. But instead, her told Cynthia the story of the message Annie scratched on her windowpane.

"'So in love, says everyone.' That's beautiful, isn't it?" she said wistfully.

"Wasn't *everyone* a bit of an exaggeration?"

Cynthia ignored him. "If it *was* Bird Song where Annie lived, perhaps the scratched window pane is still here!"

"That's more of a stretch than trying to fit Gladys Turnbull in Annie's white dress. Even if it was Bird Song where she stayed, the place must have been altered a dozen times in the last century."

"Well," Cynthia said, "perhaps her ghost survived. You said Effie claimed she saw it."

Dean smiled. "Do you believe in ghosts?" he asked.

She thought a moment before answering. "Yes and no. I don't believe in white-sheeted spirits that scare little boys or drag chains around or only come out in cemeteries on Halloween."

"So what's the 'yes' part?" he asked.

"I think places hold the past. Perhaps not real 'ghosts' but things we don't understand—some essence of what occurred there. People subconsciously realize this. That's why they visit birthplaces, places of

monumental happenings like battlefields or sites of great tragedies—
to absorb a tiny bit of what happened there. Maybe places retain all of
the past, every antecedent happening, not just the bad but the good
too. Like Bird Song. Since the first time I stepped inside I had a sense
of all of the love and happiness and peace those walls have witnessed.
Perhaps some unhappiness, too, and tragedy, but even those emotions
seemed wrapped in forgiveness. I guess there was death—but not
scary death—only inevitable, the-time-has-come kind of passing. But
more than anything else, there was love at Bird Song."

He didn't say anything. Finally, she asked, "Does that make sense?"
He nodded his assent and she continued. "Perhaps it's me. Maybe
some people sense that sort of thing more than others—that feeling
you get when you're standing in a spot where you know something
really dramatic occurred."

"Do you believe Annie died at Bird Song?"

"Yes."

"We could probably find out for sure if we kept checking enough
records."

She smiled. "I don't want to *know*. I just want to believe. That's good
enough for me."

"And her ghost lives on?"

Cynthia smiled. "Sort of. But now she's a contented ghost. I don't
sense any feeling of uncertainty or anguish. She knows Rev. Martin
really loved her. Perhaps they're together now."

"Only if St. Peter lets in hookers and hypocrites. Don't you suppose
they might both be doing time in the other place? Shoveling coal?
After all, he was a wayward man of the cloth and she did peddle her
butt for bucks, whatever the extenuating circumstances."

"That's an unforgiving male chauvinistic attitude! I'm sure God has
forgiven their little transgressions and the two of them are contrite for
their actions. Besides, it reads much better the way I want to believe
it!"

"Always the romantic," he smiled. "Okay. I'll buy that they're up
there keeping an eye on Bird Song and watching out for us. But tell
me, where does Mrs. Martin fit into this blissful picture?"

"His wife? Oh, she empathizes with what they did. See? When you
die and go to heaven, you have universal knowledge and understanding. Everyone else feels the same as you and sympathizes perfectly
with just how you feel."

"Like some kind of celestial ménage à trois?"

"Of course not! That's sacrilegious! Let me explain. You see, when *you* die, you have your heaven and I have mine. Everyone has their own heaven. The *you* in my heaven is the person I create in my mind, the perfect *you*, who never drinks his milk from the cereal bowl and remembers every birthday and holiday with the nicest card he buys the day before, and he sends roses for no reason at all...."

"I get the picture," Dean said glumly. "Meanwhile, the *you* up in my dream is—"

"...is probably usually naked and when not screwing, waiting on you hand and foot!"

"So Mrs. Martin is up there socializing with Mr. Martin in her heaven, unaware that Mr. Martin is balling his brains out with Annie across the hall—cloud—while Annie, in her heaven, is the happy homemaker up on Oak Street. I'm beginning to get the picture."

"Just take my word for it. Heaven is a perfectly marvelous place." She patted his knee. "Just be a good boy and you'll get there."

"It all sounds a bit complicated to me. It's a good thing God is omnipotent. Otherwise, he'd never be able to keep it all straight!"

"Of course it's a bit involved. You can't expect all this perfection to happen without a lot of work."

He nodded in agreement. "Maybe now things will be quiet enough so I'll have time to contemplate all those high level philosophical concepts. I can use the peace. It's been a terrible couple of weeks."

"Back to our 'don't get involved' philosophy?" she asked with a smile.

"Getting involved didn't do any good this time around. I'm not sure we didn't compound problems. At least Edith Shipton was alive before she visited Bird Song."

"You can't keep blaming yourself for that, David. Granted, we didn't stop her death, but she didn't kill herself through any direct fault of ours. Just because she threw herself at you hours before she died doesn't make you culpable."

Dean didn't answer as they left the restaurant, but the deep ache remained. Maybe he didn't stop Edith Shipton from taking her own life and maybe he couldn't have done so if he'd tried, but the bottom line scrawled in bold print said he stood idly by while it happened.

"We've got a inn to run," Cynthia said as she hugged his arm for the short drive home. "We're out of it. It's all behind us." It was a terrific speech and they both nodded in mutual agreement. However, neither entirely believed the pronouncement. But they did believe, fervently, that together they made an unstoppable pair, whatever the situation.

CHAPTER 25

When they entered Bird Song Fred was still in place on the sofa, but as soon as he saw them he jumped up and embraced Cynthia like the returning prodigal child. During the hurried explanations of her mother's condition, her trip home and hushed comments on the recent happenings, it was moments before Dean noticed Janet O'Brien sitting in the far corner. She was dressed in a tattered coat, hands in her lap, sitting as nervously as an immigrant awaiting deportation.

"Janet!" Dean said, "What brings you out so late?"

"She's been waiting for you," Fred offered, as if embarrassed at failing to acknowledge their wayward employee earlier.

Janet, with an out-of-character burst of loquaciousness asked, "Miz Dean, I got a little problem. I gotta go away a bit. Can Martha stay here?"

"This evening?"

"No. Like overnight."

"Certainly. Martha's never a problem. She's a sweet little girl. She can stay as long as she wants."

Bells started going off in Dean's mind at the same time bells started ringing in the hall telephone. Janet's request was far too studied for a simple baby-sitting gig. He smelled a rat. "How long?" he asked. The phone continued to ring while Janet contemplated an answer. Dean wanted Fred to answer the damned thing but the old man was too nosy to move. Dean was forced to quiet the persistent instrument before hesitant Janet could muster enough courage to voice her reply. The caller was a stutterer who wanted information on summer rates and a detailed description of the area. Dean tried listening to the two conversations while responding to the one, all at the same time but only managed to catch Cynthia's carte blanc offer for Martha to stay, 'as long as necessary'. Dean, fearing the worse, tried to shake his head 'no' from the hall but no one was looking.

Janet muttered, "I got sixty days." Then she added, "Starts tomorrow."

The two women moved out of sight and sound and Dean agonized through the lengthy, halting conversation before rejoining them. Janet was backing away toward a stage-right exit now that her lines had been delivered. She told Cynthia she'd have Martha carry over her 'stuff'.

"Whoa, wait a minute," Dean said, cutting off his caller. "Officially, doesn't Martha have to—"

"Huh?" was Janet's response.

"I mean, what's her status? Is she a foster child?"

"Naw, she's a Boyd kid."

Dean closed his eyes in frustration. "I don't mean her *name*. I mean legally. Are you her guardian?"

Janet gave a wave of her hand. "It's all unofficial-like. Her ma didn't tell anyone she even had a kid, so nobody cares. I took Martha in 'cause I owed Patsy a favor for some stuff. When I see Patsy I'll tell her you got her so she knows where her kid is at. Martha won't be no problem."

"How did you get her in school?" asked Fred, the detail man.

"I guess I fibbed. But she's there now. Wouldn't seem right to change her, would it?"

"Mrs. Dean and I will have to discuss this," Dean said.

"She already said yes," Janet answered, gesturing toward Cynthia as if to say, the boss has spoken, mind your own business. She turned and wiped her nose on her sleeve. "Damn head cold. Been sneezing all day. I'll be glad to be inside."

Dean turned to Cynthia who tried to busy herself picking up snack dishes from Fred's evening refreshments. He was at a loss for words. Janet, no whiz-kid, at least knew a good exit line and was out the door in a blink.

"Are you going to send me back to Indiana?" Cynthia smiled as soon as the three were alone. "I'm home five minutes and I'm getting you in trouble already."

Dean plumped down on the sofa. "Don't get me wrong—I like little Martha. She's a sweet child who deserves much more than she's ever gotten. But sixty days! And God knows what lies Janet told the school to get her in!"

"That sort of answers the home schooling bit she was trying to pull before you had Jake Weller force the issue," Fred said. "She probably tried to get Martha in class but couldn't come up with the right paper work."

"So now it's our problem," Dean muttered, and then speculated, "I wonder what Janet did to get sixty days."

"Something to do with checks," Fred said. They both looked at him. "Miss Worthington called from the islands." Then, as if explaining her long distance telephone expenditure added, "She got a free phone card for listening to a time share pitch."

"How come your senior citizen girl friend knows our employee is going to jail when she's three thousand miles away and we don't get word until they're ready to slam the cell door?" Dean asked. Fred just shrugged. "To boot, now we've lost our only outside help."

"Don't need any help if the place stays empty," Fred reminded him. "Janet will be out of the slammer before spring."

"Martha will take your mind off everything that's happened the past few days," Cynthia called over her shoulder as she strolled toward the kitchen.

"We don't have a spare room," Dean protested.

"Look around. Spare rooms are about all we've got!" Fred said.

Martha, who couldn't have run that fast from her trailer if she did have a decent pair of sneakers—which she didn't—was at the door, pulling a sled upon which was piled a bundle far smaller than any ten-year-old's belongings ought to represent.

"Guess you won me," Martha said as she dropped a duffle bag on the hall floor. "What do I got to do?"

"What do you mean?"

"Janet says I got to earn my keep. Chores and stuff. I clean pretty good but I don't want to have to do the 'death' room."

Dean and his wife looked at one another. "Feed Mrs. Lincoln," Dean offered as his cat rubbed a welcome against Martha's legs.

"And water Alice," Cynthia added, returning to the room. Alice was a geranium Cynthia had lovingly rescued from certain death by frost last September when the rest of their first year garden succumbed to the advancing seasons.

God, remembered Dean. I've killed Alice! He'd forgotten the scraggy thing while Cynthia was away. He was sure by now it was a brown tangle, ready for the trash heap.

"I saved your butt," Fred muttered, as if reading his mind.

Cynthia took Martha by the hand and led her back to the small first floor bedroom, recently vacated by Ryland. Just then, the front door opened. It was Donald Ryland, Franny and Donnie. All three looked like front of the liners at a Santa Claus hand-out.

"Donnie wanted to say good bye to you," Ryland said as Donnie came up to shake hands with first Dean, then Cynthia and Fred.

"I'm sorry about your mother," Dean said. The young boy scampered back to Ryland's side, still smiling.

"Donnie's going to get lots of help now," Franny said. "There's a real good chance he'll be living with us! Donnie's mother's family is providing for him. It has something to do with a trust fund. We talked on the phone half the day, to some lawyer guy. And, it looks like we're going to have custody!"

"That's great!" Cynthia said as she joined the group, absent Martha, who Dean could hear opening drawers and unpacking in her new room.

"What about Jerome?" Fred asked. Franny just shrugged, as if she didn't want to say anything in front of the boy.

"I'm sure Mr. Shipton will want to see Donnie, from time to time," Ryland offered half-heartedly. Donnie just grimaced, an acknowledgment that he was paying attention to what was being said, and harbored no desire to see his stepfather.

The boy took his small note pad from his back pocket and carefully wrote, "What happened to Annie?" Just then, Martha came into the room. She made a choking, gagging motion at her throat in answer to Donnie's written question. It was Dean's turn to grimace at the untimely reference to death by hanging but Donnie seemed not to understand or make the connection. His face lit up in a smile at seeing his friend and the two bounced over to the sofa together. Then he looked back at Dean, perplexed.

"Didn't you translate the final pages?" Dean asked the boy. Donnie emphatically shook his head no and tapped his pad, as if to ask the question again.

"What happened to your copy of the notebook Cynthia made for you?" Dean asked. Donnie shrugged.

"Did you show them to your mother?"

Again, the boy shook his head no. He picked up his pad and wrote, "Lost them."

"When?" He shrugged and pointed at his first question.

Dean sat down next to him. "Annie was a very sad and troubled woman, Donnie. Perhaps a little like your mother." He didn't elaborate further but the boy seemed to understand.

Franny came over and leaned down to put her arm around his shoulders. He gave her a hug back and then, at Martha's enthusiastic invitation was off to see her new room.

"We took Donnie to a doctor," Franny said when he was out of ear shot. "He said except for Donnie's refusal to speak, in every other way he appears perfectly normal."

Ryland added, "The doctor was very surprised how unaffected Donnie appeared after we described his dysfunctional family environment. The poor kid. But in spite of it, he appears to be well adjusted. The doctor thinks there's a good chance he may even get over the speech problem in time."

"Did the doctor believe Donnie's muteness went back to the death of his half-brother?" Dean asked.

"It was a quick first visit, so the doctor didn't come to any real conclusions. He did say that something as serious as Donnie's stepbrother's death would have been very traumatic to a child. Any time anyone tries to raise the subject to Donnie, he just turns away and acts as if he didn't hear the question."

"He's blocking it out," Cynthia said.

"He has a long road ahead of him, but I'd say he's now in good hands," Dean said.

Dean wandered to the kitchen for pie and coffee for the guests while the others chattered in the parlor. As he was waiting for the coffee to perk, Donnie ran upstairs for something. Dean took the opportunity to knock on Martha's door and step inside.

"Do me a favor?" he asked.

"Sure," she shrugged. "You're the boss now."

"Ask Donnie what happened up there when his stepfather fell." She looked at him, as if she didn't want to go there. "I'm not trying to get him in trouble. Mrs. Dean saw him up there when Mr. Shipton fell and she's concerned...about Donnie."

Martha peeked around the corner to see if Donnie was in sight. He wasn't. "He already told me."

"What did he say?"

"He saw him fall. He thought he was dead and he said that made him happy." She bit her lip. "He asked me if that was being bad."

"He didn't say anything about cutting the rope?"

"Naw. He didn't do that. He would have told me. Him and me are friends. He told me he took the knife, didn't he?" Then she added, "His mother took it away from him, saying she'd keep it, and stick it in his stepfather if he dared come near them."

"Thanks," Dean said, patting her on the shoulder. Then he added, "I'm glad you're staying here with us. You're a sweet girl."

She smiled, hesitantly, then looked up at him. "Ain't you going to ask how I answered?"

"No, Martha. I don't have any business asking you anything personal...about your friends."

"I'll tell you anyway. I told him it was okay for him to be happy. Shipton was a meanie."

Later, after the visitors had left and Martha was in bed, Dean, Cynthia and Fred remained in the parlor.

"Those two, Ryland and Franny—what a pair! They're certainly different," Cynthia said as she stretched back on the sofa.

"Different ain't all bad," Fred said. "They fit together as nice as hot apple pie and a scoop of cold ice cream."

"They're just what Donnie needs," Dean added. He then related what Martha told him about Donnie.

"Thank God," Cynthia said. "I was praying he wasn't involved in Shipton's fall."

"Except if he wasn't involved, who was?" Fred asked, reaching for his notes. "This whole business is getting curiouser and curiouser."

"And what happened to the transcribed pages?" Cynthia asked. "If Donnie didn't know that Annie hanged herself, how could Edith know? Unless someone else could have transcribed them. And where are the missing notebook pages now?"

"More importantly," Fred asked, "If Edith never knew Annie committed suicide, how did she just happen to hang herself the very same way?"

"Whoa!" Dean said, interrupting him. "Let's look at the givens. Edith *had* to know about Annie's death—otherwise her carbon copy suicide is just too much of a coincidence. Perhaps Edith transcribed the last few pages herself. By that time there were enough examples of the substitution code to make the job fairly simple. Maybe she read the pages and destroyed them, or someone else took them after Edith had seen them."

"One or the other of the Boston sisters?" Fred suggested.

"Not Effie," Cynthia said. "Why would Effie take the papers? We volunteered to let her see them."

"She was a big fan of the true Annie Quincy," Fred said. "Why would she try to hide her suicide?"

Dean answered. "She may have been more realistic about Annie's life, but she is very protective of sister Claire. Let's look at *why* they were taken. Maybe that speaks more about the person who took them."

Cynthia nodded in agreement. "The only people truly interested in Annie Quincy are Effie and Claire. It must have been one or the other of them."

"Claire seems to be the prime suspect for taking everything else that isn't nailed down," Dean offered. "She was desperate to hide any blemish on her version of ancestor Annie Quincy's sainthood."

Cynthia capped the discussion with a yawn. "But it doesn't really matter does it? We have the original. Let them have the copy, for whatever it's worth to them. They are about to go back to Boston. Good riddance." She rose and announced it was far past her bedtime, in any time zone.

Dean followed her, happy beyond belief to have her once more share his bed. But the peaceful sleep he'd assumed would come eluded him as his mind continued to trip over far too many loose ends in the recent happenings.

CHAPTER 26

The following two weeks were a mellowing down time. Two more Saturdays of garage sales passed by, far less bountiful than the summer versions of the same, but nevertheless stocked with enough alleged treasures to keep Fred O'Connor at his computer key board for hours on end. There was time for quiet evenings, some jazz and classical music in the Dean's quarters, country and western in Fred's and some totally incomprehensible noise from the small room where Martha Boyd and her boom box now dwelt. Bird Song remained nearly empty during the week and half full weekends when get-away folks from Grand Junction, and sometimes even Colorado Springs or Denver, left the kiddies with grandma and snuck over the mountains for a little R and R. An occasional ice climber continued to remind the group of the receding memories of the recent tragic past.

While the on-premise death of Edith Shipton remained on their minds, it was sinking to a lower level of importance. It was a time to tackle all those built up chores that had accumulated during the busy season now that life was stalled in the dark of winter. It was time for the Deans to talk, to enjoy one another, the first real time together since their May wedding and hectic summer and fall that followed their move West and the opening of Bird Song. While Cynthia's mother was recovering, they discussed what to do if and when she should become unable to care for herself. Her sudden heart attack had frightened Cynthia, reminding her as an only child she was her mother's sole resource. And there was Fred, no trouble but not getting any younger.

Then there was Cynthia's recent additional fear. She confided it to her husband late one night, awakening him from his sleep as Edith Shipton had just awakened him but a week before. This time it was a welcomed body that snuggled against him. She hadn't been able to sleep, she told him, wondering what his reaction would be, if in fact she might be pregnant.

Dean was wide awake in a flash. Cynthia carrying his child! The very thought stunned him. They were both now forty years old. Dean was childless but Cynthia was mother to a twenty-year-old college student. Bird Song, while providing a simple living for them, was never going to bring a fortune to their bank account. He didn't, however, give a quick, stock answer to the possibility. He thought about it. He thought about Annie Quincy carrying a child she would have loved to bear, but couldn't. He thought of Edith Shipton, impregnated by a man she hated and who seemed not to have wanted an intrusive fetus invading her life. And he thought of Cynthia, who loved him as he loved her.

"I'd be the happiest guy in the world," he answered. He could feel her smile in the darkness.

The Quincy sisters had left the day after Cynthia's return from Indiana. Claire, in her usual manner, said nothing as she departed, but Effie had flustered and hovered about, asking detailed questions about Annie as soon as her sister was out of ear-shot. She covertly accepted the copied transcriptions of the young woman's notebook that Cynthia presented to her. In Dean's mind, her attitude and actions eliminated any thought that she might have read or learned of Annie's final hours earlier.

Gladys Turnbull remained Bird Song's sole paying guest, at least for a couple of days longer. She had joined the three hosts for a game of dominoes when Bird Song welcomed a new guest.

The hesitant visitor was Gladys Turnbull's "publisher" from New Mexico. Mr. Arlen was a skinny wimp who introduced himself as the author and publisher of the best selling novel *Responsible Drunkdom*, his thesis and contention being drunkenness was much maligned in our society.

"Between drinking and driving, public drunkenness, wife-beating and under age imbibing, the whole subject of alcohol consumption has been considerably skewed." He looked up, through what Dean thought were reddened eyes. "Of course, all of those conditions are unacceptable to the responsible drunk." He smiled. He pronounced each word precisely, as if he was totally bombed. Which he was.

"I see." Which of course Dean didn't, in the least. But Gladys was delighted and after a night, ostensibly in adjoining rooms, the pair were off, with giggles and tears and a proud pronouncement that Arlen had agreed to present all seven volumes of Belfair and her galactic cohorts to the waiting world of letters—in paper back form. The emaciated, and now exhausted visitor presented Dean with a signed copy of his book, which Dean summarily dumped in the trash without even breaking the spine before the black exhaust of Arlen's rusty Toyota had left the street.

Martha became settled into Bird Song's routine with amazing rapidity. She made herself scarce at first, as if believing if she weren't noticed, no one could kick her out. But the Deans, and especially Fred O'Connor made her feel as if she truly belonged. Her schoolwork improved, she was responsible about helping out and generally unintrusive. Used to being alone, she was content with her own company. When she did venture forth from her digs, a favorite pastime was exploring the cyber world with Fred and his computer.

The clothing Martha brought with her was made up of a rag-tag collection of cast-offs that made most garage sale clothes look like they'd been purchased in a boutique. When the Deans tried to buy her even a minimal number of new items, she became embarrassed and pensive, no doubt a result of Janet's don't-rock-the-boat philosophy. Cynthia, in her infinite wisdom, arranged a generous monetary scale of chores-for-bucks that seemed to take care of the problem. Added to that was Fred's frequent lies about picking up at tag sales for a pittance, items that to an observant eye, still retained their much-higher new-store price.

The paper work on Martha was nowhere near as simple as clothing the child. Apparently mom, before assigned to hard time in Cañon City, had dragged the poor child over most of Colorado and the West. Janet and Ouray were but a stop on the bumpy road to nowhere. Records were nearly non-existent but the kindness of the Ouray school personnel allowed Martha's attendance until matters were straightened out. Which everyone involved realized would never happen.

During the two weeks there was a Mexican dinner at the Catholic church, a couple of movies, three evenings at the Ouray Hot Springs Pool and even a day of downhill skiing at Telluride. Martha tried the boards for the first time and was surprisingly agile. But the high cost of lift tickets and rentals made downhill skiing look like an infrequent outing. Fred picked up a pair of children's cross country skies from an ad in the paper and the group spent a number of after school afternoons on Red Mountain utilizing the free trails at Ironton.

Dean hadn't spoken to Jake Weller in nearly two weeks when he gave the law man a call. All of Edith Shipton's belongings were still packed in a closet at Bird Song. Storage space was at a premium and no one was making any signs of making claim to the stuff. Dean asked Weller to contact Shipton concerning disposition. Jake Weller said he'd look into it and that afternoon he stopped by the inn. He carried a large bundle.

"This junk is Shipton's, too," he said, as he dumped the lot on the hall floor and continued on to the kitchen.

"We wanted to get rid of what we had, not get more. Why would we want Shipton's stuff?" Dean asked as Cynthia joined him.

Weller ignored the question and handed Dean a sheaf of papers. "These are for you. They're filing papers for next summer's sheriff's election."

"Why would I want those papers any more than I want Shipton's garbage? I already told you I'm not interested in your job."

"Just look 'em over. That's all." He smiled at Cynthia who looked as if she'd been out to lunch during an important discussion but she said nothing. Weller poured himself a cup of coffee and sat down at the kitchen table. "You're supposed to get a call about sending Shipton's belongings back east. The only thing I mailed was Mrs. Shipton's wedding ring. This stuff and what you've got is the lot of it. I figured you might as well ship it all together, at one time. CBI didn't need Shipton's junk after all and I don't have the room at the office to store it. We got to leave room for important things like evidence." He looked longingly at an apple pie fresh from the oven. Cynthia obliging cut a piece—a second piece for Dean after he frowned—a third as she joined them.

"Did you speak with dear, sweet Mr. Shipton?" she asked.

"Naw, just his mother. He's too busy making money, I guess. She said she'd arrange for you to box it up. She'll pay you for your trouble."

"If he paid us for all the 'trouble' they caused us, we'd be rich," Dean muttered.

"So we're supposed to find boxes and do the packing, too?" Cynthia asked.

"Yup. There's more in the car." Between bites he added, "I even brought the white dress. I thought the old man might want it."

Cynthia gave a shiver. "I certainly don't want it. Besides, it belongs to Edith—or her family—or her estate—or someone. Not us. She paid for it."

And died in it, Dean wanted to add.

"Shipton doesn't want it. He said so."

"You talked to him?" Dean asked, as Weller eyed a second piece of pie.

"Only back when I told him his wife was dead. Lucky me. I get all the shit jobs—pardon me, ma'am. He didn't want the dress. He said the whole song and dance about his wife acting like that other woman gave him the willies."

"How did he take the news of her death?"

"Once I located him, about as you'd expect—shocked, couldn't believe it, blah, blah, blah. I finally got a hold of him at the airport in Richmond that afternoon. We talked about him coming out here but he begged off. He called back later and left word that he was staying in

Virginia and he'd arranged with a Montrose funeral home to have her cremated."

"He certainly won't be missed at Bird Song," Dean said.

"Yeah," said Weller. "Good riddance to 'em both." He added, "I'm sorry the missus killed herself but she was a looney from the word go. You never knew what to believe of when she opened her mouth. I even hear from the grapevine, there's some question she was pregnant."

"Wasn't there an autopsy?" Dean asked.

"Yeah, but I hear it didn't report anything except she wasn't a druggie and was sober."

"Can't we talk about something else," Cynthia said. "That whole business is too depressing. I'm trying to forget it."

Dean helped Weller carry the remaining articles into Bird Song. The collection was made up of Shipton's newly purchased, barely used, ice climbing gear, ropes, ice axes, pitons and various garments. Fred O'Connor strolled up just as Dean finished. He'd just returned from visiting sun-tanned Miss Worthington. Fred offered to go up to Duckett's Market for boxes and give up closet space to temporarily store the large pile. Not, Dean surmised, out of a sense of charity as much as a severe case of nosiness.

As soon as Jake Weller left, Cynthia questioned her husband about the candidate filing papers Weller handed him.

"Jake's not standing for election next August. He thinks I should file. No dice." End of conversation, except Dean noticed Cynthia fold the papers and put them aside.

For the balance of the afternoon, Dean felt pangs of guilt for summarily deciding not to even consider seeking the position of sheriff without so much as discussing it with his wife. Was he being unfair, taking the easy way out? Content with a no-sweat life made up of V-necks and corduroys and flannel shirts and music no one else listened to anymore? His season was passing like tomatoes still green when the frost hits, unable to fulfill what they've been straining to achieve through the long hot summer. But the tomato, a berry grown out of its natural proportion by the fiddling of man, at least knew redness was its ultimate goal. What was Dean's goal? Dean vacillated between the contentment of inactivity and the frustration of trying to change the unchangeable. Was he Dorvad the lazy mate as Gladys so fictionalized him? He planned to discuss it with Cynthia but other matters interrupted.

Later that evening, Fred came down to the kitchen as Martha was finishing drying the dishes. As she scooted off to do homework, he plunked down at the table, looking perplexed.

"What's the matter?" Cynthia asked.

"One of them bundles says it's Mrs. Shipton's stuff but all it has in it is the white dress."

"So?" Dean said.

"So where's the pen?" They didn't answer. "And where's her...unmentionables?"

"Her underwear?" Cynthia asked with a smile. Fred shook his head yes. "Maybe her personal effects are in another bag."

"Nope. That was all there was. And I looked again in her other stuff, the things she left in her room. No pen. No underwear either—least not Annie's." Fred assumed his senior detective mode. "As you remember," he said, "I questioned the fountain pen before, earlier in this here investigation. You thought it went to the hospital, in a pocket of the white dress. It didn't. The dress doesn't even have a pocket. So where is it? They sure didn't cremate the woman, naked as the day she was born, holding on to a fountain pen!"

"Let's chalk up another light-finger souvenir to Claire," Dean suggested. But Fred wasn't buying.

"Why would Edith put the white dress back on but no underwear?" he asked.

"Modesty?" Cynthia offered.

"She didn't demonstrate any modesty when she came to your room," Fred pointed out, reopening a road Dean preferred to detour. "Nor when she paraded up the stairs and gave the business to Claire Quincy."

Dean sighed. He wished to put everything concerning the Shiptons in the circular file of his memory and get on with a normal life. While the loose ends of both Jerome Shipton's fall and Edith's suicide itched at Dean's sense of logical completion, the matter in its entirety was so repugnant to him that he didn't want to think about it. Dean said nothing, hoping the subject would die a natural death.

"She put the white dress on because she was Annie Quincy when she died," Cynthia said.

"I'll bet Annie Quincy wore her underwear," Fred grumbled. "Edith didn't. Not even her own. Edith didn't have anything on but the white dress. She didn't wear a bra or her panties or Annie's antique drawers."

"Maybe she was in a hurry," Cynthia offered. She turned to her husband. "How long after she left you did she...do it?"

"I don't know," Dean answered, a tad on the surly side. "I sure wasn't looking at a clock when I was trying to get rid of her."

"I can answer my own question," Cynthia said quietly. "Remember? I telephoned you at four-thirty."

"Edith died before five," Fred said. "That was mighty quick."

"Why would she bother to wait?" Dean asked glumly. "There wasn't anybody to stop her. That was the point of her suicide, wasn't it? There wasn't anybody left in Edith Shipton's life for her to turn to."

Dean continued to feel miserable but Fred was on a roll. "So where are the drawers?" he asked. "They weren't in Edith's room either."

"Claire the klepto swiped them," Dean said impatiently.

"Antique undies?" Cynthia said, shaking her head. "Claire didn't express any interest in Annie's clothing earlier. She was quick enough to toss in the underthings when she sold the dress to Edith that first night. Why would she steal them back later?"

"And when could she swipe 'em?" Fred asked. "I was in that room real quick after Edith died. So were you. And a little while later the police were all over the place. I never saw Claire poking around."

Cynthia turned to her husband. "It seems to me, that Edith had a very rapid mood change from flaunting her nakedness in front of Claire to...killing herself, practically minutes later. You have to admit, that's strange behavior."

Dean tried to put the matter to final rest. "Everything about Edith Shipton was strange—her moods—her personality—the fact that she lied so easily. She said she was pregnant and now there's a question about that. She said her stepson was killed canoeing with her husband when we know he died in a swimming pool—with her nearby. She claimed Shipton was nuts to have her back, when in reality, who knows how he felt? She told Franny that Donald had dumped her as his fiancée when he never considered doing any such thing. Even though she had a bruise, we only have her word that Shipton beat her. Edith Shipton was, first and foremost, a very manipulative and self-centered woman who had a love-hate relationship with every man she ever met. Who knows what went through her mind when she died?"

"That doesn't sound to me like the type of person who takes her own life," Cynthia said.

Fred O'Connor's eyes lit up and his wheels began to spin. Dean knew the look and he put the brakes on Fred's euphoria before the rampant speculation could go any further.

"Don't forget the suicide note," Dean said emphatically. "She wrote it and no one forced her to do so. We can wonder what happened to the pen and who raided her panties but we'll probably never know the answer to either question. We can speculate all day *why* Edith Shipton killed herself, but there's no arguing the fact that she did so. That's a given. End of report." Dean rose and wandered out to the front porch but in spite of his sterling speech, and overwhelming wish that he could forget the Shiptons and all the grief they had brought him, he couldn't quite chase the unfinished business from his churning mind. Primarily, it was Jerome Shipton's severed climbing rope that remained a knotty question that wouldn't go away.

The following weekend, two and a half weeks after Edith's death, Penny and Mick returned to bird Song for a couple of days of ice climbing, a further reminder of the ice park incident. Before the couple left for their climb, Dean pulled Penny aside.

"If I wanted to rappel down and not leave a rope at the top, how would I do it?" he asked.

"That's easy," she answered. "You'd just loop your line through a set up or a fixed anchor and rappel down. Then you'd pull the free end of the line down to you."

"What happens to the ice anchor?"

She looked at Dean as if he were less than the top of his class. "It'd stay up there, of course. If there's a stationary point you could tie on to, all the better. Otherwise, you're out one anchor."

"But you've retrieved your line."

"Sure."

"But you'd have to set an ice anchor?"

"No need, in most places." She paused, then clarified. "If you can't find a fixed rappel, you have to rig one, but at popular climbing spots, like in the ice park, there's lots of choices 'cause it's climbed so much."

"But you could rig an anchor, right?"

"As a last resort. But those things cost big bucks. Why leave it up there if you've got a better choice, like a tree or iron ring to rig your station? But why would you go to all that trouble in the first place? You'd have to get back up to where you started anyway, unless you're going out in another direction. Rappelling is just getting there, a way to get down to your base. The sport is called ice *climbing*—getting back up is the challenge."

"Thanks," he said.

"So, you think Jerome Shipton cut the line so it looked like someone was trying to kill him and then used the remaining portion to loop through an anchor so he could then rappel down?"

Dean smiled at the young lady's perception. "I guess I considered it as a possibility. But it doesn't answer his injuries, does it?"

"The jerk didn't know what he was doing in the first place. He might have just fallen, luckily closer to the bottom than the top, or he'd be a dead man. It's not hard to misjudge out there, especially a rank beginner like Shipton, doing it alone."

"Why would he go to so much trouble?" Dean asked.

Penny thought a moment. "He was pretty pissed at you. Maybe he wanted to dump a little do-do on your parade...pretend like you were trying to kill him."

"He'd be taking a big risk and going to a lot of trouble just because I took a couple of swings at him."

She shrugged. "He sure didn't fall all the way down from where the line was cut and I doubt anyone cut the rope when he was half way down the cliff. No one was seen up at the top when he fell, right?" Dean nodded. "Then what you were suggesting makes sense. He himself could have cut the rope—the short end they found tied up top—set up a second rappel at a nearby spot and gone down on it. What a bastard! I'm glad he messed up and fell." She thought a moment and then turned to Dean, a puzzled look on her face. "There is one more possibility."

"What's that?"

"A second climber. No one would have seen him so he could have cut the line and then rappelled down, on a looped line, after Shipton fell. Just a thought." Before Dean could comment, she asked, "You going to try ice climbing yourself? Mick and I will take you up to the ice park if you want to give it a go. We'll teach you to do it the right way."

Dean thanked the personable young lady but passed on the invitation. But he thought he'd learned what he wanted. He could now picture how Jerome Shipton might have caused his own fall. What remained was the question why. And Penny's final observation about a second climber opened a whole new perspective. The only other party involved with Shipton who was an ice climber was Donald Ryland.

Later the same morning, Dean took advantage of the cold but clear day for a little biking. He was concentrating on the roadway, miles from Ouray, when Franny Mulligan passed him, slammed on her brakes, and waved him back to where she parked.

"I was on my way to Bird Song this afternoon," she explained as he peddled up to her car.

"Great to see you! How's Donald and Donnie?"

"That's why I was coming to see you. To invite you guys to the wedding, all of you, even Martha!" Dean set his bike down and joined Franny in her car as she continued. "And we were wondering if we could take Martha back to Grand Junction with us today? Just for a few days. Donnie would love to see her."

"I know she'd have a ball. I don't see why not."

"Donnie's starting to speak. I know seeing Martha would help. He's not saying sentences or anything like that yet. He's just forming words and sounds but the doctor is very encouraged. I'll bet the first time he really talks, it'll be about Martha! He keeps writing little stories about her. The boy is smitten."

"Come by Bird Song and we'll have to arrange for her to go back with you."

"And guess what else? We're going to have permanent custody! That's the other reason I'm down here. I have to go by a lawyer's office. Shipton the bastard agreed to sign some papers and give Donald and me full custody!"

"Where is Donald?"

"Donald isn't coming to the lawyer's office because he doesn't want to see Shipton if he doesn't have to. He's going to meet me later after he gets in a little ice climbing."

"Then you're meeting with Shipton?"

"Naw. Just exchanging papers with the lawyer. It's temporary custody at first until some court stuff takes place and we're married but the lawyer says Shipton definitely signed."

"Shipton is in Ouray?" Dean asked.

"Yeah. The lawyer said he came by personally with the papers. He has to pick up his wife's belongings, too."

"Their luggage is stored at Bird Song," Dean said. "I'm not that fussy about his coming there to get it."

"I can understand that after you guys tried to kill each other. Maybe he'll have enough sense to send someone else to pick it up."

Dean hadn't received word from the Shipton family since Weller had deposited the baggage on his doorstep. If Shipton was in town, Dean was unaware of it. His first inclination was to stay as far away from Bird Song as possible until Shipton was long gone. He hadn't set eyes on the man since he'd decked him in front of his inn and that was fine in his book. However, he was even less inclined to leave Cynthia, perhaps alone, if Shipton were to come by for the stored belongings.

"I'd better get back to Bird Song in case he shows up," Dean said.

"I'll come on over as soon as I'm finished with the attorneys. I can referee!" Then Franny added, "It'll be strange going back there. God, it was a terrible night. I'll never forget it. Me standing there half naked,

Gladys screaming her fool head off, Edith's body hanging in the middle of the room...." She gave a shiver.

Dean patted her arm. "Forget the Shiptons. You've got a whole life ahead of you." His words seemed to perk up Franny.

She smiled. "You're right. I've got too much going for me right now to be thinking about those jerks. And look," she added, "No butts! I listened to your advice. I haven't smoked since I decided not to kill Donald Ryland and let him marry me! It's pushing three weeks now and I hardly ever get the shakes anymore."

"No more midnight trips out in the snow?"

"God! I was bad, wasn't I?"

Dean climbed from her car and she was off with a wave. At least something good had come out of Edith Shipton's ill-fated stay at Bird Song. It looked like young Donnie had a chance at life, in a home where love was in residence, instead of hatred and desperation. And smoke-free to boot!

Dean was several miles north of Ridgway, fifteen miles from Ouray. Later, thinking back, he realized it was on that one-hour bike trip the first few seeds of comprehension began to sprout something besides weeds in the garden of his mind. No, the events of two weeks past didn't make total sense, at least not yet, but Dean was suddenly interested, not in avoiding Jerome Shipton, but asking him some important questions.

As Dean peddled up to Bird Song, he saw no unfamiliar cars. It was Martha who met him when he opened the front door.

"You're not alone, are you?" he asked, the concern showing in is voice.

The young girl explained Cynthia had just left for Duckett's Market to pick up a few items but Fred was up in his room, working on his computer. Shipton had come and gone. Cynthia had spotted him coming up the walk, Martha explained, and managed to remain out of sight while Fred helped Shipton lug down the belongings.

"He had some lady in the car," Martha said, just as Fred O'Connor tromped down the stairs and joined them.

"You wouldn't have recognized Shipton," the old man said with a smile. "He was as sweet as peach pie in August—shook my hand like a Sunday preacher. He even dropped off their room key and apologized all over for keeping it for two weeks and sticking us with storing all his junk."

"Where is he now?" Dean asked.

"One of the motels in town. He didn't say which. He even apologized for not calling before he stopped by and for not staying at Bird Song, like maybe he'd be welcomed. Said it brought back sad memories. If he didn't have some tootsie with him and I didn't know him for the skunk he is, I might have believed him."

"Did he pick up everything—all the items Jake Weller brought by and the luggage we were holding—and the climbing gear?" Dean asked.

"Yup. He had a car, a rental I guess. We piled it in the trunk and backseat." Fred reached in his shirt pocket and with a smile and a flourish, held out a check. "But give the devil his due, he paid his way." The check was for a substantial amount. "Shipton insisted on paying for the last two weeks even though he wasn't near the place. Said it was for all the trouble he and his wife caused Bird Song."

Dean held the key in his hand and glanced at the check. More seeds sprouted. It was plunk, plunk, plunk as little pieces began falling in place.

"No guess where he and the woman are staying?" Dean asked, sudden concern showing on his face.

"Naw. They drove off to the south." Unfortunately, most of the motels that remained open in the winter season were located in that direction. Dean picked up the hall phone, and resting the phone book on his lap began calling lodging establishments.

"What's a matter?" Fred asked. "You're not going to return his money are you?"

"No," Dean answered. "I just want to talk. Something important just dawned on me."

Fred continued to stand by as Dean found where Jerome Shipton was staying on the second try. He asked to speak with him.

"No, he's not here now," answered a pleasant voice. "They just left for the ice park." He could hear the smile in her voice. "He said something about getting back on the horse after you fall. I can't understand those climbers...." But Dean didn't let her finish before he interrupted, ending the conversation. He dialed Sheriff Jake Weller's office while Fred continued to question him, but he waved him off with a shake of his head.

Weller wasn't in. Dean slammed down the phone as he grabbed his coat and rushed for the door. "Call the City Police, too. Keep trying to locate Weller. I'm going up to the ice park!"

"Why?"

"Because if someone doesn't find him soon, Jerome Shipton is going to be a dead man!"

CHAPTER 27

Dean jogged up the hill to ice park, hoping to find Penny and Mick, and perhaps Donald Ryland, before confronting Jerome Shipton. From what he could see from the roadway bridge the upper path was empty. Up the gorge, there were no climbers tacked to the icy walls. He hesitated, wondering if they had chosen a lower climbing spot, below the bridge that spanned the gorge. No, he guessed. The others might be below, but Shipton would attempt the same climb where he had fallen two weeks before. The spot was out of sight from where Dean stood. The day was overcast and absent the warming glow of the sun, felt colder than usual. Dean wished he'd taken time to dress more warmly as he hurried down the penstock path toward where Shipton's severed line had been tethered. He moved up the steel trestle by the ice climbing area designated The Schoolroom. As he hurried down the narrow plank catwalk atop the penstock, he caught sight of a woman stumbling toward him. She clung to the metal railing as if her life depended on it, stumbling toward him, blocking his progress.

The woman, a buxom blonde about forty, Dean guessed, was clothed in a fashion magazine outfit, designed for après snow bunny activity, not actually *doing* anything in the great outdoors. She was furious. Dean pegged her to be Jerome Shipton's companion.

"If he thinks I'm going put those stupid things on my feet and swing down there like some mountain goat, he's crazier than I am for coming out here in the first place." She talked to Dean as if any fool out here in the wilderness should be fully versed in everyone else's activity. "God, I must have been drunker than I thought I was! Guys are so incredibly stupid!"

"Where is he?" Dean asked as he tried to move around the irate woman on the narrow walkway. She motioned over her shoulder.

"All I was supposed to do was take his damned picture, just because some jerk didn't believe he'd been up here and done it! He didn't say I had to climb down on some rope and hang by my thumbs! And he has the nerve to call this shit exciting and romantic! He promised to take me to Telluride, not some God forsaken place out in the effing woods where I could kill myself!" She wiped a hand across her tear stained face, smudging an abundance of makeup. "So, I'm a chicken. Big deal! Like I'm going to lose sleep over that one! Better a live chicken than a

253

dead rooster. Tell him I clucked my way back to the motel and the fire-place—if you see the bastard before he kills himself!" She shoved a camera at Dean, an expensive looking Nikon, freeing her other hand to more securely grasp the rail. "Here, you take his stupid picture." She swung by him, oblivious that she was rubbing her ample chest against him in the passing. She moved down the catwalk, swinging her design-er-encased butt.

Once off the walkway, Dean ran down the path until he spotted a pile of equipment and what had been described as fixed belay. While no one was in sight, Dean recognized the line, wrapped around a gnarled cedar, as the same color that had been stored at Bird Song. He dropped the camera and peered over the edge of the cliff but the out-cropping blocked his view of anything below. The only sound was the rush of water at the base of the canyon. Several days of unseasonable melt had boiled the river to a noisy torrent of cascading water.

"Shipton!" Dean yelled, his voice echoing up and down the now empty gorge, bouncing about the stone walls and boulders of the nar-row ravine. His own voice was the sole reply. Dean leaned over and grasped the taut line that ran unseen over the edge. He could feel the tremor of movement in his hand, the result of some motion far below. He leaned forward but strain as he might, the overhanging bulge at the top of the cliff prevented him from seeing the source of the activity. He called Shipton's name once more, but again his shout hung unan-swered in the still winter air. It was decision time. He could wait until help arrived or just wait until Shipton climbed back up—before some-thing untoward occurred. He owed the scoundrel nothing. But for most of Dean's life, hadn't that always been the case?

Dean again looked down the path but no help was in sight. His stomach knotted. It was as if every fear he'd ever encountered paled before the idea of descending even a few feet closer to the edge that yawned before him. He took a deep breath. The retreating blonde woman's rope and crampons lay discarded at the edge of the path, the bag from their recent purchase crumpled nearby. Dean blanked from his mind what he was about to do, concentrating on the task at hand. He clamped the metal spikes to his feet. Shipton had used a gnarled cedar, years dead, as an anchor for his line. Dean did the same, hoping its eighteen inch girth was sufficient to secure the two damn fools who were testing it as their sole mooring against the natural forces of nature. With shaking hands, he fumbled, affixing what were certainly not approved knots, but he tied enough of them to be confident they would hold. No textbook belay. Not by a long shot. Dean tried to remember how Ryland had described the method of securing the other end of the line to the climber's body. There was something about a belt—a harness he'd called it. Dean rummaged about in the snow among the remaining climbing articles but the leather apparatus he untangled was far too small for his waist. He glanced back once more at the void beyond the ledge and then looped the line around his body and stomped the few feet toward the cliff, trying to step without tripping in the cumbersome and unfamiliar foot wear.

Dean knew he was being foolish beyond any measure of reason to venture even the short distance that would allow him to see beyond the overhang. His gloves, adequate for snow shoveling, were poor equipment to safely grasp a rope that supported his full weight. He wound the line around his left hand twice while playing it out with his right hand. He leaned back over certain death, a hundred bouncing, smashing, flying feet below. His sole security was the loop of this rope around his body, between his legs, across his back and over his shoulder, which he then grasped as if his life depended on it. Which it did.

In his mind's eye Dean could picture climbers rappelling downward in great lunges, covering many feet in long swings, reaching the bottom in but a few mad leaps into space. He forced the picture from his mind and leaned backward, testing the rope against his weight. He gave no thought to how he'd reverse the process and return to the ledge above.

"Shipton!" he continued to yell as he paid out more of the line, moving down the short but near-vertical slope of snow-covered rock, his eyes fixed above on the receding bank of trees and safety. Abruptly the scratching sound of the crampons beneath his feet told him he'd reached the first mounds of solid ice. Stomping harder, he tried to plant the spikes, as if gravity would bow to so meager a hold against its forces. He stole a glance downward for the first time but found he hadn't cleared the edge far enough to see below. Gingerly, he played out more rope and descended lower, the slope now near-vertical so the toe of his crampon bit into the rock-hard ice. Water dripped from above and tiny snowballs cascaded down the slope, bouncing off his un-helmeted head and under his collar as his line scoured the bank of snow above him.

He was startled by a voice below him, causing him to nearly lose his grasp with its closeness. Jerome Shipton was scarcely a dozen feet lower, off to his left.

"Did you bring my camera?" he asked as he smiled up at Dean. "This would make a hell of a picture."

"Shipton, climb back up! Your line may not be safe!"

"That was a one time accident, buddy. This is another rope."

"Shipton, think about it!" Dean cried, struggling to maintain his precarious position. "The first rope was cut. Why not the second one, too?"

Shipton dismissed Dean's concern with a smile. "She wasn't that smart."

"Don't be stupid and take the chance! You've already fallen once!"

"That's why I'm here, just to prove I can do it. Call it a macho thing, but this time I'm not going to screw up and slip."

"Are you sure you slipped?" Dean said through gritted teeth, his hands beginning to ache against the strain of the tightened rope.

"I'll race you to the bottom and we can talk about it." Shipton squirmed, adjusting his position. He began to fumble with the ring of his harness.

"Wait!" Dean yelled, panic in his voice.

Dean knotted his rope with trembling hands as he looked down on the man nearly directly under him. "Shipton, listen. You can't be sure you slipped! Climb back up!"

"Edith cut my rope but she didn't do a very good job, did she? Of course she didn't do a very good job with anything in life. Especially watching my son."

"So you killed her," Dean growled.

Shipton halted what he was doing and looked up, the smile now gone. "She killed herself, remember? She was remorseful because she tried to kill me."

Dean attempted to move, turning his body for a clearer look down at Shipton but the adjustment in his position caused a shower of snow to descend on him, nearly covering his head and shoulders. Shipton laughed as Dean spit away the icy covering. Finally he steadied himself enough to respond. "I saw the check you just gave Fred. That told me how you did it. And you still had a key to Bird Song." He now had Shipton's attention. "You strangled her and pulled her body up on the cord to fake her hanging herself."

"Prove it," Shipton answered coldly.

"The crime lab guys in Denver will be able to. The pen's the key. That's all they'll need."

"You think you're pretty damn smart, don't you?"

Dean grimaced against the strain of the rope on his back, legs and shoulder. "Not as smart as I should have been. I should have remembered you still had your key to Bird Song. And you hadn't left town yet. You didn't return to Virginia until the following day."

"Who else knows about your little fairy tale?"

"Jake Weller. And Corday and the rest of them by now," Dean lied.

Once more, Shipton laughed. "I don't think so. You must have just guessed what happened after I just stopped by Bird Song. Then you came hustling up here, alone. If you'd taken time to talk to Weller and the rest of them, they'd be here, not just you."

"You bastard!" Dean snarled. "I spent two weeks of hell thinking I was a big part of why Edith died!"

"Edith was too damn selfish to ever kill herself," Shipton growled. He swung his ice ax into the wall in front of him, dug in the toes of his crampons and began to ascend toward Dean.

It was no match. Dean, absent any tools for pulling himself upward was limited to using the rope, hand over hand, impossibly slow compared to the man now pursuing him. Each pull upward would require Dean to release his grasp on the line that secured him should he slip and fall backwards! Dean had no doubt about Shipton's ultimate intention. He tried to move laterally, away to his right, but the gnarled branches of a now-dead bush blocked his path.

Shipton swung his ice ax again, inching up closer to Dean. "She would have killed me if she could have, wouldn't she? Fair is fair." He swung the ax once more, now only half a body length away.

"Shipton! You don't get it, do you? You're line *was* cut!"

Shipton paid him no mind. One tug on the rope confirmed to Dean his sole route of escape was down, not up. He closed his eyes briefly and began loosening his tight grip on the line, readying himself to rappel downward. Glancing over his shoulder at his advancing pursuer, he knew he'd have to drop far enough and rapidly enough to pass Shipton before the killer could swing out with his deadly ax. He had no idea if he possessed the strength to stop his fall once the loosened slack had expired.

Shipton's ax bit the ice scarcely a foot below Dean as the man glared up at him, a snarl on his face. It was now, if it was to be at all. Dean released his grip and dropped backward into space. The line burned across his shoulders and exposed neck. When the stopping jolt came, it nearly knocked the wind out of him with its abruptness, but he'd fallen only to the level of Shipton's knees. Shipton flailed out at him with his ax, missing his head by inches as Dean leaned sideways and frantically fumbled with his line to drop again. Shipton, sensing now that Dean had not simply fallen, began to work at the ring on his harness where his line was secured.

Dean dropped once more with the same bone-jarring result, this time slamming against the cliff-side with his entire right side and arm. Searing pain shot through his shoulder and he realized he barely had the strength to halt another rappel. Shipton leaned to his right and began to chop away at a large outcrop of ice directly above Dean, laughing as a loosened piece tumbled downward, striking Dean's exposed head, nearly knocking him senseless. Shipton continued to chop, as if deciding this and not a direct blow from the ice ax was a far better way to remove this annoying impediment to his foolproof plan.

Dean gritted his teeth and dropped once more, just as a block of frozen mass as large as his head struck a glancing blow to his already aching shoulder. Shipton swore and began to fumble with his line to rappel again, down to the now injured and trapped form hovering below him. As he was about to drop, Dean saw Shipton's half-severed line begin to part!

"Don't," he screamed at Shipton, "the line's been cut!" But his cry came an instant too late as Shipton plummeted past him, his ice ax swinging in a rip across Dean's calf as he plummeted backward into space, and down to the rocks and churning river below. Dean momentarily opened his eyes to the swaying end of the cut line across from him. He couldn't bring himself to look down before a wave of dizziness overtook him.

Dean vaguely remembered the eternity before voices above called his name and rescuers gracefully dropped down next to him. There was a sense of cold and the ooze of blood filling his boot, and a reeling wave of lightheadedness, but little pain. Unconsciousness must have paid its call before hands secured him and lowered him to the waiting rescuers below. He recalled none of this, nor his damaged body being placed on a litter at the narrow edge of the cascading water and lifted upward from the depth of the inaccessible gorge to the penstock path above. The only sound he remembered was ambulance siren on its long journey to the Montrose hospital.

CHAPTER 28

It was Monday. Two days and nights had passed since Dean's siren-serenaded ride to the Montrose Hospital and subsequent forty-eight hour stay in its friendly confines. The leg wound from Shipton's flailing ice ax had been an eight-stitcher of no permanent consequence but the clump of frozen mountain Dean caught on the head kept him fuzzy and blurred his vision for a day and a half, necessitating the stay. An hour earlier a nurse wheeled Dean to Cynthia, Fred and their waiting Jeep. Now, thanks to an early February thaw, it was warm enough to haul out the front porch rockers and pretend it was summer in the warmth of the mid-afternoon sun.

Cynthia, Fred, and Dean with a cane nearby, rocked in unison, albeit bundled and mittened, but content to have Bird Song to themselves, at least until the weekend.

"Are you going to fill us in or just keep rocking until you wear a hole in the porch?" Fred asked, his patience hitting the wall. The trip from hospital to Ouray excluded any mention of the earlier happenings as Dean's health took precedence but now that wellness was established, it was open season.

Dean chuckled. He'd been waiting for just such an outburst. During his in-and-out-of-it hospital stay both his wife and stepfather had refrained from questioning him. This noble restraint wasn't entirely out of respect for Dean's condition. A police guard blocked Dean's door for the first twenty-four hours, precluding visitors. Once it was established the law wasn't there to jail Dean as soon as he'd recuperated, Cynthia relaxed. Shipton was dead—he had tried to kill Dean. Beyond possessing those meager details, wife and stepfather were clueless.

Shipton's traveling companion, Penelope Something, hysterically filled in what little she knew to Jake Weller and Emile Corday, both of whom visited the patient at the hospital. Dean's spoon-fed explanation to the two, served between naps and medical visits, satisfied officialdom enough to free Dean from any hint of culpability. If Corday had apologized, Dean was napping at the time.

Dean continued to pump his rocker a few moments longer, trying to set up his response in some sequence of understandable order.

"It's a bit confusing and a lot of it's speculation on my part, but bear with me and I think I have enough of the answers to make some sense of what happened. The bottom line is Shipton killed his wife." Dean turned to his stepfather. "It wasn't the amount of the check Shipton gave you that caught my attention, it was the ink. The check was written with an old fashioned fountain pen. If the pen were Edith's, how, or why would Shipton have it?"

"Why would he take the fountain pen?" Fred asked, checking his notes.

"It wasn't the only fountain pen in the world," Cynthia said. "Maybe the Shiptons had a matched pair, like his and hers? I can't see why the fact that he used a pen would send you dashing up to the ice park and half kill yourself."

Dean cringed at this first admonition for his impulsive actions. "Don't give me hell just yet darling," he said with a smile, patting her arm. "The pen was just too much of a coincidence. That and the key to Bird Song. The key told me Shipton could have been here that night. The noise at the locked front door I heard when Edith was in my room wasn't Franny going out for a smoke as I'd assumed at the time. It was Shipton sneaking in. Of course it wasn't Franny. How stupid could I be? All she was wearing was her underwear a little while later when she ran up the stairs when Edith's body was discovered. Even if modesty wasn't at the top of Franny's traits-list, it *was* January! Even the most ardent smoker wouldn't be outside in those skimpy duds."

"That may be a neat theory," Fred said, "but it ain't proof. Not by a long shot. Just because Shipton had a key don't mean he used it. Besides, he was back in Virginia when Edith died."

"We never considered Shipton might not have left town until after Edith died," Dean answered. "Jake Weller told us he had difficulty locating Shipton to inform him of Edith's death. He finally spoke with him at the airport. Shipton hadn't left town the day he checked out of the hospital. He waited until the following day, after he killed his wife."

Cynthia turned to him. "There was no reason to care when Shipton left town, was there? No one ever considered it because it wasn't important. Edith's death wasn't murder. The suicide note cut off any reason for investigation."

"Right," Dean answered.

"I don't understand," Cynthia continued, a perplexed look on her face. "If Shipton did kill Edith as you say, how did he get her to leave a suicide note?"

"Think about the missing pen," he answered.

"What was so important about the pen?"

"Think about the ink. The suicide note was written in blue ink. The pen has black ink in it now. That's the color of the ink on the check Shipton signed."

Fred looked as bewildered as Cynthia. "So?"

"Able Whitehouse, the guy we spoke to back in Virginia gave us the clue, only we didn't realize it. Edith Shipton had attempted suicide once before, after her stepson drowned in her presence. Had she written a suicide note then? Probably. Who might still have that note? Her husband! What a perfect way to kill someone when they've conveniently given you a suicide note indisputably in their handwriting!"

Cynthia and Fred began to nod their heads, understanding what Dean was saying.

"Shipton must have been smart enough to notice the different color inks. Buying fountain pen ink now-a-days is a little tricky. Nearly everyone uses ball point pens. Besides, Edith had the pen in her possession so he lacked any opportunity to change it back to the color she used years earlier when she wrote the suicide note. Better to have the pen missing than to have the wrong color ink some one might notice."

"Couldn't the CBI guys over in their Denver lab tell the suicide note was written years before?" Fred asked. "I've read up on some of the stuff those fellas can do. Pretty amazing. And that ain't just fiction."

"You'd have to ask them, but I'm sure they could. However, someone would have to question the note in the first place. Who would ever bother to check? A woman is dead. There's a note in her handwriting. The whole business with Annie Quincy leads up to a similar suicide. End of case. We bought it, didn't we? Granted, Shipton was taking a slight chance, but a mighty slim one."

"So you're guessing he was the one who took the Annie papers, the ones Donnie lost?" Cynthia asked. "But how could he translate them?"

"By the time we got to the end of Annie's notebook, there was more than enough pages transcribed that anyone could decipher the last few pages. I think Shipton found the pages and decided to follow Annie's method of death."

Cynthia shuddered. "What about the missing underwear? Did Shipton steal that, too?"

"Yes," Dean answered. "I'm pretty sure he did."

"Why? Why not put them on her, too? He must have put Annie Quincy's white dress on her. You said she came back upstairs naked and he probably killed her as soon as she entered the room." She thought out loud. "Then he dressed the naked corpse, and pulled her up on the drapery cord. God! It sounds so gruesome! What a monster!"

"It *was* gruesome, but that's what he did. Annie's white dress would easily slip over her head. It was readily available. Edith was carrying it when she came into the room but he probably didn't want to take time to search for underwear. Or shoes. She was barefoot too, remember?"

"But why would he take the underwear?" Cynthia repeated.

"A sick souvenir?" Fred asked, disgusted.

"Do you want another guess?" Dean asked. They nodded. "Think what those hundred-year-old drawers looked like to someone who didn't know what they were. An old cotton rag. I wouldn't be surprised he used them to mop up something, blood perhaps. She must have struggled and may have hurt him. Even if it was just a scratch or a bite it wouldn't do to have blood at the scene, especially someone else's blood." Then he added, "Or, perhaps he used it, to stuff it in her mouth and silence her while he chocked her to death."

"God," Cynthia said, turning away.

Dean continued. "I should have guessed what happened a long before now. I was too busy feeling sorry for myself."

"But it's all still just that, isn't it?" Cynthia said. "A guess? Granted, what you're saying *could* have worked, but that doesn't mean it did. I don't see how noticing a different color ink on Shipton's check made you so positive you set off after him the way you did."

"It was the proverbial straw. Once I had a means of discounting the suicide note, everything else made much more sense. I'd had a problem myself all along, not seeing Edith as being on the brink of suicide. Now there was a chance she didn't kill herself. When a person dies, the prime suspect is always the surviving spouse."

"If you do any more ice climbing we can put that to the test," she answered. But Dean saw a hint of a smile. "You've spent a pretty miserable two weeks beating yourself and taking responsibility for her death," Cynthia said, placing a consoling hand on her husband's arm. "If you're right about what happened, there must be some consolation in knowing Edith's death had nothing to do with you."

"Oh, I'm right about it. Now I'm just kicking myself for not figuring out the whole business earlier."

"How could you?" Fred asked. "We were all bamboozled."

"There were any number of hints. I was too tunnel-visioned to dismiss the inconsistencies. I just wanted to put the whole business out of my mind, behind me. Fred here was the guy who wouldn't let go. He was the one who kept at it. Edith's death was constantly on my mind, but I never for a minute considered anything but suicide. If I had tried to figure it out logically, things might have fallen into place. Take the time factor. It was the noise from the falling chair that woke me up. I rushed up the stairs but when I arrived, Edith was stone dead. Strangulation isn't a nice way to die. It isn't instantaneous. It takes time. If she had just kicked away the chair, we all would have made it to her room in time to save her."

Cynthia looked about to cry. "God, I'm so glad I wasn't here to see it." She looked up, as if believing the truth of what her husband was saying for the first time. "So he'd have to stuff something in the poor woman's mouth for fear she'd scream or cry out before she died."

Fred added, "Then Shipton had to set the whole scene up before he knocked over the chair. But we came up so quickly! Why didn't we pass him coming down the stairs?"

"Another guess?" Dean offered. "I don't think he came down the stairs. Not then. I think Shipton hid in the next room—perhaps in the closet. The room was empty and there was no reason for anyone to look in there. To the best of my knowledge, no one did."

"You think he was in Bird Song all the time?" Fred asked.

"It's the only thing that makes sense to me. You're correct that there wouldn't be time for him to race downstairs and out of the building. It was far too risky for him to even attempt it. It's possible he waited around hours, until the afternoon when the police had left and it was quiet. Then he could slip out unnoticed. Later, we complained about Janet's sloppy cleaning when we found traces of mud in an unused room. I'd guess Shipton left it."

"While I can buy all this as possible, it would be the dickens to prove it." Fred gestured to Dean's injuries. "Why would Shipton try and kill you?" The old man picked at his red suspenders. Santa Claus in civies, dressed by GQ, the senior edition.

"He knew once someone questioned the suicide note and seriously examined it, he was all finished. He also knew I was the only person who guessed what had transpired."

"But I still don't understand. Why did he kill her?" Cynthia asked. "I thought he was obsessed with his wife. He traced her all the way out here, like some love-sick stalker."

"Ah," Dean said. "But remember, he never acted very love-sick, did he? Anything but. Furious at her, yes. But he didn't display an iota of love toward her that I picked up on. Just a sick sort of dominance."

"He was a despicable slug," Cynthia muttered.

"Edith Shipton wasn't a saint either, nor do I think she was near as bewildered about life as she let on. A certain amount of planning and calculation went into all of her actions. For instance, I don't think it was a mistake that her husband followed her to Ouray as easily as it seemed. We just took her word for the fact he chased down the credit card charge so quickly. That one point always bothered me. There was something TV about it. If Shipton traced the credit card to Bird Song, why would he call to confirm she and Donnie were here? All that would do is warn them he knew and he would be coming out to get her. My guess is Edith left lots of little subtle clues around her house, letting hubby know where she was going."

"Why would she do something stupid like that?" Fred asked.

"I think she wanted a confrontation between Ryland and her husband all along. She threw herself at Ryland, practically under Shipton's nose."

"And at you," Cynthia offered. "But her husband didn't want her dead," she continued. "He desperately wanted her to bear his son."

"Says who? Think about that."

"Donald Ryland said so," Fred answered.

"Besides," Cynthia added, "Even if she did make it easy for her husband to follow her, Shipton did chase her out here. Look how obsessive he was!"

"She was a very obsessive woman too, a far different person than we were all led to believe."

"What do you mean?"

"Stop and think. Everything we knew about Edith Shipton came either from her directly or through Donald Ryland. But Ryland's personal knowledge of her was limited to a couple rolls in the hay a dozen years ago. Her life with Shipton was solely based on what she told Ryland and he conveyed to us. Once you realize that, you have to question everything she said. Especially about Jerome. Aside from our personal observation that he was a first class son of a bitch, everything else about him came from Edith."

"I'm getting confused," Cynthia said.

"I'll grant you, it is confusing and there's a whole lot more about their relationship we don't know and probably never will know. But we do know Edith did do some very calculated things. I don't believe

Jerome beat her when she showed up Sunday morning all bruised and cut. I think she did that to herself."

"You don't think Shipton was a wife beater?" Cynthia asked, her deep hatred of the man bubbling to the surface.

"Having met him, I'd have to say he was capable of it. The point I'm trying to make is, we lack confirmation, especially in view of subsequent events. We only have Edith's word."

"God, David! You sound like every cop and judge who doubts every battered and raped woman victim! She asked for it—it was her fault!"

"Whoa! I'm not writing any letters to the Vatican proposing Jerome Shipton for sainthood. He was a woman-chasing, obnoxious bastard in a dozen different ways. Don't forget he killed his wife in cold blood and tried to kill me! All I'm trying to do is sort out the real man from the image his wife created. Look at the facts. Aside from what we observed ourselves, everything we thought we knew about Jerome Shipton came from his wife, a dedicated liar. She told Franny Mulligan that Ryland was dumping her. A bold-faced lie. She was pregnant. Probably another lie. The whole fable about how her stepson died was a fabrication. So tell me, what was truth and what was fiction?"

"Did she ever believe she was Annie Quincy?"

"Who knows? I don't think we'll ever learn when reality took over from fantasy. My guess is she acted out of some inner desperation. She turned to Ryland, throwing herself on him, but that didn't work. It was an impossible situation for her. She hated her husband who in turn despised her. I'm sure she believed, perhaps rightly so, she couldn't just leave him. His ego and sense of dominance over her wouldn't let him allow her to be the one walking away. Look at the way he treated her—always embarrassing and belittling her. He practically raped her the night he first stayed in Bird Song. It's like he needed her to be his punching bag, at least verbally if not physically. Why, I don't know, but I'm sure the shrinks could tell you."

"What about the death of Shipton's son? Was that Shipton's basis for everything?"

"I honestly don't know. There's no doubt he blamed Edith for his son's death. If both boys were struggling in the water, I suppose her natural impulse would be to first save her own child. Perhaps that's what she did. What else happened out there at the pool? Who knows? I do think the intimation Donnie's lack of speech was a result of that incident may be overrated. My guess is Donnie's muteness may be far more complicated. I wouldn't be surprised the Shipton marriage was a disaster from the start and Donnie's silence is a result of that tension."

"There's no doubt Donnie hated his stepfather," Fred said. "I always figured dad might have murdered his son and frightened the boy into silence. I read an English caper about that happening one time."

"I'll leave Donnie's problems for the guys in white coats to sort it out," Dean answered. "But given the pair of parents the boy was forced to live with, it's a wonder he's as well adjusted as he is. Donnie needs a prolonged dose of professional help and an environment absent the stress he's been living under. It sounds like he's getting it now. Hopefully he'll come around."

"So you think Shipton came out here to Ouray with the intention of killing his wife?" Cynthia asked.

"At first I didn't think so, but the fact that he had the old suicide note with him makes me think he at least considered it, if the opportunity presented itself . When he read about Annie Quincy's death, that must have seemed too perfect for him to pass up. He may have even realized what happened up at the ice park."

"You still haven't told us why you went climbing down the cliff trying to kill yourself," Cynthia said, a touch of chill still in her voice. "Or what happened up there."

"The first time Shipton fell or the second time?"

"Both," Fred said, then added, "I suppose Edith did cut his line. Or did he do it himself to blame her?"

"Both," Dean answered. They just looked at him. He smiled before he continued. "This is part guess, part fact, with both parts complicated. Shipton was mad as hell at me for knocking him down. He was vindictive by nature and—this is the 'guess' part—he cut his line and left my knife which he'd picked up from his wife's room."

"So how did he get down to the point where he fell?" Fred asked.

"Penny showed me how. When you rappel down, you loop the rope over your anchor, your fixed point up top, so in effect, it's secured in the *middle* of the line. Shipton cut a short section of rope and left it up there so it would look like someone cut it when he was part way to the bottom. He then descended down using the remaining good section intending to fake a fall or otherwise call attention to what supposedly happened."

"But he messed up and fell too far," Fred offered.

"That's what I thought at first. But it didn't make sense, even though I think Shipton himself continued to believe that's how he fell."

"Would you care to expand on that a bit?" Cynthia asked.

"Edith *had* cut the line and he fell, injuring himself. I'm not sure, but I'm guessing his head injury caused him to not understand, or even remember what happened. He may have continued to think he'd slipped, never realizing what she'd done."

"That's bizarre," Cynthia said. "Doesn't it make more sense that the whole bit about the cut rope was Shipton's sole doing? Perhaps Edith wasn't involved at all."

"Earlier I considered that, but when Edith was with me, she said she tried to kill her husband. We kept trying to make more of the statement than a simple declaration of fact. Shipton might have begun to consider that Edith tried to kill him, but I'm inclined to believe he saw where he could use the attempt on his life to give reason for her remorse and subsequent 'suicide'. Remember, he changed his story about blaming me for his fall. Blaming Edith fit nicely with his plans to kill her."

"That's pretty ironic," Cynthia said. "Here's Jerome Shipton concocting a story, blaming his wife for something she really did!"

"Wouldn't Shipton have seen where she cut the line?" Fred asked.

"Here's where Edith's cleverness comes into play. Remember the candle in her room? She used wax to bind the partially severed ends together, just enough that a cursory glance wouldn't disclose what she'd done. Sheriff Weller told me that later. She didn't cut the rope all the way through, but enough that it wouldn't bear her husband's full weight."

Cynthia thought about it. "Edith cut the rope too close to the end so he didn't fall far enough to be killed," she said.

"Not exactly. When Shipton looped the rope to descend, after he faked cutting it, Edith's cut was then positioned differently. Fortunate for him it was then near enough to the end of the line that his fall wasn't far enough to kill him."

"Wouldn't the police have examined the rope after Shipton fell?"

"This part gets confusing. The rope *was* cut. The fact that the other end was also cut must have looked like the natural end of the line."

"But there would have been a shorter severed piece, wouldn't there?" Cynthia protested.

"Yes. But Weller told me in the hospital that in the confusion of getting Shipton out of the gorge, no one examined the bottom of the cliff, where he landed. Remember, the police were sure the rope was cut when Shipton was part way down. The crime scene was the top of the cliff, where the rope was slashed. My guess is the missing piece of line fell into the river."

"But Shipton had two ropes," Cynthia said. "How could Edith be sure which rope he'd use?"

"Bingo!" Dean said.

It dawned on both of them at the same time but it was Cynthia who said it. "She cut both ropes! That's how he fell to his death when he was after you!"

Dean nodded his head in agreement. "That's why I ran off to the ice park. I guessed the second rope might be cut, putting Shipton in serious danger. But he wouldn't believe me."

"So Edith Shipton killed her husband from the grave," Fred said.

"I guess you could say that," Dean answered.

"Why would he be fool enough to go back up there and climb again?" Cynthia asked her husband.

Dean remembered the Ride the Rockies bike tour, when he had fallen, nearly killing himself, but put his bruised and cut body back on a bike, just to finish.

"It's a macho thing," he answered

"Men!" Cynthia snorted. "How can anyone be that macho, or stupid is a better word!"

"Am I forgiven for trying to warn him?" Dean asked with a smile.

"Perhaps. But I'm required to be standoffish a little while longer. Otherwise you might take up ice climbing as a sport."

Fred stood up and stretched. The others followed and the trio went back inside where Dean began building a fire.

Cynthia settled into the sofa where Dean joined her, putting his arm around her shoulders. "I realize in most ways Edith isn't deserving of too much sympathy, but I still think of her as a tragic figure. She was a lot like Annie. In a way, this whole business started with Annie Quincy. Neither one of them had any place or anybody to turn to." She reached over and picked up the translated pages of Annie Quincy's notebook and began reading aloud.

CHAPTER 29

Love is so strange, my dearest Joshua. It is a feeling I've not had nor scarce dreamed could exist in such intensity before you entered my life. Love is a craving hunger while it fills me to satiation like no mortal fare could ever satisfy. It pains and it heals, it wakens me while it lulls me to the most peaceful sleep imaginable. Just a touch, a smile from you can do so much to brighten my every day. I am miserable in your absence yet the simple memory of you is enough to sustain me during those interminably long intervals when we are apart. I know in my heart we can never truly be, and yet we are. Always. Verily this I know, with all my being. So in love says everyone....

Cynthia set down the page after reading the paragraph aloud to her husband. Fred was off to Miss. Worthington's so they were alone in the parlor. The fire ebbed to glowing coals in the silent old building and she snuggled against him.

"What a sad and tragic life poor Annie led."

"As intelligent as Annie Quincy was, I still have trouble rationalizing her exit. Suicide is cheating. It's a coward's way out. And she took an unborn child with her."

Cynthia didn't disagree as much as Dean expected. "She realized she had no future with the reverend. He was married—had children. She loved him too much to interfere in his life. The best she could hope for was a few hours in his arms. She had no self image and was ashamed of being a prostitute." Cynthia turned and looked up at her husband. "Most of all, she feared for her baby."

"Are we going to have a baby?" he asked. They hadn't spoken of the possibility of Cynthia's pregnancy since the topic was first mentioned.

She shook her head. "I still don't know."

"There's ways of finding that out, you know," he said, giving her a squeeze.

She bit her lip. "I'm scared too. Like Annie, and Edith, if she really was pregnant. But I'm frightened for a far different reason."

He betrayed his surprise at her reply by his movement. He worded his response with caution. "It must make you concerned. Your age is pushing the envelope—"

"Careful...." she smiled.

He laughed. "Forty is beautiful! It's just that I'm concerned about your well being. I can understand it must be scary to think of giving birth."

She pulled away and looked him in the eye. "I'm scared I might *not* be pregnant. I just want a little more time to bask in the beauty that perhaps I'm carrying a life. Your child. I know it's silly...."

"No, it's not silly at all," he answered as he kissed her cheek. "We'll know soon enough." Then he added, "As long as this is let's-be-honest time, I have an apology to make." She turned expectantly. "I should have discussed Jake Weller's suggestion about my running for sheriff before dismissing it. A decision like that should involve you. I was being selfish."

"Do you feel that strongly about not getting back into law enforcement?" she asked.

"To be honest, I didn't even take time to think seriously about it. But if we are to have a larger family, maybe I should consider. We could use the money. I notice the difference in the grocery bill just feeding Martha."

"Wrong reason," she answered. "Money shouldn't govern your decision. But the election isn't until August and that's a long way off."

"Either way," he said, "'So in love, says everyone.'"

She smiled, and repeated the phrase. "'So in love, says everyone.' Would you scratch that on a window pane for me?" she teased.

"Give me your ring."

"No, you'll damage it!"

"It's a diamond. It won't hurt it. At least I think it's a diamond. That's what the guy in the alley said when he sold it to me for ten bucks." She gave his arm a whack but surrendered the ring. He took her hand and led her up the stairs. "It won't hurt to look," he said with a smile as they began to climb to the now-empty upper floors.

"Every time I come up these stairs, I look up to see if a white-dressed figure is standing at the top," he said.

She turned to him. "Remember, Annie is a friendly ghost!" She squeezed his hand playfully.

He started to enter the first room, on the northwest corner, but Cynthia tugged him further down the hall until they reached Edith Shipton's room on the southeast corner. Cynthia had avoided it since the woman's death and now entered, hesitation in her step. She crossed herself and bowed her head.

"Scratch the message in this room," she said. "Perhaps it will expunge the hate and tragedy this room has seen." She moved off to examine the other windows as Dean knelt to do her bidding.

"David!" she exclaimed. "It's here!"

He smiled as he began scratching the message in the tiniest letters he could muster at the very base of the pane—just as he had done on the other window, days earlier, after she'd left her ring on the kitchen counter to wash dishes. Cynthia turned toward him, then realizing what his smile didn't deny. He couldn't keep a secret from this woman he loved.

"Thank you," she said as she snuggled her arms about his neck. "That was the sweetest thing to do." She kissed him. "Now scratch this one so there are two messages! I'll pretend the other one was really what Annie wrote here so long ago!"

Later, as they descended the stairs to the hall, Dean commented, "It's nice to think Annie and her friends are up there in heaven smiling down on us, probably thinking that we're nuts for always taking on everyone's problems."

"Yes," Cynthia answered. "So much for not getting involved."

Dean paused to turn out the lights as his wife walked ahead of him toward their room. He turned and glanced up at the top of the stairs. There, in the fog of semi-darkness, stood a white-clad figure, smiling down at him. At least in his mind's eye.

ABOUT THE AUTHOR

R. E. Derouin is the author of a number of award-winning plays and two previous David Dean novels, *Time Trial* and *San Juan Solution*, the latter a finalist for the Colorado Book Award and the recipient of a silver medal from the Colorado Independent Publishers.

Derouin lives in beautiful Ouray, Colorado where, when not working on the latest David Dean mystery, he occasionally helps out in his family toy store.

For more information, visit www.rederouin.com.

Printed in the United States
1470900001B/486